I0690498

# DIVINE
# JUSTICE

**Cheryl Kaye Tardif**

**DIVINE JUSTICE**

http://www.cherylktardif.com

FIRST EDITION
Imajin Books - http://www.imajinbooks.com

ISBN: 978-1-926997-00-1 (trade paperback edition)

eBook editions also available at various ebook retailers

Cover designed by Sapphire Designs - http://www.designs.sapphiredreams.org

For my mommy-in-law Francine,
the one person who sells more of my books than I do and supports
me in all that I do—thank you and I love you.

## ACKNOWLEDGMENTS

I'd like to thank my early editors and readers. You always keep me on my toes and your honest feedback is irreplaceable and much appreciated.

Thanks to author Kelly Komm for her creative input and proofreading. And for her continuous support and friendship.

Thank you to my editor, Lisa Hazard, for finding those sneaky gremlins that find their way into my work when I'm not looking.

A special thanks to Jennifer Johnson, cover artist extraordinaire, who always makes me look good by creating the most wonderful book covers.

My sincere appreciation to author Art Tirrell for sharing his nautical expertise. Now I can pretend I know what I'm talking about—even when I don't.

A very special thank you to every bookstore I have visited or held book signings at over the years—especially to Audrey's Books (Edmonton), Coles (Millwoods Town Centre and Southgate Shopping Centre in Edmonton), Chapters (South Point in Edmonton), Indigo (Edmonton) and other Indigo Books & Music, Chapters and Coles Bookstores in Edmonton and beyond. And to every patron who has entered these bookstores, whether you've bought my books or not.

Thank you always to my family, especially my husband Marc and my daughter Jessica, for all their support and enthusiasm.

# *Prologue*

Jasi McLellan drifted in and out of consciousness, her thoughts like waves lapping restlessly against the shore. When she opened her eyes, distorted faces flashed past her and indistinct words assaulted her ears. She reached for the names that belonged to those faces, but they eluded her. She tried to swallow, but her mouth and tongue were sandpaper-dry. She inhaled slowly, trying to place the smell, a mix of antiseptic and sweat.

*Where the hell am I? And why is it so dark, so cold?*

She blinked once and everything changed.

Before her lay a long, murky corridor. At her feet, the bare hardwood floor was polished to a reflective shine. Her sandals clicked as she headed toward the door at the end of the hall. A crack of backlighting outlined the door's shape. As she moved toward it, the door appeared to drift further away.

She paused and leaned down to look at her reflection in the gleaming floor. A face she didn't recognize stared back at her. Amidst charred skin, blue eyes blinked at her.

*I have green eyes.*

She cried out in terror when the face became two.

The dead girl from her closet was coming for her.

Jasi faced the girl. "Why can't you leave me alone?"

"I can't leave. You need me, and I need you."

The girl's accent was soft—from South Carolina maybe—and the pink skipping rope noose cut deeply into her lolling neck with every word she spoke.

"He keeps callin' me," the dead girl whispered.

"Who?"

The girl began to sob and Jasi reached out to touch the child's blistered shoulder. She snatched her hand back when it encountered skin that was morgue cold.

"Who are you?"

"Emily," came the soft reply.

"What do you want, Emily?"

The girl's next words turned Jasi's blood to ice.

"I want you to find me."

Confused, Jasi shook her head and took a few steps backward. "What do you mean? You're right here."

The girl said nothing.

"I've seen you ever since I was a child," Jasi said. "You've never spoken to me before. Why now?"

Emily lowered her head. "You jes never heard me before. Now you're open-minded. Now you're hearin' me fine."

A light flickered at the end of the hall and Jasi glanced over her shoulder.

"It's okay, Jasmine." Emily smiled weakly. "Go."

The girl drifted backward toward the shadows.

"Emily, wait!" Jasi cried. "How do I find you?"

"When you're ready, I'll find you."

As Jasi drifted off into a peaceful, healing sleep, she made a solemn vow to the dead girl in her closet.

I'll find you, Emily. I promise.

The dead girl finally had a name—Emily.

# *1*

Natassia Prushenko was scared—*really* scared.

She looked down at the woman lying motionless in the bed. *She's so pale, so still. Like death.*

The door opened behind her. Someone stepped into the room.

"Is Jasi awake yet?"

Natassia glanced over her shoulder. "No, she hasn't moved an inch. I'm worried about her, Ben."

Benjamin Roberts crossed the room, bringing with him an air of calm authority. When he reached Natassia, they stood side-by-side, keeping vigil over the woman in the hospital bed.

It had been nearly two weeks since their partner and team leader Jasmine McLellan had taken a bullet high on her left arm. She'd been doing well, was even out of Vancouver General Hospital for nearly a week, but then she'd taken an unexpected turn for the worse. Her arm had swelled painfully, the bullet wound festering. Without warning, a blood infection invaded Jasi's body, causing serious complications and a sudden trip back to the hospital. That's where they discovered she had a concussion and mild swelling of the brain, probably from when she hit the ground after an explosion during the last case.

Natassia stared down at Jasi. "I don't think she's getting any better, Ben. She looks like she's barely breathing." She reached out to touch Jasi's arm, but snatched back her hand as if she'd touched a hot flame.

Ben raised a brow. "Natassia…"

"You know what can happen if I touch her. After all she's been through, the last thing she needs is me poking around in her mind. Anyway, we already know what happened during the Gemini Murders.

It's not as if we need to know any more."

She studied the woman in the bed, taking in the tangled mane of shoulder-length auburn hair and the sprinkle of cinnamon freckles that appeared much darker against the creamy whiteness of her face.

"It's up to Jasi now," Ben said quietly. "We both know how stubborn she is."

He turned away, but not before Natassia saw tears in his eyes. "Where are you going?" she asked.

"I want to check on her status. I'll get her doctor."

Natassia felt a void in the room as soon as he was gone. She couldn't help but feel a little better when he was around. If there was one thing she'd learned, Ben knew how to take care of things—especially the people he cared for.

She watched Jasi. "And he sure cares a lot for you, my new friend."

Although she'd only known Jasi for about three months, she'd grown fond of her. The slender redhead had a lot of spunk. That was something she could appreciate.

Natassia had spent a few years consulting with a Russian agency similar to the Canadian Federal Bureau of Investigation, which had been formed in 2003. As a Victim Empath capable of receiving cryptic flashes from the minds of victims, she was responsible for bringing down some notorious criminals. After a brief scandalous affair with a married field agent, Natassia was 'traded' to Canada's CFBI. Recently, she'd been assigned to the PSI Division and relocated to Vancouver, B.C.

"Remember when we first met, Jasi? You thought I was an escort hitting on Ben." She laughed. "The poor guy practically fell over in his chair when I sat down with you two."

It had been an awkward first meeting.

Natassia let out a sigh.

She still felt like the new kid on the block, having only been a Psychic Skills Investigator with the CFBI for the past three months. As a PSI, her gift of reading victims, live or dead ones, had helped crack the last case. But not before Jasi had been shot. Natassia hadn't been able to prevent that. Or Jasi's subsequent heartbreak.

She pulled the chair up to the side of the bed. "Get well, my friend. We've got cases to solve, murderers to catch and good-looking men to tease."

There was no answer.

She leaned closer. "Jasi? Can you hear me?"

No reply.

"Jasmine McLellan, it's time to wake up now."

The woman in the bed remained still.

Out in the hall, footsteps approached. Ben entered the room, followed by Jasi's father and Brady, her brother. Dr. Mohinder Habib entered the room after them and immediately picked up the chart at the end of Jasi's bed.

"So?" Natassia said impatiently.

When the doctor looked up from the file, his expression was guarded. That made her nervous.

"When is she going to wake up?" she blurted.

"We've been monitoring her stats closely," Dr. Habib said, his black eyes drifting to the bed. "Ms. McLellan has been only slightly responsive to antibiotics."

Natassia frowned. "But she's getting better, right?"

"Your friend is too exhausted to fight off the infection, and the swelling in her brain is impeding her recovery." Dr. Habib tried to smile. "She's in a very deep sleep."

"You mean she's in a coma," Ben stated.

The doctor nodded. "Yes, but she's still breathing on her own."

Jasi's father looked stunned. "When will she wake up?"

"I'm afraid we don't know when," Dr. Habib said gently. "The body often reacts this way when it's under attack. Some people wake up within days, once an infection is under control. Some remain in a coma for longer periods of time." He made a note on Jasi's chart and adjusted the IV drip.

"What's the worst case scenario?" Ben asked.

Natassia knew it was the one question everyone had on their minds.

"Well, worst case—and I mean very worst—would be that we can't control the swelling in her brain or the infection in her arm." He turned away from his patient. "And if the infection travels up her arm toward her heart, we might have to take more aggressive action."

"What kind of action?" Jasi's brother demanded.

"Brady," his father warned. "Let him finish."

Dr. Habib's expression darkened. "If the infection spreads upward, it could reach her heart or brain and that would complicate matters. There is a slim possibility that we might have to amputate her arm."

Natassia let out a soft cry. "No!"

"We might not have a choice," the doctor said quietly.

Natassia moved closer to the bed. As she gazed at Jasi, her mouth tightened. *I won't let them take your arm.*

"For now, her vitals are good," Dr. Habib said, moving toward the door. "We have every reason to believe she'll fight the infection and regain consciousness. When she's ready. I'll check in on her in a couple of hours, but I can assure you we're doing everything we can for her."

Brady and his father followed the doctor out into the hall, while Natassia sank into the chair by Jasi's bed.

"They might take her arm, Ben. Oh, God…"

Ben placed a gloved hand on her shoulder. "Hey, you heard the doctor. She's stable and she's a fighter. She'll wake up soon enough, and when she does, she'll be bossier than hell."

Natassia studied the woman in the bed, yearning for Jasi to open her green eyes. "Come on, Jasi. You've gotta fight this thing."

Behind her, Ben said, "She's probably dreaming about lying on a tropical beach somewhere, sipping mojitos and getting that tan she always wanted."


While her partners discussed tropical beaches and tanning, Jasi drifted on a turbulent river of unconsciousness, reliving flashes of conversations and glimpses of past murder scenes that all led her back to the one case that had hit close to home.

*Too close.*

She'd let her guard down, opened herself to a personal connection instead of her ordinary measure of distance, something she always strived for.

In her drug-induced world, faces flashed before her.

*Brandon…Ben…Natassia.*

A burnt corpse floated past her on a cresting wave.

*Monty Winkler.*

The dream took her closer to the water. She saw her reflection. And something else just below the surface.

She scrunched her eyes. *What is that?*

Suddenly, a hand broke the surface. Fingers clawed at empty air, yet as quickly as it had appeared, the hand sank below, returning to its watery grave.

*No!*

A rush of emotions assaulted her. Death…loss…pain.

Jasi was suddenly transported to the day she had returned to Divine Operations, the covert location of the PSI Division. Divine Ops was cloaked within an isolated, heavily guarded complex in the Rocky Mountains. Not even the one hundred or so residents of Divine, BC, knew what went on inside the complex—or underground. They believed the signage that stated it was a company called Enviro-Safe Research Facility.

In her dream world, Jasi found herself standing in front of Matthew Divine, the mysterious creator of the PSI Division. With shoulder-length gray hair tied in a ponytail and old-fashioned tortoise-shell glasses, the man could be easily mistaken for an aging hippie or a computer geek.

The latter was true.

"Hi, Matthew," Jasi said.

She knew he wasn't pleased. Why should he be? She had another dead body on her hands, someone who could've been saved if she'd bothered to call for back up. Plus, she had a wounded friend who wouldn't have been shot if it wasn't for her stubborn refusal to follow protocol.

"I-I'm sorry," she told him.

A bright flash sent her muddled mind back to the case that still haunted her. The Parliament Murders. Memories flooded her mind. She couldn't fight them, or stop them. All she could do was remember.

As usual, everything had started with a dead body.

## 2

Jasi first met Monty Winkler at the Ottawa Forensics Unit, but shaking his hand was definitely out of the question. From the look of his bloated, blistered and undeniably dead corpse, Winkler wouldn't be shaking hands, hugging women or kissing babies any time in the future.

As she approached the metal table, she was forced to do a double-take. Her gaze drifted from the corpse's face to the photo on her data-com screen.

She frowned. "You sure this is my floater?"

"The one and only," the pathologist said. "All week."

"A slow week?"

"Dead slow. For him anyway."

Jasi held out a hand. "Agent Jasmine McLellan, CFBI."

The woman removed a latex glove and wiped her hand on her lab coat before offering it. "Dr. Faith Copeland, keeper of the dead. Also known as the chief pathologist."

Copeland was small and neat in appearance, her ash-blond hair twisted into a tight bun. Gold-rimmed glasses made her brown eyes appear even larger and softened the small lines that feathered the corners. She wore no makeup and didn't need any to maintain an attractive, yet serious, appearance.

The pathologist yawned loudly, then blushed. "Sorry. I've been on this case almost twenty-four-seven. We're a bit short-staffed. You know, government cutbacks and all."

"No need to apologize."

Jasi knew all too well the hazards of a case like this one.

"This victim is our number one priority," Copeland stated. "And I doubt any of us will get much sleep until you find his killer."

Jasi turned her attention back to the body on the table.

Winkler was unrecognizable. His unanticipated swim in the icy waters of the Ottawa River had put on an extra twenty pounds or more of bloated tissue. That was after someone had tried to fry his flesh—extra crispy. His body was unevenly burned and blistered, with most of the damage to his head, face and right side. Fish had feasted on one side of Winkler's head, and the underlying skin tissue clung loosely to muscle and bone, falling away in places like meat from the bone of an overcooked turkey.

Jasi's stomach lurched and she studied the photo again.

*What happened to you?*

The smiling—and alive—Monty Winkler in the photo reminded her of someone, a comedian. The father in *American Pie*. He had the same curly black hair, a prominent nose, bushy eyebrows and dark intelligent eyes circled by black frames. A man like him with average height, weight and looks would normally blend into a crowd, except that he had a charismatic personality that most people found very appealing.

Married, with no kids, Winkler was a dedicated Member of Parliament and a firm supporter of gun rights, and although women hovered around him like flies, he'd always appeared committed to his wife.

What was her name?

Jasi consulted a file on her data-com. *Ah, Marilyn!*

"Marilyn's going to take this hard, Monty."

Her eyes wandered across the photo again and she glanced back at the decomposing body. "How can you be the same man who wielded such charm that you had college girls and married women practically swooning at your feet?"

"Pardon me?" Copeland said, distracted.

"Don't mind me. I have a habit of talking to the dead."

"As long as they don't talk back."

"So you're sure this is Monty Winkler?"

Copeland nodded. "We made a positive ID from the DNA I pulled from his hair and matched to a hairbrush his wife brought in."

Jasi tried to picture Monty Winkler as she'd last seen him on television. He was a well respected man, for a former lawyer. Unlike many of his fellow MPs, Winkler had kept himself in shape with a regimented routine of low-carb health food and running and weightlifting every morning. He'd looked damn good for a man nearing his fifties.

*But you don't make a very good-looking corpse.*

She hovered over the table, scanning every inch of Winkler's body. Unfortunately, the fire and the river had destroyed most of the physical evidence. And sitting in cold storage for almost three days didn't help either.

"COD?" she asked without taking her eyes away.

"In layman's terms, he drowned in freshwater," Copeland said. "There's a substantial amount of fluid in his airway and stomach, and his lungs are inflated. We were able to confirm the presence of diatoms, which we identified and were able to match to a specific section of the Ottawa River."

"Which section?"

"From Mud Lake—that's west of the city—to the MacDonald Cartier Bridge to the north. Ironically, he would have died soon anyway."

"Why?"

"There was blunt force trauma to the neurocranium. His brain was hemorrhaging."

Since rigor mortis was fading, Copeland was able to carefully turn Winkler's partially shaved head so Jasi could view the injuries. The back of the skull was exposed. Fragments of parietal and occipital bone were embedded in a frenzied array of circular indentations, some of them overlapping.

"Any idea what caused these wounds?"

Copeland shook her head. "Never seen anything like it."

"Could they be accidental? From the river maybe?"

"No, not with this grouping so close together."

"So he was hit on the back of the head numerous times."

"With a heavy circular object," Copeland added, "approximately an inch and a half in diameter."

Jasi chewed her bottom lip for a moment.

"Why do you say he was hit with a *heavy* object?"

Copeland strode across the room to a workstation. She tapped on a touch screen and brought up a 3-D hologram of Winkler's wounds.

"There are ten of these impressions, Agent McLellan. Notice their depth. They're small in circumference, yet deep, meaning two things. The perp was enraged and the weapon had some weight to it, otherwise it would've broken or folded under pressure and left uneven marks, not these perfect circles."

The pathologist zoomed in on the occipital region.

"Each impression shows a slight angle of impact. I believe he was either hit from behind by a very tall man or he was kneeling or sitting."

Jasi studied the hologram. "Maybe the killer used a metal pipe?"

"Could be. But it's an odd way to wield a pipe."

Copeland was right. Most pipe injuries were made with the side or length of a pipe, causing long, cylindrical wounds.

"Maybe he was jabbed with a martial arts weapon," Copeland said.

"What about defensive wounds?"

"He couldn't have fought back. Toxicology report came back positive for flunitrazepam."

"Flunitrazepam?"

"You'd know it as Rohypnol."

Jasi's heart skipped a beat. "The date rape drug?"

"Flunitrazepam has sedative, paralytic and amnestic properties, which is why it's been a popular in rape cases. The victim loses muscle control and often ends up with anterograde amnesia and can't recall what happened."

"Winkler wasn't raped, was he?"

"No. My guess is someone wanted him docile."

Jasi paced the floor. "Rohypnol isn't easy to get."

"Not anymore. Ever since drug manufacturers started adding noticeable dyes to the tablets, we've seen less of it in the clubs and on the streets. It *is* available in injectable liquid, but you'd have to acquire it in Mexico or overseas."

Copeland tapped the screen and brought up a holographic image of Winkler's upper left arm.

"This is the injection site," she said, pointing to a small dark spot. "He was given a large dose."

Jasi peered over the woman's shoulder at the body on the table. How could someone have gotten close enough to Winkler to stick him with a hypodermic?

"The drug was administered about a half hour before the scalp wounds were inflicted," Copeland said. "He wouldn't have felt much, but he was conscious enough to know what was happening. Shortly afterward, he was lit on fire."

"Jesus!"

"The burn pattern is consistent with the use of an accelerant. What's unusual is that the regions here and here weren't burned to the same extent."

Jasi studied the area the pathologist had indicated. The left side of the body was less burnt than the rest.

"Do you think something was covering him?"

The smile Copeland gave her had the effect of taking ten years off the woman. "Watch closely, Agent McLellan."

The pathologist tapped the touch screen and the hologram began to fold in as if Winkler were sitting down. Then the 3-dimensional form rotated on one side.

"He was lying on his left side when the accelerant was poured on him," Jasi observed.

Copeland nodded. "In a small, restrictive space. He didn't die from smoke inhalation, although there was some smoke damage to his lungs. He was dumped into the river shortly afterward, still breathing."

"What's the estimated time of death?"

"TOD is between eleven p.m. and two a.m. on April 13." She grimaced. "Friday the 13th, to be exact."

"Did you send your report to the CFBI?"

"Yes, and I uploaded an image of the wound pattern."

Jasi did something next that made the pathologist gasp. She strode toward the corpse on the table and leaned forward, her nose barely an inch from the scorched flesh. Shutting her eyes, she inhaled deeply.

"Agent McLellan?" the woman said, concerned.

"I have a keen sense of smell. Oversensitive olfactory nerve."

She wasn't really lying. Then again, she couldn't exactly tell the woman that she was hoping traces of smoke still lingered on Winkler's body, enough to set off her psychic abilities so she could enter a killer's mind.

She inhaled again.

Nothing. Not one flash. Not one sick, twisted thought.

She shivered.

*The dead won't speak to me.*

She thought of the young girl who had haunted her nightmares ever since she was a child. The girl waited each night in the closet of her dreams, a pink skipping rope strangling her last breath. She'd never said a word either.

"You okay?" Copeland asked.

"Yeah."

The woman eyed her suspiciously. "I hope you don't mind me saying this, Agent McLellan, but you look awfully—" She broke off, closed her mouth.

"Young?" Jasi chuckled. "I get that all the time. But trust me, Dr. Copeland, there isn't much I haven't seen."

The look Faith Copeland gave her was one Jasi had seen a million times before. In her father's eyes. The look said, "Why in God's name would a young woman go into such a depressing and dangerous line of work?"

Because of Mom, she wanted to tell him.

The pathologist patted her arm. "Seeing death the way we do, day in and day out, has a way of making you value your own mortality."

Jasi raised a brow. "Meaning?"

"Life is for the living, Agent McLellan."

"Yeah, but I have to find justice for the dead first."


Out in the hallway, Jasi pushed Copeland's dire warning to the back of her mind and searched for her partner. She found him standing near the information desk, chatting with a smiling blond who looked fresh out of college and eager to make his acquaintance.

"Hey, partner!"

"Took you long enough," he said, moving toward her. "I was getting bored."

She smiled wryly. "Didn't look like you were bored."

Eleven years her senior, Agent Benjamin Roberts gave off an air of quiet confidence. At thirty-six, he had several commendations for solving some of Canada's most gruesome, high profile murder cases. Jasi counted her blessings that she'd been paired with Ben and not one of the older PSI agents. Most of them thought she was too young to be a good field agent. Except Ben. He was a patient team leader, a top-notch profiler and her best friend.

While he led her to an empty alcove, she studied her partner. Lean, six and a half feet of muscle and agility—and a Psychometric Empath to boot—Ben wore a navy blue Armani suit with ease. Not many men could it pull off, but Ben was at home in a well-fitted suit, the way most men practically lived in their favorite pair of old jeans. Armani was his middle name.

Or it should be, she thought.

She was sometimes tempted to ask him how he could afford such clothes. Sure, they made good money, but not that much. Regardless, there was more to Ben than he let on. One day she'd find out his secrets.

"So what did you get off Winkler's suit?" she asked.

He shook his head. "What little was left of it was tainted by fire, water and decomp. What about you?"

"The pathologist was very helpful. Can't say the same for Monty Winkler."

"No vision?"

"Not a flicker. The river washed away all traces of smoke. I couldn't smell a thing other than decaying body parts, but we did get a COD. Monty Winkler drowned, and there was prior blunt force trauma to the back of his head."

She described the strange circular wounds.

"Pretty brutal," he said. "Sounds like a rage killing."

"He was also drugged."

"With what?"

"Rohypnol. He was given an injection to immobilize him." Her mouth thinned. "Copeland says there are no signs of rape. Later, someone pounded on his head with an unidentifiable weapon and set him on fire."

She told him about the uneven burn pattern on the body and Copeland's theory that Winkler had been placed into a restrictive space before an accelerant was poured on him.

"He was dumped in the Ottawa River," she said.

They were silent for a moment.

"A trunk of a car is quite restrictive," Ben suggested.

She shook her head. "Smaller. He was practically in a fetal position. Maybe a box of some kind."

The blond from the information desk strolled past, giving Ben a coy look that said, "Call me! Day or night."

"You going to call her?" Jasi asked when the woman disappeared into an office.

Ben shook his head and glanced at his gloved hands.

She let out an irritated huff. "You can't let *those* get in the way—"

"You know what can happen, Jasi."

"That doesn't mean you have to live like a monk."

"Monks aside," he retorted, "let's stop discussing my personal life and focus on what we're going to report to Matthew."

"I think he wasted his time sending us." She looked up at him. "Or at least me."

"Matthew knows what he's doing. He sent us here for a reason."

"Because the government takes care of their own."

"It's been almost a week since they found Winkler. The Ottawa Police Service conducted the preliminary investigation before it was handed over to the RCMP. They've interviewed anyone who came into contact with Winkler before he went missing. Every alibi checked out. Everyone is stumped. That's why we were called in." He smiled. "Besides, Matthew thinks you're ready to lead your own team. This is good prep for you."

She pursed her lips. "What if I don't want my own team? Did anyone ever think of that?"

"Jasi—"

"No, don't *Jasi* me," she snapped. "I like working with you, Ben. We're good together. With our skills, we complement each other. We make a great team. I don't get why Matthew doesn't see that."

"He knows what's best."

Frustrated, she changed the subject. "Did Winkler have any personal belongings?"

"Nothing in his pockets, no wallet, no identification. Whoever did this even removed his wedding band."

"Didn't want an ID made."

She steered him down the hall, making for the doors to fresh air and life. Morgues always gave her a chill. Death lingered in the air, in every corner.

Around 9:30, they crossed the gloomy parking lot. One streetlight at the far end provided the only light. She noted that two others weren't working.

"Remind me to mention something to Copeland about the poor lighting out here," she said.

They located the rental, a black SUV with dark tinted windows, the CFBI's definition of inconspicuous transportation. Ben unlocked the doors and slid behind the wheel, and Jasi climbed into the passenger seat.

"We'll have a full pathology report from Dr. Copeland by tomorrow," she said. "For now, we know that someone drugged Winkler, beat him, doused him in an accelerant, set his body on fire and threw him into the river."

Ben frowned. "Kind of overkill, don't you think?"

"That's exactly what I was thinking."

"Intense rage and overkill. What does that tell you?"

"It tells me that someone wanted Monty Winkler deader than dead." She looked Ben in the eye. "And Winkler knew his assailant."

"So the question is…who?"

She gave him a scornful look. "Are you kidding? He's a politician. Probably had people lining up at his door, just waiting for an opportunity."

"Yeah, I think you're right about that." He fastened his seatbelt, started the car and inched it out into the busy traffic. "Well, since you're in training for team leader, why don't you tell me what we should do next?"

Ben was testing her again. He'd been doing that a lot the last two weeks. On his say-so, she'd be ready to lead her own team. Something she'd been waiting for. She'd been going through all the manuals, studying past cases, listening to and watching recorded testimonies for weeks. She was more than ready to lead her own team.

"We should start with his last known whereabouts and last contacts. Next, we should interview witnesses, make a list of known enemies, find out if any death threats had been issued and look into his political—" She broke off. "Hey, wasn't Winkler the swing-vote in the small arms rights bill a few months ago?"

"Winkler pushed it through before anyone could blink."

"And a lot of people were pissed."

Monty Winkler was responsible for the new law that now gave Canadians the freedom to carry handguns. As long as they carried permits, of course. The gun law had created a surge of dissention across Canada. Some thought it was a long time coming, considering the US had implemented a similar law decades ago. Others thought it would lead to higher crime rates.

For weeks afterward, thousands of people gathered on Parliament grounds across Canada, some in support and some in protest. The pro-gun crowd wanted fewer restrictions on licensing, while the anti-gun crowd protested Canadians carrying weapons at all. Ironically, three people were injured two months ago outside Ottawa's Parliament Hill. They'd been shot by an enraged pro-gun advocate, while the anti-gun crowd carried around massive signs showing dead teenagers in a high school cafeteria and a blood-soaked Toronto alley sealed off with crime tape.

One particularly gruesome sign was a screen capture of Brett Laughlin slumped on his bed, brain matter pooling on the blanket beneath him. After being taunted mercilessly by a group of cyber-bullies, the shy, overweight sixteen-year-old had logged into an online video chat room, then sat down on the bed with his stepfather's newly purchased Walther PPX semi-automatic pistol hidden behind his back.

"Today is my last day of suffering. And I'm glad."

Brett spoke about his persecutors, about the beatings in the boys' change room, about the time he'd been forced to lick one boy's feet clean. Sobbing uncontrollably, he told the world how difficult it was to not fit in.

"It's not easy being the most unpopular kid in school. I'm afraid every day of what they'll do to me. But no more. I can't do this anymore."

He described how he'd suffered at the hands of his stepfather, who beat him for being weak and not fighting back.

"I just wanted to be liked. I didn't care if I was super popular, but maybe just some respect. Instead I was treated worse than an animal, and no one gave a shit. Not my mother, and especially not that asshole she married." He swiped at the tears on his face. "So why should I care? I'll never be popular. I'll never even be liked."

With millions of horrified people—mostly unsuspecting teens—watching live, Brett Laughlin put the gun to the side of his head and pulled the trigger. The gunshot was deafening.

In a matter of seconds, his grisly death had become the most popular cyber-suicide video to hit VidWurld, with over thirty million world-wide views before the Laughlin family got a court order to shut it down.

It was ironic. Brett had gotten his wish to become popular. But what a price he paid for it.

Jasi still couldn't get the kid's face out of her mind. He reminded her of her brother Brady—young, impetuous, troubled and filled with resentment. The perfect recipe for disaster.

Pro-gun supporters didn't seem to care what guns were doing to the youth on the street, and no one bothered to look at what gun rights had done to the USA. The United States of *Arms*, as some called it.

She sighed. "No one outside of law enforcement would be carrying if it weren't for Winkler and that other MP. What was his name?"

"Ravinder Sharma," Ben replied. "They sure surprised everyone with their votes."

"Wonder what made them change their minds."

"Who knows? Some people believe they have a God-given right to protect themselves at all costs."

"Well, they're half-right," she said dryly. "They just don't realize they increase the chance of violence by simply having a gun in their possession. The people shot at the Ottawa protest have proven that."

Ben nodded. "Nothing worse than an angry mob."

Jasi thought of the corpse lying in the morgue.

"I don't think Monty Winkler would agree."

## 3

The Embassy Hotel & Suites, a regal hotel located on Cartier Street, was cradled in the heart of Ottawa. It had served military and government officials for decades, and the security was impeccable. Security guards and cameras made it virtually impossible for someone to walk into the hotel, carry out any nefarious plan and then get away without being detected.

The sun had gone down by the time Jasi and Ben checked in. They took the elevator up to the twenty-seventh floor. Their rooms were side-by-side, with windows facing Parliament Hill and the Rideau Canal.

When Jasi opened the door to her room, she eyed the two queen-size beds. Recycled airplane air always made her tired and she'd give anything to just crawl into bed and sleep the rest of the day away.

"First things first."

She locked the door behind her and tossed her tote bag and backpack on the bed near the window. Shrugging off her jacket, she hung it on the back of a chair. She removed her shoulder harness and quickly inspected the M9 Beretta holstered in it. The double-action semiautomatic was ancient compared to the newer Glock models most agents were fitted with, but Pop had given it to her when she graduated from CFBI training. She'd cleared it with Matthew under the strict rule that she'd have it inspected by a weapons tech every three months.

She slipped the gun into the holster and draped the harness over her jacket. "Time to check out the view."

Crossing to the window, she pulled the cord and the gold satin drapes parted, revealing a sensational night skyline and the Ottawa River. City lights glinted off the Rideau Canal, the 125 mile long waterway that was designated a UNESCO World Heritage Site back in 2007.

Jasi recalled that in the winter the canal was closed down and turned into the world's largest skating rink, but because global warming had initiated an earlier spring, a warm spell during the first two weeks of April had melted most of the river ice. Ships and personal watercraft now dotted the Ottawa River, which was back to business as usual.

She left the drapes open and moved to the bed where she opened the backpack and took note of the field supplies in various pockets. A full canister of *OxyBlast*, two flashlights, extra batteries, bottled water, evidence markers and other items. Everything was in order, so she unpacked her tote bag and hung her clothes in the wardrobe.

She was about to toss the tote bag in a corner when she spotted a gourmet truffle on the pillow.

"Dark chocolate. My favorite."

Paying no heed to the inner voice that reminded her she hadn't gone for her run yet, she removed the wrapper and stuffed the decadent candy into her mouth before her conscience could argue. She let it melt, slowly, savoring the treat.

She ate the chocolate from the other bed too.

*I'll add ten more minutes to my morning run.*

She tossed both wrappers into the wastebasket.

A beeping sound caught her attention. Unclipping her portable data-communicator from her belt, she read a message from Ben. *Have a good sleep, Jazz.*

"You too," she texted back. "Tomorrow the investigation begins."

She peeled off her jeans and blouse and sniffed them. They smelled of death. From the morgue. She stuffed the clothes into a laundry bag and set it by the door.

In the bathroom, she stripped completely and opened the glass door to the double shower. Inside was a digital panel set up for touch or voice command. Most modern hotels had these showers now. Jasi had one recently installed in her apartment, a luxury most people couldn't afford. She'd learned a long time ago to splurge on the few things that brought her comfort or pleasure.

"Shower on."

The shower obeyed, but the water was cold.

"101 degrees."

She stepped inside and heaved a sigh of relief. As steaming water washed away the morgue blues, she took a deep breath and released it, watching her tense morning swirl down the drain.

She reached for the shampoo bottle. "Damn."

In her haste to catch the flight from Vancouver to Ottawa, she'd forgotten to pack shampoo and conditioner. She picked up the hotel's mystery sample, opened it, gave it a sniff, then shrugged.

"Note to self," she said as she lathered her shoulder-length hair. "Buy shampoo and conditioner in the hotel gift shop."

She wondered how much Monty Winkler had spent on hair care products. Any time she'd seen him on TV, he'd always appeared immaculately groomed, as if he'd just stepped out of a Vidal Sassoon salon.

As she rinsed her hair, she thought about his wife. Marilyn Winkler had supported her husband, followed him everywhere. The woman would be devastated.

*At least she doesn't have any kids to break the news to.*

She instantly recalled her own father's grief-stricken face the day he had taken her aside and told her that her mother was dead. Her life had changed forever after that. She couldn't recall events from her childhood before that, much less what happened exactly on the day her mother was brutally murdered. There was only one thing she could remember with perfect clarity. The sound of her mother screaming.

That sound still haunted her at night.

On that horrible day so many years ago, eight-year-old Jasmine was the only witness to a home invasion gone wrong. It had happened on Brady's second birthday. Everything she knew was from what her father had told her years later. He had returned from an outing with Brady and found Jasmine on the floor. She was covered in blood, holding her mother's limp hand, singing a lullaby. Her father had placed Brady in his playpen, then pulled Jasmine into his arms and carried her into her bedroom, where he broke down, sobbing.

Jasmine had said nothing. She was in shock, nearly catatonic. Realizing he needed to also tend to Brady, Pop tucked her in bed, kissed her forehead and left the bedroom. Ten minutes later, while uniformed officers and a crime scene unit invaded their home, Pop had sat on her bed, stroking her hair. He tried to explain that her mother was gone, that she'd never be coming back. Ever.

Her mother's death had left a gaping hole in Jasi's heart. Over the years she'd tried to remember, but every time she thought of that horrible day, all she could recall was her mother's scream.

*And the blood. There had been so much blood.*

In the shower, Jasi blinked away the tears and tipped her head back under the cleansing spray. But all the water in the world couldn't wash away that memory of death.

# 4

While waiting for Jasi to arrive, Ben used the in-room menu on the touch screen plasma TV to place a breakfast order from room service—two omelets, crisp Canadian back bacon, toast and coffee.

He set up his laptop on the small table near the window. Attaching a short cord from the laptop to his data-com, he transferred the secure files he'd received from Divine Ops to the laptop.

While waiting, he removed his leather gloves, massaged his hands and frowned at their paleness. He rarely removed his gloves during the day. The last time he'd been careless and left them off, he'd had an unexpected vision. Jasi had caught him off guard and he grabbed at her ponytail to give it a teasing pull. With a bare hand.

Big mistake.

He had an instant vision, a flash of a woman lying on the floor, her body bruised and beaten beyond recognition. It haunted him. As did the image of large black shoes. Something about them gnawed at his mind, like an irritating sliver that wouldn't dislodge itself.

"You saw my mother," Jasi said when he told her what he'd seen. "The night she was murdered. A night I can't remember clearly and one I desperately want to put out of my mind."

They'd spent the evening together, lying side-by-side, not touching, just talking. It was the beginning of a deep friendship.

Ben was reading the file on Monty Winkler when the door opened. Jasi entered, looking flustered but refreshed. Her hair was damp and she wore no makeup. Then again, she didn't need it.

"Hey," he said. "I was about to call you."

"Sorry, I was sleep-showering after my morning run. I could've stayed in there for another hour."

"You'd come out looking like a shriveled prune."

"With ratty hair." Jasi smoothed her ponytail. "This hotel needs to get new blow driers."

He smiled.

"What are you grinning about?" she muttered.

"Nothing."

Jasi's pet peeve was her hair. She preferred it straight, but she grumbled that it took too long to straighten with a hot iron. The natural waves always crept back as soon as the humidity soared. So every morning, up it would go into a ponytail that swung when she walked.

"You look great," he said, pulling on his gloves.

Jasmine McLellan always looked great, as far as he was concerned. She was a beautiful woman with striking green eyes and flaming red hair. A Scottish wench with a wicked temper, he thought with a smirk. He should know. He'd been on the receiving end of that temper many times.

"You're a sight for sore old eyes," he said, turning back to the monitor.

Jasi snickered behind him. "Yeah, you're so old, Ben. That bit of gray hair above your ears is spreading. Might have to get you a walker soon." She dragged a chair beside him. "Where's the coffee?"

"It's coming. I ordered breakfast for us, so we can start wading through all the files. The RCMP really didn't have much to give us. I can see why they're stumped."

She nudged the laptop. "What have we got so far?"

"Stats on Monty Winkler." Ben clicked on a folder. "He's married, no kids. A member of some exclusive social clubs, including the Ottawa Hunt & Golf Club."

"Membership to the Hunt Club isn't cheap," she said. "Even for an MP. What's his wife do again?"

He scrolled through the file. "Marilyn Winkler is the CEO of Paragon Research Corporation, located at Shirleys Bay." He frowned. "Hmm, this is interesting."

"What?"

"Paragon is funded by three generations of family money."

Jasi's brow lifted. "Winkler money?"

He shook his head. "*Dailey* money." At her blank look, he said, "Warner Dailey?"

"I have no idea who you're talking about, Ben."

"Warner Dailey was a business tycoon who made it big back in the late 40s. He funded companies that sold weapons and ammunition to the US and Canadian military during the war."

"And he owned Paragon?"

"Dailey founded the company in 1952. His son Stephen took over when he passed away." He glanced at the monitor and a chuckle escaped. "You'll never guess who Stephen Dailey was."

"Who?"

"Marilyn Winkler's father."

"And now she's CEO."

"Her father died last year and left her the family business, plus all of his investments."

"That's some inheritance."

He watched as Jasi moved to the window. There was a calm grace in her movements, like a dancer. Of course, she was completely unaware of this and if he ever said anything, she'd deny it and probably tackle him to the ground.

*You're one tough cookie, Jasmine McLellan.*

"Money and a position of authority are a powerful mix," she said without looking at him. "It gives her freedom to travel with her husband."

"And keep an eye on him. The file says two women publicly accused him of adultery."

Jasi turned. "Who?"

"Karen Hampton and Deirdre...Dailey. Now that can't be a coincidence."

Jasi's eyes widened. "I remember hearing about Deirdre. She's Marilyn Winkler's sister."

"We'll have to check both women out. His wife too."

"Anyone else stand out as a possible suspect?"

Before he could answer, there was a knock at the door.

Jasi's face brightened. "Food."

He opened the door and a uniformed room service attendant pushed a wheeled cart inside. On the cart two silver-dome lids covered their meals. Along with the plates and condiments, there was a glass pitcher of ice water with lemon slices, a carafe of coffee and two mugs.

"Do you want all this on the table?" the attendant asked.

"Just leave the cart," Ben replied. "We'll put it out in the hall when we're done."

"Fine, sir. Please sign here."

Ben signed the electronic receipt.

"Thank you, sir. Here's a complimentary newspaper."

Ben took the newspaper and gave the man a ten dollar bill. He'd write it off as an expense later.

"Here." He tossed Jasi the newspaper. "See if there's anything in there on Winkler." He pushed the laptop to one side of the table to make room for their breakfast plates.

"There's an article on page two," Jasi said, pouring coffee into the mugs. "And we're in it, complete with a photo of us."

"Great," he muttered.

"Nothing new in the article. I can't believe they found out about us so soon. They mention us by name."

"So much for keeping a low profile, but I guess it's to be expected, considering who was murdered."

This new development did nothing but darken his mood, and he knew Jasi felt it too.

"Smells awesome," she said, adroitly changing the subject. She lifted the lid and grinned. "You know me so well."

He watched as she doused the omelet in ketchup and dove into it. Jasi always ate like it was her last meal.

"You're the only woman I know who can pack away food like a guy."

She almost looked hurt. "I burn it all off."

"Yeah, you're lucky that way. If I ate like you, I'd gain ten pounds a month." He picked up his fork.

"This is heavenly," she said, her mouth full. "Great choice. Thank you, Ben."

He was tempted to wipe the spot of ketchup from the corner of her mouth, but he didn't. It was too intimate of an action. Plus, she'd probably hit him.

"You're so ladylike, Jazz," he teased.

"I was raised by a man. What do you expect?" She picked up a piece of bacon with her fingers, stuffed it in her mouth, then licked her fingertips. "Shouldn't we get back to Winkler?"

Between bites of food and sips of coffee, they reviewed their respective files, Ben on the laptop and Jasi on her data-com. Ten minutes passed before he saw something interesting.

"Monty Winkler might have been well respected, but he did butt heads a few times on certain controversial issues."

Jasi raised her head. "Which ones?"

"Gun rights and gay marriage seem to be the hot spots."

"So it's possible that one of those hot spots set off a killer." She paused. "I'll look into Ravinder Sharma, the MP that voted with Winkler on gun rights. Maybe someone was threatening them."

"The locals have no leads yet," he said, picking at his salad. "Which is why Matthew sent us here. Today we get acquainted with Monty Winkler until we know everything about him. Tomorrow we'll head out to the crime scene, see if there's anything they overlooked."

"Secondary crime scene," she corrected. "We don't know where Winkler was killed."

He grinned. "Good catch. I thought you'd miss that one. We'll check it out first thing tomorrow morning.

"Sounds like a plan. Maybe we'll get lucky."

"Really?" he teased, one brow arching devilishly.

She swatted his arm. "You've got a one-track mind. You know, I pity the woman who ends up with you. She'll be lucky to get out of bed each morning."

"Aw, Jazz, you know there's only one woman for me."

Before she could pull away, he tugged at her ponytail, thankful he'd remembered to put on his gloves.

She scowled at him. "Enough of that."

"But we're best friends, remember?"

She clinked her mug against his. "Bestest."


By mid-afternoon, they'd gone over more than half the files related to the case, plus some that delved into Winkler's political career. It was dry reading and Ben could tell that Jasi was getting impatient. Every now and then she'd let out a frustrated sigh, emphasizing it to make sure he heard.

He chuckled when she did it again. "Take a break, Jasi."

"I want to get this over with. You know I hate politics."

"Hey, you might actually learn something."

"Learn something?" She scowled. "I'd rather have a root canal done. Without anesthesia."

Ben was about to say something when his data-com beeped. He answered, then activated the speakerphone so Jasi could hear.

"Have you solved the case yet?" a gravelly voice asked.

"Ha-ha, Matthew," Jasi replied.

Ben watched as her smile brightened. Matthew Divine was almost a surrogate father figure, and he knew their boss held a special place in his heart for her.

"Are you both settled in?" Matthew asked.

"It's a very comfortable hotel," Ben replied.

"I've arranged for another SUV to be delivered to the hotel. For Jasmine. It's in the underground parking. Keys are at the front desk."

"I can't drive in an unfamiliar city," Jasi argued.

They heard Matthew sigh. "You drive in Vancouver."

"That's different, sir. I know Vancouver like the back of my hand. Anywhere else and I'm—"

Ben smiled innocently. "Directionally challenged?"

Even Matthew had to laugh at that.

"Half the time I'm with Ben," she said. "Any other time, I'm perfectly fine taking a taxi. At least they know where they're going."

"Traffic's too busy in Ottawa," Matthew said.

"Yes, it is," Ben agreed, ignoring his partner's flashing green eyes. "She'll survive, Matthew. It's everyone else in Ottawa I'm worried about."

Jasi tipped her head to one side. "Gee, thanks for the vote of confidence. My driving's not *that* bad."

"Tell that to the granny you side-swiped last month."

He grinned and held up his hands in surrender. She was fun to tease, but she had her limits.

"The SUV has a voice-activated navigational system," Matthew said. "All you have to do is say your destination out loud and it'll track your route for you."

Jasi scowled at Ben. "You think of everything, sir. Thank you."

"I'm looking at the police report right now," came the reply. "Some things are definitely out of whack."

"What do you mean?" Ben asked.

"Well, for one thing, Monty Winkler went missing two days before his body was discovered."

"Missing? I don't recall hearing anything about that."

"Marilyn never reported him missing until the day before his body was found."

Jasi cut in. "Where was his wife on the night Winkler disappeared?"

"At a charity fundraiser," Matthew said. "She called him that Wednesday night, April 11, but he never answered."

"His body wasn't found until Friday morning, April 13," Jasi murmured. "So where was he for those missing two days?"

"That's what we need you and Ben to figure out."

Ben frowned. "I don't get why Marilyn didn't report him missing right away. Didn't she think it was strange that he never came home after two days?"

"Apparently, it's a habit," Matthew said. "Winkler often came home late at night. Sometimes he'd be gone the next morning before she woke up. That's what she figured happened."

"So she never heard him come home, yet she still did nothing?" Jasi asked. "She must sleep like a log."

"Marilyn takes amitriptyline to help her sleep," Matthew said.

"What about the next day?" Ben asked. "Didn't she at least try to call him?"

"Marilyn tried his 'com both mornings. No answer. That's when she started to get worried. So she called his office."

"And?"

"Monty Winkler never showed up for work Monday or Tuesday. That's when she called the police."

Ben scratched his chin. "So he went missing Sunday before the charity event, but no one knows where he was until his body washed up on the beach." He checked the file. "Any sign of his vehicle?"

"Not yet. He drives a light tan colored 1972 Mercedes Benz 280SE. There's an APB out on it." Matthew gave him the license plate number.

"What about comparative cases? Has anything like this happened before?"

"Nothing conclusive. There was one case about nine months ago. Darlene MacKenzie, another Member of Parliament and a divorcee with no children, went missing for three days. When she resurfaced, she said she'd taken off for a much needed rest and was sure she'd notified her work. Her VISA bill recorded her stay at a bed and breakfast outside the city."

"You want us to talk to her?" Ben asked.

"OPS and the RCMP have already questioned her. I'll send you their reports."

"Did you get Jasi's report?"

"Yes. It was very detailed. Good job, Jasmine."

Ben smiled. That was about as much praise as anyone would get from Matthew Divine.

"I just sent you the report from the RCMP, Ben."

"Thanks, Matthew. Does Marilyn have any idea where her husband might have gone?"

"No. She says he's never disappeared like this." Matthew cleared his throat. "You need to find out where he was. As discreetly as possible."

"So we have two mysteries to uncover," Jasi said. "We need to find out where Winkler was for those two days and—"

"Who killed him," Ben finished.

Matthew cleared his throat. "There's one other thing. The Winklers have friends in high places. Director Petrie called in a Russian psychic."

"Why would the director do that?"

"Monty Winkler was a longtime friend of the Petrie family. It's some kind of peace trade. This psychic has been in Canada for just over a year, finished basic with the CFBI and was transferred to Quebec City five months ago."

"What's his name?"

"*Her*," Matthew replied. "Natassia Prushenko. She'll be meeting up with you the day after tomorrow."

"Should we pick her up from the airport?" Jasi asked.

"No. She'll contact you at the hotel. She should be there around four-thirty in the afternoon. Ben, I want her to pair up with you or Jasmine at all times."

"No problem."

"Oh, and one more thing. I think you'll work well together. Prushenko is a highly skilled VE. A Level 1."

Ben heard Jasi's sharp intake of breath. He could practically read her mind.

A few years ago the PSI Division had designed a system of testing and documenting psychic skill levels. There were five levels in total. The average tarot card reader or palm reader scored a Level 5. Those with vague premonitory dreams or waking visions might score a Level 4.

PSI agents scored in the top three levels. Level 1 was the highest, most dependable and the rarest. Ben was a Level 3 Psychometric Empath. And Jasi was the only Level 1 he'd ever met.

However, that was about to change.

# 5

Jasi stood on the shore of the Ottawa River, miles from the city center. Being near water always made her think of home...the salty scent of Vancouver air, the roar of the ocean. She loved the ocean.

She inhaled the crisp air and watched cotton puffs sail overhead. On the river, four speedboats and a sailboat glistened like tiny jewels dancing on the waves. A wintry wind whipped through her hair, plucking at the burnished strands like a voracious lover.

Despite her lined jacket, she crossed her arms. "I hate this time of year."

"Do you want to sit in the car for a while?" Ben asked.

"No, I'm fine. My run this morning is keeping me relatively warm."

"You ran?" He eyed her. "By yourself?"

"Yeah, Ben. All by my lonesome."

Back home, her morning routine usually consisted of a set of fifty sit-ups and push-ups, plus a morning jog along the Stanley Park seawall. This morning she'd gotten up at six, done her sets, then gone for a run. She needed to forget about death and work, if only for a few minutes.

The route around the hotel had been hindered by early morning rush hour traffic and impatient pedestrians who stared at her as though she were a member of an alien species bent on taking over the world. Hardly anyone jogged in Ottawa anymore. Maybe it was a new law. Outside of personal vehicles, buses and taxis, bicycles and Segways were the popular mode of transportation, and there was a health club every four blocks for those who had time to run.

Once she'd found her way onto the wide promenade that framed the Rideau Canal, Jasi had forgotten all about Monty Winkler's corpse and the five circular wounds on his scalp. Ignoring a few catcalls from young men racing down the walkway on their bikes, she'd pushed herself forward. The biting wind made her calf muscles work harder, but the sight of the water calmed her nerves.

Jasi was a *water soul*.

That's what her mother had called her.

Now, wearing comfortable navy pants, a v-neck sweater and a heavy jacket, she stood along the Ottawa River and let her eyes drift across the shoreline. She should have gone running here. No people to dodge, no waiting for traffic lights to change, no exhaust fumes to gag on.

She glanced to her right. "I'm ready."

Dressed in a dove-gray Armani suit, open-collared shirt, no tie, Benjamin Roberts looked out of place as he stood in a grassy area a few feet from the rock-lined shore. Next to him, the stocky silver-haired man in his distinctive red uniform gave her a veiled nod. Constable Finn O'Malley from the RCMP was their liaison on the Winkler case. Thankfully, they'd have no trouble from him. He seemed relieved to hand the case over to the CFBI, probably because he was only a few months to retirement.

"Thank you for securing the scene," she said to him.

"If you need anything, let me know," O'Malley replied, his voice gruff. "I'll stay up here."

"Thank you. I think we're good."

When O'Malley stepped away, Ben said, "Have you got *OxyBlast* on hand?"

"A small canister. But I don't think I'll need it. Police found no traces of a campfire or brushfire." She saw his worried look. "I'll be fine."

It wasn't difficult for them to find the secondary crime scene. A few yards down the beach, the area where Winkler's body had been found was secured by four perimeter beacons. The heavy neon orange cones were two feet high and resembled traffic pylons. Two of them rested in about four inches of water. Six-foot high screens of orange light connected the high-tech beacons, creating a large rectangular wall of light, to warn away the public.

The beacons used instant GPS tracking and facial recognition identification. If anyone tried to move them, enter the wrong code, or if a screen was broken by anything bigger than a sparrow, the beacon would lock onto the person's face and track them anywhere. It also emitted an ear-piercing alarm that would drive even the most resilient criminal to his or her knees.

There was some controversy over this, just as there had been over the use of police Tasers a few years ago, and certain activists felt it would be better to let someone corrupt a crime screen rather than to risk a city lawsuit for hearing impairment.

Three officers from OPS stood at various positions on the beach. They had thoughtfully cordoned off the area surrounding the beacons, just in case some idiot couldn't see the bright orange light. In the daylight, the light was more yellow than orange, but it was still hard to miss.

Jasi moved toward the bushes, followed closely by Ben.

A thorough search uncovered nothing but a few trampled patches of grass and broken branches.

"Probably from investigators," she said.

"Or curious onlookers," Ben added.

The wind and rain had swept away any footprints, and there were no drag marks, nothing to indicate that Winkler had been carried to the shore and dumped.

On the beach Jasi stepped over the rope, then moved to one of the perimeter beacons. She pulled out her data-com, retrieved the code and entered it on the beacon's panel. The light screens retracted and she clipped her 'com to her jacket pocket. She didn't expect to have anything to report, but better to be safe than sorry.

"You ready?" Ben asked.

She nodded. "Voice record on."

She gave a brief description of the scene. Three gray boulders jutted out of the water about four feet from shore. Winkler's bloated body had been discovered wedged between two of them. A small red flag marked the spot.

"*Shake 'n bake* time," she muttered.

She made her way to the water's edge, thankful she'd worn her CFBI-issue steel-toed boots. She moved into the river and even though the boots were waterproof, she flinched from the sudden chill that surrounded her feet.

Holding onto a boulder for support, she crouched over the flag and examined the rocks. Each boulder was polished smooth from years of erosion, and there was no trace evidence. She circled each boulder, prodding beneath the water with her boot. She found nothing but sand and pebbles.

With a sigh, she looked at Ben and shook her head.

"I want to walk further down the beach."

Ben signaled O'Malley. "Make sure we don't have any unexpected visitors while the screen is down."

O'Malley nodded. "Will do, Agent Roberts."

"Wait," Jasi said. "Were there any witnesses?"

"Just a couple of teenagers. They're the ones that found the body."

Jasi blew out a breath. "Did they see anyone else?"

O'Malley shook his head.

Ben followed her as she walked the shoreline, inspecting every bush, every square foot of beach and every piece of driftwood. A few yards ahead, a rickety boat dock jutted out into the water.

"Winkler could've been dumped off the dock," she said.

As they walked the length of the wood contraption, Jasi imagined someone tossing Monty Winkler off the end of it.

"Maybe his body got caught in the beams under the dock," she suggested. "Then brought back to shore by the current."

"Why would someone dump him in the river?" Ben said. "Why not bury him?"

"Animals could dig up a body, which means early discovery. The river might take the body out of range of the dump site, which is what the perp would want."

"Any other reason?"

Another test.

She smiled up at him. "The combination of fresh water and marine life destroys a lot of trace evidence. If it were summer, the river would've sped up decomposition of the body. Still, the river is…convenient." She glanced over her shoulder. "Did I pass?"

He ignored the question. "Who uses the river?"

"Tourists, fishermen, shipping companies…"

A silver speedboat with a blue stripe across the body cruised past, maybe forty yards from shore. In its wake, lapping waves swept up the beach and washed over Jasi's boots.

"And boat owners," she added.

She shielded her eyes and squinted at the boat. There was one person aboard, a man in a hooded maroon-colored jacket and reflective sunglasses. She switched her data-com to camera mode and took a few pictures, although she thought it unlikely that their perp would be so foolish as to come back to the crime scene when it was still under investigation. However, she had captured some really stupid criminals in the past.

She turned back to the task at hand—finding the murderer responsible for putting Monty Winkler in a body bag.

"Voice record off."

"So what are your conclusions?" Ben asked.

"I'm thinking he might have been tossed off the dock, but there's no evidence to prove that theory."

"I'll get some divers to check around the beams."

"Have they done a sweep with an X-Disc yet?"

"Yeah. OPS said they'll send us the data as soon as it's in."

While Ben reset the perimeter beacons, she pocketed her data-com and checked her watch. "It's almost one."

"Let's go back to the hotel, have some lunch. Then we'll figure out what we're gonna do next."

"I think we need to talk to some of Winkler's family. And his associates." She paused. "Why would someone go to all the trouble to drug him, beat him, set him on fire, then dump him in the river?"

"Maybe they didn't like his political policies."

"Or it was someone with a personal score to settle."

She mulled this over in her mind.

"So who had it in for Monty Winkler?" Ben asked.

"And what could anyone hope to gain from his death?"

She glanced back at the man in the speedboat and allowed herself a moment to envy his freedom.

*Winkler is free too. You can't get freer than dead.*


The Nook Coffee Shop in the Embassy Hotel was quiet and quaint, with only a handful of guests occupying tables. Ben asked the hostess for a table in the far corner and Jasi followed him, her stomach gurgling in anticipation.

"I'm starving," she said apologetically.

She sat down immediately to Ben's right. That way they were both facing the room, a habit born from the desire to stay alert and alive. When the waiter arrived, she ordered the Eggs Benedict special and coffee, while her partner ordered a more traditional lunch, a cheeseburger and fries.

"I need to wash my hands."

She grabbed her purse and strode across the room. She pushed open the washroom door and moved to the sinks. That was when she noticed the other occupant at the opposite end.

Jasi probably wouldn't have given her a second thought except that the woman's attire seemed out of place for a classy hotel. The woman's long legs looked like they had been painted into the black jeans. A black short-sleeved sweater with a plunging neckline showed off her ample assets. A simple gold chain with a small cross hung low, lost in her generous cleavage.

"*Merde!*" the woman muttered. Her hand shook as she tried to apply a dark shade of lipstick.

Washing her hands, Jasi eyed her surreptitiously.

Tall and slender, the woman was about Jasi's age. Her pixie face and high cheekbones were framed by jet-black hair, cut short, choppy.

"Can you pass me a tissue?"

Startled, Jasi handed her the box of Kleenex.

"Thank you," the woman mumbled.

Brilliant blue eyes enhanced by dusky gray eye shadow examined her for a brief moment. Then the woman turned away to dab at the corner of her mouth, stopping suddenly when her hand trembled again.

"Are you okay?" Jasi asked hesitantly.

The woman let out a snort. "I'm supposed to be meeting someone. I'm a bit nervous." Her voice held a trace of accent, a mix of French and something else.

"Blind date?"

"More like a job interview."

Jasi was surprised. *There's only one job I can think of that warrants a neckline like that.*

It didn't surprise her to find an escort in the hotel. It wasn't uncommon for visiting dignitaries to use such personal *services*. However, it did surprise her that the woman was starting so early. It wasn't even lunchtime.

Drying her hands, she glanced over her shoulder.

The woman was leaning with her back to the sinks. She looked as if she were about to throw up.

Must be one hell of an awful client, Jasi thought.

"Uh, good luck on your, uh…interview," she said, heading out the door.

The woman grunted. *"Merci beaucoup."*

Back at the table, Jasi quickly dove into a plate of poached eggs, ham and hash browns, all slathered in rich Hollandaise sauce. It took mere seconds before she forgot all about the nervous escort in the washroom.

Until Jasi saw her again.

# 6

"Let's go over the report on Winkler," Ben said.

Pushing his empty plate aside, he read the screen for a minute, then sighed. The report was less than he'd hoped for.

"The accelerant used was regular gasoline," he said. "Remnants of his clothing match the suit that his wife reported he was last wearing. No trace."

"What about the wounds on his scalp?" Jasi asked.

"No match to any identifiable weapon." He paused as something in the report caught his eye. "Well, this is interesting. Someone called Monty Winkler at his home nearly every night for the past two weeks."

"Who?"

"Don't know. They used a payphone. Same one every time." He leaned back in his chair, his gaze drifting across the room. "When we're done here, we'll have a talk with Marilyn Winkler. Actually, you can ask the questions. She might open up more to a woman."

He froze when his gaze fastened on something.

Or some*one*.

A tall, slender woman dressed entirely in black was making her way across the floor. Her hair was short, blue-black and messy, as if she'd just woken up. Her lips were painted a deep crimson—too much lipstick for his liking—but she was drop-dead gorgeous. And she knew it.

The black knit sweater with its low v-neck showed off all her curves. She had a lot of them. Her entrance didn't go unnoticed by the various diners seated in the coffee shop. Every man in the room was practically salivating as she passed by.

"Jesus, she's starting early," he muttered.

Jasi followed his gaze. "I saw her in the washroom."

His mouth curled in distaste. If there was one thing he had zero tolerance for, it was hookers or 'legal escorts.' He thought they spelled trouble. With a capital 'T.'

As the escort approached, he noticed her eyes. They were a deep sapphire blue framed by thick black lashes. When her gaze swept over their table, her eyes locked on Jasi and there was a flicker of recognition and what seemed like...surprise.

That's odd, he thought.

The woman wiped her hands on her thighs and moved toward them, chin held high. Every set of male eyes trailed after her.

"Ben!" Jasi whispered. "Did you hire someone?"

"Hire someone for what?"

"For some...you know." She jerked her head in the woman's direction. "She's heading straight for you."

"I don't know what she's thinking."

The escort paused a few feet away, suddenly seeming unsure. She watched them for a moment, gave a subtle nod and strode to the table.

"Are you Benjamin Roberts?"

Annoyed, he set aside the data-com. "Obviously there's been a mistake. As you should be able to see, I'm already with someone. You'll have to find another mark." His eyes rested on her breasts. "One who's actually interested in all that you are so openly offering."

The woman's face turned bright red. "I'm afraid you've misunderstood. I'm not here to offer my...uh...self. At least not in the way you're suggesting."

Beside him, Jasi gasped. "Ben, I think she's—"

"What other way is there?" he interrupted.

Jasi dug her elbow into his side. "Ben!"

He ignored her and stared up at the intruder. "Well, off you go now. Run along." He gave her a mocking smile, hoping she'd take the hint.

She didn't. Instead, she flicked a cursory look around the room. People were staring.

What she did next drew a muffled curse from him.

She sat down.

"What the hell are you're doing?" he demanded.

"Following orders."

The woman leaned on one hip. The movement caused her sweater to pucker and all of a sudden Ben had a clear view of a lacy black bra barely restraining two very round breasts. He glanced away as she fished something out of her jeans pocket.

A shiny object landed on the table.

He gaped at the CFBI badge until comprehension set in.

"N-Natassia Prushenko, I take it." He felt like an idiot.

The woman raised a brow. "So you *were* told I was meeting you. I was starting to wonder." She turned to Jasi. "Is this how he greets all new team members?"

"Usually he's more civil. Not much more, mind you."

He cleared his throat. "We, uh, weren't expecting you until this afternoon, Agent Prushenko."

"Natassia. I took an earlier flight from Quebec City."

"Ah, that's why I pegged you as French Canadian," Jasi said.

"Sorry, it slips out every now and then. I've obviously spent too much time there." Natassia held out a hand. "You must be Jasmine. I've heard so much about you. You too, Benjamin. Although, Matthew Divine told me you'd welcome me with open arms."

"Open arms?" He'd have to have a talk with Matthew.

Natassia smiled, flashing perfect teeth. "Well, I *was* expecting a slightly warmer welcome."

"And I was expecting someone who wasn't dressed so," he waved a hand toward her, "provocatively."

She gave him an innocent look. "Don't all Canadian women dress like this?"

"Not unless they're—"

"Going out," Jasi cut in. "Clubbing, maybe."

Suddenly, it hit him.

"You knew who she was all along. Didn't you, Jasi?"

"I knew as soon as she looked at you."

Natassia frowned.

"When you saw Ben's gloves, you nodded," Jasi explained. "Just briefly, mind you. But it was obvious you knew the importance of his gloves."

"I'll have to work on that."

Ben held out his hand. "I'll admit I was expecting someone more…"

"Russian?" Natassia shook his hand briefly, then shifted smoothly into a heavy accent. "You're wondering where my Russian accent has gone, da? I'm fluent in five languages. English, French, Spanish, Japanese and Russian." She looked directly at him. *"Vy zhenaty?"*

He was sure she'd just called him something nasty.

She switched to a perfect Canadian accent. "Oh, and I speak a bit of German, but not enough to fool anyone."

"Must come in handy," Jasi said in admiration.

"With a little help from a good makeup artist, I can pass for all five nationalities." Natassia fastened her gaze on him. "Looks can be deceiving, eh?"

Ben clamped his lips shut. The woman had made her point. And he didn't like that. She had firmly set him in his place, and at this particular moment, he wasn't exactly sure where that was.

"I'll do some background checks while you two visit Marilyn Winkler."

Jasi gave him a surprised look. "Don't you want to come too?"

"I'll go see her later."

He needed some time to assess the current situation.

*And Natassia Prushenko.*

The only way he could do that was if he distanced himself from her. For the good of the case, he told himself.

Natassia stared at him. "I'll need case details."

"What did Matthew tell you?" Jasi asked.

"He said a dead politician was found on the beach."

"The victim's name is Monty Winkler. He's an MLA."

"Any suspects?"

"Not yet," Jasi replied. "And no primary murder scene."

While she filled Natassia in on the details, Ben sipped his coffee. He tried to eat the last few fries, but they were tasteless and cold. His attention kept wandering—much to his dismay—to a gold cross that was playing hide and seek between black lace and flawless skin.


"A job interview, huh?" Jasi said to Natassia as they made their way to the elevator. They'd left Ben back in the coffee shop to sulk.

"It was the only thing I could think of saying."

"And what was that you said to him? *Vy…*"

*"Vy zhenaty?"* Natassia laughed. "I asked if he was married."

From the corner of her eye, Jasi peeked at her new partner. She was about to say something, warn the woman, but the elevator stopped at their floor.

"I still don't understand why you were so nervous to meet Ben," she said, swiping the hotel key in the lock and making a mental note to get one for Natassia. "He's a great supervisor, very patient and not overly demanding."

"It wasn't *Ben* I was nervous about meeting."

Jasi was taken aback. "Me?" She laughed. "You've got to be kidding."

When they entered the room, Jasi spotted a red light flashing on the phone.

"Someone's left us a message," she said, curious.

She called down to the front desk. "I have a message?"

"There's a small package down here for you."

She frowned. "Who's it from?"

"It's from a Matthew Divine, at the CFBI."

"I'll be right down."

When Jasi returned to the room, she showed Natassia the small box she'd retrieved from the front desk.

"I have no idea why Matthew sent me this."

"What's inside?"

"I don't know. I haven't opened it yet."

Natassia smiled. "Is it your birthday or something?"

"No," she frowned. "Not for a couple of months."

The box was about the size of a triple pack of soap bars and the postal stamp had yesterday's date. When she opened the package, she found an envelope and a note from Matthew. As usual, he was a man of few words.

*Jasi, someone sent this to you, so I'm forwarding it on.*

She studied the envelope. Someone had carefully printed her name in block letters. That was it, nothing else.

*Who sent this?*

She'd have to ask Matthew later.

"Well, aren't you going to open it?" Natassia asked.

She did just that and a lighter slid into the palm of her hand. She showed it to Natassia. "Just what I need."

"I take it you don't smoke?"

Jasi made a face. "No, and I sure hope you don't."

"I only have healthy vices. So who's the lighter from?"

Jasi shook her head slowly. "I haven't got a clue." She stuffed the lighter in her purse, then looked at her partner's tote bag. "Aren't you going to unpack?"

"I'm thinking I should get my own room," Natassia said.

Jasi blinked, stunned. "You don't like sharing?"

"Not at all. I just thought…"

"What? Have I grown two heads?"

"No," Natassia said with a sigh. "Jasi, you're the only Level 1 PSI I know. Besides me. And you're team leader. That makes you very important."

With a derisive snort, Jasi said, "*All* PSIs are important."

"You know what I mean."

"Listen, I don't care who is what rank. It's easier if we share. I can pick your brain and you can pick mine."

Natassia relaxed and settled into a chair. "Fine. I wanted to give you the option."

Jasi gave her a wary look. "Why? Do you snore?"

Natassia laughed. "I don't think so."

"You better not."

With the mood lightened, Jasi hung up her jacket and dug her favorite long t-shirt from her bag.

"So…" Natassia drawled, watching her. "You're a Pyro-Psychic, huh? I've met a couple in Russia. Is there anything I need to know?"

"I carry OxyBlast with me."

Natassia nodded. "Do you pass out?"

"Not if I'm careful. I usually wear an oxy-mask if the scene is fresh or if there's a lot of smoke. If you're with me and there's smoke, keep an eye on me. What about you?"

"At times I need a reality line. Depends on the victim."

Jasi studied Natassia carefully. Victim Empaths were known to get deeply entranced by victim's memories. It was an ugly business. Most VEs could read only live victims. Level 1s could read live and dead.

*What is it like to feel what a victim feels, feel their fear?*

"Let's get caught up on the case," she said. "Matthew sent over the missing persons report that Winkler's wife filed with the local PD. Tomorrow we'll pay her a visit. After that I'll take you to OFU."

"OFU?"

"Ottawa Forensics Unit. The morgue."

"Nothing like a little sightseeing in a new city."

Jasi settled on the bed and combed through Winkler's file on her data-com. As she did so, she thought of Ben's bizarre reaction to their new partner. Sure, Natassia dressed a bit provocatively, but that could be an advantage. Especially during interrogations.

A movement caught her eye. *What is she doing?*

Natassia was frisking the other bed, looking under the covers and pillows. With a scowl, she got down on her knees and checked under the bed.

"What in God's name are you looking for?" Jasi asked.

"They usually leave chocolates on the bed. I thought maybe mine had fallen on the floor. Did you see any?"

Jasi tried not to look at the wastebasket.

"Nope. Housekeeping must've missed our room."

# 7

Winkler Manor was located northeast of downtown Ottawa in Rockcliffe Park, a neighborhood that was reserved for the very wealthy and for government officials, including the Governor General and the Prime Minister of Canada. Generations of money had been pumped into the area by various ambassadors, computer software companies, Internet entrepreneurs and more than a few politicians.

It had been a few years since Jasi had driven through this area. Things had changed. A year ago, the former Canadian Forces Base CFB Rockcliffe had added a new expansion to Rockcliffe Park. Some of the existing buildings had been converted for other uses. Many had been demolished so that new homes could be built. The Winkler's lived in the original area, in an older estate home.

Grateful for the SUV's state-of-the-art GPS system, Jasi slowed the vehicle so they could take in the gated mansions that nestled in the trees. Somewhere behind them were endless immaculate lawns, azure swimming pools, extra-large hot tubs, outdoor bars and tennis courts.

"Welcome to Ottawa's version of 'Lifestyles of the Rich and Famous,'" Natassia said in a British accent. "I'm your host, Robin Leach."

Jasi grinned. "Champagne wishes…"

"And caviar dreams," they said in unison, laughing.

"I think caviar is disgusting," Jasi said, making a face.

Natassia released a contented sigh. "Caviar and sushi. Two of the four food groups. Or they should be. You don't know what you're missing."

"I'll live just fine without sludge in a tin. Give me a charbroiled steak any day."

Jasi maneuvered the SUV along the perfectly paved main road, then turned down a secondary street lined with pruned black willow, red maple and hundred-year-old hackberry trees, and assorted trimmed bushes, no doubt the responsibility of an expensive lawn care service. In Rockcliffe, the lack of sidewalks stood out. People liked their privacy at Rockcliffe Park. They expected it.

She slowed the car in front of two brick pillars. There were rough iron gates on either side. An ornate wooden plaque was centered on the pillar on the right side.

*Winkler Manor*, it proclaimed in a floral scroll.

"That's odd," she said.

"What is?"

"Most people in this neighborhood keep their gates closed."

The Winkler's gate was wide open.

Natassia frowned. "Did you call Marilyn Winkler to let her know we were coming?"

"Nope. I prefer the element of surprise."

"It looks like she's expecting someone."

"I wonder who."

Jasi turned down the long driveway and was silent for a moment, taking in the rich green lawn and colorful flowerbeds. She envied people with yards like this. She couldn't keep a houseplant alive for more than a month.

"Matthew said you're training for the position of team leader," Natassia said hesitantly.

"Uh, yeah. They think I'm ready."

"What do you think?"

"I know I'm ready. Ben's been drilling me for over a month."

"You're lucky to have someone who believes in you the way he does."

"I know." She studied her new partner. "So, how shall we do this?"

"I'll follow your lead."

Well, Natassia was certainly accommodating.

"Since Marilyn is a victim of sorts, can you read her?"

Natassia shrugged. "I do better with people who have directly experienced a violent crime. I feel the energy from their trauma."

"So you probably won't get anything from her then."

"I doubt it."

The scenery suddenly flared open and an impressive coffee and cream brick house, roughly five thousand square feet, lay before them. Owning the land with its grandeur, Winkler Manor resembled a medieval castle with two towering turrets and a peaked roof. An oversized balcony looked down over the driveway.

Natassia whistled. "That's some house."

Jasi couldn't agree more.

The driveway circled around in front of the estate, with a three-car garage forking off the main curve. A one-lane paved road continued past the garage and disappeared between the bushes. Parked in front of two garage doors were a silver Sebring and a blue Cadillac.

"The Winklers like their toys," Jasi observed.

They climbed out of the SUV.

Flat slabs of beige and gray stone carved a sidewalk to a porch with two white columns that framed arched double doors inlaid with etched glass panes.

"Custom built," Jasi determined.

Natassia nodded. "There's some serious money here."

Jasi found the doorbell and pressed it. They were rewarded with a familiar waltz tune that played inside and out. Mid-tune, one of the heavy doors opened, the archway appearing even larger as it dwarfed a bone-thin bald man in a disheveled burgundy suit.

Wordlessly, he glowered at them with cold eyes.

Jasi glared back. *Why is he so annoyed?*

"We're here to see Mrs. Winkler."

The man squinted at her badge. Without a word, he turned away, leaving the door ajar.

Natassia gave her a questioning look.

"Good help is so hard to find," Jasi quipped.

Inside, they followed the clicking of the man's dress shoes. The scent of roses lingered in the air as he led them across a marble floor and into a carpeted sitting room decorated in pale shades of lavender and pink. Pink roses in crystal vases graced every surface, along with potted African violets of various shades. A quick once-over of the room told Jasi that it was rarely used by anyone other than the lady of the house.

Like an old-fashioned Victorian parlor, everything was delicate and flowered, from the Queen Anne sofa and loveseat, to the embroidered pillows and window valances, to the ruby and gold decanter set that accented an elaborately carved mantle over the wood fireplace. Massive oil paintings in intricate gilded frames hung on the far wall, threatening to buckle the pastel mauve wallpaper behind them.

"Please tell Mrs. Winkler we're here," she said, eyeing the bald man.

The look he gave her wasn't any warmer than the one they'd gotten at the door. With a shrug, he turned on one heel and left the room.

"What a strange man," Natassia whispered.

Jasi had to agree.

While they waited, Jasi studied the paintings. She was sure they were all originals, probably handed down from generation to generation. They had that air about them. Valuable. Old money.

"My husband's collection is impressive, isn't it?"

The lady of the house breezed into the room, her entrance marked by a scented cloud of rose, vanilla and a hint of sandalwood. She moved slowly across the floor as though she had all the time in the world, as though her husband wasn't lying dead in the city morgue.

"Welcome to my home."

*My* home, not *our* home, Jasi observed.

Marilyn Winkler was not a beautiful woman, but she commanded attention. People would notice her because of the severity of her appearance. Her hair, an indefinable black or dark brown depending on the lighting, was sleeked back from a high forehead, then twisted at the back and fastened with a jeweled clip. The combination of pale iridescent foundation, razor-thin black eyebrows that were drawn on, cold brown eyes and thin blood-red lips made her face look harsh and unfriendly.

*Otherworldly.*

Red lips lifted into a stiff smile. "I'm Marilyn Winkler."

The woman might not be attractive, but she sure knew how to dress, regardless of the extra thirty or so pounds she was carrying. The two-piece navy skirt suit reeked of New York City. It probably cost more than one of the many rings that adorned her hands. A single string of assorted pearls circled her thick neck.

Marilyn nervously touched the necklace. "So you're with the CFBI."

"Yes," Jasi said. "I'm Agent Jasmine McLellan and this is my partner Agent Natassia Prushenko."

"Please have a seat. James will bring us some coffee."

The bald man who had answered the door stood a few feet behind Marilyn. His subservient posture screamed *'domestic.'* James, the butler? If so, Marilyn's dress code for the hired help needed some work. James' suit needed dry-cleaning.

The man shifted under Jasi's concentrated inspection. Then he spun on one heel and left the room.

Jasi activated the voice recorder on her data-com. She set it on the coffee table, then settled beside Natassia on the sofa.

"Now..." Marilyn said, perching on the edge of loveseat across from them. "Let's get this nasty business over with, shall we?"

*Nasty business?*

"Thank you for seeing us, Mrs. Winkler," Jasi said. "We're very sorry for your loss."

"Monty is everyone's loss," came the hushed reply.

Readjusting the pillow under her arm, Jasi studied the woman before her. "Were you and your husband together a long time?"

"We married late in life," the woman answered, clasping her hands primly in her lap. "Both of us were well past thirty. My mother called me a spinster. Said I'd never catch a man. Well, what did she know? I ended up with the biggest catch of the decade." She glanced away, her attention on something else.

Propped against the wall a few feet from where Jasi sat was a briefcase made of high quality leather. It had an unusual design stamped on the top, maybe a family crest. A corner of paper protruded from one side, as if someone had hastily stuffed it inside the case.

Jasi couldn't quite make out the words on the paper, but she did see two interesting things. Monty Winkler's name and a number. $2,000,000.

*Monty Winkler's insurance policy?*

"Did your husband take out a life insurance policy?" she asked bluntly.

Marilyn gazed down at her hands. "Yes."

"For how much?"

Jasi saw the woman visibly wince.

"I-I'm not quite sure exactly."

Winkler's wife was lying.

*Interesting.*

Jasi thought about the two vehicles outside. Other than the rude butler, there was no sign of anyone else in the house.

"Is there anyone else in the house right now?"

"No. Just the four of us."

"The police already searched the garage out back. Your husband's Mercedes wasn't among them."

"That's Monty's favorite. Do you think you'll find it?"

"I hope so."

Ottawa was a big city. Finding Winkler's car would help narrow down the search.

"How many vehicles do you own, Mrs. Winkler?"

"Twelve." Marilyn chuckled. "Monty's passion is cars. He likes to collect older models, rebuild them."

"What did he do with them afterward?"

"Oh, he sells them usually. To other collectors."

"And he stored them here on the grounds?"

Marilyn smiled. "In his car motel. That's what Monty calls the building out back. The cars in there are worth a small fortune. He says they're his investments." She paused. "Occasionally, he donates a car to a fundraiser."

Jasi nodded, her attention diverted by the woman's constant use of the present tense. She'd been around death enough to recognize the stage of grief that Marilyn was in—denial. She knew that stage all too well.

After her mother's murder, it had taken her months to realize that her mother was never going to walk in the front door again or tuck her in at night. And it had taken years to get over feeling abandoned, betrayed.

Betrayal was something Marilyn Winkler knew about.

"I'm sorry to ask this," Jasi said, "but is there any truth to your sister's allegations?"

"You mean the so-called affair with Monty? He swore that nothing happened."

Jasi waited.

"Deirdre has a vivid imagination. She's always wanted what I have. I'm the oldest, you see, by nearly eighteen years. Deirdre was what my parents liked to call an 'oops.' Daddy left me in charge of my sister's inheritance. Deirdre has never forgiven me for that."

"So you think she started that rumor in spite?"

"I think she made it up because she doesn't like to see me happy. Sibling rivalry." Marilyn shrugged. "Monty would never touch my sister."

"What about other women, like Karen Hampton?"

Marilyn's eyes narrowed. "That bitch—pardon my French—was someone I trusted. My former secretary. She used to come to parties and benefit galas with us."

"So you think she lied too?"

The woman looked away. "No. I knew about Karen and Monty. All the late nights, phone calls at all hours. It wasn't too difficult to put two and two together. I knew he was seeing someone. I had no idea it was my secretary until I caught them together in his office."

"What did you do?"

"What do you think I did? I fired her ass." Her eyes settled on Natassia. "That woman knew how to use her body to get what she wanted. Not unlike my sister."

"Deirdre was promiscuous?" Jasi asked.

"When it got her something."

Jasi allowed the comment to sink in.

What would sleeping with her sister's husband get Deirdre? Not much, if what Marilyn said was true. She held Deirdre's purse strings. Not Monty.

"Monty knew I draw the line at family," Marilyn said, reading her mind. "Besides, my sister is in a *relationship*." On the last word, curled fingers made quotation marks in the air. "Or at least that's what she told me. I never know what to believe with her."

"Where does your sister live?"

"Downtown." Marilyn gave the address. "But you won't catch Deirdre there today. She's in Niagara Falls until late tomorrow night." Her mouth curled in distaste. "She said she needed a break, that she wasn't coping with Daddy's death."

"We'll have to confirm all this with her."

"Just be careful what you believe, Agents. My sister has a plethora of *stories*. Sometimes I don't think even she knows what's true and what's not."

"Would she have any reason to kill your husband?"

Marilyn's eyes widened. "Is that what these questions are about? You think Deirdre killed Monty?" She smoothed her skirt with her hands. "My sister might be a bit of a pain, as sisters usually are, but she wouldn't know the first thing about killing someone. Except maybe herself."

Jasi raised a brow. "What do you mean?"

"Deirdre started smoking again, after being a non-smoker for nearly six years. I don't understand the attraction of poisoning yourself daily like that. She says she's trying to quit, but I'm not sure I believe her."

"Is she under a lot of stress?"

Marilyn shrugged. "I guess."

"Stress can make people do terrible things."

The woman chuckled. "Well, my sister didn't hate Monty that much. He was too good to her."

"If she had anything to do with your husband's death, it could get ugly," Jasi warned.

"Everything in Deirdre's life is ugly. At least, according to her. She's young, impetuous, immature, and she's always been rather messed up."

"What does she do for a living?"

"She's a research technician at PRC."

Jasi tried to hide her surprise. "Paragon Research Corporation? You work together?"

"It's a family project," Marilyn said with a shrug. "Daddy had no sons to follow in his footsteps, so I went to work for him eight years ago. He left me in charge when he died."

"And your sister?"

"Deirdre joined us about three years ago."

"Do you get along with her?"

Marilyn's mouth curved into a dry smile. "Like sisters."

*Or brothers…*

With startling clarity, Jasi pictured her brother Brady and his constant struggle to gain Pop's approval.

Maybe Deirdre wanted to get back at her sister, make her pay for taking away Daddy's attention and approval. Maybe she was so jealous of Marilyn, who seemed to have it all, that she thought she'd take something away, make her suffer.

*Did Deirdre kill Monty Winkler?*

Jasi gave her new partner a quick nod. *Your turn.*

Natassia leaned forward. "It isn't easy to lose a parent, and I can only imagine what it must be like to lose a husband."

"I don't even remember the last thing I said to Monty."

"I'm sure he knew you loved him."

Jasi had no idea if her partner's words were true. But she did know one thing. It didn't really matter what Marilyn Winkler had said to her husband on his last day on earth.

Words were never enough.

## 8

Using the guise of needing a testimonial release form signed, Natassia sat down beside Marilyn. "Just sign at the bottom, please."

Marilyn obeyed. "Monty was everything to me."

Natassia reached for her hand and patted it gently. The caring part of her felt for the woman, but the PSI part wanted only the truth. She closed her eyes briefly when Marilyn turned her face away. She could feel the woman's energy. It radiated with a low hum. Marilyn was exhausted, unfocused, confused.

Within seconds, Natassia was inside. She *was* Marilyn.

*"We have to talk, Monty."*

*A mirror reflected Marilyn Winkler's angry face.*

*Her husband's eyes burned with anger. "Can't you see I'm busy?" A hand waved across his empty desk.*

*"What are you busy with?" Tears welled in her eyes and her throat burned. "Or maybe I should ask...who are you busy with?"*

*He must be seeing someone again. She knew it.*

*The phone rang, but Monty ignored it. It rang a second time and she was about to tell him to pick up the damned thing, but the ringing stopped.*

*"For God's sake, tell me who she is," she begged.*

*"Not this again. Marilyn, I'm waiting for a call."*

*She turned away just as the phone rang.*

*This time Monty picked it up. He listened for a minute, then in a perfectly calm voice said, "Yes...I understand." Without another word, he hung up.*

*"I'm not going to stand here and be made a fool of while you go off gallivanting with some slut," she said.*

*He smiled as if he hadn't heard her. "I have to go, dear. We'll talk when I get home." Whistling a tune, he shrugged on his jacket.*

*"Maybe you shouldn't come home," she snapped.*

*He gave her a cool look. "Careful what you wish for."*

*Marilyn gasped.*


Natassia hissed in a breath of air. Marilyn had released her hand and was staring at her with concern.

"Are you okay, Agent Prushenko?"

"I, uh…sorry, I was thinking about something else."

She caught Jasi's eye and gave a subtle smile to indicate she'd seen something.

"Mrs. Winkler," she continued, "did your husband have any known enemies, past or present?"

The woman shook her head. "I don't know. He never really discussed work with me."

"Any financial problems? Did he owe anyone money?"

"You mean besides the bank?" Marilyn glanced uneasily at a briefcase on the floor. "We're in decent shape, financially. I make very good money too."

Natassia caught the tightness in her voice. Money made the Winkler world go round. Marilyn Winkler had lived her life in the shadows of her well-known husband, yet she probably made twice the income.

"What exactly does Paragon research?" she asked.

Marilyn shrugged. "A bit of this and that. We started off looking for UFOs." At Natassia's raised brow, she chuckled. "Yes, we're looking for E.T., but we haven't found him yet. Seriously though, we're involved in satellite research, boring stuff to most people."

"Was your husband involved in your work?"

"No, Monty steered clear of PRC. He and Daddy had never seen eye-to-eye. Monty told me the company was in my hands alone. He was very adamant about that. Said if it sank it would be my fault and mine alone."

"Did you or Monty receive any unsettling or threatening letters or emails?"

"I don't think so."

"Did he have any problems at work that you know of?"

Marilyn's gaze traveled across the room and rested on one of the paintings. "There were always problems. *Issues*, he called them. Not everyone agreed with his policies or how he ran his campaigns."

James entered the room. His hand trembled as he placed a silver tray on the table. Resisting the temptation to help him, Natassia stared at him, waiting for the man to leave. He glared back at her, his face pinched and stubborn.

"That's fine, James," Marilyn said. "I'll call you if I need anything else."

His chin rose ever so slightly as he hobbled to the far end of the room.

Once the door closed, Natassia said, "Did your husband receive any threatening phone calls?"

Marilyn poured cream into a mug of coffee. She stirred it for a long time. Finally, she shook her head. "He never said anything to me. I think he would tell me if anyone was threatening him. But..."

Natassia leaned forward. "But what?"

"He received phone calls the same time every night for the past week. It was kind of strange. The phone would ring twice and whoever it was would hang up. Then a few minutes later someone would call again. Monty always picked up on the first ring."

"What time was that?"

"Around six-thirty."

Natassia turned to Jasi. "That coincides with the phone calls from the payphone."

"Payphone?" Marilyn sounded surprised.

"Is there anyone you can think of who'd call your husband from a payphone?" Natassia asked.

"No. Everyone we know has a cell phone or one of those data-communicators."

"Did you ask your husband about the calls?"

"I asked him point-blank after the third call."

"What did he say?"

"He gave me a blank look and said he didn't get a call. I was getting worried. I thought maybe he had Alzheimer's."

"Did he always have problems with his memory?"

"Not usually. But..."

"But what?"

"About six months ago, something happened. I don't know what exactly, but...Monty started to change."

Natassia flicked a look at Jasi. "In what way?"

"He became distracted, less patient. With me mainly. And he stopped discussing his day with me. That wasn't like him." Marilyn took a sip of coffee. "He always shared everything."

"Six months ago…" Natassia recalled something. "That's right before he voted for the gun rights bill. Perhaps he was preoccupied with that."

"Or with someone," Marilyn said dryly.

"You thought he was having an affair?"

The woman's gaze hardened. "I was sure of it. Then one night last week he was in his office and I walked in with his evening tea. You would've thought I'd caught him with another woman, the way he jumped out of his chair."

"What was he doing when you walked in?"

"Sleeping in his chair. With the TV on. That wasn't like him, not one bit. My Monty is a night owl. He'd stay up until well past midnight every night."

"What time did you bring him the tea?"

"Seven o'clock. That's our nightly ritual." Marilyn's eyes locked on hers. "But every night for the last three weeks, I found him sleeping in his office. And he refused his tea."

Natassia mulled over the woman's words. Winkler's regular routine had changed right around the same time as the suspicious payphone calls.

*Something's definitely off in the Winkler world of Oz.*

Natassia glanced at Jasi. Her partner gave a bob of her head, so she continued.

"Did your husband have any health problems?"

"Monty had osteoarthritis in his back, hips and knees. Some days he could barely get out of bed, much less make it through the day. One of his friends told him he was moving like an old man."

"Was he on any medication?"

"Tylenol 3. Two every night. He's been doing that for years, but ever since he *changed*, I have no idea what he's been taking. He stopped asking me to pick up his prescription. I suppose he could have gotten it himself."

"How was he sleeping at night?"

"That's the odd thing. He was sleeping better than he'd been in years. He told me that." She closed her eyes and rubbed her forehead. "I'm sorry, but I'm very tired."

"I know this isn't easy," Natassia said. "Thank you."

"We need to see your husband's office before we go," Jasi said, rising to her feet. To Natassia, she added, "Matthew is sending an evidence team over in about an hour. They'll catalog everything in Mr. Winkler's office and bring us anything they think is useful to the investigation."

"What kind of things?" Marilyn asked in a weary voice.

"We'll need to look at your husband's computer, laptop, data-com—basically anything that might give us a lead or reveal the identity of your husband's killer."

"Monty always carries his data-communicator with him." Marilyn flinched. "Did you find it?"

Jasi glanced at her partner. "No."

"Well, take whatever you need."

"Why don't you go rest?" Natassia suggested. "We can let ourselves out when we're done." Her foot *accidentally* brushed up against the briefcase. "Interesting design."

Marilyn blinked. "The Winkler family crest."

"Did Monty usually take this to work with him?"

"Oh, that's not Monty's. It's James'."

At that very second, the bald man appeared.

"James," Marilyn said with a gasp. "I'm so sorry. I didn't make proper introductions before. Agent McLellan and Agent Prushenko, this is James Winkler, my brother-in-law. Monty's younger brother."

Natassia studied James with careful consideration. He looked nothing like his brother. Not only was James tall, bald and reed thin, his skin sagged with an unhealthy gray glow.

"I don't know what I'd do without him," Marilyn said, smiling at James. "Show the agents Monty's office, dear. I have some things to take care of."

James nodded once, his gaze resting for a moment on Natassia's pendant before drifting toward her face. He led them from the room, his back rigid, almost angry.

*What's gotten under his skin?*

"He's awfully quiet," she whispered to Jasi.

"Maybe he can't speak."

"Do you think he's mute?"

James whipped around. The look he gave her silenced any further conversation. All the guy needed was a riding crop to complete the image of Icabod Crane—*after* his run-in with the Headless Horseman.

He escorted them to a formidable oak door and paused, one skeletal hand on the knob.

"Thank you, James," she said.

But he was already walking away.

She glanced at Jasi. "A man of few words."

"Makes me wonder why he's hanging around his brother's widow. It doesn't seem like they're mourning a common loss. Marilyn treats him like the hired help."

"Brother James does make a good butler."

"Yeah, but the question is, did he make a good brother?"


Jasi's first impression of Monty Winkler's home office was that it was like stepping into a cold, gloomy cave. Every piece of furniture was black and the walls were navy blue. A man's room, and a complete contrast to the floral garden of Marilyn's sitting room.

In the dead silence, a clock ticked loudly above the door.

She pulled on a pair of latex gloves. "Glove up."

Natassia blushed. "I left mine in my tote bag."

"No problem." Jasi pulled another set from her jacket pocket. "Here you go."

"I'm sorry. I don't know what I was thinking. I'll be more prepared tomorrow."

"Don't worry about it. I've got your back."

The look her new partner gave her was one of surprise.

"What? You think we don't watch out for one another?"

Natassia shook her head. "It isn't that. I'm used to...well, you know...it takes time to connect with an already established team."

"Established." Jasi snorted. "You make Ben and I sound like an old, married couple."

In some ways, that wasn't far from the truth. Ben certainly knew her better than anyone else did.

"Now tell me," she said. "Did you see anything when you touched Marilyn's hand?"

"I saw a wife accusing her husband of being unfaithful."

Natassia described her brief vision.

"Marilyn sees herself as a victim of her husband's infidelities. She didn't trust him. When she confronted him, Monty acted disconnected."

Jasi's mouth thinned. "Marriage has become as unstable as a house built directly over a fault line. One quake can bring it down in a heap, until all that remains is nothing but destruction and garbage."

She ignored the curious look Natassia gave her and moved toward a bookshelf.

"Do you think Marilyn did it?" her partner asked.

"Killed her husband?" Jasi shook her head. "I can't see her doing all that. In a drugged state, Winkler would have been a dead weight. No pun intended. There's no way she would have been able to move him."

"What if she had help?"

Jasi chewed on this for a moment. "Who?"

"Maybe James was tired of being demoted to hired help. Maybe he's in love with her, or wants a piece of the pie. Someone's going to inherit a lot of money."

Natassia was right. It wouldn't be the first time someone was murdered for money.

"Marilyn does seem close to her brother-in-law," Jasi agreed. "We'll look into the insurance policy when we get back to the hotel."

"I think that's what was in the briefcase."

"I saw that too. The bit of paper sticking out said something about two million dollars."

Natassia stopped rifling through the papers on Winkler's desk. "You think that's the beneficiary payout?"

"That's exactly what I was thinking. But I'm curious why Marilyn would lie about it."

"If James is her lawyer, maybe he hasn't shown it to her yet."

Jasi surveyed the room, frustrated by the lack of clues.

"Didn't anything in your vision stand out?" she asked.

"The phone call Winkler got seemed important."

"Any idea of a timeline?"

"I'm guessing it was the night he disappeared."

"Why do you say that?"

"He was wearing the same suit he wore that night."

"Great catch, Natassia."

"Thanks."

Jasi wandered over to the massive desk, one of those modern interlocking styles. On the right side of the desk was a filing cabinet. She tugged on it. It was locked.

Keys will be in the desk drawer, she thought.

Sure enough, a set of five keys rested in a small tray in the top drawer of the desk. Beside it was a handheld device.

"We're in luck," she said. "Winkler left his 'com behind." She removed the device from the drawer. "It's an older commercial model. Nothing like the high tech ones we have."

"His wife said he always took it with him."

"What I'd like to know is why he'd leave *this* behind?" Jasi held up a worn brown leather wallet. "He's got about two hundred bucks in here. *And* his driver's license."

"Winkler drove his Mercedes without his license? Not very law-abiding, was he?" Natassia held out a hand. "Can I see the data-com?"

"Gladly. I'm not very tech-savvy."

"Then it's a good thing I'm on your team."

"You know something about computers?"

"Some people consider me a techie."

Jasi let her comment slide. For now.

"Hmmm," Natassia murmured.

"What?"

"He has a lot of entries in here."

"Anything jump out at you?"

"He had eight meetings the week before he died. His entries are hard to read though. He abbreviates everything. He met with *P.M.* on Monday—"

"The Prime Minister?"

"Could be. He had other meetings during the week, a couple of doctor appointments, dinner out with his wife and a FR gala, whatever that is."

"Busy man. What about the day he went missing?"

"Nothing. That's kind of strange, don't you think? He has something for every day, even weeks in advance. Yet there's nothing on that day."

"I guess even politicians take a day off now and then."

Natassia released a heavy sigh. "So what now?"

"Take the 'com. We'll dump the info at the hotel."

"What about these?" Natassia pointed to the computer and laptop on the desk.

"I'll have an evidence team send the files from the PC to our data-coms. You can take the laptop."

Jasi unlocked the filing cabinet and leafed through the files. Nothing stood out. She took a quick photo of the open drawer with her data-com, then stood back, her eyes wandering over the room.

*Damn!*

She wasn't any closer to finding out who killed Winkler.

"I've got nothing," Natassia said behind her. "These shelves are filled with books on politics, war and history. Plus there's a stack of legal forms awaiting his autograph."

"I guess he won't be signing them now." Jasi closed the cabinet. "If you take the forms, we can go over them later."

"Winkler has interesting taste in music." Natassia held up a CD with butterflies on the label. One butterfly was emerging from a cocoon. "*Relaxation for the Soul.* Hmm, well that explains why he kept falling asleep."

Jasi chuckled. "What did you expect—Metallica?"

"You know, you look like you could use some relaxing. Maybe you should borrow it."

"Last thing I need is to be falling asleep in the middle of an investigation."

As they moved toward the door, Jasi hesitated. She flicked a backward glance across the room. A powerful man had sat behind that desk. He'd looked at the clock, answered a phone call, scheduled a meeting, then...what?

Winkler's ghost seemed to linger close by.

"I think we're re done here, Jasi." Natassia prodded.

Jasi shivered. "I think we've only just begun."

When she stepped out into the hall, James was waiting for them. His eyes narrowed when he spotted the data-com in her hand.

"I think we've got everything we need for now." She pulled a piece of paper from her purse and handed it to James. "You'll have to sign this acquisition form. It says we've borrowed your brother's data-com and laptop for the duration of the investigation. We'll return them as soon as we can."

Without a word, James scribbled his signature on the bottom line and handed the form back. Escorting them to the front door, he moved swiftly, as if he couldn't wait to get rid of them.

*What's your hurry?*

Jasi made a mental note to check out the brother.

She stepped outside, turned and planted one hand in the doorjamb. James couldn't close the door without catching her hand in it. Looking into his eyes, she wondered for a moment whether she would lose a finger or two.

*Sometimes you gotta take a chance.*

"My sincerest condolences," she said. "I'm very sorry for your loss."

James' pale blue eyes clouded. Whether from anger or sadness, she couldn't tell.

"Some people aren't," he said in a flat tone.

She pulled her hand away as he closed the door.

"Wonder what's got his knickers tied in a bunch?" Natassia said.

"Knickers?"

"Sorry. I spent most of my childhood and early twenties in London, before moving back to Russia. Where did you grow up?"

"Vancouver. Born and raised. I never really did much traveling until Matthew recruited me."

When they climbed into the SUV, Natassia said, "Why do you suppose Monty changed his nightly routine?"

"I don't know. It does seem strange though."

"Well, he went *somewhere* that night."

"And he met someone," Jasi said. "But who?"

There was one thing she knew for sure.

*When I figure out the answers, I'll find a killer.*

## 9

To Natassia, a morgue was a daycare for the dead, until someone claimed them for burial or cremation. The Ottawa Forensics Unit was no different. It held stainless steel sinks and counters, multi-functioning computers, a forensics body scanner and a wall with stainless steel compartments for the dead. The room smelled the same as every other morgue, a combination of sanitizing cleaning products and formaldehyde that fought to mask the unmistakable stench of decay.

Natassia sprayed some *Mentho* in both nostrils to ward away the intense odor of decomposition. She read the nameplates on the wall.

When she found Monty Winkler's name, she pressed the red button beside it. There was a soft hum. A drawer slid out, revealing Winkler's body. It hadn't been bagged yet, but the stapled Y incision told her that an autopsy had already taken place.

"Dr. Copeland sure didn't waste any time," she murmured, thankful the pathologist had agreed to leave them alone.

"A high profile case like this means a lot of press," Jasi said. "Last thing our government needs is another scandal."

Natassia knew full well the devastating effects of scandal. She'd unearthed plenty. The morgue was a place that held so many last thoughts. Few people went peacefully. There was usually some kind of pain, loss, regret...guilt.

*Or burning secrets waiting to be revealed.*

She moved closer to the body. "Well, Mr. Winkler, are you ready to share your secrets?"

"Let's hope he saw his killer," Jasi said.

Sitting next to Monty Winkler's body, Natassia studied him for a long moment, her hands finally resting on his bloated face.

"What do you need me to do?" Jasi asked.

Closing her eyes, Natassia began to trace each facial feature with butterfly strokes, ignoring the slightly sticky feel of bloated, rotting skin.

"If I'm not out in ten minutes, pinch me hard and yell 'yeah, baby' at the top of your lungs."

"That's your safety phrase? Yeah, baby?"

Natassia didn't answer. She couldn't. She was already slipping away. She was as light as a feather, drifting above the corpse of Monty Winkler.

In a flash, she was staring out through his eyes, an observer of his final memories.

And a witness to murder.

*Terror gripped her, making it difficult to breathe. She couldn't move anything except her eyes.*

*Monty Winkler's eyes.*

*She—he— was lying on one side. On a sofa.*

*Where was he?*

*The last thing he remembered was...*

*James! His brother wanted something from him. What was it? It was something very important. Think!*

*James' image flashed before him.*

*"Monty, you need to sign this. Today."*

*A piece of stark white paper fluttered in the air. It disintegrated into dust before it touched the ground.*

*Wait? What was that, James?*

*An image of Marilyn fluttered past him.*

*Come back, he yearned to say.*

*They'd had a fight. What was it about? Why couldn't he remember anything?*

*He thought of Marilyn.*

*Marilyn, my love. I'm so sorry. I hope you'll forgive me.*

*From the corner of his eye, he peeked at the shadow that hovered over him. He tried to make out a face.*

*There wasn't one.*

*The shadow carried something shiny in one hand.*

*A hammer?*

*Whatever it was, it rushed toward Monty's head with lightning speed. He tried to back away, but his body didn't cooperate. He heard a sickening thud and his head jerked close to the edge of the sofa.*

*Oh God...*

*As another blow fell, an enraged shriek filled the air.*

*But it wasn't Monty's.*

*He felt a rush of dizziness. He gasped, and his lungs sputtered. No, please...*

*No sound came from his mouth.*

*The shadow moved away and Monty drifted between unconsciousness and death. He felt no pain. The drug in his system took care of that.*

*In the flickering light, he saw that his wrinkled hands were covered in blood and tied with coarse rope. He couldn't move his fingers. He couldn't even feel them.*

*Someone was approaching.*

*Help me, he tried to cry out.*

*Arms reached down. He was lifted and carried out into the night air. He couldn't focus on anything, not the person who carried him or his surroundings. The shadow unceremoniously leaned down and dropped him in some kind of...box?*

*Monty struggled to blink as his limbs were maneuvered until they fit inside the cramped space. Fear gripped his heart and he could hear its frantic beating.*

*Wait! No, please...why are you doing this?*

*He wanted to cry, and for a moment he thought the cool droplets on his face were tears until he smelled their overpowering scent.*

*Gasoline.*

*Oh Jesus. He's going to burn me to death.*

*Bile rose in his throat. Dizziness overwhelmed him, and he felt his entire body ebbing and receding. He heard a haunting violin composition, a sputtering engine and a slapping sound. Music symbols floated through his mind.*

*He wanted to relax, give in. Surrender.*

*Fingers of fire scorched him. Intense heat engulfed the top of his body. He screamed silently. He was melting, burning...dying. He could smell his flesh burning, but he couldn't move, couldn't do anything but lie there.*

*God help me!*

*The violin melody merged with the pitter-patter of rain, the bittersweet sound calming him.*

*Maybe the rain would put out the fire. Maybe not.*

*Marilyn, I love you. I always have. James—*

*A gasoline tear on his cheek sizzled and ignited.*

*His life flashed before him.*

*Did my life mean anything?*

*The glow that encircled him was brilliant and he fought for air, while a sudden cold permeated his skin.*

*This is it then. End of the line.*

*Gradually, the blazing light was extinguished and Monty released his fear and floated away. It was peaceful in the great Nothing. He could float there forever.*

*No, you can't!*

*The part that was Natassia struggled to gain control and return to her body, but the calmness seduced her, threatening to pull her back.*

*Something stung his arm—her arm.*

*She heard a muffled yell and spiraled away from the iron grip of Monty Winkler's spirit. But not before she felt another painful twinge. Finally, Natassia began the painful task of separation.*

*Time to go...*


"Yeah, baby!" a woman yelled.

Even in her half-conscious state, Natassia grinned. When she opened her eyes, she saw Jasi standing beside her, a worried expression on her face.

"It's been twelve minutes," Jasi said.

"I'm fine."

"Your pulse was slowing."

Natassia shrugged. "That happens sometimes."

She realized Jasi wasn't going to leave it alone, so she said, "I'm really fine. You got me out. That's all that matters."

Jasi's expression was dead serious. "I did exactly what you told me."

Natassia chuckled. "I can't believe you fell for it."

"For what?"

Natassia couldn't hold back any longer. Her eyes watered and she burst into laughter. Jasi watched her, confusion filtering across her face.

"Come on," she said. "I'll explain on the way back to the hotel. Then I'll tell you what I saw. Maybe you can make sense of it." She pushed open the door. "Shit."

A crowd of five men backed away from the door. When they saw the two women, there was a mix of gasps and snorting laughter.

"What's their problem?" Jasi whispered.

"I'll tell you outside."

Muffling a snicker, Natassia dragged her down the hall, praying that her partner had a sense of humor.

"So, spill it," Jasi demanded once they reached the car.

"Yeah, baby?"

Jasi eyed her suspiciously. "That's not what brings you back. Is it?"

"Nope."

"The pinch?"

"Yup."

"So the 'yeah, baby' was…"

"Just for kicks."

Jasi's cheeks turned red. "Oh God. Those men in the hall. They'll think we…"

Natassia winked. "Yeah, baby."

"You aren't…uh…"

"Gay?" Natassia shook her head. "No, I like men."

Her partner seemed frazzled.

"Well, now that we've got that out in the open," Jasi said, "let's focus on the man of the day. What did you see?"

Natassia gave Jasi the details of her vision, then allowed her thoughts to dwell on another man. Benjamin Roberts. She'd read up on him during the flight from Quebec City. He fascinated her almost as much as Jasi did. But for different reasons.

With Jasi, she felt a kinship born from their extreme abilities. Ben, on the other hand, was touted as one of the best CFBI profilers. His gift as a Psychometric Empath was understated, mainly due to the fact that his was an unreliable skill. He never knew if he'd get a vision or not. So he saved his energy and his visions for the most important witnesses. Or suspects.

*What would happen if he touched me?*

She pictured him. Tall, dark, serious.

*And very handsome.*

She wondered what he was doing.


At that very moment, Ben was thinking about a certain CFBI agent. One with dark, messy hair and piercing blue eyes. He sat on the bed, three pillows bunched behind him as he read through Natassia Prushenko's file. Over the past four years, the woman had been credited with breaking sixteen major cases, some with live victims, some with corpses. A Level 1 who could read a victim was invaluable.

A vision of Natassia's sultry eyes and shapely curves flashed through his mind. Was that what they were churning out in Russia now? Sexy female detectives?

"Damn," he said softly.

He was certain about one thing. Someone had slacked off on dress code regulations during her basic training. He'd have to talk to her about that. Lay down the law, show her who was in charge.

Except *he* wasn't in charge. Jasi was.

# *10*

While Jasi and their new partner went to interview some of Winkler's associates, Ben perused the files on his laptop. The police hadn't found any usable evidence outside of Winkler's body.

He blinked a few times to moisten his dry eyes.

*If we don't get a break soon, this case will be shelved.*

His data-com beeped. "Matthew, what's up?"

"Another politician is missing," Matthew replied grimly.

"Shit." Switching to speaker mode, Ben clipped the 'com to his jacket pocket and brought up a new folder on his laptop. "Who is it?"

"Porter Sampson."

Ben labeled the folder. "The Minister of Finance?"

"The one and only. His wife just reported him missing."

"How long's he been gone?"

There was a brief pause.

"Since Monday night," Matthew said.

Ben opened a document file and made some notes.

"You think the two cases are connected, Matthew?"

"It's too much of a coincidence not to think that."

"Give me a quick overview."

There was a rustle of paper before Matthew answered.

"Lorraine Sampson said she went to bed Monday night, shortly after eleven. Porter was in his study going over some documents. That's the last time she saw him."

"Anyone try calling him?"

"Lorraine's been calling him nearly every hour. So have some of his associates on Parliament Hill. We've tried too, but he's not answering."

"News has already leaked out about Winkler," Ben said. "Why did she wait so long?"

"She called it in yesterday afternoon when she couldn't reach Porter at work or on his cell. Someone at OPS dropped the ball and told her she had to wait twenty-four hours. They didn't make the connection."

"Jesus, you've gotta be kidding. He's the Minister of Finance, for crying out loud."

"I know," Matthew said tiredly. "We put a trace on his cell phone, but it's probably been dismantled and disposed of already."

"What about phone records?"

"I have them in my hands as we speak. There are no unusual phone calls on his cell, nothing we could trace back or triangulate."

"What about at home?"

"That's where it gets interesting. There were numerous late night calls, all originating from the same phone number. One of the calls came in the night Sampson disappeared. But we won't get too far with that."

"Let me guess. They came from a payphone."

"You got it. The same payphone where Winkler's calls had originated from."

"Did you get the phone records from his office there?"

"We're still waiting for those."

"So Monty Winkler gets a series of calls from a payphone, then disappears and ends up dead. Then Porter Sampson, the Minister of Finance, gets phone calls from the same payphone, then mysteriously disappears without a word to anyone, not even his wife."

"I know you're thinking what I'm thinking, Ben."

*There's a serial killer loose in Ottawa.*

That's what Ben was thinking.

"I hope we're both wrong, Matthew."

He strode to the window, parted the hotel's plush drapes and stared down at the busy street below before glancing across to the mammoth Parliament buildings.

Ben paced the room for a moment.

"What the hell is going on, Matthew?"

"Hell if I know. But one thing's for certain, we'd better find out soon. God knows what'll happen to Porter Sampson if we don't."

"Someone has a hate-on for our esteemed lawmakers, and we don't have one solid lead."

"Speaking of leads, that photograph Jasmine sent to Ops might help. The speedboat near the crime scene came back registered to someone high up on the political food chain."

Ben perked up. "Really?"

"Victor Cahill, Chief Justice of the Supreme Court. See if he's connected to the case."

"I suspect that if he is, this case won't remain quiet."

"Not in the least," came Matthew's reply. "To change the subject, I take it Jasmine and your new partner are out following leads on the Winkler case."

"Yeah. I'll fill them in when they get back."

"How's Prushenko working out?"

Ben straightened, his eyes wandering across the room. Should he tell Matthew about his misgivings, or just suck it up?

"Ben, you still there?"

"Yeah. Prushenko will be fine. It's only temporary, right?"

"Far as I know, she's here for this case only. She'll be sent back to Quebec when it's over."

Ben let out a slow breath. The thought of Natassia Prushenko leaving once the case was closed made him feel relieved. She made him nervous.

"I'll send you the files on Sampson," Matthew said.

"After I visit his wife, I'll head over to Winkler's house. Did the X-Disc pick up anything at Winkler's scene?"

"Not a thing. Makes me think that area wasn't the primary crime scene."

Ben let that sink in for a moment.

"Anything else?"

"Let's just hope you get a vision."

Matthew wasn't chastising him. But still…

"I'll start cross-researching when I get back," Ben said, knowing that his psychometric skill wasn't nearly as developed or reliable as Jasi's gift. "There has to be a connection to these men outside of the phone calls."

Matthew grunted. "Politics is an incestuous world."

"Yeah, that's enough of a connection right there. But you're right. Someone has an obvious distaste for the lawmakers in this country. We'd better find Sampson before he ends up on a slab like Winkler."

"There is one piece of good news, Ben. The RCMP found Monty Winkler's Mercedes."

"Where?"

"In the river, east of the city."

"You think he was dumped in it?"

"No. All the doors were closed and the trunk was locked. It's quarantined in the police impound lot. A trace team is on their way."

Ben heaved a frustrated sigh. "I bet they won't find much. This perp has been too careful. Any trace would be washed away or contaminated, just like with Winkler. Which reminds me...has the pathologist released Winkler's body yet?"

"She signed off on it this morning," Matthew replied. "Marilyn has arranged a funeral service the day after tomorrow. I want you all there. And be alert. They're expecting quite a crowd."

"I take it you haven't found Porter Sampson's car?"

"The RCMP is searching the river, near where we found Monty's car."

Would Winkler's killer be stupid enough to use the same dumping grounds?

"We've got this under wraps for now," Matthew said. "Try to keep it that way, Ben. The last thing we need is the media to get their claws into these cases. They'll make mincemeat out of the CFBI for not protecting these MPs."

"I won't say a word."


As Ben approached the driveway of 501 Linden Terrace, he let out a muffled curse.

*Someone's let the cat out of the bag.*

Porter Sampson's driveway was buzzing with activity. The paparazzi had caught the scent of a story, and like a pack of mangy wolves, they weren't about to let go of their prey.

"Shit, shit, shit," he muttered.

He lowered the window and flashed his badge at a couple of burly police detectives. They quickly pushed back the crowd, allowing him through. Stepping out of the SUV, he gritted his teeth in frustration.

"Okay, people! There's nothing to see here!"

That didn't stop the rapid flashing of cameras in the slimy palms of trigger-happy photographers. A dozen questions were fired at him, shot from the mouths of news-hungry reporters.

"What exactly is the nature of your business here?"

"Are you a friend of the deceased?"

"Do you know Mrs. Sampson intimately?"

Ben smoothed his Armani jacket, suddenly wishing he'd changed into something less ostentatious. He set his mouth in a firm line and moved with purpose toward the front porch.

An Ebonic woman opened the door before he had time to knock. She resembled a slightly older, rounder version of Oprah Winfrey. Not that he ever watched the TV icon's show or anything.

"Are you the CFBI agent?" she asked timidly.

"Yes, I am, ma'am. Agent Benjamin Roberts. You're Lorraine Sampson, I presume?"

"Come inside, please" she said. "Before those vultures have you on the front page of the Ottawa Sun."

He stepped inside the L-shaped bungalow. The sweet scent of baking wafted toward him. His stomach grumbled as Lorraine led him into the living room.

"I bake when I'm stressed," she said in a quiet voice.

He didn't even try to smile. "I eat."

Lorraine's eyes watered and her hands shook as she motioned for him to sit. "Are you here to give me bad news?"

"We have no news yet."

"No news is good news, I guess."

A soft *ding* came from the kitchen.

"Cookies are ready," she said, standing slowly. "I'll be right back."

A moment later he heard quiet sobs coming from the kitchen. This was always the hardest part of his job. Dealing with secondary victims of crime, the survivors. The ones who had to somehow learn to cope with their grief and move on with their lives.

Padded footsteps announced Lorraine Sampson's return.

"Here we go." She gave him a brave smile, but her swollen eyes betrayed her. She placed a plate of warm brownies—their edges slightly burnt—on the table. Then she handed him a mug of coffee. "I added some cream," she said apologetically. "I'm sorry I forgot to ask you. That's how Porter takes it. I could get you a fresh cup if—"

He took a sip. "It's just the way I like it."

The little white lie wouldn't hurt anyone.

"Don't you want to take your gloves off?" she asked.

"Cold hands," he replied.

Lorraine nodded. "Warm heart."

She settled into a colonial style armchair and slid her hands down the carved oak armrests, as if it were her only connection to the real world.

"Porter carved this chair himself," she murmured, staring off into space. "It was his gift to me on our last anniversary. We've been married forty-five years."

"You must have been kids when you married."

"We were high school sweethearts, Porter and I. He was on the track team, a long distance runner. I was just clumsy. The first time I met him I tripped and he caught me." She chuckled. "He always says I fell for him, literally."

Ben leaned forward. "I have some questions for you, Mrs. Sampson. I know the police probably asked you the same things, but people often remember more when some time has passed."

Lorraine clasped her plump hands in her lap and waited expectantly while he activated the voice recorder on his data-com. He set the device in the center of the coffee table.

"Interview with Lorraine Sampson, wife of Porter Sampson, politician. Mrs. Sampson, can you tell me when you last saw your husband?"

"Two nights ago."

"And where was he?"

"Porter was in his study, like he usually is after supper."

"What was he doing?"

"Going over the federal government's budget. He's always bringing work home with him."

"Do you have any idea what was in those files?"

Lorraine shook her head. "I'm not much into politics, to be truthful. Never did understand it all. Porter usually keeps to himself about these things. All I can say is that I always see him with files in his hands. Beige ones, blue ones, red ones. Sometimes he gets real riled up reading them."

"What do you mean?"

"Well, the other night I heard him muttering and cursing away. When I walked in, he was cramming a folder into the wall safe."

"Was this the same night? The last time you saw him?"

"Yes."

"Can you show me his study?"

The woman stood reluctantly. "It's at the far end of the house. Porter likes his privacy. I'm not sure I should—"

"I need to see it, Mrs. Sampson." he said gently. "I might notice something that'll help us find your husband."

Lorraine sighed heavily. "Of course. It's right this way."

The bungalow was an older style, brick fireplace, two bedrooms. Someone, probably Sampson, had added on an attachment that stretched into the backyard. It made up the lower part of the L-shape. Two French doors led into a spacious study.

When Ben stepped inside, the first thing he thought was that the room screamed *expensive* and *powerful*. The walls were painted forest green. Every piece of furniture was mahogany, polished to a gleaming shine.

He inhaled deeply. The room even smelled rich.

"Obsession," Lorraine said.

"Excuse me?"

"What you're smelling. Obsession Cologne for men. You could say Porter is a bit obsessed with it." A small smile struggled to the surface. "I always tease him, tell him he smells like he bathed in it. He spends most of his time in this office."

"It speaks a lot to his personality, this room. Organized, proud of his success and of his family." He indicated the family photographs on the wall. They'd been taken in various locations, mostly holidays from their carefree, relaxed expressions.

When Lorraine spoke, her voice was tinged with something primal. Fear. "It's hard not to wonder if I'll never see him in here again." She chocked back a sob. "I can't imagine where he is, Agent Roberts. He's never disappeared like this before. Do you think he's been kidnapped?"

"Let's not borrow trouble," he said. "There could be a logical explanation for his disappearance." *Although I don't know what that could be.*

Lorraine tried to smile. "You're right. I should be patient."

He wandered into the middle of Porter Sampson's office and carefully surveyed the room. A mammoth executive desk was paired with a high-backed leather chair. Items on the desk were carefully lined up, everything in its place.

A CD player sat on a shelf behind the chair, the remote control centered in front of it and a handful of assorted CDs stacked to the left. Ben glanced at the top CD. Looked like one of those new age albums—probably his wife's.

To the left of the shelf were a small office fridge and a humidor. He was tempted to explore the latter. It had been years since he'd savored an expensive cigar. Or even smelled one.

Solid mahogany bookshelves lined two walls. On one shelf was a collection of framed photographs. One in particular caught Ben's eye. A photo of Porter Sampson and two younger men in their twenties dressed in army fatigues.

"Denzel and Terrence," Lorraine said proudly. "Our sons. They're on tour in Afghanistan."

"Twins?" Ben asked.

"A year apart actually, but everyone thinks they're identical twins." She took the photo from him and gently set it back on the shelf. "I haven't called them yet. It's better to wait until I know for sure what's happened to their father. They don't need any distractions over there."

Another shelf was filled with dozens of books, mainly fiction.

Authors included Bowen, Crichton, Gross, King, Koontz, Mofina and Patterson, all arranged in alphabetical order by title. Below them was an assortment of legal tomes, shelved alphabetically as well.

Ben's brow furrowed. *Someone suffers from OCD.*

"Your husband has an interesting collection," he said.

Lorraine Sampson snorted. "He treated these bookcases as if they were made of gold. Always filing the books and binders just so. God forbid if he found one out of place."

"So everything here looks as it should?"

Scanning the shelves, she frowned. "Hmm…that's strange."

"What is?"

The woman ran her hand lightly over the top of a row of legal binders. "There's one missing."

"Are you sure?"

"I dust these shelves every day, Agent Roberts. I think I'd know if a binder was missing." She nudged a red binder and pointed to the empty space beside it. "There's usually a blue one right here."

Ben removed his gloves and examined a binder. It contained mostly legal mumbo-jumbo. He pulled out the next binder. It was much the same. Maybe Natassia could make sense of them later, after an evidence team picked them up.

He'd hoped to get a vision, but he didn't sense a thing.

He picked up the red binder. It was dated 2011 and contained notes on the year's federal budget and prospective bill proposals. The missing binder must hold similar paperwork for the current year.

His pulse quickened. "Do you know what's in the blue binder?"

Lorraine shook her head. "Like I said, Porter's been keeping to himself these days. I never read these anyway. Never wanted to." She released a sad sigh. "I'm sorry I can't be of more help."

"Can you tell me if anything else is missing or not where it should be?"

Lorraine opened a desk drawer. Her fingers skimmed across the contents and she picked up something small and round. "Porter's one-year coin."

"For…?

"My husband is an alcoholic, Agent Roberts."

When she handed him the coin, his psychometric senses immediately kicked in. He could feel Porter Sampson's struggle with alcoholism, his intense shame and his eventual relief. Sampson was proud of his accomplishment.

Lorraine smiled. "He's been sober for over a year, God bless him."

"You mentioned a wall safe," he said.

Lorraine pointed to a four-foot mirror in a leafy brass frame. "Behind that."

He examined the mirror. It was hinged to the wall for easy access to the safe behind it. He swung it open, exposing a Brinks wall safe, an older model with a touch screen access panel set for a seven-digit combination.

He touched the safe with bare hands.

*Not one flash. Damn.*

"Do you know the code, Mrs. Sampson?"

The woman shook her head.

He tried their phone number first.

Nothing happened.

"When did you get married?" he asked.

She told him and he tried the date. He tried birthdays next—hers, Porter's and their sons'. Still nothing.

"Can you think of any numerical code your husband would use?"

"Not really." She glanced at the shelf beside the safe. "Unless he used a date from one of these. He was a long-distance runner in university."

Ben picked up on of the trophies. "1975 National Senior Championships," he read.

"Our first date was the night of the Championships," Lorraine said in a soft voice. "Porter looked so handsome. It was the first time I ever saw him look nervous. We both were. And we've never forgotten that day."

"What was it?"

"June 30, 1975." Lorraine's face lit up. "Such an exciting night. He picked me up in his Corvette and drove me to the field. It was so exciting watching him run like he had the devil on his tail."

Ben was no longer listening. He tapped out the date, month first. Nothing. He entered the day first. Still nothing. Then he tried year, month and day.

*Bingo!*

The door to the safe gave a soft pop.

As he eased the safe door open, he glimpsed a manila folder. However, he never got a chance to examine it because they were abruptly interrupted by an angry voice behind them.

"Just what the hell do you think you're doing?"

A shriek filled the air.

# 11

Ben spun around.

Lorraine Sampson clung to a handsome man with milk chocolate skin, wide receiver shoulders, a sleek bald head and piercing black eyes. Her shrieking had stopped. Through her tears, she clasped the man's face between her hands and kissed him soundly on the lips.

Ben couldn't help but stare. The man was intimidating.

*Not someone I'd like to bump into in a dark alley.*

Of course, there was no denying who the unanticipated specter was. Porter Sampson. In the flesh.

The man reeked of alcohol, and his clothes had seen better days. The gray dress pants were wrinkled and the white shirt was unbuttoned at the collar and stained with either red wine or blood.

Ben hoped it was wine.

Sampson peered over his wife's head and shot him a menacing glare. "Who are you?"

"Agent Benjamin Roberts. I'm with the CFBI."

"What the hell is the CFBI doing in my home, going through my things?"

Ben forced a smile. "We were investigating your disappearance."

The man opened his mouth to reply, but his wife cut in.

"You scared me, Porter. Where have you been?"

Sampson shook off his wife. Without a word, he plucked a cigar from the built-in humidor, snipped the end and lit it. A stream of fragrant smoke poured from his mouth.

He scowled in Ben's direction. "You haven't answered me, sir. What were you doing poking around in my safe?" The cigar dangled from the corner of his mouth, bobbing up and down as he spoke.

"We were worried about you. Your wife reported you missing. We were looking for a clue as to your whereabouts."

"And you thought you'd find it in my safe?"

"We didn't have anywhere else to look."

Ben caught the overpowering scent of alcohol.

*Uh-oh, Sampson's been on a bender. Guess his days of sobriety are over.*

Porter Sampson dropped into the leather chair, asserting a position of control. "Well, you don't have to worry any more. As you can perfectly see, I am *not* missing. And I'll thank you to keep out of my personal belongings."

Ben gritted his teeth. The man was starting to irritate him. "I'm just following procedure."

"Listen, Agent Robins—"

"Roberts," Ben said in a tight voice.

Sampson inspected the cigar, then took a long drag. Finally he said, "Anything else I can help you with?"

Ben sank into the chair across from him. "Well, for starters, you can tell me where you've been."

"I was…out. I had a meeting to go to." Pause. "I think."

"You *think*?" Lorraine snapped. "You'd better explain yourself, Porter Lee Sampson. Don't think I can't smell the booze on you, 'cause I can."

"I know that, Rainey!"

"How could you?"

The hurt in Lorraine's voice made her husband wince.

"I'm sorry," he cried out. "I slipped up somehow, but I don't remember any of it."

"That's mighty convenient," she said in a quiet voice.

"I'm telling the truth."

"Sure you are." Lorraine shook her head slowly and moved toward the door. "I'll make you something to eat."

After she'd gone, Sampson said, "I used to lie to her all the time, back when I was drinking at the bars every night, but I haven't gone near one in over a year. Not that I know of anyway. I assure you, I'm not lying, Agent Roberts." He yawned and Ben noticed a gold-capped tooth. "I have no idea why I smell like a brewery."

"Where were you then?"

With a sigh of defeat, Sampson slumped down in the chair, the gravity of his situation finally sinking in. A bead of sweat rolled down his brow, past a dark mole below his right eye. A quick swipe of a beefy hand took it away.

"I'm not sure exactly. Last thing I remember was working here last night."

"*Two* nights ago," Ben corrected.

"What?" Wild, dark eyes betrayed the man's confusion and fear. "I've been gone two days? That's not possible. I was in my office last—"

"What day is it?"

"Tuesday."

Ben shook his head. "Wednesday. You've been missing for over thirty hours."

Sampson stared at the cigar for a long moment. Finally he tamped it out in a glass ashtray.

Ben leaned forward. "Mr. Sampson, I need to ask you these questions while everything is fresh in your mind."

"But that's what I'm trying to tell you. I don't remember anything. In fact, I don't remember a thing since working in my office two nights ago." Sampson's mouth thinned. "I don't know where I was, or who I was with. All I know is that I woke up on the concrete floor of the concert stage at Britannia Park a few hours ago, with nothing but the clothes on my back."

Ben was vaguely familiar with the park. He'd seen it on the map in his hotel room. The park spread out adjacent to the Ottawa River, southwest of Parliament Hill.

"Did you go see a concert?"

"No. They don't start up until June."

"How well do you know Monty Winkler?"

"Not well. I know who he is, and I may have met him at Parliament or at a social event, but other than that, we're involved in different things." His eyes narrowed. "Why?"

"You haven't heard?"

"Heard what?"

"He was murdered a few days ago, burnt beyond recognition and dumped in the river." Ben kept quiet about the strange scalp wounds.

"My God," Sampson said. "And you think his murder is somehow linked to what happened to me?"

"At this point we have to look at any possibilities. At least until you remember something."

"I don't understand. Why can't I remember?"

"You might have been drugged, like Monty Winkler. He was injected with a paralytic. If you were given the same drug, you'd be awake yet unable to move. You wouldn't be able to retain memories of the event either."

"Jesus! Why would someone do that to me?"

"That's what the CFBI is here to find out." Ben switched tactics. "On the night you worked here, do you recall getting a phone call?"

Sampson's forehead creased. "No."

"Are you sure? Someone called your home office number that night, from a payphone."

Sampson shook his head. "I remember going over some paperwork that night, but I didn't get any calls. And no one I know would call me from a payphone."

Ben studied the man carefully. Either he was a first-rate liar or he really didn't remember. *Interesting.*

"So you don't recall leaving the house, in your car?"

"I drove somewhere?" Sampson asked, stunned. "How can I not remember driving my car? Good God! Where the hell did I go?"

"To meet someone, maybe. At a bar."

"I don't go to bars." But even as Sampson said this, his voice registered a tremor of uncertainty.

Ben was baffled. The man's story didn't make much sense. Why couldn't Sampson remember?

"You have a tan 2009 Lincoln MKZ," he said, consulting the file on his 'com. "Maybe you met someone at a bar and the bartender took your keys afterward."

"I wasn't in a bar! I just don't…remember anything."

Ben was getting nowhere.

"I'll drive you to the hospital," he said.

"No way. Hospitals are for sick people. I'm not sick, Agent Roberts. I'm sure that once I've had some time to rest, I'll remember where I was."

And who you were with, Ben wanted to say.

One thing for sure, a guy didn't get this drunk by himself. Someone else must have been with him. Another woman maybe. Or maybe the drinking was only part of it. Perhaps a little recreational cocaine stuffed up the nose was Sampson's drug of choice. He certainly wouldn't be the first politician to go that route.

"You really should get checked out," Ben repeated. "Unless there's something you don't want your wife to know."

Sampson's eyes narrowed. "I know exactly what you're thinking, Agent Roberts. And no, I wasn't out cheating on my wife. I love Lorraine and I would never do anything to hurt her."

"Except start drinking again. You don't think that hurts her?"

"Of course I do! I'm not an idiot, you know." He stood shakily, his large hands gripping the desk. "I've been sober over a year. I've stayed sober because I love my wife. I have no idea why I started back again. I've asked myself that question a million times since I woke up on that park bench."

"Then come with me to the hospital. Maybe they'll find an answer."

Sampson moved to one of the bookcases. One hand hovered over the binders. His body stiffened suddenly.

"Something wrong?" Ben asked.

"Uh, no," the man said in a shaky voice.

"Your wife said there's usually a blue binder there. Is it missing?"

"It's probably at my office." He didn't sound too sure.

"What's in it?"

Sampson faced him. "Every bill or policy I've worked on this year. But like I said, I'm sure it's at my office. Now, back to our earlier discussion." He took a breath. "Nothing's wrong with me, Agent Roberts. At least, nothing that some sleep won't cure."

"But we need to know what happened to you."

Sampson turned away. "Anything more you need from me will have to come with a warrant, Agent. Right now, what I need is sleep."

Ben didn't need a warrant to take evidence in plain sight. He snatched something from the man's desk with a tissue and stuffed it into his jacket pocket.

"We'll be in touch, Mr. Sampson."

"You do that. I'll be here. I'm taking a few days off."

As Ben made for the door, he paused to study a photo of Porter and the Prime Minister, one of those *'stand side-by-side, shake hands and smile like you're best friends'* publicity shots common with prominent figures.

Sampson's dark eyes twinkled back at him, as if he had a secret he couldn't wait to tell. It probably didn't hurt for the younger *Caucasian* Prime Minister to be seen exchanging gracious handshakes with an *Ebonic*—or formerly politically correct *African American*—politician whose major platform was the elimination of racial discrimination.

*Probably won the PM a lot of votes*, he thought.

As Ben drove toward downtown, he thought about Sampson's bizarre memory loss. Having glimpsed a wounded man, one who was confused and devastated by his actions, he actually felt sorry for the man. Alcoholism was an insidious disease and recovery was a constant uphill battle, and there was no doubt in Ben's mind that something or some*one* had given Porter Sampson a downhill push.

*But who?*

Ben replayed their conversation. Sampson seemed honestly confused. No head games there. The man had disappeared for thirty odd hours and knew nothing about it.

*Is this connected to Winkler?*

"Time to pay Marilyn Winkler a visit," he decided.


On his way to Winkler Manor, Ben decided to take a short detour. He stopped at the park where Porter Sampson had woken up from his drug-induced sleep.

The concert stage at Britannia Park, he'd said.

The stage was situated on the bank of a duck pond. To the left of the stage was a bench made of wrought iron with weathered wooden planks for the seat, which had seen a lot of wear from Mother Nature and passers-by who'd stopped to admire the view. All around the bench grew short, scruffy-looking grass.

Ben checked the area thoroughly, especially the floor of the stage. He found nothing of notable importance. The city police had done their job. They'd already collected garbage and prints from around the stage.

He sat down on the bench and gazed out over the pond. Patches of algae marred its otherwise perfect mirror finish, but that didn't matter to the three young ducklings that followed their mother into an overgrowth of waving reeds and cattails.

*Witnesses?*

Ben peered over his shoulder, observing the other occupants of the park. A young woman jogged along the paved path, a golden retriever at her side. The woman's ponytail swung from side-to-side. Her limber legs seemed to barely touch the ground. A couple of teenaged girls giggled nearby while taking long drags off a shared cigarette. Skipping school, most likely. The only other occupant of the park was an old woman dressed in layers of ill-fitted clothing that screamed 'street person.' She was busy feeding the ducks and talking to them.

He strode toward her. "Excuse me, ma'am."

The woman spun around unsteadily.

"What do *you* want?" she snapped, her cold hazel eyes drilling into him. "You gonna tell me it's against the law to feed my babies?"

"No, ma'am." Ben held up a photo of Porter Sampson. "I want to know if you've seen this guy around here."

The woman's eyes narrowed. "Why? He kill someone?"

"Why would you say that?"

She shrugged and turned back to feeding the ducks.

"He's a Member of Parliament, ma'am. He woke up on the floor of the concert stage this morning, with no knowledge of how he got here."

"Must've been plastered then. Or on drugs."

"Did you see anything suspicious, anything at all?"

"I ain't seen nothing." She peered over her shoulder at him. "And the only suspicious person 'round here is you. Who comes to the park in a suit like that? You can't be a cop."

Ben chuckled. "I'm with the CFBI."

"CFBI, CIA, CSI...it's all a conspiracy, you know."

He thanked her.

"You wanna thank me proper, leave me a tenner."

Without a word, he tucked a ten dollar bill into her outstretched palm. The skin on her hand was raw and red.

The old woman examined the bill. "Better not be fake."

"It's good," he said.

She beamed a smile at the ducks. "Babies, I'm going to get you the best lunch today." To Ben she said, "I heard music in the park this morning."

"What time?"

"Around five o'clock. I followed it here, but it was already gone. I never saw no one though. And I didn't go up on the stage."

"What kind of music was it?"

"Dunno. It was kinda hard to hear."

He left her to her ducks and headed back to the parking lot. The music the woman had heard could have come from anywhere. More than likely, someone had driven past the park, with music blasting and windows down.

*Another dead end.*

He mulled over his earlier conversation with Sampson. Something about Sampson's disappearance stank, and it wasn't just the man's sweat-stained and booze-soaked clothes. He'd woken up here, yet had no idea how'd he'd even gotten to the park.

"No, there's more to this than meets the eye."

In the SUV, Ben carefully pulled the tissue from his pocket and unfolded it, revealing Sampson's discarded cigar butt.

"Perhaps this will shed some light on the truth."

Removing a glove, he held the cigar stub loosely between his fingers and closed his eyes. A wave of emotions coursed over him. Confusion, uncertainty...fear. Blurred images crept into his mind. Two of them came into focus for a few seconds.

*A Canadian flag falling into water.*

*A glowing silver sun.*

He opened his eyes and waited for the feeling of disorientation to disappear. When it did, he wrapped the butt in the tissue and started the car.

On his way to meet Marilyn Winkler, he thought of the fleeting images. It frustrated him that his visions were always cut short. He'd spent a month in intensive training, working with psychometric specialists, doing everything to refine his gift.

"And this is what I get," he muttered. "A Canadian flag and a silver sun. Great."

When he arrived at Winkler Manor, he put aside all thoughts of his vision and took in the formidable surroundings. He was impressed by the stately home, but the lady of the house was even more extraordinary.

Marilyn Winkler welcomed him with the grace of a woman accustomed to entertaining. There was no sign of her brother-in-law James.

"I'm sorry I'm such a mess," she said, one hand patting the bun in her hair. "I wasn't expecting company."

That wasn't how it looked from his perspective. Marilyn was dressed for business. For success.

She offered him tea, but he declined.

"If you don't mind," he said, "I'd like to check your husband's office."

"Of course I don't mind."

She showed him the way.

"Would you like me to stay?"

"That's okay," he said, but not before he caught a faint glimmer of distrust in her eye.

"Are you sure, Agent Roberts?"

"I'd like to get a sense of Monty," he said, purposefully using her husband's first name. "I promise I won't take anything without your permission."

That seemed to have the effect he was hoping for.

Marilyn retreated, the door closing softly behind her.

He released a breath, then turned to the business at hand.

Monty Winkler's office had the aura of a man's world. He imagined that this was where the politician had conducted a lot of business, tying up deals, making policies that affected the Canadian life.

He removed his gloves and tucked them in his jacket pocket. He picked up a golf trophy. It was cold and he got nothing from it. He set it down, careful to place it exactly where it had been.

A framed newspaper clipping hanging on the wall near the window caught his eye. He carefully took the clipping down. The photo was familiar. It had run on the front page of the Ottawa Sun.

The headline read: *Victims of Violence Gun Gala.*

Suddenly an image flashed before him. A road splitting in two. Winkler was walking down one side, while a ghostly twin strolled down the other.

Ben jerked, and the vision vanished. Returning the clipping to its place on the wall, he thought of Monty Winkler. Somewhere in his career, the man had taken a detour, a decision that quite possibly had resulted in his brutal murder.

*So what had he decided?*

# 12

Jasi knew something was up the second she saw Ben. He was seated at the table in his room, scrolling through documents on a laptop. He was so engrossed by whatever he was reading that he didn't realize that she and Natassia had entered the room.

She was about to say something when Natassia dropped her purse on the tile floor. It landed with a loud thud.

Ben's hand reached for the gun on the table.

"Good thing I'm not a bad guy," Natassia joked.

"Well, you're not a guy," he quipped. "The jury's still out on the *bad* part."

"Ha-ha."

Natassia flashed him a saucy grin and Ben looked away.

Jasi hid a smile. *Very interesting.*

"I think we need a pow-wow," she said.

Natassia's brow arched. "Pow-wow?"

"It helps to talk the case through out loud." Jasi perched on the bed. "So what do know so far?"

"Winkler had a fondness for butterfly music," Natassia said.

Ben frowned at her. "What?"

Natassia glanced at Jasi. "Forget it. It was an inside joke. You had to be there."

Jasi watched them with curiosity. The air was electric, sizzling with tension. Or perhaps something else.

*Something's happening here.*

Whatever it was, she wasn't sure she liked it.

After they rehashed everything they knew about the two cases, Jasi sent a written report to Matthew via her data-com. Then she activated the phone number search. Within seconds she was connected to Ravinder Sharma's office on Parliament Hill.

"We're investigating Monty Winkler's murder," she told him. "I'm wondering if someone went after him because of the gun rights bill. Have you received any threatening phone calls or letters on this?"

"I've received some threats, Agent McLellan," Sharma replied in a heavy accent. "Mostly emails. But I don't take them seriously. It comes with the territory. A kind of political karma and all."

*Political karma?* That was a first.

"I had lunch with Monty a couple of weeks ago," the man added. "He seemed content and happy, no worries. If he was being threatened, I think he would've told me. We were very good friends."

"I'm sorry for your loss." She paused. "I have one more question. It's about the gun rights vote."

"You want to know why I voted for and not against the new law." Sharma's voice grew quiet. "I can't answer that, Agent McLellan."

"It's not like it's confidential information," she argued.

"No," he said calmly. "I mean, I can't answer you because I'm not sure *why* I voted for it. I planned to vote against guns. So did Monty."

Jasi was shocked. "Then why did you both vote yes?"

"I think we were just overworked at the time. Anyway, by the time we'd realized what we'd done, it was too late. And frankly, we both felt a little stupid."

*Stupid and irresponsible,* she thought.

"Is there anything else?" Sharma asked.

"No. If I have any other questions, I'll call back."

"I hope you find whoever did this. Monty was one of the good guys."

"That's what everyone tells me."

After she hung up, she turned to Ben. "Neither Sharma nor Winkler seem to have received any direct threats relating to the gun law."

"Then perhaps someone's harboring a grudge about something else." He filled them in on his visit to the Sampson residence.

"It could be exactly as it looks," Natassia said. "Maybe he went out and got drunk."

Jasi turned to Ben. "What's your take on Porter Sampson? Do you think he's lying, trying to cover up where he really was?"

"I don't think Sampson voluntarily went out and got so stinking drunk that he can't remember anything." He grabbed a can of cola from the small fridge, then returned to his chair. "I wanted to read him, but he wasn't in a friendly sort of mood."

Natassia gave Jasi a questioning look.

"When Ben reads someone," she explained, "they have to be relaxed and open."

"Ah," Natassia replied. "And unsuspecting."

"Uh, yeah," Ben said. "I did, however, read two inanimate objects, although I didn't get a lot from either of them."

He told them of his vision from the cigar butt.

"We're surrounded by Canadian flags here," Jasi said.

"And the silver sun?"

She thought about this. "A full moon or new moon, maybe."

"Or coins," Natassia added.

"Maybe," Ben said.

"What about your other vision?" Jasi asked.

"Before I left Sampson's office, I took a photo of a newspaper clipping." He brought the photo up on his data-com. "When I touched it, I saw Sampson walking along a road that veered off in two directions."

"He hit a detour," Jasi guessed. "Or had to choose."

"Yeah, but what's weird is that I saw him clearly on one road and a paler ghost image of him on the other."

"Maybe it's related to the gun vote. He chose yes, but wanted to vote no."

"Or it could be unrelated."

She hated seeing him so unsure. "Do *you* think your vision is connected to the case?"

"Honestly? I don't know."

Jasi felt for him. Lack of clarity was a common problem with Ben's gift. He usually saw cryptic symbols, which made interpreting his visions extremely difficult.

"Well, let's keep it in mind," she said.

"Oh, and speaking of photos," Ben said, "the one you took of that boat is registered to Chief Justice Victor Cahill."

Jasi initiated a quick phone number search on her 'com. Within seconds she was connected to the judge's office and lined up an appointment the following day with the esteemed Chief Justice.

"All taken care of," she said when she hung up.

"Anything else we need to know?" Natassia asked Ben.

"Yeah, Sampson's missing a blue binder. He thinks he left it in his Parliament office, but his wife says it was on a shelf at home. I'll check with him later on that." He released a pent-up sigh. "I wish to hell we knew what was going on here."

"I have a feeling," Jasi said, "that things are going to get a lot worse before they get better."


From beneath her lashes, Jasi spied on her partners and tried not to laugh. Ben sat in the armchair near the window, as far away from Natassia as he could get. But he couldn't stop staring at her. Natassia was oblivious.

"See anything interesting?" Jasi asked Ben.

His head whipped around. "What?"

"In the files."

Ben's task was to read through the missing person's reports that had been sent to his laptop.

"Uh, nothing yet."

"We should look for connections the men may have had. There has to be a reason why these men were chosen."

On her own laptop, Natassia was screening the main folders from Winkler's computer, checking for recently updated files. Jasi sat at the table across from her and poured over the victim's emails and the brief report on Darlene MacKenzie, the woman who'd gone missing for three days. MacKenzie's credit card showed charges for the room and a couple of meals. Nothing there.

With each passing hour, she became increasingly frustrated. Nothing jumped out at her. Nothing unusual, anyway.

"I don't see anything in Winkler's correspondence," she said with a sigh. "Everything seems to be either innocent conversations or a lot of boring political mumbo-jumbo that I can't even understand."

She'd already contacted everyone Winkler had emailed the week before his death. Nothing had panned out, and they weren't any closer to solving his murder.

She studied her partners. From the looks on their faces, they weren't having any better luck at finding something useful.

Ben caught her eye. "What?"

"Now I know why OPS and the RCMP were stumped. And they didn't even have half the information we have."

Ben's eyes drifted toward Natassia. "What about you? Any luck?"

"Nope," their new partner muttered. "Nada."

Jasi groaned. "So what are we supposed to do now? Wait around for a killer to make his next move?"

No one said a word.

"We need more to go on," she muttered.

"I agree," Ben said. "But we still have to keep looking."

Natassia glanced up. "I'm done with these files. The only ones Winkler created in the past three months match the forms we found. He revised a few of them somewhat, then printed and signed them. Most were attachments that he saved in separate files."

"I've got nothing," Ben said. "Everything the wives say checks out with the reports they filed when their husbands went missing. And there weren't any witness reports to give us any leads."

Jasi nodded. "The only connections outside of their disappearances are that both men are members of Parliament and they're well respected with few complaints lodged against them."

"What about police records?"

"Squeaky clean. Both of them."

"Nobody's that clean," Ben argued. "Not in politics, that is."

Jasi agreed. "So what ties them together? They hang around with different crowds, are members at different country clubs and have no interests in common."

"They're both married," Ben said. "But I can't picture Oprah getting her husband drunk and dragging him to a park bench."

"Oprah?" Jasi said, her mouth crinkling in a half-smile.

"Lorraine Sampson." He shrugged. "Hey, she looks like Oprah to me."

"Who's Oprah?" Natassia interrupted.

Jasi and Ben were stunned into silence.

Natassia cocked her head to one side. "Well?"

"You're not serious, are you?" Jasi asked. "Oprah Winfrey? One of America's most influential women?"

No response.

"Queen of television talk shows?" Jasi prodded.

Natassia gave them a bland look. "I don't watch TV."

"I take it you're not a member of her book club either."

Ben released a muffled sigh. "Back on track, you two. We've got one dead politician and one who was missing for nearly two days. We have to trace Sampson's steps, find out where he was, where he was drinking. Someone had to have seen him."

"Tomorrow I'll check out the bars near the park," Jasi said. "Why don't you two visit Sampson?"

"Natassia should go with you," Ben said quickly.

Jasi smiled. "Well, since I'm team leader, I think she should go with you."

Ben's face reddened. "Jasi—"

"Yoo-hoo!" Natassia cut in, waving a hand at them. "I'm right here. Why don't you ask me who I want to go with?"

Ben cleared his throat. "Sorry. Go ahead."

Natassia smiled at Jasi. "I'll go with Ben. That way we can both try to read Sampson."

"Good," Jasi said. "Well, now that we have that settled, what shall we do the rest of the night?"

Ben seemed lost in thought and she prodded him with her elbow. "Up for some cards after dinner?"

"As long as it isn't Texas Hold 'em."


"I win!" Jasi said, letting out a whoop of victory as she spread her cards out on the table.

*These two are just too easy to beat.*

Natassia tossed her cards down on the table. "That's five wins in a row."

"Now do you see why I didn't want to play this game?" Ben said dryly. "Jasi's too damned good at keeping a poker face. Wish I was a mind reader."

"There are only three Level 2 mind readers in the world," Jasi said absentmindedly. "And they're banned from any gambling establishment."

Natassia broke out in a fit of laughter. "My God, you're so damned serious. Loosen up."

Jasi blushed.

"This is really refreshing," Natassia said, leaning back in her chair.

Ben's brow arched. "What is?"

"This. Playing cards with my partners."

Ben's eyes widened. "What the hell do you usually do to pass the time? Some cases are virtually endless."

"Like this one?"

Jasi cut in. "How did your other teams do things?"

Natassia shrugged. "We met like you do every night to discuss the case. Then we went to our rooms and went to bed. That way we could get up the next morning and do it all over again."

"Sounds boring," Jasi said. "How do you get to know each other then?"

"We're given files on every member of our team. My team leader doesn't encourage fraternization outside of work."

"Michael Dorsey?" Ben said.

Natassia looked at him, surprised. "You know him?"

"We met. Years ago."

Ben didn't say any more. Jasi had a feeling he was leaving something out intentionally.

"Well, as long I'm team leader," Jasi said, "we can fraternize all we want." She placed a hand on Natassia's arm. "When it's time for business, we're there. One hundred percent. But in between we need to relax, chat, play cards."

Natassia glanced from Jasi to Ben, then back. "I can tell you're very close."

"Ben's my best friend," Jasi replied.

In fact, Ben was more like family to her. A big brother that she could always rely on. One who would always be there for her, just as she would for him.


It was late when Jasi and Natassia finally left, just after midnight. He removed his gloves and put them on the bedside table, next to his data-com and gun. Then he undressed and climbed into bed. But sleep evaded him.

Staring up at the ceiling, he thought of Monty Winkler. The man had an enemy, someone who hated him enough to burn him alive and make him suffer.

Then there was Porter Sampson. Was he simply a victim of over imbibing? Or was there something more to it? It sure seemed like there was. Nothing added up, and he had a sneaking suspicion that a serial killer lurked on the streets of Ottawa, searching for his next victim.

He sighed. *I hope we get him first.*

Having a new member on the team was a bit disconcerting and it was throwing him off his game. For some reason every time he looked into Natassia's deep sapphire eyes, he was reduced internally to a bumbling schoolboy who couldn't think straight.

Why did Natassia have such an affect on him?

*Natassia.*

Now there was a conundrum. She might dress as if she's ready to go out partying until the wee hours of the morning, yet she exhibited some reticence. Bold, yet shy at times. He suspected that she knew exactly what she was doing.

*And what is that exactly?*

He sank into a deep sleep, disturbed only by a face with sapphire eyes, dark lashes and lips that made him ache to kiss her.

# 13

After breakfast, Ben and Natassia left for a meeting with Porter Sampson, while Jasi decided to take the CFBI files on Winkler and Sampson down to the coffee shop. She was seated in the far corner near a window. In most cities the morning rush hour would have been winding down by now. But not in Ottawa. The streets were still packed, bumper to bumper.

First, she pulled out Monty Winkler's file. She leafed through it until she found the information on the man's political standing and placed it on the table. Then she did the same with Sampson's file.

"Different platforms, different circle of friends." She bit her bottom lip. "So what did they have in common?"

She was four paragraphs into Winkler's education background when someone tapped her on the shoulder.

"Jasmine, my love."

A man with sun-kissed blond hair and eyes the color of a pale spring sky leaned down and kissed her cheek.

Jasi couldn't breathe.

When she finally spoke, her voice came out in a squeak.

"Zane?"

Zane Underhill, ex-lover and brilliant psychologist, was the last person she expected to see in Ottawa. He had worked closely with the CFBI for many years, consulting on cases prosecuting dangerous criminals. That's how they'd met. He thought she was an expert profiler with the CFBI. He didn't have a clue what she really did.

"It's been a long time," he said, the warmth of his voice melting her frozen heart.

"Yes, it has."

Three years ago, Zane had left for Washington, supposedly for a one month teaching assignment. He called her every night for the first two weeks. Then his phone calls and emails became less frequent, and one month dragged into two. Four months later, she heard through the grapevine that he had gone on to New York, working with the CFBI as an expert witness in the field of psychology. Not long afterward, she gave up trying to keep track of him, or waiting for him.

She stared up at him now, trying not to remember how heartbroken she'd been, how utterly devastated she'd felt. He was someone from her past, someone she had tried long and hard to forget. And now, here he was, smiling at her as if it had only been three days instead of three years.

"I can't believe my good luck," he said, his Australian accent still as charming as ever. "Mind if I join you?"

Without waiting for an answer, he pulled out a chair and dropped into it with a lazy smile. The same disarming smile that had drawn Jasi into a tempestuous relationship. The same smile that had betrayed her when he promised he'd only be gone a month.

"What are you doing here?" she finally managed. "I thought you were still in New York."

Zane stretched his legs. "I came back over a year ago."

There was an awkward silence.

"So what are you doing here?" Jasi blurted.

"Chatting with you, love." He grinned. "You're the last person I expected to see here."

Her mouth felt dry. "Ditto."

"You living in Ottawa now?"

"No, I'm still in Vancouver. I have a new apartment."

He frowned. "I tried looking you up last year, but your number wasn't listed."

She shrugged. "I was getting too many crank calls."

And none from you for three years, she wanted to say.

The conversation seemed forced, at least from her end, and right now she'd give anything to be someplace else.

"Zane, I'm kind of in the middle of something right now." She stared pointedly at the papers on the table.

"No problem. We'll catch up at dinner."

"Sorry. I have other plans."

"Cancel them," he said, his tanned hand covering hers. "I've missed you, Jasmine."

As she gazed into his eyes, long buried memories teased at her mind. Candlelight, roses, wine and writhing bodies.

"I've missed you too." The words were out of her mouth before she could stop them. "Sorry, but I can't, Zane."

"Come on," he pleaded. "Dinner. That's all I'm asking for. You can't work all night long without sustenance. Besides, when was the last time you had some fun?"

She blushed. Fun, by Zane's definition, meant hot, steamy sex that lasted well into the night. She wasn't about to tell him he'd been the last man she'd slept with.

"Give me a chance to apologize," he said. "We both know I owe you that much."

*You owe me more than that.*

"Fine," she said with a sigh. "One dinner. Nothing more, Zane. I've moved on."

He raised a finely arched brow. "Yet here you sit, alone without any of your mates around, looking as gorgeous as the day I met you."

She couldn't resist a slight smile. "I was covered in soot when you met me. And profiling an arson case."

He stood. "Ah, but your smile lit up the crime scene."

"Dr. Underhill, you're so full of shit."

"That was the moment I knew."

He leaned down and kissed her slowly, deeply.

She came up for air, gasping. "Knew what?"

Zane strode across the room, heading for the exit.

"Knew what?" she shouted, ignoring the other diners who were scowling at her.

Zane grinned over his shoulder. "That you were the only woman for me."

Then he was gone.

The air in the room seemed to thicken. The couple at the table nearest Jasi smiled. They were probably dreaming up all sorts of romantic explanations.

"Great," she muttered.

The last thing she needed was Zane Underhill back in her life. He represented chaos, because when she was with him, nothing else mattered except being with him, skin on skin.

She shifted uncomfortably in the chair.

*Jasmine McLellan, you agreed to dinner. Nothing else!*

In the foyer of the Sampson residence, Ben took Natassia aside. "Follow my lead, Agent Prushenko."

Flashing blue eyes met his and for a moment he thought she was going to argue. The woman would have to learn her place, and he'd have no problem reminding her. New partners were at the bottom of the status ladder—especially *temporary* partners.

"Aye, aye, *capitaine*," she said, saluting him.

He turned to Porter Sampson. "Thanks for seeing us."

"Whatever it takes to end this."

"This is Agent Natassia Prushenko. She's temporarily assigned to your case."

The man gave Natassia a brief nod. Then he led them into his office. "Have a seat, please. Lorraine is bringing us some refreshments."

As if on cue, Lorraine Sampson entered the room. She carried a wooden tray with a pot of French pressed coffee, three mugs, sugar and cream. Setting the tray on her husband's desk, she poured the coffee without saying a word.

"Thank you," Ben said, accepting a mug.

With a nod, Lorraine quietly retreated.

"You have a lovely home, Mr. Sampson," Natassia said. "Have you lived here long?"

"About eight years. I built this house for my wife and I after the boys were gone. We didn't need a four-bedroom house anymore."

"I think smaller homes are quite cozy. My parents have a home about this size, right outside Saint Petersburg."

"Russia?" Sampson asked in surprise.

*"Da."* Natassia smiled. "That's where I'm from originally. Have you been there?"

"I visited Russia once many years ago, when I was in my early twenties. A friend and I backpacked across Europe and we stopped in Saint Petersburg and Moscow." The man chuckled. "We got into our fair share of—what shall I call them—adventures."

Ben eyed Natassia. She'd ignored his order and charged in full-speed, but he had to give her credit. She had immediately put the older man at ease.

Of course, that could have had something to do with how striking Natassia looked. She wore simple navy blue pants, with a white and blue striped blouse. The top three buttons were left undone and revealed perfect, unblemished skin.

He needed a distraction.

"You only have the two sons?" he asked Sampson.

"Yes."

"It must be difficult to be here, waiting for news from Afghanistan. Is either of them married?"

"Denzel was married for about two years, but they got divorced. Such is life nowadays." The man glanced at the door. "It's hard to keep a marriage going."

"It looks like you and your wife have managed to keep the spark alive." Ben paused. "What about grandchildren?"

"Denzel has a son with Sheri, the girl he married. The baby's name is Tyrell. He's two. We see Ty once a month. My wife spoils him rotten."

"I bet you're just as bad," Natassia teased.

Sampson's mouth curled up at the corners. "I guess I am. Playing with little Ty is the only time I can get away with being...well, silly."

Ben envied the man. Silliness wasn't part of his life either.

"How do you get along with your boys?"

"We're better than we used to be. We had rough patches when they were teens, like most fathers and sons." The man caught his eye. "Do you have children, Agent Roberts?"

"No."

"Well, when you do, you'll learn that being a father is the toughest job there is. It makes boot camp seem like a Disney holiday. But once they're on their own, that's the real test. Rainey and I are real proud of our boys."

"Have you had any problems with them lately? Any arguments?"

Sampson gave him a hard stare. "Agent Roberts, don't go looking down this alley for trouble. My boys had nothing to do with what happened to me. I guarantee you. We may have our occasional disagreements, but I love them and they love me."

Natassia cut in. "I'm sure Agent Roberts didn't mean to imply that your boys had anything to do with this case."

Ben shot her a frown. "Mr. Sampson, we need a clear picture of the people in your life. Whoever is responsible for abducting you could be someone you know, or have ties to someone close to you."

Sampson rested both hands on the desk. "I don't believe anyone I know would do such a thing."

"You're not the first victim to tell me that."

And you won't be the last, Ben thought.

Sampson drummed his fingers on the desk. "I talked to Denzel and Terrence before they shipped out. Denzel was worried about Ty and asked me to check in on him. And no, we never argued. Neither of my boys is in any trouble. No one's after them. No gambling or drinking problems."

Ben believed him. But he'd still run a security check.

"Can you walk us through what you remember on that last day? Don't leave out anything, not even the smallest detail."

"I remember everything I did during the day. I had meetings in the morning and—"

"Who did you meet with?" Ben interrupted.

Sampson's gaze drifted. "My lawyer. Joe Zhang. He's drafting up some legal documents for me."

"What kind of documents?" Ben asked.

"Nothing to do with work. It's strictly personal. I've been meaning to draw up a new will, make sure my Rainey is well protected." He flicked a sad look at the door. "She's my life."

"My father says that about my mother all the time," Natassia said gently. "Where did you go after the meeting with your lawyer?"

"I went to work. I had a pile of papers waiting to be signed, and my assistant Martin Fonteyne gave me a stack of notes, calls I needed to return."

"We're going to need those," Ben said.

"I'll have Martin fax them to you."

"What time did you arrive back home?"

"It was a little after four, I think. I had supper with Rainey, then came in here to do a little research." Sampson pursed his mouth. "That's it. That's all I remember."

"Thank you," Ben said. "You've been very helpful."

"Is there anything else you need?"

"A list of everyone you met or talked to that day and their phone numbers."

"Will do, Agent Roberts." More scribbling.

Ben's data-com beeped.

It was an unfamiliar number. Local. The call display read Ottawa C. Mg.

"I'll take this in the hall, if you don't mind."

Sampson shrugged. "Go ahead. Agent Prushenko can keep me company. I'm sure she has more questions for me."

In the hallway, Ben answered the call.

"Is this Agent Roberts?" a woman asked.

"Yes, but you have me at a disadvantage."

"Sorry. This is Dr. Faith Copeland."

Ben smiled into the 'com. "Ah, our resident mortician."

"Actually, I prefer *pathologist*."

He could tell she was smiling.

"I tried to reach Agent McLellan, but her line was busy. OPP gave me your number."

"Has something come up?"

"That cigar butt you sent to Tox came back positive for alcohol, like you suspected. They sent me the report as soon as they saw the connection."

"What connection?"

"There were traces of Flunitrazepam in his saliva."

The same drug found in Monty Winkler. *Damn!* He had hoped he was wrong.

"Saliva tests only show positive for up to six hours after the drug is taken orally," Copeland said.

"He wasn't injected like Winker?"

"No, he probably drank something laced with it."

"This isn't enough of a deviation from the method used on Winkler to suggest Sampson was drugged by a different perp."

"Exactly," she said. "And you know what that means."

"Yeah, we're looking for a killer who hates politicians."

"Agent Roberts?" Copeland's voice was edgy.

"Shoot."

"Mr. Sampson should be examined by a doctor. He needs a rape kit done. It's important to rule out any kind of…abuse."

"Monty Winkler's came back negative."

He heard her sigh. "Just because his results were negative doesn't mean Porter Sampson's will be. Take him to the hospital, Agent Roberts."

Ben hung up.

How the hell would he be able to convince Sampson to go to the hospital for a rape kit?

When he re-entered the office, Natassia was laughing at something Sampson had said. She took one look at his expression and her mouth snapped shut.

"Mr. Sampson," Ben said slowly. "I'm going to have to insist that we take you to the hospital for a physical examination."

Sampson jumped to his feet. "I already told you. I'm fine."

Ben gave Natassia a helpless look.

"What did the tox screen say?" she asked.

"He tested positive for Rohypnol," he replied. Turning to Sampson, he said, "Mr. Sampson, you were given a paralytic drug that causes memory loss. If a larger dose had been used, you would've been completely unconscious. Or dead."

The older man seemed baffled. "How could you know I had drugs in my system? I didn't give you any of my blood to test."

"We borrowed your cigarette stub." Ben lowered his voice. "We need to know if anything was done to you while you were unconscious, Mr. Sampson."

Sampson turned a sickening shade of gray. "Are you saying I was…?"

"We don't know that yet."

"Oh God."

There was something pitiful about Sampson's voice.

"Let's wait until all the reports are in," Ben said.

Natassia patted the older man's arm. "It's better to know, Mr. Sampson. One way or the other."

"We'll take my vehicle," Ben said when he saw Sampson fish his keys from a jacket pocket.

As they left Sampson's office, Lorraine gave them a surprised look. "Porter?"

"I'm going out for a bit, Rainey."

His wife's worried gaze followed them to the door.

Outside, Sampson paused in front of the SUV, his eyes barely meeting Ben's or Natassia's. "This is between us. Okay?"

Ben removed one glove. "Our team is very discreet."

As the man opened the vehicle door, Ben rested a bare hand on the man's arm. His vision immediately shifted until all he saw was a cloudlike fog. In the far distance, a shape moved, but Ben couldn't make it out. He felt a cool breeze brush against his face and a mist of water wash over him. Then…nothing.

"Agent Roberts?" Sampson was staring at him, a look of concern on his face.

"I'm fine," he lied.

Sometimes his 'gift' infuriated him. It came and went without any rhyme or reason, and that made him a liability. One day, his unreliable visions would get him into trouble.

# 14

"Maybe Rohypnol was only used to keep him quiet, so the perp could transport him to the park," Natassia said to Ben.

They were seated in the waiting area of Ottawa General, awaiting the results of Sampson's examination. Sampson was getting dressed.

"I hope so, Natassia," her partner said absentmindedly.

She smiled. He'd used her given name for the first time. Mr. I'm-so-serious Roberts was warming up to her.

"What are you grinning about?"

"Nothing," she replied.

Cool eyes gazed at her. "By the way, when we're interviewing a witness, or anyone for that matter, follow *my* lead, Agent Prushenko."

*So we're back to being formal.*

"You mean be quiet?" she said dryly.

"And don't defend me."

She scowled at him. "I was just trying to help."

Ben was being pigheaded. All she'd done was try to smooth things over with Porter Sampson. Why was he so touchy?

"I'm fully capable of explaining myself," he told her.

"Of course you are."

Just then, Sampson stepped into the waiting room, his face three shades of red. He glanced around, noting the empty seats beside Ben and Natassia.

"Well," he said. "If I didn't feel violated before, I certainly do now."

"We're very sorry," Ben said. "But we had to know."

"Now what?"

"Now Agent Prushenko is going to talk to you alone for a few minutes."

"Why?"

"I may be able to help you recover some of your memories," Natassia said, standing. "Come with me."

Ben pulled her aside. "Do you want me to be your reality line?"

Surprised by the offer, she shook her head. "Not necessary. He was drugged and that makes his energy weak. Thanks, though."

She led Sampson into an empty examination room and closed the door. "Have a seat, please. I promise this won't hurt."

"What are you going to do?"

"I'm going to help you remember." She dragged a chair in front of another. "Sit."

Sampson sat down, eyeing her suspiciously. "You gonna hypnotize me or something?"

"Something like that. Trust me." Sitting across from him, she rested her hands on both sides of his head. "Just relax, Mr. Sampson. Think of this as a kind of relaxation massage."

Once she felt some of the tension drain away, she moved her fingertips down to his jaw, stroking his face softly.

"That feels…nice," Sampson said, his voice distant and tired.

"Shh…no talking. Close your eyes and picture yourself at home in your office on the night you went missing. It's after supper and you're working."

With that, she was in.


*She was in Sampson's office, seeing it through his eyes, living it through his actions, inside his body.*

*The phone on the desk rang twice then went still.*

*Minutes later it rang again. Sampson's hand picked up the receiver after the second ring.*

*"Hello?" she said in Sampson's voice.*

*"Justice," a voice whispered.*

*Yawn. "Sorry. You've got the wrong number."*

*Sampson hung up.*

*His hand reached for a blue binder on the shelf. Nothing was legible inside the binder. It looked like someone had taken an eraser and rubbed it over every page in diagonal lines, canceling out letters and words along the way.*

*His body suddenly felt very heavy.*

*I need a break. Maybe I'll watch a little TV.*

*He slumped into the chair behind the desk. Placing the binder in front of him, he picked up the remote control and turned on the television. The screen was blank and all he heard was static, but he was too tired to bother changing channels. Besides, the static was kind of soothing.*

*I'll rest my head. Just for a moment.*

*The binder felt cool against his face. He closed his eyes.*

*It seemed like only seconds had passed before he awoke to the sounds of a loon crying in the distance.*

*He lifted his head. "What the—?"*

*He was lying on cold concrete.*

*It took him a few minutes to recognize his surroundings. He was on the floor of the concert stage at Britannia Park.*

*Panic overwhelmed him.*

*How the hell did I get here?*

Returning to Ben's side, minus Porter Sampson, Natassia was wearier than she'd anticipated, probably more from jet lag and a bout of insomnia during the night.

Ben frowned. "You look exhausted."

"Thank you, kind sir. It's not easy inhabiting someone else's mind, body and memories."

"No. I don't suppose it is. Do you need to lie down or something?"

"Trying to get rid of me already?" In her best Sarah Palin impression, she added, "Don'tcha worry your head about little ole me. I'm just peachy."

It was a lie, but she wasn't going to show him any weakness. Her energy wasn't always reliable or sustainable.

"Did you get anything?" he asked.

She told him what she'd seen.

"Well, that confirms the presence of the blue binder in his home. I wonder why he doesn't recall bringing it home." He shook his head, frustrated. "And you didn't see where he went?"

"It was really weird, Ben. One minute he was in his office asleep at his desk; the next he was laying on the stage floor in the park."

"The phone call seems weird."

"I agree. I don't think it was a wrong number. I think Sampson knew who called him."

"Do you think you'd recognize the voice if you heard it again?"

"I doubt it. He whispered that one word." *Justice.*

Ben leaned his head against the wall and closed his eyes.

"The only thing that makes any sense," he said after a moment, "is that someone snuck into his house, found him sleeping and drugged him. It's the only way anyone would be able to get him out of his house without him knowing it."

"This just gets stranger and stranger," Natassia said, peering down the hallway. "I feel so bad for Porter Sampson. No one should have to go through this."

"At least he didn't wind up like Winkler."

"True, but doesn't it make you wonder why?"

"It sure does. So what did the perp have to gain? What did he want from these men?"

"And did he get it, whatever *it* is?"

Ben's gaze hardened. "I'm not going to stop until I find out why Winkler was brutally murdered, while Sampson was dumped, alive, in the park."

"We," she said in a firm voice.

Ben looked confused.

"You said '*I,*'" she said. "We're a team, Ben. And *we're* not going to stop until we solve this case."

His intense gaze rested on her mouth and a shiver tingled up her spine.

"You're right, Natassia. Sorry."

They waited in silence until the doctor appeared. Behind him stood Porter Sampson, his unshaven face pale and his breath shallow. Fear was etched into every furrow on his brow.

"Maybe you should sit down," she said gently.

Sampson puffed up his chest. "Just tell me."

The doctor consulted a file. "The test came back negative. No bruising or injury. No sign of sexual assault."

Sampson deflated instantly, heaving a visible sigh of relief. His eyes watered and he turned away.

"We'll take you home now," Ben told him.

On the drive back to Sampson's house, Natassia studied the man in the passenger seat. Porter Sampson was a man of power and authority, a Member of Parliament, someone who followed the laws and helped set legal standards in Canada. Today was his wake-up call. He'd have to be more careful, maybe hire a bodyguard since he often spent time with the public, co-workers, his assistant or Lorraine. He couldn't take any unnecessary risks now. Someone had gotten to him, taken advantage of him. Not sexually, but someone had managed to drug him, move him without his knowledge and take away his memories.

When they finally reached the modest house at 501 Linden Terrace, she watched Sampson stumble toward the door, then hesitate on the porch. He seemed smaller, less sure of himself. At last, he went inside.

"He's going to have a long, tough recovery," she said.

"It always is for a victim of crime," Ben replied.

Natassia heaved a sigh. "What does this perp want?"

Jasi was wondering the same thing as she checked out the bars near Britannia Park. There were five in total. She had already visited an Irish pub and a hotel bar.

No one had seen Sampson.

The next place on her data-com checklist was the Britannia Yacht Club, located on Cassels Street. It was worth the visit just to see the uniquely designed bar counter constructed from an authentic 30-foot Dragon sailboat. She'd never seen anything like it.

A stooped man with a bushy white beard appeared in a doorway behind the bar. When he noticed her, he slid on a pair of thick-lensed glasses and gave her a wide smile, revealing crooked, tobacco-stained teeth.

"Can I help you, young lady?"

She slid Porter Sampson's photo toward him. "Have you seen this man in here recently?"

The bartender scrunched his eyes. "Don't think so. Is he a member?"

"No. But he might have been meeting someone here."

"Haven't seen him. Sorry." He paused. "I'm only here during week days. Maybe the night bartender's seen your man."

"When will the night guy be in?"

"He's already here. Paul Cahill. The kid over there." He pointed to a preppy college kid sitting at a table with an older man.

"Who's the guy in the suit?"

"Paul's father."

"Well, isn't that ironic?" she murmured.

Victor Cahill, the owner of the speedboat she'd spotted near the Winkler crime scene. She had him slated for an interview later that day.

*Now I can kill two birds with one stone.*

The bartender leaned close, his breath a mix of pepperoni and beer. "Victor Cahill's the Chief Justice of the Supreme Court of Canada, and one of the richest men in the city."

"Is he a member of this yacht club?"

"Whole family is. The Cahills have three crafts docked here. Two fancy yachts and one of them racing boats."

"Thank you for your help."

She briefly scanned the room. Other than the bartender, who was possibly the oldest person in the bar, there were two male customers occupying the barstools and a few others sitting near the pool tables. She was the only woman.

As she approached, Jasi carefully observed the younger Cahill. From the expensive gold-trimmed pool cue that rested against a nearby wall and the reversed ball cap on his head, she guessed that Paul's occupation would best be described as 'slacker.' Even from a distance he had that spoiled rich kid attitude, an attitude of entitlement.

"Paul Cahill?" she said.

"I'll be anyone you want, sweetheart." he drawled, eyeing her from head to toe.

There was no denying that Paul Cahill was a handsome young man. Too damned handsome for his own good. He was also well-built and naturally bronzed, the kind of tan one would get from habitually lazing by a pool, horseback riding and boating. Based on his clothing style and intelligent eyes, she'd bet anything he was educated at one of Canada's best colleges or shipped overseas

*Probably has a hefty trust fund from dear Daddy.*

She slapped her badge on the table.

Paul Cahill jerked back in his chair, then guiltily gazed at his father. "I didn't do anything. I swear."

"Probably not," she agreed. "Have you seen this man in here?"

"Never. Guaranteed. I've been working here for two years. I know all the regulars and most of their guests."

From the corner of her eye, she saw Paul's father staring at the photo. "What about you?"

Victor Cahill was an older version of his son. Good looking, wealthy and educated.

"I haven't seen him here, but I do recognize him. That's Porter Sampson."

She nodded, unsurprised by the man's admission. As a judge, Cahill would be familiar with many of the MPs.

"Can I see your badge again?" Victor Cahill asked.

She handed it to him and his eyes lit up.

"Ah...Agent McLellan. Don't we have an appointment this afternoon?"

"Yes. I had no idea you'd be here."

"You might as well pull up a chair."

"Thank you, but I'd rather stand. I have a few quick questions."

He studied her with heavy hooded eyes. "Ask away."

"Do you know Porter Sampson personally?"

"No, but I've seen him around."

She angled her 'com so he could see a second photo. "Recognize this?"

The judge shrugged. "Looks like my boat. Why?"

"It was spotted near a recent crime scene."

"Well, it might be mine, might not. But I haven't taken it out in over two weeks." His gaze narrowed and he glanced at his son. "Paul, did you use the speedboat?"

Jasi sensed that Daddy wasn't too pleased with Junior.

"You know I'd never take it out without your permission first," Paul Cahill said defensively. He looked Jasi in the eye. "I swear I didn't use it. My father has the only key."

Her eyes narrowed in the Judge's direction.

"Like I told you," he said. "I didn't take it out either." He rummaged through his jacket pocket, then tossed his keys on the table. "The silver one is for the speedboat."

"Does anyone else have access to your keys?"

"They could," Paul cut in. "He usually hangs his jacket up over there." He pointed to an open wall cupboard with hooks.

"Where were you between eleven p.m. and two a.m. Friday evening?" she asked the younger Cahill.

"I was here. I work weekends." He scratched his chin. "I don't get out of here until close to two."

She wasn't sure whether she believed him.

"I can vouch for him," his father said.

"Of course you can."

Victor Cahill frowned. "I'm not sure I like what you're implying, young lady."

"Simply an observation. And it's Agent McLellan, sir." She eyed both Cahills. "Thank you for your time. If I have any more questions, I'll be in touch."

She had moved a few steps away when angry voices rose over the music. Peering over her shoulder, she saw the Cahill men facing each other. Neither looked happy.

"I told you, someone stole it!" Paul Cahill snapped, tamping the end of the pool cue on the carpeted floor for emphasis.

"Who would steal an old dingy?" his father demanded.

"I haven't got a clue. Maybe you forgot to secure it to the yacht and it drifted away."

Victor Cahill pursed his lips. "I doubt it."

"Why? You think I'm the only one who slips up and makes mistakes?"

The judge said nothing.

"Fine, Dad. I'll buy you another one. But so you know, I never touched the Goddamn dingy." He slammed the cue into the carpet one last time.

Paul Cahill stalked past Jasi. His father followed close behind, barely acknowledging her. That was fine with her, though. Her mind was elsewhere. Something bothered her. The problem was she couldn't quite put her finger on it.

Outside the Britannia Yacht Club, Jasi activated the recorder on her data-com and left some notes. She'd add them to the official file later.

"Not enough to pull a warrant on either Cahill regarding their speedboat seen near the crime scene. And neither appeared to be lying. Also, look into Paul and Chief Justice Victor Cahill. Is there a connection to Winkler or Sampson?"

She pulled up the checklist. The stripper bar was only two blocks away, so she walked. Signage outside the bar boasted dollar drinks after midnight and five dollar lap dances. The marquis above the bar door read 'Bottoms Up.'

"Why didn't I let Ben take this one?" she groaned.

Taking a deep breath, she pushed open the door and stepped inside. The first thing that hit her was the smell. Stale beer and sex. The lunch she'd eaten earlier on the pier threatened to end up on the floor and join the miscellany of unrecognizable stains on the worn burgundy carpet. Even though smoking had been banned from public places years ago, the stench of old cigars and cigarettes still wafted from the carpet.

"They need an Extreme Bar Make-Over," she mumbled.

Even the four intoxicated businessmen who sat around the raised dance floor were oblivious to the sad state of the bar. They were too busy ogling a half-naked redhead with cellulite buttocks and over-inflated bare breasts. The stripper hung upside-down, her legs wrapped around a pole in a position that no human body should be able to accomplish.

Jasi strode toward a man sweeping the floor.

"Is the owner of this…uh, lovely establishment here?"

"You're talkin' to him."

Jasi was a bit surprised. The man looked more like a banker than a bar owner.

"And you are?"

"Ernest Hemmingway," the man snapped.

"Well, *Ernie*...I have a few questions for you."

"Shoot." He gave her a sly look. "Officer."

"I'm not with OPS. Agent McLellan, CFBI."

Ernest, or whatever his name was, shrugged and continued sweeping. "Same thing. One look at you and I knew you were a cop."

Ignoring a sudden throbbing pain in her left arm, she shoved the photo of Sampson in his face. "Did you see him in here this past week?"

"I don't see anyone." He snorted. "This ain't the kind of place where we get all friendly, you know. Guys who come here wanna be left alone. Well, except by the girls, if you know what I mean."

"Take another look."

The man leaned the broom against the wall. His pudgy fingers reached for the photo, then he pushed it into her hands. "Nope, couldn't tell you if he was here or not." He turned his head away. "Stella! Get over here!"

The buxom redhead slid down the pole and staggered to her feet. With a giggle, she patted one of her customers on the shoulder and whispered something in his ear.

"You want a lap dance?" Stella hollered as she approached. "Don't get many ladies here, but I'm game if you are."

Scowling, Jasi showed the stripper the photo.

"Don't know him, lady. Sorry."

"Maybe one of the other dancers—"

"There aren't any others," Ernest said impatiently.

Stella laughed. "Yup, I get these men all to myself."

"Lucky guys," Jasi muttered under her breath.

"Back to the customers, Stella," Ernest snapped.

With that, the stripper sashayed back to the dance floor, her breasts bouncing in time to the dance music. A second later, she was gyrating in one man's lap.

Jasi looked away, catching Ernest's gaze. "Nice place."

He shrugged. "It pays the mortgage and alimony."

Imagining Ernie with a mortgage and possible family didn't quite fit. But the ex-wife sure did.

She stepped outside and gulped in a huge breath of fresh air. Well, as fresh as the city could get. Even the smell of vehicle exhaust was a welcome reprieve from the reek of the stripper bar.

"Note to self. Give Ben the stripper assignments."

Walking back to the car, she sat with the engine idling and thought of Porter Sampson. So far, she'd struck out. No one had seen him.

*So where the hell did he go to get drunk?*

# 15

The Belle Fleur Hotel, distinguishable by its green Normandy copper roof and prime riverside location, was located a few blocks east of the yacht club. Only four years old, the Belle Fleur was a luxurious hotel that catered mainly to celebrities and foreign diplomats.

She'd stayed here once, shortly after it opened.

With Zane.

She entered the hotel's elegant bar. Crossing the dimly lit room, she stopped halfway to admire the view of the river from a floor-to-ceiling window.

"Can I get you something, ma'am?"

The man behind the bar was young—early twenties probably—and not bad on the eyes, but she still wanted to smack him for the, *"ma'am."*

She held out her badge. "I need some information."

"How about a drink first?" He gave her a Tom Cruise smile and tossed a towel over one shoulder. "You look like you could use one."

"I'm on duty." She slid a photo of Porter Sampson across the bar. "Have you seen this man recently?"

"Almost every night."

"Really? Does he come here alone?"

The bartender chuckled. "I never said I saw him here. He's the dude that's always on the news. Politics, right? Minister of something or other."

Jasi scowled. "So he wasn't in here the past week?"

"Not on my shift. Lysette takes over after six. She's in the back. I'll go get her." He vanished for a moment, then reappeared with a bleached blonde at his side.

"Bonjour, mademoiselle," the blond said. "Can I help you?"

At first glance, Lysette seemed to be in her early thirties, but upon closer inspection, Jasi realized she was probably closer to fifty.

*If that's what facial rejuvenation does for you, I might have to reconsider in twenty years or so.*

"Do you recognize the man in this photo?"

"No, I never seen him before," Lysette said in a heavy French accent.

"Thanks anyway."

Jasi tossed a twenty dollar bill on the counter and eyed the bartender. "Buy a book on Canadian politics."

In the lobby, she mentally crossed the Belle Fleur Hotel bar off the list. *That's it then. No other bars in the area.*

She decided to grab a quick salad and iced tea in the dining room. Seated at a table near a window, she thought about the case while enjoying the mesmerizing view of the Ottawa River, the same river that Monty Winkler had drowned in.

*Does it hold some kind of special meaning?*

Winkler had made some enemies along his climb up the political ladder. Yet no one stood out.

She was lost in thought, trying to put the pieces of the puzzling case together when someone called her name.

She looked up. "What are *you* doing here?"

Zane Underhill flashed his perfect white teeth. "Jasmine McLellan, are you following me?"

"Not likely."

"You couldn't wait for dinner?"

"I thought you were staying at the Embassy Hotel."

"I am. I had a meeting with a client near here." His eyes captured hers. "Ottawa sure brings back good memories. Remember?"

"No," she said.

She knew exactly what he was referring to. That one hot summer three years ago when Zane had coaxed her into taking a vacation in Ontario. He'd rented a yacht and they cruised around the Thousand Islands. He'd even taught her the basics—starting the twin engines, steering, navigation. She decided she was better at driving a car. A few days later, they had rented a Porsche and toured the Niagara Falls area before making their way to Ottawa for the Canada Day celebrations.

A sudden image of sweat-soaked bodies writhing in passion amidst tangled sheets and spilled wine came to mind. Sex with Zane was like an intoxicating drug, and she'd responded like an addict, always hungry, always wanting more.

"What I'd like to know is how you found me," he said with a grin. "I don't recall telling you I was coming here."

"I'm not here for you," she said bluntly. "I'm following some leads."

"Ah, I should've known. You're here for some secret CFBI case." He sat in the chair across from her. "Let's have some coffee and you can tell me all about it."

"You know I can't discuss an investigation with you."

Zane ran a hand through his hair. "You can trust me, Jasmine. I won't breathe a word to anyone."

"Sorry, Zane."

"How about a coffee then? We can catch up."

She shook her head. "I agreed to dinner. You'll have to wait until later."

"I see you are still as committed to the CFBI as you've always been. You know, I've helped put away my share of criminals."

Zane was right about that. He had interviewed numerous serial killers, rapists and con artists. His psychological profiling had resulted in a high rate of convictions.

"I can't talk about any case I'm investigating, Zane. Not even with you."

Zane's smile faded. "There was a time when you could tell me anything."

Not everything, she wanted to argue. She had never told him that she was a psychic in the PSI Division. As far as he knew, she was simply a CFBI agent. And that suited her just fine.

"I'll see you at dinner then," he said, standing.

She watched him go. She wanted to stop him, but she knew that doing so would only lead to her emotional destruction.

*I'll deal with him later.*

She rubbed her arm again.

*Why does it ache so much?*

# 16

Natassia stood aside as Jasi's father and brother approached the hospital bed. There was no change in Jasi's condition. She was lost somewhere in a comatose limbo.

It broke Natassia's heart.

*Come on, Jasi. Wake up.*

"Let's get a bite to eat, Natassia." Ben touched her arm. "You need more than just coffee in you, and Jasi needs to be with her family."

"You're both as much her family as we are," Jasi's father interrupted gruffly. "You've seen more of my girl than I have in the past year."

"Pop's right," Brady said. "You're family too."

Ben patted the younger man on the back. "Thanks, bro."

"We'll come back in an hour," Natassia said. "We can take turns watching her today."

She stood up shakily. She'd been at the hospital since 7:00 that morning.

"Lunch in the cafeteria?" she asked Ben.

He nodded, then leaned forward and kissed Jasi's cheek.

"Don't go anywhere, Jazz."

Natassia gave him a wry look. "Where would she go?"

There was a pained expression in his eyes. She knew that he was petrified that Jasi wouldn't pull through.

"She'll be right here when we get back," she insisted.

Following him out of the room, she stared at the worn carpet during the ride in the elevator and thought about Jasi and Ben. They'd been good friends for almost four years. Just friends, Ben had insisted. Yet, sometimes she wondered if they'd ever been more than friends. Sometimes she had to restrain the green-eyed monster when she saw them together, laughing and so much at ease in each other's company. It was impossible not to be jealous.

*She's interested in someone else. Brandon.*

As Ben steered her toward the cafeteria, she thought back to the previous case. *The Gemini Murders*, nicknamed by the press because of the Gemini lighters that a vengeful murderer had left at each arson scene, had ended with the arsonist's death. Afterward, Brandon Walsh, the Chief of Arson Investigations, disappeared with his tail between his legs, abandoning Jasi when she needed him most.

*The coward!*

Natassia had known that something was going on between the two of them. If there was one thing she could spot a mile away, it was sexual tension.

She peeked under her lashes at Ben.

*Like the tension between us.*

"Soup or sandwich?" he asked without looking at her.

"Both. I'm starved."

She heaped up a tray with two bowls of clam chowder, two sandwiches, a veggie tray and two bottles of ice tea.

"I hope that's not all for you," he teased.

She handed him the tray. "Watch it, mister. I'm hungry enough to eat everything on that tray. Lucky for you, I'm in a sharing mood." She stifled a yawn.

"You look exhausted. You need a good night's sleep."

"Is that all I need, Ben?"

She was thinking of something else, and it wasn't sleep.

"Yeah, at least ten hours," he said, oblivious.

"I can think of something even better than sleep."

She grinned, knowing her not-so-innocent words would push a button.

"Natassia…" He gave her a warning look.

"I know, I know. Our relationship is taboo."

"Only when we're out in public."

"You know, I don't really understand what the big deal is. No one's going to care if we're together." She set her hands on her hips. "Are you worried about what Jasi will think?"

She'd already let it slip to their partner that she and Ben had kissed. Jasi didn't need to know that things had progressed beyond kissing. Not yet anyway.

"Jasi will be happy to see me happy," he said.

She raised a brow. "You're happy then?"

"Of course I am." But his expression was anything but happy. "I'm afraid for her, Natassia. I've never seen her look this..."

"Vulnerable?"

He nodded and veered off toward an empty table. As soon as they were seated, he removed his gloves and set them beside his plate.

"My, you're being bold today," she said, grinning.

She remembered the first time they had made love. It had happened a week ago. He'd driven her back to her apartment in Burnaby and she'd invited him in. They hadn't even made it to the bedroom. Instead, she found herself lying on the oriental carpet in front of the fireplace.

Ben hadn't even removed his gloves.

When she had mentioned this, he warned her that his visions were unpredictable, often sparked by touching skin or an object close to a victim. Both of them knew that Natassia carried enough baggage to qualify as a 'victim.'

"I can't take my gloves off around you," he told her.

She never pushed the issue. The last thing she wanted was for him to stop doing all the tantalizing things he'd been doing to her body. If truth be told, she rather enjoyed the sensuous feeling of cool leather on her bare skin.

"What's up?" he asked, interrupting her thoughts.

She smiled. "I'm just remembering."

"Remembering what?"

"The first night you stayed over. In my apartment."

"I wasn't expecting to stay over, you know."

"I know." She chuckled. "But I'm glad you did."

"Me too." He examined his bare hands. "I wish..."

There was a brief silence.

"I know," she said in a quiet voice. "I wish you could touch me, skin on skin. Maybe one day."

Ben picked up a glove. "These are getting thin."

"We'll be careful then."

"I used to wear two or three pairs of department store gloves before I signed on with the CFBI," he said. "I was only nineteen and my gift had developed almost over night. If it weren't for Matthew, I'd probably have gone insane."

"He trained you personally?"

"He tried," he said dryly. "He had these gloves made."

"Tell me about Matthew."

"Not much to tell. I don't know much about his personal life." He took

a breath. "All I really know is that he created the PSI Division. Every
Prime Minister for the past thirty years has supported its existence, but
they'd each deny they knew anything about us if questioned."

"It's the same in Russia."

"The public thinks we're regular CFBI agents. Meanwhile, Matthew is
constantly seeking out people with psychic abilities—like me and
Jasi—and recruiting them if they test positive."

"And Jasi tested as a Level 1."

He nodded.

A depressed calm washed over them and they ate their lunch without
a word to each other.

Finally, she broke the silence. "Jasi has to get better."

"She will."

"If they take her arm…"

"Don't," he snapped. "You can't think like that."

She couldn't imagine what Jasi would do if she woke up and found
that her arm had been amputated. If that happened her career as a CFBI
field agent would be over.

A doctor rushed past them, a serious look on his face.

She gasped. "Oh God."

"That's not Dr. Habib," Ben assured her. "She'll be fine, Natassia. Jasi
is a fighter."

"I know. I hate seeing her like that. A week ago we were talking
about what we'd do when she was better." She locked eyes with his. "We
have cases to solve."

"And you will."

"How can you be so sure? You get a psychic vision?"

Ben slipped on his gloves. "I feel it in my gut. Jasi's got too much to
do, too many criminals to catch. And she's got some unfinished business
to take care of with Walsh."

She scowled. "He certainly hightailed it outta here."

"She told him to go. What else could he do?"

That much was true. Jasi had ordered Brandon to leave, and he'd done
just that.

*Idiot.*

"I don't get why she would push away a perfectly sexy man like
Brandon." She gave Ben a rueful look. "He's not as sexy as you, of
course. But still…"

"Maybe we should call him."

"Uh, I already did," she said, biting her bottom lip.

Ben seemed taken aback. "Really? Is he coming back?"

"I don't know. I've left four messages on his voicemail and he hasn't called me back."

"Walsh's feelings are a bit hurt."

She scowled at him. "I don't care about *his* feelings."

All she cared about was Jasi. Her partner wasn't happy with Walsh gone. Not one bit. And Brandon Walsh should have known that. His absence was making her partner miserable.

When Ben took her hand, the leather was cool against her skin.

He squeezed gently. "Have faith, Natassia."

"I could strangle the guy," she muttered.

"Don't worry. Walsh will come back. Guys like him always do."

"But what if he doesn't?"

Ben shrugged. "If he doesn't, I'll hunt him down and strangle him myself."

# *17*

Meanwhile, Jasi's coma-induced memories took her back to just after her unexpected run-in with Zane Underhill. She began remembering with perfect clarity.

*Zane's back.*

As she hurried back to the hotel, she tried to quell her concerns about their pending dinner engagement.

She found Natassia in Ben's room. The first thing she noticed was the excited expression in her new partner's eyes.

"Got something?"

Natassia nodded. "I've been comparing Winkler and Sampson's data-com appointment books. Look." She turned the monitor.

Jasi studied the open files of Monty Winkler and Porter Sampson. They were placed beside one another for easy comparison. The *doctor* tab had been used on both data-coms.

*Not unusual considering their ages.*

"They both had a lot of doctor's appointments," she noted. "Sampson is seeing two doctors. Dr. Friedman and Dr. Li. Winkler's doctor was Dr. Zuniga."

"I was distracted by those entries too," Natassia said. "But look at this." She pointed to an entry marked *dog groomer*. "Every month for the past six months, they've both taken their dogs to a groomer. Maybe the same one."

Jasi scrolled back through Winkler's schedule. Every month on the first Tuesday at 1:00 p.m., he'd blocked off an hour to take his dog to be groomed. Sampson had a similar appointment booked on the first Wednesday of every month. Also at 1:00 p.m.

"Different days but the same time," Jasi said.

"It's too strange to be coincidence," Ben added.

"I agree."

"We'll have a chat with Sampson first. He said he only knew Winkler in passing and from reputation." He picked up his data-com.

"We have you on speaker," he said when Porter Sampson answered.

"What do you need?"

"We're going over your data-com entries," Jasi said. "We noticed that you and Monty Winkler both had dog grooming appointments, different days, but we thought maybe you had the same groomer, maybe even met each other there. It would give us a connection."

"Well, there are two problems with your theory," Sampson said. "First, I've never had a conversation with Monty Winkler, not that I can remember."

"And what's the second problem?" Ben asked.

"I don't own a dog, Agent Roberts."

Natassia broke in. "But you have it listed in your appointment book on your data-com."

"You must be mistaken. I have no reason for such an appointment. We can't have a dog. Or a cat, for that matter. Lorraine's allergic."

Jasi glanced at Natassia. "You sure this was uploaded from his 'com?"

"I know what I'm doing, Jasi. Especially when it comes to computers. This," she pointed at the left side of the monitor, "is everything from Winkler's data-com, and this is from Sampson's."

Jasi gave her an apologetic look. "Mr. Sampson, who else knows your data-com password?"

"No one. Not even my wife."

"Have you ever left your 'com out in public?" Ben asked. "Maybe on a desk during a meeting?"

"Never. I keep a lot of sensitive material on it."

"Have you ever misplaced it, even temporarily?"

"No. The only time it's not in my pocket or my briefcase is when I charge it at night." He paused. "You don't think someone broke into my house just so they could leave bogus appointments on my data-communicator, do you?"

Jasi looked at Ben. "He does have a point. Why would someone do this?"

"There has to be a better explanation," Natassia said. "One that actually makes sense."

"Okay, Mr. Sampson," Ben said. "Thank you for your assistance."

"I don't know what help I've been," the man grumbled before

disconnecting.

"So what do you make of this?" Jasi asked Natassia.

"The entries were made directly on the 'com, on both of them. They weren't transferred or uploaded from another computer. Both men had a few appointments that were uploaded from their office, meetings they had to attend. Probably sent by their secretaries. But not these."

"So the only explanation is that someone took the 'coms, hacked in and added the appointments," Jasi said.

Natassia shrugged. "Unless Sampson is lying."

"I don't think that's it," Ben said. "There was evidence that someone disturbed Sampson's office. And don't forget about the missing blue binder."

Jasi had almost forgotten about the binder. It certainly suggested that someone had been inside the Sampson home.

"Did you dust for prints?" she asked Ben.

"Matthew sent an evidence team in."

She pocketed her data-com. "Well, we haven't gotten the report yet, but one way or the other, we're going to find this guy."

*Hopefully before he kills someone else.*

Jasi dressed carefully for dinner. Black slacks, a teal satin camisole with a scooped neckline and a short black denim jacket. Light makeup, no jewelry. She didn't want Zane to get the wrong idea.

*It's not a date.*

Then why had she agreed to have dinner with him?

Zane Underhill had always had a hold on her. He had a certain kind of charm that was hard to resist. But he'd left her, walked away without an explanation, no goodbye.

She sighed.

They'd been good together. Once. But that was years ago. Zane had never returned or called her. He'd apparently moved on. So had she.

*I'm over him.*

Was she?

She shoved the doubts aside and focused on fixing her unruly hair. It had decided on its own that curly was 'in.' After a few minutes of fighting with her hair, she gave up.

Exiting the bathroom, she saw Natassia and Ben hovering over an unfamiliar laptop.

"Whose laptop?"

"Sampson's," Ben said without looking up. "An evidence team

dropped it off with three boxes of documents while you were in the shower."

Jasi felt a surge of guilt.

"Do you have a date?" Natassia asked, eyes widening.

"I, uh…" She glanced at Ben. He wasn't smiling. "No, I'm meeting an old friend." Changing the subject, she said, "Ben, can you and Natassia go through those boxes tonight without me?"

His brow arched. "Getting a bit pushy, aren't we?"

"I have to be if I'm going to be team leader." She gave him a wry smile. "Anyway, I learned from the best."

He let out a huff. "Fine."

"Look, I can cancel my—"

"No." Natassia shook her head. "We'll hold down the fort."

"We're having dinner at Red Lobster tonight," Ben said, jerking his head in Natassia's direction. "To discuss the case, of course."

Jasi held back a chuckle. Based on the glint in Ben's eyes, he was finally warming up to their new partner.

"Of course."

"You could always join us later."

Ben had a half-scared look on his face. Like a kid who was about to perform in front of a live audience. She'd never seen him so vulnerable. She liked it.

"Sorry." She glanced at her watch. "I've gotta run."

Natassia walked her to the door.

"Do you think this outfit is too much?" Jasi whispered.

"Depends on what look you're after."

"What does this outfit say?"

"Smart and sexy."

Jasi buttoned the jacket.

"Okay," Natassia said, making a face. "Skip the sexy."

"Perfect. And by the way, I won't be late."

"Stay out as long as you want." Natassia arched a brow. "This old friend of yours, does he have a brother?"

"No."

"I guess I'll have to make do with Ben's company."

Jasi hesitated, wondering if she should say something. She glanced over Natassia's shoulder. Ben was watching them, probably wondering what they were whispering about.

"Ben takes this job very seriously," she said finally. "He's focused on solving every case that comes his way. And he likes things a certain…way."

"You mean he's old school."

Jasi chuckled. "I guess you could say that."

"Got any tips on how I can get on his good side? Providing he *has* a good side"

"You might want to dress more…uh, conservatively."

Natassia's eyes flared in mock outrage. "What, no skinny jeans or cleavage? Hell, that's no fun."

"If it's fun you're after, Ben isn't your guy."

Natassia nudged her into the hall. "Yeah, whatever you say. Have fun, Jasi. Don't come back early." She waved once, then closed the door

In the hallway, Jasi mulled over Natassia's words.

*Have fun?* She wasn't sure she knew what fun was.

A quick look at her watch made her curse. She was nearly twenty-five minutes late—half an hour by the time she'd reach the dining room.

On the way down to meet Zane, she thought of Natassia. Obviously her new partner was attracted to Ben. Did he return the interest?

At the entrance to The Study Lounge in the Embassy Hotel, Jasi slipped past the customers who were waiting to be seated.

A young woman intercepted her. "Can I help you?"

"I'm meeting someone and I'm late."

The hostess smiled. "Ah, this way please."

She led Jasi toward a table in the back corner. Zane was sipping a glass of red wine, looking rather relaxed and as handsome as ever. He smiled and stood as she approached.

"Sorry I'm late," she said hurriedly.

"I thought maybe you'd changed your mind."

He pulled a chair out for her. She sank into it, suddenly realizing that she was famished. The hostess passed her a menu, but Zane slipped it from her hands. "Allow me."

With the suaveness that bespoke of a lifetime of dining out, he said, "We'll have the crab-stuffed mushrooms to start and a bottle of your best champagne."

"Iced tea for me," Jasi said.

Zane flashed a set of perfect teeth. "Champagne. We're celebrating, Jasmine. Besides, you're off duty now, right?"

She sighed. "Yes, I'm off duty."

When the hostess left, she said, "What exactly do you think we're celebrating, Zane?"

"Being together, of course. Tonight it's just you and me."

The light above their table shone down on Zane, illuminating the pale golden streaks in his hair.

He's almost angelic looking, she thought.

She suddenly recalled one of the steamy showers they had taken together in her old apartment. Nothing either of them had done that day was very angelic.

Her face grew hot.

"Something wrong, love?" he asked.

"No, I…it's a bit warm in here."

A waiter approached with a plate of mushrooms, two crystal flutes and a silver bucket containing the bottle of champagne on a bed of crushed ice. He efficiently set everything on the table and poured the champagne into the flutes.

"Are you ready to order, miss?" he asked Jasi.

"Two of your finest steaks, mate," Zane said without missing a beat. "Medium rare. Baked potatoes with the works and two Caesar salads."

Jasi's mouth thinned. "I'm perfectly capable of ordering my own food, thank you."

Zane gave her a wide-eyed look. "Of course you are. I happen to remember that we like the same things."

"That was three years ago," she snapped. To the waiter, she said, "I'll have the shrimp fiesta pasta and a tossed salad with lemon juice."

When the waiter was gone, she gritted her teeth. "Some things have changed, Zane. You shouldn't presume you know what I want."

He reached across the table. "Come on. Truce. Let's just enjoy each other's company."

Annoyed, Jasi picked at a mushroom. It probably would have tasted heavenly if she had been dining with anyone else, but for some reason the mushroom caught in the back of her throat and she had to wash it down with—what else?—the champagne.

She took a sip and made a face.

"Now what's wrong?" Zane asked.

"You forgot. I don't really care for champagne."

"I'll order some wine for you then."

She sighed. "No, I'm good."

There was a momentary lapse in conversation.

"So tell me," she said finally. "What are you really doing here?"

Zane's eyes burned into hers. "I'm here for business mostly. I'm meeting with a few clients this week, then heading back to New York for about a week. Actually, it could be a bit longer."

"Ah, good ole New York, New York." She couldn't control the sarcasm that oozed from her words.

Zane sighed. "Look, Jasmine…I'm sorry that last time I was away longer than I promised."

"Away? You make it sound like you were only gone a week."

"I did try to call you. A few times."

"I never got any calls."

"Every time I got your voice mail, I hung up. Call me a coward—"

Her eyes narrowed. "I did."

The waiter came back with the salads. As soon as he left, Zane said, "Yeah, I *was* a coward. I apologize. You deserved better."

You're damn right, she wanted to say.

Resentment clawed at her throat and she swallowed hard, willing her feelings into the background.

"It's really good to see you again, Jasmine," Zane said softly. "I've missed you."

"Could've fooled me. You seem to have moved on quite easily." She stabbed at a piece of cucumber with her fork. "You've been a busy boy. I heard that you testified in some heavy cases."

He gave her a surprised look.

"We do get the news in Vancouver," she said dryly.

"Did you know that I no longer consult for the CFBI?"

Now that surprised her.

"No. What happened?"

He shrugged. "I decided it was time to move on, work as an independent."

"Really? So you're doing what—family therapy, couples counseling?"

He smiled. "It's far more rewarding and definitely less stressful than dealing with serial killers."

They were briefly distracted when their dinner arrived.

"I saw your face plastered all over the news," she said. "You know, the Dubois trial?"

Zane nodded. "Now that was one sick bastard."

Sixty-year-old Andre Dubois owned a cattle ranch outside Edmonton's city limits. 'The best beef in Alberta' was his motto. 'Organically fed.' It took investigators years before they had enough evidence to charge Dubois, exposing him as one of Canada's most ruthless serial killers.

Dubois had raped and decapitated his victims—twenty-seven prostitutes—over a period of nine years. He kept the heads as trophies, wrapped them in brown paper and stored them in the freezer, alongside the grade A t-bones, ground beef and ribs. He even labeled the heads. 'Blade Roast.'

She glanced at his steak and shivered. "I couldn't eat beef for months after they found out what he'd done with the bodies."

"Is that why you don't eat steak any more?"

"I never said I didn't eat steak. I said I could order my own meal."

"I really thought he'd buried the bodies or dumped them in the river," Zane said. "So much for organically fed cows. I'm glad I'm not a beef inspector. Can you imagine finding human remains in the feed?" He sliced off a juicy piece of steak and put it in his mouth.

She picked at her salad. "No, I can't imagine."

"Sorry," he said. "Not good dinner conversation, is it?"

"Not really."

She focused on removing the eight jumbo shrimp from a bamboo skewer and mixed them into the pasta. The linguine noodles were tossed in a white wine and cilantro cream sauce. Light and satisfying.

Zane topped up her champagne glass.

"I'm good," she insisted. "I still have notes to go over."

He pouted. "The night is young, Jasmine. And so are we. I'm going to take you dancing afterward."

"I don't dance."

"Sure you do." He grinned. "I remember distinctly holding you in my arms. What was that song you liked so much?"

"I don't remember. I have work to do tonight."

"All work and no play—"

"I know, I know. I'm a dull girl, Zane. But I don't have time to play."

"The Jasmine I remember was anything but dull."

She tried not to let his words affect her.

"I'm not the same Jasmine." *I'm not a pushover who sits by the phone every day waiting for you to call.*

"No, you're a workaholic," he said dryly. "There's more to life than work. You should go out, have fun, live life."

"I *am* living my life. The way I want to."

She couldn't allow Zane to gain any ground with her. Underneath all of his charm, he was a guy who would never commit to her, and she wasn't going to be used and tossed aside again.

"It's obvious you still have trust issues," he continued. "You should work on that."

"Don't analyze me, Zane," she said, gritting her teeth. "I am not one of your patients."

"I know that. I'm trying to help you."

"Help me?" She put down her fork, afraid that she might throw it at him.

Why the hell had she agreed to have dinner with him?

*Why? Because you want closure, you idiot.*

"I have everything I want or need, Zane."

He gazed at her for a long moment. Then he gave a nod and turned his attention to his meal. While they ate, she studied him discreetly.

Zane Underhill was her Greek Adonis. That's what she used to think. Everything about him was too damned perfect. He had a smile that could melt even the most stubborn of hearts. His blond hair was luxurious and wavy. His body was fit, defined by daily workouts in his home gym. And his hands...

She stared at them now. Tanned hands with long fingers. Piano player hands, she used to joke, even though Zane couldn't carry a tune, much less play a musical instrument.

*But he sure played me.*

Those hands had done things to her. They had caressed every inch of her, making her ache and cry out for more.

She bit her lip. *Stop it! Nothing good will come from thinking about what was, what used to be. It's over!*

However, one look in Zane's eyes told her she was wrong. He wanted her. A tremble swept over her as she realized something else. She wanted him too.

"Fine," she said. "I'll go dancing. For one hour only."

*What the hell am I doing?*


"Jasi went out? With who?"

Natassia eyed Ben. *Was he jealous?*

"An old friend," she said. "She didn't mention a name."

Ben stood near the window, glancing at the street below, making it impossible to judge his expression.

"Are you hungry?" she asked.

"Sure. Take out? Or do you want to go downstairs?"

"Let's order in. I know a good Japanese restaurant. You like sushi?"

"Good God, don't tell me you're into raw fish." His mouth turned down. "I'll have something cooked, with beef and noodles...or rice."

Natassia grinned. "Chicken?"

"No," he said, distracted. "Beef."

She hid a smile.

"I doubt Jasi will stay out late," he said. "We'll go over the case until she gets back."

"Who says she'll be back tonight?"

Ben eyed the door, a worried look on his face.

"Here." She handed him a data-com. "It's Monty Winkler's. I've got Sampson's. I'm making notes on what I find."

"I'll do the same then. We can compare notes later."

His data-com beeped.

"We've got a text message from Matthew," he said. "He finally got a hold of Deirdre Dailey. She's driving back from Niagara Falls tomorrow morning. She should be here in the afternoon."

"She's number one on my list of possible suspects."

"We also have a warrant for Winkler's legal documents. If that was a will Jasi saw in the briefcase, then we'll have a copy of it tomorrow."

"It'll be interesting to see who Winkler's beneficiaries are," Natassia said.

"I'm more interested in who killed him," Ben replied.

*And why.*

# 18

Jasi awoke to the sound of running water.
_Natassia's already in the shower._
That meant she didn't have to hurry to get out of bed.
With a groan, she rolled over. She wasn't ready to wake up. Not yet.
She still had to shake away the night's grip on her consciousness. She'd
had the strangest dreams and her head felt foggy.
_Maybe I'm coming down with the flu._
She stretched her arms before opening her eyes. The first thing she
saw was the ceiling of the hotel room. She shut her eyes again. At the
same time, a door opened and she heard footsteps padding closer. She
was about to ask Natassia to make coffee when she felt warm lips on
hers.
Her eyes flared open. "What the—"
Zane stood over her, one hand leaning against the bed frame. Her
gaze swept over him, taking in his tousled, wet hair and the towel that
was slung low across his hips. A drop of water trickled down the side of
his neck and rippled down the contours of his well defined chest. She had
a sudden urge to lick it off.
"Good morning, love," he said with his usual Australian charm. "Rise
and shine. Breakfast will be here in about fifteen minutes. I have to pack
for New York. When I get back, we can continue this."
Flustered, she sat up. The blanket slid into her lap and she gasped.
"I'm naked!"
"And beautiful. Maybe I should join you."
"No!"
She scrambled out of bed, tripping over the clothes scattered across
the room. She found her bra draped over a lampshade. Her blouse and

pants were on the floor near the bathroom. She eyed the bed uneasily and flung back the covers. Her panties lay crumpled at the foot of the bed.

"Oh, shit."

Zane chuckled. "Something wrong, love?"

She gawked at him. "We didn't…"

"Oh, yes we did." His grin widened. "And we can do it a third time if you want."

*Oh, Jesus…I had sex with him. Twice.*

As she quickly dressed, memories flooded over her. The wine at dinner. More wine in Zane's room. His seductive voice, easing her into conversation, relaxing her completely. Her carefree, intoxicated mind urging her to surrender to him.

"What time is it, Zane?"

"Almost six-thirty."

"Damn!" She fastened the last button on her blouse and tugged on the jacket, mismatching the buttons in her haste to get dressed.

"What's the rush, Jasmine? Why don't we—"

"I have to get back to my room. I'm here on a case. Business, not pleasure." She let out a moan. "Oh, God. This didn't happen, Zane."

He grabbed her arm, his fingers digging into her. "But it did. We always were good together. You know that." He cupped her face between his hands and leaned close. "We can be good together again."

"No." She pulled away, her heart hammering. "I didn't want this. I'm over you, Zane Underhill."

He smiled confidently. With one quick tug, he whipped the towel from around his waist. "I'm not over you, Jasmine McLellan. I think that's rather obvious, don't you?"

She strode to the door, snatched up her purse and yanked the door open. "This was a mistake." She turned to face him, doing her best to ignore his perfect, golden Adonis body. "One I won't make it again."

Zane cocked his head. In a cool voice, he said, "You still want me, Jasmine. We're not done. Not by a long shot."

She stormed from the room and slammed the door behind her. Her breathing didn't slow until she was alone in the elevator heading for her floor.

"Jesus!" she muttered. "How stupid can you be?"

She'd be useless for about twenty-four hours. No psychic abilities. Sex always put them on hold. She'd have to face Ben, and he'd know immediately.

*And he won't be happy.*

Ben had been there after Zane had left her. He'd picked up the pieces of her shattered heart and helped her see that Zane was just not good enough for her. He'd told her numerous times that Zane Underhill was not the kind of guy to stick around.

Ben had been right. Yet, he'd never said, "Told you so."

Jasi pursed her lips and ran her fingers through her hair.

*You should've learned the first time around, stupid.*

She stepped from the elevator and brushed her sweaty hands against her thighs. If she was lucky, Natassia would still be sleeping and she'd be able to slip into their room, unnoticed.

But Lady Luck wasn't on her side today.

When she entered the hotel room, Natassia and Ben were waiting for her. They didn't look too happy.

"What's up?" she asked, trying to sound nonchalant.

"We've been waiting for you," Ben said.

Natassia rolled her eyes. "I told him not to worry about you."

"Thank you," Jasi said. "Ben, I'm a big girl now."

"Who's here on a case," he added.

"Sorry. I stayed out a bit longer than I planned."

"A bit? You were gone all night."

She glanced from Natassia to Ben. "You haven't waited up for me all night, have you, Dad? I didn't think I needed to report to you where I'd be and for how long."

Ben sighed. "What you do on your own time is your business. You know that."

"Listen…" She sighed. "I'm sorry. I know you worry about me, Ben. But you don't have to. I'm a big girl now and I can take care of myself."

He watched her, his eyes narrowing. "So who were you out with?"

Jasi hesitated. If she told Ben the truth, she'd have to endure another lecture about why Zane wasn't the right guy for her. And she just couldn't take that right now.

"Yeah," Natassia said, grinning. "Tell us. Who's this mystery man?"

"Who said it was a man?" she quipped.

Ben stood, hands on hips, and cocked his head, waiting.

"Just an old friend, Ben. Nothing you have to worry about. I won't be seeing him again."

Ben gave her a hard look. His mouth curved into a frown. "Don't let this guy affect your work."

"I won't." She turned away, knowing that he suspected she'd done more than sleep. "Anything new on the case?"

"Prints came back from the Sampson residence," Natassia said, coming to her rescue. "No other prints except ours, Sampson's and his wife's."

Jasi flopped into a chair. She was frustrated by more than Zane Underhill. They needed a break, a clue, something to point them in the right direction.

"The evidence team did an X-Disc sweep," Ben said, sitting down across from her. "We're waiting on those results. We do know that there were no unusual footprints and no other obvious trace."

"So if someone went into Sampson's home," Jasi said, "they knew how to get in and out without leaving any evidence behind."

"If that's the case, our perp could be familiar with police procedure and evidence collection," Ben said.

Jasi leaned forward. "Any word on the blue binder?"

"It's still missing."

"Doesn't that seem odd to you?"

Ben nodded. "Makes me think there was something in it that someone wanted very badly."

"Badly enough to kill for," Jasi added, scanning a text message from Marilyn Winkler.

"Deirdre's back from Niagara Falls," she said. "She's at Winkler Manor right now. Marilyn suggests we come over and talk to her now."

Ben gave her a disapproving look. "Are you going like that?"

"No," she snapped. "I'll be ready in half an hour."

"Me too," Natassia said quickly. "I need to freshen up. We'll meet you in the lobby in thirty minutes."

"Fine," Ben said, heading out the door. "Half an hour."

Jasi grabbed some clothes and headed for the bathroom.

"You okay?" Natassia asked through the door.

"Yeah."

"You sure."

"I'm positive," Jasi said, a little too sharply. *Am I okay?*

Between Ben's inquisition and Natassia's concern, she felt like she'd dodged a bullet.

As she showered, she thought about her night with Zane. It was all coming back to her now, the warmth of his hands on her body, his mouth on hers.

*How could I be so stupid?*

She closed her eyes and let the water pound down on her head and body, washing away every physical trace of Zane. But it wasn't the physical she was so worried about.

She'd learned years ago that there was a heavy price to pay when she had sex. It drained her of every ounce of psychic energy and left her unable to do her job. Even if she walked into a still smoldering fire, she wouldn't be able to read it for about twenty-four hours. No matter how hard she tried.

"Damn you, Zane."

But it wasn't really *his* fault. He had no idea what he'd done. He didn't know what she was, what she could do. She'd never told him.

"You're an annoying snag, Zane Underhill. An obstacle I have to avoid at all cost."

She didn't need any more complications in her life. She'd have to learn to say 'no' to him. She could do that. She was a self-reliant woman now, not some sniveling girl who needed a man in her life to fulfill her.

As she stepped from the shower and pulled on a plush hotel robe, she glared at her reflection in the mirror.

"Just say *no*. How hard can that be?"

# 19

I covertly studied the CFBI agents as they gathered in the hotel lobby.

"They have no idea who they're messing with," I said beneath my breath.

My eyes followed Agent Jasmine McLellan as she approached the other two. She was a gorgeous woman. Sexy and smart. Too damned smart for her own good.

How much does she know?

The media was dutifully following Winkler's murder and the mystery surrounding Porter Sampson's disappearance and memory loss. But even those unscrupulous reporters had no idea what was really going on. My plan was in motion. Any deviation from the plan, like Winkler, would be taken care of. Permanently.

"Do you need some assistance?" a voice interrupted.

I turned and smiled in the direction of a young woman. Her polished nametag read 'Simone.' She stared back. She seemed nervous.

She should be.

My eyes traveled down to her v-neck blouse, then back up to her graceful neck. I could almost wrap one hand around that neck.

"I'm just leaving."

When I smiled at her, she smiled back.

Don't tempt me, my dear.

I watched her leave and caught sight of the predators that were hunting for me. They'll never catch me. I'm smarter than they are. I have control.

I grinned, recalling the look of horror on Monty Winkler's face when he had caught sight of the hypodermic needle in my hand. All those questions in his eyes. He didn't know he was one of my failures. Must *have been awful knowing that he was going to die and not being able to move or do anything about it.*

*Poor Monty. He was shocked when I poured gasoline over him. The most satisfying part of that evening was lighting the match and tossing it into the dingy, before setting it adrift on the current.*

*I thought of Porter Sampson. It had almost worked with him.*

*"So close..."*

*I let out a frustrated sigh. Porter was a problem and that was a shame. All those months of work.*

*"Why are some so resistant?"*

*I thought of my other subjects, my converts, as I liked to think of them. Everything was going perfectly with them.*

*But I'm running out of time.*

*"Damn it! I needed Winkler and Sampson."*

*With the CFBI watching Sampson so closely, it would be hard to get close.*

*Shit. Sampson's a definite problem. I'll have to take care of him. The sooner, the better. Before he recalls something.*

*I glanced at the CFBI agents. They were going to be a problem.*

*"If so, I'll take care of them."*

*As I left the hotel, I thought of my plan. I smiled. There is justice in this world. As long as I carry it out myself.*

*Divine justice.*

*The irony made me laugh out loud.*

# 20

Ben drove one SUV, while Jasi and Natassia took the other. That way they could interview Deirdre Dailey and get a look at Monty Winkler's will, then split up afterward if they got any good leads. It had been Jasi's idea. Kill two birds with one stone.

From the look on Marilyn Winkler's face, Jasi realized birds weren't the only thing in danger. The woman perched on the edge of the sofa, hands clasped in her lap, all the while scowling at her sister, who sat as far away as possible.

The file stated that Marilyn was almost forty-seven years old. That would put Deirdre at twenty-nine. It could be one reason for their obvious rivalry. Plus the younger woman was very pretty, not to mention model-thin.

Deirdre sat in the armchair, looking completely at ease. Her rich brown hair was sleek and freshly styled in a bob that was longer at the front, with a one-inch section on the right bleached to a pale blond. But her eyes were her best feature. Thickly lashed, they were a brilliant shade of green, far brighter than Jasi's.

"I had a sectional eye enhancement done," Deirdre said, catching her off guard. "My eyes used to be the same dirty brown as Marilyn's." She frowned in her sister's direction. "I wanted mine to be different. So I chose green."

Green, the color of jealousy, Jasi thought.

"Sorry, I didn't mean to stare."

Deirdre smiled. "I'm used to it. When I went for my SEE treatment everyone thought I was crazy."

A movement near a doorway caught Jasi's eye. *James.*

He hovered there, looking uncertain as to whether he should join them or walk away.

"James, be a dear and get us all a drink," Deirdre said, as if she were the lady of the house.

James glanced at Marilyn.

"Fine," she said. "I'll have a glass of lemonade."

"Rum and coke," Deirdre said without missing a beat.

"Isn't it a bit early for alcohol?" her sister asked dryly.

Deirdre shrugged. "I'm on holiday."

Marilyn turned to Jasi. "Would you care for a drink?"

"Nothing for me, thank you."

Ben and Natassia also declined and James left the room.

"Deirdre, you left the day before Monty disappeared," Ben began. "What prompted your sudden holiday?"

"I've been having a difficult time adapting to my father's death. And I've been overworked."

Marilyn let out a derisive snort.

"I decided to take off for a few days," Deirdre continued. "Is that a crime?"

"Someone murdered your brother-in-law," Jasi said. "That's a crime."

"I had nothing to do with that. I wasn't even here."

Absentmindedly, Deirdre pulled a pack of cigarettes from her purse. She caught her sister's disapproving look and smiled. "Marilyn is the perfect sister. She has no bad habits." The cigarettes went back in the purse.

Ben consulted his data-com. "We understand you work at Paragon with your sister."

"I'm in a different part of the building. The satellite research department. I rarely see Marilyn." She gave her sister a disparaging look. "She's too busy securing government contracts so she can study atmospheric deterioration."

"How would you categorize your relationship?"

"Marilyn's the boss. Just like Daddy wanted."

Ben leaned forward. "Your father passed away last year. Is that correct?"

"*Passed away* is a mild way to put it," Marilyn interjected.

"Why do you say that?"

"He was killed in a boating accident, trying to repair the engine. It blew up. When the Coast Guard found him he was still alive. He was covered in burns. It was awful." Deirdre reached for a tissue. "He died a week later."

There was a moment of silence.

"I'm very sorry," Jasi said.

The woman shrugged. "What's done is done."

Jasi glanced at Ben, who gave a small nod.

"Mrs. Winkler," she began, "have you got a copy of your husband's will? I'm sure you're aware that we have a warrant for it."

"It's in Monty's office. I'll go get it. Excuse me."

When she was gone, Jasi turned back to Deirdre. "Is there anything you want to tell us about your relationship with Monty while your sister's out of the room?"

The woman shook her head. "Nothing I can think of. I was a bit troubled a few years ago. I'm sure my sister told you all about it."

"You mean the affair you lied about?"

"I'm not proud of that time in my life. I was angry at my sister. She seemed to have it all, while I had nothing." Deirdre smiled. "But I'm past that now. I'm very happy now."

"How was your relationship with Monty?"

"He forgave me. He was a great brother-in-law, very patient. Couldn't ask for better."

"Do you know Porter Sampson?"

Deirdre considered the name. "I don't think so. Was he a friend of Monty's?"

"You haven't heard about him in the news?"

"I rarely watch the news. Besides, I've been on holiday. Remember? I have more exciting things to do than watch the world crumble to pieces bit by bit."

Marilyn returned with James' briefcase, followed by James who carried a tray of beverages. He set the tray on the side table, while Marilyn placed the briefcase on the coffee table and sat down again.

"All of Monty's life insurance forms and his will are in here," James said, unlocking the case and withdrawing a folder. "The payout on the insurance policy is two million, to Marilyn."

Jasi eyed Marilyn. Her expression remained unchanged.

"That's a lot of money, Mrs. Winkler. You're not shocked."

"I already knew about it." The woman smiled tightly. "I didn't mention it before because I was afraid."

"Afraid of what?"

"I thought it might make me look guilty."

"Are you?"

The look the woman gave her was unwavering. "No."

Jasi wasn't sure if she believed her.

"When did you find out about the life insurance policy?"

"I always knew about it. It was my idea." Marilyn straightened. "We each took out two million dollar policies."

Jasi's gaze drifted to James. "Did you know about this?"

The man nodded. "My brother didn't keep much from me. I handled all his legal matters."

How convenient, she thought. *For James.*

Brother James was looking more and more like their number one suspect. Perhaps he wanted everything his brother had, including Marilyn. It was certainly motive enough for murder.

"You handled his will then," she said.

"I drew this one up about two weeks ago," he said.

"Didn't he have one before that?"

James shifted nervously and she swore she could almost hear his bones rattle.

"Monty wanted to change some of the beneficiaries."

Marilyn's calm composure snapped. "Why would he do that?"

"Wait a minute," Jasi said slowly. "Are you saying you haven't read the will yet?"

Marilyn shrugged. "Monty specified that Deirdre had to be present for the reading, so we've had to wait."

Jasi bit back a smile. *This could prove to be interesting.*

Ben quickly scanned Monty Winkler's will, then passed the entire folder to Jasi. Her eyes latched onto the payout clauses.

*Yes, very interesting indeed.*

"Mrs. Winkler," she said, "your husband left a million dollars to Paragon Research Corporation."

Marilyn's anger deflated. "Well, that's more like it."

"Actually, he left it specifically to the satellite research department." Jasi shifted her gaze to Deirdre. "That's your department, isn't it?"

The look on Deirdre's face was one of stunned surprise.

"Oh my God. I can't believe it."

"What do you mean, you can't believe it?" Marilyn demanded, jumping to her feet. "I know you, Deirdre. You had something to do with this. What did you do, ask him for money for a new house or another car?"

Deirdre laughed. "I didn't ask him for a cent. I guarantee you, dear Sis, I had nothing to do with Monty's will."

Marilyn clenched her fists at her side. "Shut up! I don't want to hear your lies." She took a deep breath. "Agent McLellan, what else does the will say?"

"It looks like your husband left all the cars except yours to charity."
Jasi perused the will, then glanced at James. "And your brother-in-law
here was left a comfortable amount—"

"How much?" Marilyn demanded.

"Fifty thousand."

"What about the rest? His investments, properties, all that?"

Jasi handed the will to Natassia before replying, "Mrs. Winkler, I'm
not sure how to tell you this."

"What?"

"It seems that your husband amassed some large debts. Most of his
investments will be used to pay off that debt. He did, however, leave you
this house and everything in it, plus your car and ten thousand dollars in
a high interest savings account."

"Ten thousand dollars?" Marilyn's face paled. "That's it?"

"And the house," James said quickly.

"Plus the life insurance," Jasi added.

Sure seemed like a lot of money to her.

Marilyn appeared to be on the verge of collapsing. She sat down
again and blinked back tears, while James moved to her side and rested a
bony hand on her shoulder.

"Alrighty then," Deirdre said. "Am I done here?"

Jasi nodded. "For now."

Deirdre stood quickly and headed for the door.

"We may have more questions," Jasi called after her.

"I'll be at my apartment. Please call ahead."

After Deirdre was gone, there was a long silence. In the calm, Jasi
heard the ticking of a clock. *Tick...tick...tick.*

It made her think of a ticking time bomb.

*Who will explode first—Marilyn or Deirdre?*

"I apologize for my sister," Marilyn said with a long sigh. "And for
my outburst."

"No worries," Jasi said. "We understand that things can be difficult at
a time like this."

"I haven't been getting much sleep." She gave a derisive laugh. "I'm
turning into my husband."

"He had trouble sleeping?"

"Except when the television was on after supper."

Ben smiled. "Sounds like a guy thing."

"That's what I thought at first, but when I'd try to wake him he was
always in a nasty mood. Then he'd go to bed later and have awful

dreams."

"Was he always like that, Mrs. Winkler?" Ben asked.

The woman shook her head. "He used to sleep like a baby. I thought it was his job that was keeping him up all night, but...I don't know." Her gaze drifted from Ben to Jasi. "I thought he wasn't happy. You know, with me."

"Were you arguing a lot?" Jasi asked.

"No, not really. Except about the TV. Every night he'd hide in his office. I thought he was watching...you know...porn." She whispered the last word and her face reddened.

"Was he?"

Marilyn's eyes widened in outrage. "Of course not! Monty wasn't like that."

"How do you know?"

The woman took a deep breath. "I listened at the door one night. All I heard was static, so I went in. Monty was just sitting there, staring at the TV. He didn't even notice I was in the room."

This piqued Jasi's interest. "What was he watching?"

"The emergency broadcast channel," Marilyn said with a snort. "Or should I say, static. The next time I walked in it was later, a bit after seven. Monty was passed out in his chair."

An invisible alarm went off in Jasi's mind. There was definitely a connection between the two men now. Winkler and Sampson had both received calls from a payphone around that time. They had both fallen asleep at their desks.

*But what does that mean?*

"I know," Marilyn said, catching her eye. "It doesn't make much sense. I asked him once if he was waiting for an emergency report."

"What did he say?"

"He never answered me. He acted like I wasn't even there. He kept staring at the damned TV." She eyed Ben. "And don't tell me that's just a guy thing too. Monty never used to treat me that way. We used to go for a walk every night after dinner and talk about our day."

"So what you're saying," Jasi said gently, "is that your husband's habits changed in the past couple of months."

Marilyn gave a nod.

Jasi felt a tremor of anticipation. They were on to something. She just wasn't sure what.

From the corner of her eye, she saw Ben remove his gloves and shove them in his pocket. He rose to his feet, holding out both hands to Marilyn. She glanced up, gave him a timid smile, then wordlessly placed her hands in his.

As Ben helped Marilyn to her feet, his smile faded, and Jasi's eyes narrowed. *He saw something.*

"We're sorry for intruding on your grief," Jasi said. "We'll need a copy of these documents."

"Take the folder," Marilyn offered. "I know we can trust the CFBI to keep them safe."

"I'll make a copy of anything we need and have this returned to you tomorrow morning."

"That's fine, Agent McLellan." Marilyn's bottom lip trembled. "When will Monty's...body...be released?"

"Later this afternoon."

"I have so much to do," the woman said, frazzled. "I'm worried I'll forget something. I have to make arrangements for the memorial service and call the pastor. Then I have to call Monty's friends and family." She eyed her brother-in-law. "Don't let me forget, James. And I'll have to buy Monty a new suit for the funeral."

Watching Marilyn and James, Jasi had one thought.

*A new suit is the least of your worries.*


Ben hesitated on the front porch. Time to see if Monty's brother was harboring any covetous thoughts about his brother's widow.

"Thank you for all your help, James," he said. "I'm very sorry for your loss." He held out his hand.

When James took it, Ben felt a sharp flash of sorrow and despair. The feelings intensified and took the form of a smiling face. Marilyn Winkler's.

Two objects came to mind. A heavy lock and a heart.

Ben smiled. *Too easy.*

There was no doubt in his mind that James harbored powerful feelings for his sister-in-law. He was in love with Marilyn. But he'd never told her the secret he kept hidden deep in his heart, locked away.

Marilyn's face quickly faded and was replaced by Monty's. James' emotions toward his brother were equally as strong and resulted in a symbol of two hands joining in a firm handshake. James had idolized Monty and was proud of his brother's accomplishments. He was devastated by his murder. The sooty cyclonic cloud that surrounded him was evidence of that.

Ben released his grip. He felt a twinge of guilt, as if he'd intruded on a deeply personal moment. In a way, he had.

"I hope you find who did this," James said.

Ben tugged on his gloves. "We will. Count on it."

When he reached the driveway, Ben motioned Jasi and Natassia to join him. From the expectant look on Jasi's face, she knew he'd seen something.

"James isn't our perp," he stated bluntly.

"Are you sure?"

Jasi sounded disappointed.

"Fairly." He peered up at the house. "James loved his brother, looked up to him, even though he was in love with Monty's wife."

Jasi grinned. "I knew it!"

"He wouldn't be the first guy to kill someone for love," Natassia said.

Ben shook his head. "James doesn't have the strength, emotionally or physically. And he's never told Marilyn how he feels. He's not our guy."

Jasi let out an impatient huff. "What about Marilyn, then? Maybe she's in love with James and wanted Monty out of the picture. Did you see anything when you touched her?"

"Yeah, I saw a tall brick fence. Marilyn was on one side, her sister on the other."

"So there's no love lost between them?" Jasi asked.

"None at all."

"Well, we know one thing for sure. There's a solid connection between the two victims."

Ben nodded. "Their TV habits and the phone calls."

"Why do you think they were watching the emergency broadcast channel?" Natassia asked.

"I don't know," he said. "But I do know that something very strange is going on."

"It's too bad you didn't get a chance to read Deirdre," Natassia said. "There's something about her I don't trust."

"I was watching her," Jasi said. "She was stunned that her brother-in-law had left such a large sum of money for her research at Paragon."

"Do you have a copy of the first will?" Ben asked.

Jasi passed him the folder. He ruffled through the papers until he found two copies of the current will, the original and a photocopy. At the bottom of the stack was a will dated over ten years ago.

"This is interesting," he murmured. "Ten years ago, Winkler listed his wife as the *sole* beneficiary of all his assets, with the exception of James' modest inheritance and twenty thousand going to select charitable and political avenues."

Jasi's eyes lit up. "What if Marilyn thought she was still the main beneficiary? Maybe she has someone else on the side. Not James, but another man?"

"I'm not feeling it."

"That's because you're a guy, Ben. You always want to see the poor, helpless widow as an innocent."

He bit back a retort. She was right. But still, he didn't get the sense that Marilyn Winkler had offed her husband for money, even with help.

Jasi's data-com beeped. From the one-sided dialogue, he surmised that the trace report on Winkler's Mercedes was in.

"Anything?" he said after she'd hung up.

Jasi shook her head. "The car was clean."

Cursing under his breath, he opened the door of her SUV and waited for her to climb into the driver's seat. When she rolled down the tinted window, he said, "I'll have Matthew check out the emergency broadcast channel, see if maybe something had been broadcasted."

"I still say we need to take a closer look at Deirdre," Natassia said. "Don't forget, she managed to walk away with part of the Winkler fortune. And her sister wasn't too happy about losing a million dollars."

"We'll dig deeper into Deirdre's history," Jasi said, taking the file from Ben. "Technically, the money's still within Marilyn's control if it goes to Paragon, but she's bound to feel resentful toward her sister, even if she does have the life insurance money."

Natassia moved closer to the SUV. "What if Marilyn wanted it all? What if she didn't know Monty had changed his will?"

"He had quite a fortune," Jasi said. "Some people would kill for that kind of money."

"Maybe someone did," Ben said, thinking of Marilyn's taste for the rich life. "You could be right about Marilyn Winkler. Perhaps Paragon Research Corporation isn't as virtuous as its name suggests. We'd better check out Marilyn's financials, see if she has any outstanding debts."

"I have a question," Natassia said.

"Shoot."

"Why would Marilyn go after Porter Sampson?"

"Maybe Sampson was a decoy, to throw us off track," Jasi suggested.

"Frankly," Ben said, "I don't think Marilyn is strong enough to lift either man."

"Maybe she had help. James seems very devoted to her."

Ben snorted. "James wouldn't be capable of dragging his own body across the shore, much less a man the size of Winkler or Sampson. No, if

Marilyn is involved and has a partner, I don't think it's the brother-in-law."

"Who else could it be?"

"That, my dear Jasi, is the question of the day."

# *21*

While Ben and Natassia drove to the Sampson residence, Jasi decided to question the other woman in Monty Winkler's life. Karen Hampton.

She programmed the SUV's navigation system for Karen's address, an apartment on the east side. When she arrived, she had to park on the street. Between the security doors, she located the buzzer for room 1702.

"Okay, Karen. Let's see what you have to tell me."

She pushed the buzzer.

"Yeah?" The woman sounded in a hurry.

"Karen Hampton?"

"Yeah, what do you want?"

"I'm with the CFBI. I'd like to ask you a few questions about Monty Winkler."

The only answer was the droning buzz of the door.

As Jasi rode the elevator up to the seventeenth floor, she consulted her data-com for stats on the woman. Karen Hampton, also known as Monty Winkler's former mistress, had a clean record, no arrests, not even a parking ticket. She'd been a nobody until she went public about her relationship with Monty. This announcement came after tabloids released photographs of the two of them dancing very close together in a nightclub. According to one article, Hampton openly professed, "*I love everything about Monty, his kindness and humor, but mostly he knows how to treat a lady.*"

Jasi almost gagged.

*Funny thing, love. It makes you do stupid things, things you often regret later.*

One knock brought the apartment's occupant to the door, and Jasi was caught off guard. Karen Hampton's head and face were wrapped in bandages. Only her deep teal eyes and augmented lips were visible. She wore a navy-blue satin robe and matching slippers with three-inch spiked heels.

*Hollywood starlet* came to mind.

Jasi showed her badge. "Ms. Hampton?"

"Hurry up. I don't want my neighbors to see me." An impatient hand pulled her inside.

Jasi couldn't help but stare. "Were you in an accident?"

Karen Hampton laughed. "No. I had a rejuvenation lift."

Facial rejuvenation, SEE eye color enhancements, liposuction, vaginal and sexual sensitivity rejuvenation...

*Christ! No one's happy with how they look anymore.*

Jasi studied her. "I honestly don't get why you'd put yourself through such torture."

"Why, to look beautiful, of course."

"Then my definition of beauty must be a bit off."

The woman shrugged, then led Jasi into a cozy living room. Sliding doors led outside onto a small balcony. The view was so breathtaking that Jasi couldn't resist taking a peek.

"Ottawa is a beautiful city."

"You should see it at night," Karen said behind her.

Jasi turned to her host. "I have." *With Zane.*

"Have you ever had facial surgery, Agent McLellan? Your skin is so smooth."

"Ivory soap."

Karen flinched. "You're kidding, right?"

"I never kid about such things."

Jasi caught sight of three black and white photographs on the nearby wall. The girl in them had luxurious dark hair and eyes. She was exceptionally beautiful. And very young.

"You?" she asked Karen.

"Yeah. I was seventeen and at the beginning of my modeling career. Then I hit a few roadblocks."

"I hear it's a tough business."

"Yeah, you have to stay young and beautiful forever." She indicated her bandaged face. "And youth and beauty don't come cheap."

"I suppose not."

"So...shall we start, Agent McLellan?"

Jasi reassessed the woman. She was used to hesitation, stalling. Not head-on confrontation. This made Karen Hampton stand out.

As a suspect.

*Let's see what you've got to hide.*

"Have a seat," the woman said, pushing an obese Garfield wannabe off the sofa. The cat left behind a clump of pumpkin colored fur the size of a mouse. "Sorry. Max started shedding in clumps the day I got home from my surgery. I hope you're not allergic."

"No problem." Setting her data-com on the coffee table, Jasi kept a wary eye on the monstrous feline. "I'd like to record our conversation."

"I'm guessing you want to know about me and Monty."

"I understand you used to be Marilyn Winkler's secretary at Paragon Research Corporation. Is that when you first met Mr. Winkler?"

Karen settled into the armchair across from Jasi. "Yes. Monty would often drop by PRC to see Marilyn. Since I took her messages, I often talked to him. He always took the time to ask me how my day was."

Karen's voice was wistful and her expression seemed sad, from what Jasi could make of it behind the bandages.

"When did you start seeing Monty? Personally, I mean?"

"It started innocently enough. We'd duck out together during political galas. Monty said they were 'pretentious stuffy affairs for pretentious stuffy people.'" Karen laughed. "I had to agree. We'd often go to the nearest bar and just chat. Then we'd go back to the gala and Monty would act as if he'd never left."

"And the affair?"

"It started a few months after I began working at Paragon. We'd left another boring party together. One minute we were at a bar discussing the difference between a good merlot and a fruity cabernet; the next we were in a hotel room making love." Her voice grew quiet. "He was always caring and thoughtful. It made it easy to overlook the fact that he was much older than me."

Jasi smiled thinly. *And married.*

"When was the last time you saw Monty?"

"About a month ago." She saw Jasi's surprised look and smiled. "We'd broken it off six months ago. After that, I only saw him at mutual affairs." She bit her bottom lip. "Get-togethers and events, I mean."

"Did Monty break things off with you?"

"Yes. But we both felt things had come to an end. There's no future with a married man." She turned away, but not before Jasi noticed the tears in the woman's eyes. "I guess Monty had no future anyway."

"You cared a lot for him."

"Monty was the kind of guy that everyone loved."

"Not everyone," Jasi corrected. "At least one person wanted him dead."

The woman flinched. "I can't imagine why."

"According to reports, it wasn't always *good* between you. You did, after all, come clean about your affair to the press." Jasi watched her for a reaction. "Some people say you wanted the public to know. That you were trying to ruin his marriage and his career."

Karen shrugged. "You know how the press is. They take your words and twist them around to suit them. To sell more newspapers."

"So you expect people to believe you harbored no ill will against him. For choosing to stay with his wife, I mean."

"Monty and I loved each other, Agent McLellan. But we both knew that a divorce would compromise his political career. Once I realized there was no future with him, I let him go and moved on."

"Where were you the night of April 13th?"

Karen's eyes widened. "You can't think I had anything to do with his disappearance or murder. I loved him."

"People have killed for less, Ms. Hampton."

Karen tilted her bandaged head. "I was having a face lift, Agent McLellan. If you'll excuse me for a moment, I'll get you my doctor's contact information."

While Jasi waited, she took a moment to study Karen Hampton's apartment. Located in a ritzy area, the building boasted an exercise room, spa and swimming pool, according to the flyer she'd seen posted inside the elevator.

"What do you do now that you've left PRC?" she called out.

Karen reappeared with an older model data-com in hand. "I went back to modeling. For Suzi Wang Fashions."

"You must be doing well to afford such a place as this," Jasi said while copying down the surgeon's information.

"I'm doing all right."

"Did Monty ever mention getting strange phone calls?"

"No."

"Did he ever mention friction between himself and anyone else?"

"You mean besides Marilyn and her sister?" Karen chuckled. "No. Monty was pretty easy going. And one thing we didn't do was talk about his job or marriage. We had *other* things to keep us occupied."

"What about you? Did you harbor resentment against him for staying with his wife?"

"I did at first. I'll admit it, it's hard being the 'other woman,' but once the press got hold of the story, I did what any woman would do. I made the most out of it."

"But the press wasn't very flattering."

"No, but it got my name out there." She smiled. "Suzi Wang called me personally and offered me a modeling job when the story hit the tabloids. I wouldn't be modeling again if it wasn't for Monty and my affair with him."

"That's a bit shallow, isn't it? You say you loved him."

"A girl's gotta do what a girl's gotta do."

Later, in the SUV, Jasi replayed their conversation on the data-com. The woman had been brutally honest, and if her alibi checked out, Jasi could cross Karen off the suspect list.

*"A girl's gotta do what a girl's gotta do."*

Karen Hampton was right. Sometimes you had to take the bad and turn it into good. Jasi's *bad* had hit rock bottom with the violent murder of her mother. Now she was a CFBI agent with an uncontrollable urge to save the innocent and put away the bad guys.

As she drove back to the Embassy Hotel, she thought of the current case. Would a killer strike again? Or would they catch him first?

# 22

Twelve days passed with no breaks in either the Winkler or Sampson case. Karen Hampton's alibi checked out, along with an alibi and background check on Marilyn and James. No new clues or evidence were available. The investigation was at a standstill.

A media frenzy had begun to wreak havoc in Ottawa and across Canada. The press had caught wind that two Members of Parliament had been drugged and abducted, resulting in one case of partial amnesia and one violent death. Everyone was screaming for justice, with pressure coming from all angles, from relatives and friends of the deceased, Parliament and even the Prime Minister.

Jasi welcomed the pressure. It kept her too busy to think about Zane. He'd left messages at the front desk, but she refused to answer them. She'd seen him in the Embassy Hotel's foyer before he left for New York. He walked away as soon as he saw Ben and Natassia. Neither had noticed him.

She spent time chatting with Natassia, getting to know her, as Matthew had insisted. _Your partner or partners will be your best friends._

Jasi didn't do so well in the friend category.

"So..." Natassia said that morning. "How'd you find out about the PSI Division?"

"I didn't. They found me."

She told Natassia how she'd left home at eighteen and taken a job as a researcher for a high-powered lawyer.

"One night someone set fire to the office. There was one casualty, my boss. He was working late."

Natassia's finely shaped brow arched. "Alone?"

Jasi nodded. "The CFBI was called in, but after nearly a week they had no leads. Until I walked into the building to pick up some files."

"What happened?"

"The smoke overwhelmed me."

"No one showed you how to protect yourself?"

"No, not back then. I was still trying to hide what I could do. You know, pretend to be normal."

"What about your parents? Didn't they try to help you?"

Jasi laughed derisively. "My father prefers to stay in denial over what I can do. He's never seen what it does to me."

"And your mom?"

"She died when I was young."

The words were automatic, as was the small twinge in her heart that always came with them.

"Before my gift surfaced," she added.

"Sorry," Natassia murmured. "It must've been tough."

"It was." Jasi shrugged. "But I got through it."

There was an uncomfortable silence in the room, the proverbial elephant. Until Natassia made it vanish.

"So what happened when you went to get the files?"

"I passed out. A judge found me, half-unconscious, on the floor in the hallway. Apparently I told him that my boss's business associate had set the fire to cover up his involvement in defrauding the company."

"They caught him?"

"In the act of transferring hundreds of thousands of dollars to an offshore account."

"Case closed," Natassia said with a grin.

"Yup. He was carted off to prison while I was rushed to the hospital. When I woke up the first person I saw was an older man with long gray hair tied in a ponytail."

"Matthew Divine."

Jasi nodded. "He was wearing faded jeans and a blue suit jacket. I remember thinking it was an odd mix for an old guy." She chuckled. "Then I saw the guy standing beside him. Ben. He was wearing a custom-fitted suit that made him look unbelievably tall."

Natassia made a soft growling noise. "And more handsome, I bet."

"Hey, who's telling the story here?"

"So what happened next?" Natassia asked.

"Matthew said they had a proposition for me. They wanted to train me, show me how to use my gift and take control of it."

"*Et voila!* Here you are. "

"I couldn't turn him down. Or Ben."

"I don't think I could've turned Ben down either."

Jasi smiled faintly, recalling the rush of emotion she'd felt the first time she was welcomed by everyone at Divine Ops. It had been the first time in her life that she felt completely accepted for who she was and what she could do. No one else understood her the way her PSI family did.

*Not even Zane.*

His face came to mind and she wanted to smack it.

"Yes, they were both very persuasive," she said, pushing Zane to the background. "And now I get to use my gift to help others. Like Monty Winkler and Porter Sampson."

Natassia touched her arm. "We're going to get this guy."

"I sure hope so."

With her mind on Winkler and Sampson, Jasi felt more in control. Something had happened to these two men and she was going to find out what. So far, the investigation had hit a brick wall, but she was determined to dismantle it, one brick at a time if she had to.

She peeked at Natassia from under her lashes. Her new partner was developing a crush on Ben.

*I wonder if Ben knows.*

Ben wasn't always the most observant when it came to matters of the heart. He'd built up his own wall, allowing only a few people in. He often came across as curt, unfriendly and unappreciative.

"By the way, Natassia, I think you're an asset to this team and the case. I'm glad you're working it with us."

Natassia's eyes widened. "Thank you."

"I'll be back in a minute. I need to talk to Ben."

She left Natassia in their room. In the hallway, she saw Ben leaving his room.

"I was just coming to see you. Where are you off to?"

"Porter Sampson's house," he said. "He's been having some weird dreams."

"Does he think they're connected to his abduction?"

"He's not sure. But he's had the same dream for the last week."

"He could be having flashbacks. I'll come with you."

"What about Natassia?"

"She has some reports to go over."

"Did she miss something?"

She shrugged. "You know how it is, Ben. Nothing is cut and dry in what she sees. She has to decipher her visions like we do, and I'm sure she's very good at what she does."

"I guess we'll see about that, won't we? I just hope she doesn't mess up one of the clues."

As they drove to Porter Sampson's house, Jasi thought about Ben's behavior toward their new partner. He'd been acting kind of odd for the past day, avoiding Natassia whenever possible. He wasn't usually this hard on a fellow agent, particularly a PSI.

*We've both misinterpreted visions before, Ben.*

She thought about her last assignment—a corporate espionage and fraud case. Someone had not only stolen project files from a leading computer game company in Edmonton, he or she had also embezzled millions of dollars after hacking into payroll. By the time anyone noticed what was happening, it was too late. One of the company partners died in a bomb explosion that was programmed to explode the moment a particular file was entered, the game's weapons file.

After the explosion, Jasi was called in. When she caught the first whiff of smoke, a vision came fast and cryptic. For weeks she was convinced that one or more of the partners were responsible, or at least the ones without alibis. She almost missed the last piece of the puzzle and two con men nearly got away in a lavish private jet destined for Fiji, a country with no extradition treaty with Canada.

In her vision, she'd seen a golden ladder with two missing steps, and it wasn't until she was interrogating the five partners that she realized the ladder represented someone who *hadn't* climbed the ladder of success. She discovered that two brilliant techs had been voted out of the partnership three months earlier and were subsequently let go from the company because their ideals were so different from the partners. Still, everyone else in the company was under the misguided assumption that it had been a diplomatic resolution. Until the fire, they had no idea that some people hold grudges far longer than is healthy. And *that* can prove to be deadly.

"I hope we catch a break soon," Ben said, interrupting her thoughts.

"Me too." She hesitated, not knowing how to broach the subject of Natassia. "Ben, I…uh…"

"What?"

She took the plunge. "Natassia is a hard worker and very dedicated. I really like her."

Ben gaped at her. "You *like* her?"

"Yes," she said, lifting her chin.

He laughed. "Why Jasmine McLellan, I do believe you have a new friend."

She swatted his arm, hard. "Shut up. I mean that she's nice and I—"

"Like her. Okay, I get it. I'm being too hard on her."

She grinned. "You said it."

Ben sighed. "Fine. I'll try to be…uh, nicer."

"You do that."

"So," he said, "any thoughts on this case?"

"Yeah. I've never felt this useless before."

"You're anything but useless, Jasi." He tugged on her ponytail. "Except when it comes to cooking."

"Hey! Leave my cooking alone or I'll never invite you over for dinner again."

He grinned. "Promise?"


When they reached the Sampson residence, Jasi noticed that the driveway and sidewalks were vacant. Porter Sampson was old news now, especially since he couldn't recall what had happened to him. The media had gone on to more important stories, like the masked corner store bandit who had made off with a few hundred dollars. He'd left the scene on a silver ten-speed and was caught four blocks away, pedaling merrily down an alley. He probably would have gotten away unnoticed if he'd removed the mask.

With Ben two steps behind, Jasi strode to the door and gave it three sharp raps. No answer.

She glanced at Ben. "You sure he's home?"

"Hey, he called me. He should be expecting us."

Ben reached around her and rang the doorbell. Twice.

A few minutes later, Porter Sampson's face appeared. He glanced behind them, as if expecting an entourage.

"CFBI, Mr. Sampson," Jasi said, flashing her badge.

"Yeah?" He flashed them a confused look.

She frowned. "You expecting someone else?"

"Uh, no…I don't think so."

The man opened the door just wide enough for them to pass inside and Jasi took in his sunken eyes and haggard face. From the look of his wrinkled clothes and coffee-stained shirt, Porter Sampson hadn't slept or showered in a couple of days.

"What can I do for you?" Sampson asked, wiping his forehead with the back of a trembling hand.

She exchanged baffled looks with her partner.

"You called us," Ben said calmly. "You're having some strange dreams. That's what you told me."

"Oh. Right."

As they followed him into the living room, Jasi leaned close to Ben. "He seems a bit out of it."

"Maybe he just woke up."

She sat down on the sofa and placed her data-com on the coffee table. "Voice record on." To Sampson, she said, "Are you feeling okay?"

"I can't sleep," the man muttered, sitting across from her. "Whenever I close my eyes, I feel nauseous and dizzy. And I keep having the same blasted dream, over and over again."

"Have you seen a doctor?"

"Yes, and little good *that* did. He gave me some pills to take before bed. They don't do anything except make my mouth dry." He rubbed his eyes. "I saw my therapist yesterday. He gave me some relaxation exercises to do, but that seemed to make things worse. I think I got maybe two hours of sleep last night. And not much more the night before."

"You need sleep, Mr. Sampson," Jasi said, concerned.

"I know that," the man grumbled.

"Is your wife home?" Ben asked.

Sampson shook his head. "She went to her book club meeting. Do you need to talk to her too?"

"Maybe later," Jasi said. "Tell us about your dream."

"There's not much to tell. In between feeling sick and dizzy, I get these glimpses of something shiny, so shiny I have to look away. Then I feel cold, really cold."

"What else?" Jasi pressed.

"That's it. I wake up."

"What about sounds? Do you hear anything, or anyone?"

Sampson closed his eyes. "No, no voices, but I did hear music. Classical. Maybe Bach or Beethoven, I'm not sure. And I heard someone humming."

"Do you see anything else in your dream?" Ben asked.

"No, that's it." Sampson leaned forward, holding his head and rocking slowly. "Except this overwhelming feeling that I have to do something." His gaze latched onto Jasi. "I can't—"

The phone rang.

"I know there's something I've forgotten," Sampson muttered, more to himself. "Something important."

"You wanna get that?" Ben asked when the phone rang again.

Sampson shook his head.

The fact that he ignored the phone call made Jasi take notice. There was something familiar about this scenario.

The phone went silent after the second ring, so she consulted her notes. "Where were we?"

"I think I was saying I—"

The phone rang again.

Sampson jumped to his feet and abruptly left the room.

Jasi raised a brow. "Okay…"

Ben shrugged. "He's exhausted."

When Sampson returned minutes later, he seemed preoccupied. "I'm sorry but I have nothing more to add." He beamed them a bright smile. "Now if you'll excuse me, I have some papers to sign."

"Certainly," Jasi said, moving toward the door. "If you recall anything else, please call us."

She handed the man a card. It had two 'throwaway' phone numbers on it that were temporarily transferred to either her data-com or Ben's.

"Have a good day," Sampson said in a cheerful voice.

She watched him from the corner of her eye. The man had gone from weary to cheery in minutes.

*What the hell?*

As Ben backed the SUV out of the driveway, Jasi chewed her bottom lip. "Well, that was strange."

"You noticed it too?"

"Yeah. One moment he looked like he needed a nap—"

"The next, he looked like he'd been told he'd won the lottery."

"I know. What the hell happened?"

"Your guess is as good as mine." The words were barely out of his mouth when his data-com beeped.

Matthew's voice crackled through the speaker. "Any leads with Sampson?"

"We think he's having some kind of flashback," she answered. "In his dreams."

"Stay on him. He's the strongest lead we've got."

"Will do."

"Stay safe," Matthew said before disconnecting.

Ben glanced at her. "What do you make of all this?"

*Another test.*

"I think we'll discover the phone call Sampson just got came from a payphone near Parliament Hill. And I think someone is either blackmailing or threatening him."

Ben's head bobbed in agreement. "I think you might be on to something. What now?"

She chuckled. "Well, since you made fun of my cooking earlier and since I said I'd make you pay, you're going to buy Natassia and me the best dinner Ottawa has to offer."

Alone in her hotel room that evening, Jasi carried out her evening ritual of Pilates stretches on her bed, then sat cross-legged, eyes closed, breathing deeply.

*In...out.*

She kept her mind clear. No stress, no worries.

Fifteen minutes later, she felt calm. Tonight, she'd sleep.

She reached up and carefully disengaged the tight elastic band from her hair. Freed from confinement, wayward curls and waves bounced past her shoulders. She massaged her scalp and released a long sigh. For a moment she wished that it was someone else's strong, tanned fingers running through her hair.

The phone rang.

There was only one person who would call her on the hotel phone—*Zane*—and she had no desire to talk to him.

Against her will, her eyes were drawn to the phone. The message light flashed. She grabbed the phone, sucked in a breath and dialed the code for message retrieval.

"You have five messages," announced an automated male voice. "After you have listened to each message, please press 1 to save. To delete, press 2. To upload messages to your cell phone or data-com, enter your phone number followed by your room number."

She was tempted to delete all five messages, but she was curious so she stayed on the line.

"Hi, love. It's Zane. I was hoping we could talk. About last night. Call me tonight." He left his cell phone number.

Jasi pressed 2.

"Hey, it's me again." Zane sounded breathless. "I need to talk to you before I leave for New York."

Delete.

She quickly deleted the next two identical messages, but the fifth message made her pulse skip a beat.

"Come on, Jasmine, love. We can't leave things like this. I was hoping that I meant more to you than a one night stand. It did to me."

There was a long pause and she thought that was the end of the message, but then he said, "I know I messed things up last time, but seeing you again—*being* with you again—made me realize that I don't want to be without you. I need you, Jasmine. I'll be back soon."

Zane's voice was soft and tender, and his words singed her, burning into her heart. The only thing missing in her life was someone to share it with.

*Someone to love.*

She saved his message, then wandered to the fridge.

"Great," she said, peering inside. "No iced tea."

She grabbed a glass from the bathroom and strode out into the hall. The pop and ice machines were at the far end near the elevators. She dug in her jeans for some change and purchased a bottle of iced tea.

She turned to the ice machine, one of those ancient storage chest models with a spring-loaded lid to prevent people from leaving it open.

She opened the lid. "Aw, damn."

Someone had knocked the switch and inadvertently turned the ice maker off. There was a shallow pool of water in the bottom of the chest and a pile of half-melted cubes in the far corner.

But that didn't stop her.

She propped up the lid with her hand, the one holding the tea bottle. Then she leaned down so she could scoop ice into the glass in her right hand, but the further in she leaned, the harder it was to keep the lid from closing and smacking her on the head. She gritted her teeth. Praying that no one would walk by her and see her butt in the air, she leaned lower.

She probably would have been fine if she hadn't heard someone clearing their throat behind her. Before she could say anything, she heard the one thing that made her face grow heated. Someone was laughing at her.

And she knew exactly who it was.

"Stop laughing at me!"

"Nice view," Zane said, chuckling behind her.

Jasi raised her head. Too fast. Her hair caught on a hinge and she let out a loud yelp. The lid thudded against her head and the glass of ice and the bottle flew out of her hands, landing with a splash in the water in the storage bin.

"The least you could do is help me," she snapped.

Warm fingers moved over her head and she felt a small tug and then her hair was free. She came up, breathless and embarrassed.

Zane leaned against the wall and gave her a lazy smile.

"What?" she demanded.

His gaze drifted from her eyes to her blouse. "Cold?"

"What do you want?"

"What do you think I want?"

She crossed her arms defiantly.

"You didn't return any of my calls, Jasmine. I was hoping…well, you know what I was hoping. I'm in the city indefinitely now."

"Well, good for you." She turned away. "Have fun in Ottawa."

He grabbed her arm.

"Hey! What the hell—?"

Before she could utter another word, he kissed her, hard. He gathered her in close until she could smell the musky scent of his aftershave. God, she loved how he smelled. And how he kissed.

"Zane," she murmured under his caressing lips.

"Shut up, Jasmine," he whispered back. "Kiss me."

With a soft sigh, she gave in. The kiss deepened and grew more persistent, hungrier. Her skin was on fire, itching to be stroked, and she felt desire building until she thought she'd explode.

A door opened. A young woman stepped into the hall, her eyes widening when she saw them.

Zane grabbed her hand, tugging her into the elevator. His mouth barely left hers. As the doors closed and the elevator began to rise, he pressed her against the wall. Hot hands slipped under her blouse. In a flash, her bra was unhooked and replaced by Zane's hands. His thumbs stroked her breasts lightly, teasing them. His tongue slipped into her mouth, eliciting a moan of passion.

"Zane…"

"You want me. I know you do."

He pushed her blouse up and his mouth fastened on one nipple. Her breath came in quick gasps as heat built up between her legs. He kissed her lips again and she immediately missed the heat of his mouth on her breast. He shifted and she heard a zipper open.

"No," she moaned against his mouth.

He pulled away, but his eyes stayed on her lips. She knew exactly what he wanted. She wanted it too.

"We can't make love, Zane. It makes me too…" She struggled to find the right words. "…tired."

She wondered what he'd say if she told him that making love interfered with her psychic gift.

*Don't do it.*

The elevator jerked to a stop and it took a moment before Jasi realized that Zane had pressed the emergency stop.

She gave him a questioning look. "Why did you—?"

Zane kissed her again and began unbuttoning her blouse.

"Didn't you hear me?" She groaned. "We can't make love."

His warm lips found the ticklish spot behind her ear.

"Then we'll do what we can."

The blouse parted and Zane swooped in.

"No, Zane..."

*Oh God, yes...*

# 23

Her data-com beeped, jarring her from an erotic dream about Zane and a spray can of whipped cream. She blinked twice and caught sight of a bare glimmer of dawn between the curtains.

_Buzz!_

From the other bed, Jasi heard a groan.

"You gonna get that?" Natassia mumbled.

Jasi sat up when the 'com buzzed again. Figuring it was Ben or Matthew with some news, she activated the call.

"Is this Agent McLellan?"

"Yes. Who—?"

"It's Lorraine Sampson. I'm so sorry to wake you, but I didn't know what else to do."

The woman was on the verge of hysteria.

"Mrs. Sampson—Lorraine—you need to calm down."

The woman took a deep breath on the other end of the phone. "I'm trying to."

"Okay," Jasi said, "now tell me what's going on."

"Porter's been tossing and turning all night long, _every_ night. And he's been waking up between three and four, moaning and talking in his sleep. I can't make out what he's saying, but whatever he's dreaming about is keeping him awake. In the morning he looks awful and he snaps at me every time I open my mouth." Lorraine choked back a sob. "I'm sorry I'm calling so early, but I can't take much more of this, Agent McLellan."

"Has he mentioned why he's waking up early or why he's so...upset?"

"He says it's his dreams."

"What exactly is he dreaming of?" Jasi asked, sitting up.

"I don't know. He won't tell me. That's how I know they're really bad. He used to always tell me what he dreamt."

Jasi turned the lamp on low. "Mrs. Sampson, I don't know what to say. We don't have anything to go on, and without a lead..." She heard a tired sigh.

"I know, but I'm scared. I've never seen him like this."

"Has he been back to his therapist?"

"He said he went the day before yesterday, but he's getting worse. He's not eating. He locks himself away in his office every day, refusing to come out."

"Perhaps he needs to see his therapist more often."

"His therapist isn't doing a very good job," Lorraine said. "I think he should see someone else, someone better. He's supposed to be going back to work next week."

Jasi didn't know what to tell her.

"Please, Agent McLellan, you've got to help us. We can't live like this. I'm afraid Porter will have a heart attack." She lowered her voice. "Or do something crazy."

"I have a friend," Jasi found herself saying. "He's a psychologist. He's worked for the CFBI before. I'll see if he has time to talk to your husband."

"Thank you. I really appreciate this" Relief was evident in the woman's voice. "I want my husband back."

After Jasi disconnected the call, she turned off the lamp, lay back in bed and stared at the ceiling. She was ambivalent about getting Zane involved. Even though he worked closely with the CFBI, she'd made a point of keeping him away from her work.

*He can't find out what I am.*

As far as he was concerned, she was a CFBI investigator, nothing more. Zane needed to be kept in the dark. It was the only way.

She released a pent up sigh.

A light flicked on.

Natassia was wide awake, her blue eyes watching her.

"So, Jasi, who's this psychologist friend of yours?"

"Dr. Zane Underhill." She tried to be casual.

"Is he the guy you've been seeing?"

"I'm not *seeing* him. Well, not really. We just...uh..." She groaned. "Okay, yes I've been seeing him. He's an old..." She didn't know what to call him.

"Boyfriend?"

"For lack of a better term."

"Is he hot?"

"He's, uh…"

"That hot, huh?" Natassia grinned, then slid from the bed, her oversized t-shirt hanging almost to her knees. "Well, dear partner, time to get up. You can tell Ben and me all about him over breakfast."

"You can't tell Ben."

"Why not?"

"He hates Zane."

"Why would Ben hate your boyfriend?"

"Zane is not my boyfriend. We're—it's complicated."

"Relationships usually are."

"Ben thinks Zane is a player, and he doesn't want Zane to hurt me again."

"Again? He broke your heart before?"

"Once, a long time ago." Jasi crossed her arms defensively. "But it won't happen again."

Natassia's brow arched.

"It won't," Jasi repeated. "I'm in control this time."

"If you say so, Miss Control." Natassia smiled sweetly and headed for the bathroom. "Dibs on the first shower."

"Just leave me some hot water," Jasi called after her.

As soon as she was alone, Jasi grabbed her 'com. She had programmed Zane's number into it the night before, after their *ride* in the elevator.

"Call Zane." She brushed the tangles out of her auburn hair while she waited for Zane to pick up.

On the fifth ring, he answered, his raspy Australian accent sounding sexier than ever.

"Ah, Jasmine. I told you you'd want more."

"Zane, I have a favor to ask." He chuckled and she felt a stir of heat. "Not that kind of favor."

"Whatever you want, love, it's yours."

"I need a consult."

"You want to see me professionally?"

"Not for me, Zane. We have a victim who was drugged, found unconscious on a park bench and can't remember what happened to him."

There was a long pause on the other end.

"He's having awful nightmares and isn't sleeping. His wife is really worried."

"I thought you couldn't tell me about your cases," Zane said quietly.

"Normally I can't. But I think you could help us."

"You can't force therapy on someone."

"I'm sure I can get approval from the victim. Besides, he's already seeing a therapist."

"Then why doesn't he make a few extra appointments?"

"His wife doesn't think his therapist is helping him." She sighed. "Look, Zane, you're one of the best. I'm sure we can convince him to have a few sessions with you."

"So who is this victim?"

"Porter Sampson. The politician they found drugged in the park."

"I can see him at two this afternoon. Give him my room number. And Jasmine?"

"Yes?"

"I'm doing this as a favor to you."

"I know. I guess I'll owe you one."

"I'll find some way to collect."

The smirk in his voice was evident, and she smiled.

"Thanks, Zane."

She hung up, for the first time feeling hopeful. Porter Sampson needed someone to break down the invisible wall in his mind. She didn't have to tell Zane anything more about her involvement in the case. As far as he knew, she was a damned good CFBI profiler.

*Maybe not as brilliant as Ben, but I am good.*

She called the Sampson residence next. Porter Sampson picked up right away. He sounded pissed.

"What do you want now, Agent McLellan?"

"I heard you aren't sleeping well."

"My wife needs to mind her own—"

"I'd like you to talk to a friend of mine," she blurted. "He's an excellent psychologist and he's worked with us before."

"I have my own therapist."

"Zane has worked with the CFBI before. He's an excellent hypnotherapist. You do want to find out who drugged you, don't you?"

Sigh. "Of course I do."

"Mr. Sampson, you obviously need help dealing with your nightmares and the sleep deprivation, and we need to know what really happened to you when you went missing. We can either work with your therapist or you can use my friend."

There was a lengthy pause.

"If this gets out it could ruin my career," he said. "No one trusts a politician who's seeing a shrink."

Jasi bit her tongue. *No one trusts a politician, period.*

"I'm sure we can keep this quiet," she said.

"You better." There was a razor-sharp edge to his voice.

"I can promise you, Zane is very discreet. He'll only share with us anything he discovers that pertains to the case."

"Well, maybe I could see your guy. I have a lady doctor and she doesn't seem to be helping much. Maybe it'll be easier talking to a guy."

"That's a good way to look at it," she told him. "You have an appointment with Dr. Zane Underhill at two today." She gave him the details, then hung up.

She threw back the blanket and slipped into the plush hotel robe. As she prepared the coffeemaker, she thought of Porter Sampson. Zane had his work cut out for him. But if he got through, maybe they'd find out who had taken Sampson.

*And why.*

A knock at the door interrupted her thoughts.

She crossed the room and peeked through the spy hole in the door. A distorted Ben grinned back at her. She opened the door and ushered him inside.

Ben glanced at the second bed. "Where's Natassia?"

"In the shower." She scurried over to the coffee pot, feeling suddenly nervous. "I have an idea, Ben"

"I'm up for anything at this point."

"I think Sampson should see a CFBI psychologist."

"Good idea. I'll contact Matthew and have him recommend—"

"I've already got someone in mind."

Ben gave her a surprised look.

"I know someone here," she said. "A friend."

"The only psychologist you know is…aw, Jazz, please don't tell me *he's* back in the picture."

She swallowed hard. "Zane is here in the city. On business. We can use him."

"Use him? Like he used you?"

"This isn't about me, Ben. This is about finding justice for Porter Sampson, Monty Winkler and their families. If Zane can help Sampson remember, then it'll be worthwhile. I've talked to him and—"

Ben's eyes widened. "That's who you've been seeing. I knew it. How long has this been going on?"

A door opened behind them before she could answer.

"Morning, Ben." Natassia emerged from the bathroom, thankfully wearing a robe. She gave Jasi a worried look when she saw Ben's dark demeanor. "Everything all right here?"

"I told him Zane's in town."

"Zane's an ass," Ben snapped. "He'll use you and toss you aside, like he did last time. For Christ's sake, he almost got you killed."

"I know you hate him, Ben, but you don't have to worry. We'll use him on this case. Afterward, he's gone, out of my life."

"You were a mess after he left you. I picked up the pieces back then. I won't do it again."

"Zane won't hurt me. Not this time."

Ben let out a tired sigh. "What's going to stop him?"

Jasi raised her chin. "Me."

"I hope you're right."

She smiled. "I'm always right."

"Except when you're wrong," he said with a half-smile. He turned to Natassia. "Breakfast?"

"I thought you'd never ask. I'm starving."

Natassia casually leaned over to pick her jeans off the floor and her robe gaped, revealing her ample breasts.

Jasi nearly laughed out loud when she saw the shocked expression on Ben's face. Then the shock turned to something else.

*Good grief. And he's worried about me getting hurt?*

Natassia disappeared into the bathroom. A few minutes later, she reappeared, fully dressed in a lightweight sweater and navy slacks.

"I'll catch up with you two later," Jasi said, herding them toward the door.

Ben frowned. "Jasi, maybe you should—"

"We're going to take whatever help we can get. And that's final." Her voice softened slightly. "Don't worry, Ben. I can handle Zane Underhill. This is strictly a business meeting."

"For you, maybe." He playfully tugged on her ponytail. "Play with fire, you'll get burned."

She let out a slow breath when the door closed. She'd avoided another argument about Zane. She wondered how long she could keep that up.

Her data-com beeped. *Zane.*

"I was about to call you," she said. "Porter Sampson agreed to meet you at two."

"I'll do my best," Zane replied.

"You always do," she said, before realizing how it sounded.

A throaty chuckle. "I aim to please, love."

She tried to get Ben's warning out of her head. He was worried, and rightly so. She'd always been weak when it came to Zane.

*But I'm not weak now.*

"Just help me get some answers," she said wryly. "The poor guy isn't sleeping."

"What about you, love? How have you been sleeping?"

Images of Zane's naked body pressed against hers crowded her mind.

*Stay focused, Jasi.*

"I'm sleeping just fine, Zane."

She filled him in on Porter Sampson's case.

"So he doesn't remember anything?" Zane asked.

"Nope. We're stalled. We know he was drugged. We know he consumed a fair amount of alcohol. But we haven't got a clue where he was for those missing days. We're hoping you can help."

"I'll give it a try."

"Thanks."

"You can thank me later."

"Zane…"

"Have dinner with me again."

"I can't."

"You mean you won't."

"We have to keep this strictly business."

"We'll talk business then. I'll give you my report on Porter Sampson."

She couldn't pass up an opportunity like that.

"This is a business dinner," she said. "Understand?"

"Crikey, you're a tough one." There was a pause. "Fine then. It'll be all business, as long as you still want it that way. G'bye."

Things hadn't gone quite the way she expected. Zane had gotten the upper hand. Again.

She took a determined breath. She had to keep control.

*And above all…I have to keep my clothes on.*


Although she'd visited Parliament Hill countless times in the past, Jasi was still awed at the sight of the regal buildings and immaculate grounds. Those viewing the Hill from the Ottawa River saw the impressive structures sitting high on the bluffs, representing ancient wisdom and power. Home to the Senate, the House of Commons, the Library of Parliament, the Hall of Honour and the majestic Peace Tower that was proudly topped by the Canadian flag, the Nepean sandstone buildings with their striking, green copper roofs were considered to be among the most beautiful government buildings in the world.

They'd decided to take both cars, just in case they needed to check out various leads. Jasi and Natassia were in the lead SUV, while Ben followed a short distance behind.

"It never fails to amaze me the power this area of Ottawa holds," Jasi said. "To think that laws are made here, becoming part of our history, and mortal men are made into great men."

"And women," Natassia interjected.

"Women and men with the power to change a country's future."

"And with power comes great responsibility."

Jasi chuckled. "You're quoting from *Spider-Man*?"

"Hey, it's the truth."

"And the truth shall set you free," Jasi murmured.

They approached the West Block of the parliamentary grounds, which housed the offices for Senators and Members of Parliament. This area was closed to the general public, but a careful scrutiny of their badges gave Jasi and Ben clearance into the secured underground parking lot.

When they stepped into the elevator, Natassia turned to Jasi. "What's the plan?"

"You and I will check out Winkler's office. Ben can take Sampson's."

The elevator dipped, then pulled to a stop on the first floor. They were immediately escorted by a broad-shouldered armed guard to a security station. Depositing their weapons into a bin, they submitted to a quick pat-down and then walked separately through the metal detector. Jasi and Ben passed through with no problem. Natassia wasn't so lucky.

"Jewelry," the guard said as he reset the alarm.

Natassia stripped off her rings, bracelets and the heavy pendant around her neck, then walked through again. The alarm went off and the guard motioned her to one side. He waved a handheld monitor over her. When it reached the button of her jeans, the monitor chirped.

The guard cleared his throat. "Piercings?"

"Belly button." Her brow arched as if daring the guard to make an unsavory comment. "I could show you if you want."

The red-faced guard waved her on.

Once Natassia had gathered up her jewelry, they took another elevator to the second floor where they split up. Jasi and Natassia followed the signs to Winkler's office, which was at the far end of the second floor.

"Does Ben ever take off those gloves?" Natassia asked.

"When he has a reason to."

"And he has no reason to with you?"

"Natassia, if you're interested in Ben, you should know that he doesn't like to mix business with…"

"Pleasure?" Natassia grinned. "I think I could change his mind."

"Maybe. Maybe not."

"Let's say I wanted to try. How would you feel?"

Jasi paused in front of the door to Winkler's office.

"Ben's my closest friend. I don't want to see him get hurt. Or you." She patted Natassia's arm. "Trust me, it wouldn't be a good idea. Especially for the team. Anyway, you're here temporarily. What'll happen when you go back to Russia?"

"They won't send me there. I'll be sent back to Toronto. But I understand what you're saying."

They entered the waiting area for Monty Winkler's office. Overlooking the front lawn, it was small and held four plush chairs and a coffee table. A desk in the far corner was occupied by an attractive Latino woman.

"Excuse me!" the woman said. "Who are you?"

Jasi held up her badge. "CFBI. We need to ask you a few questions," she eyed the woman's name tag, "Bonita."

"Me? I don't know how I can help."

Jasi set her data-com on the desk. "Voice record on."

Bonita eyed the device. "Do I need a lawyer?"

Jasi smiled. "I doubt it. We'd like to ask you about Mr. Winkler's schedule."

Bonita seemed relieved. "Oh, well let me see…" She turned the monitor so it faced them. "He always has—*had*— me record his schedule here. That way I could remind him if he's running late." She brought up the calendar program.

"Compare Winkler's data-com entries," Jasi said to Natassia. To Bonita, she said, "Can you state your name?"

"Bonita Valdez."

"And how long have you worked for Mr. Winkler?"

"Three years on Saturday. You know, the police already asked me these questions."

"Has Mr. Sampson always updated his data-com himself, or does he have you do it?"

"Oh no. He did that first thing every morning. He had his routine. Every morning he'd ask for a coffee, double cream, then we'd sit in his office going over the week's appointments. I'd tell him what I have booked in here." She pointed to the computer. "And he'd upload it to his appointment thingy."

Jasi held back a laugh. *Appointment thingy?*

"His data-com?"

The woman nodded. "Yeah, that's what I said."

Natassia interrupted. "The appointments match, Jasi. Except for the ones for the dog groomer. There's no record of them on her computer calendar, only the letters *PT*."

"Dog groomer?" Bonita frowned. "The Winklers don't have a dog."

"That's what I figured," Jasi said. "So where did he go every Tuesday at one?"

"He never told me. I always recorded it as personal time." The woman looked at Natassia. "PT. If it was business related he'd have told me."

"The PT and groomer appointments match," Natassia replied.

Jasi sighed. "What was he doing for those hours?"

"Maybe he had someone on the side."

Bonita let out a loud snort. "Not Mr. Winkler. That was all in the past. His wife would have his you-know-what in a knot if he'd ever strayed. He was as loyal as they come, that one."

"Did he have any enemies that you know of," Jasi asked. "Anyone get pissed off at him recently, maybe make a scene?"

"No. Everyone liked Mr. Winkler. Everyone I see, anyway. It's pretty quiet around here. Things really only get heated at the House meetings."

"We'd like to see his office."

"The police already went through his things." Bonita let out a huff, then motioned to the double doors. "It's through there. Do you want me to come with you?"

"That's okay. We'll let you know if we need anything."

"Sure."

Winkler's office here wasn't much different from the one at home. Cool, dark colors and piles of paper. A computer monitor with a cordless mouse and keyboard sat in the middle of the desk. Beside it was a small stack of colored folders. They were all empty and unmarked.

Natassia sat down in the leather chair and turned on the computer. "I'll see if I can find anything here."

"Damn."

"What's wrong?"

"You'll probably need a password."

Natassia grinned. "A little old password isn't going to be a problem. I have an IHD." She held up what looked like a regular flash drive.

"How'd you get that?"

"I had it expressed here, overnight."

"I thought Investigative Hacking Devices weren't being issued to the

CFBI until next year."

"Hacking is one of my…uh, special skills."

Jasi snorted. "Nothing psychic about that. You sure you're a PSI?"

Natassia chuckled. "I knew you were going to say that."

"So someone just *gave* you an IHD? Without CFBI authorization?"

Natassia plugged the device into the front of Winkler's hard drive. "I'm testing it. Kind of like Beta testing. I know the woman who designed it." She turned on the computer and tapped on the keyboard.

Jasi watched, amazed. "Friends in high places, huh?"

"If you only knew."

"How does it work, this IHD thing?"

"You plug it into a computer and it'll bring up a menu of systems it can hack into. It can even unlock secured doors if you plug it into your data-com. Great for breaking into places." She looked up and grinned. "Not that I'd ever do that."

"Of course not."

The monitor in front of them flickered.

"Check it out, Jasi. Here's a file on proposed budget changes, saved as individual pages. Winkler was working on it the week before he went missing. Some of the pages have been deleted."

"Completely?"

"Not even a comma left."

"What was he working on the day he went missing?"

Natassia scrolled down the page. "Nothing."

"Nothing? He had to have done something that day."

"That's what I'm thinking too." Natassia's fingers paused on the keyboard. "That's strange."

"What?"

Jasi peered over her shoulder, not really sure what she was looking at. The calendar had changed to a screen of code.

"Two hours before Winkler was found dead, someone transferred a file, then deleted it from the hard drive. They replaced it with a dummy file, but they forgot to change the properties."

"Well, we know Monty Winkler didn't do it. He'd been missing during that time. Any idea what was in the file?"

"All I have is the file name. PSI-0512."

"PSI? Really?"

"It's probably a coincidence, Jasi. It could stand for anything."

"Can't you dig it out with the IHD?"

"I could have if it hadn't been replaced."

"Where was it transferred to?"

"I'm not sure exactly. It was a mobile transfer. Whoever stole the file had to have done it from a three block radius of this building. They were probably parked right outside."

"So they accessed Winkler's computer from the street?"

"Yup."

"Can anybody do that?"

"Not exactly. With all the new security measures in place, especially for government officials, you need the IP address of the computer you want to hack, plus the password. And they would have needed an IHD to do the file transfer."

"How many IHDs did this woman you know make?"

"About two dozen, for testing purposes only at this stage. Another company will manufacture them as soon as some of the glitches can be worked out."

"And that's what you're doing. Working out the glitches."

"Yeah." Natassia gave her an apologetic look. "In this case the IHD is limited. I can get into any part of the hard drive, but I'd need the portable device used in order to get that information. It's one of the drawbacks of this version, something my friend is working on."

"Damn. We just can't get a break."

"Hold on. We know one thing for sure."

"What's that?"

"Whoever did this had access to an IHD. There are only a dozen prototypes being tested at this time. I have two. That leaves ten more out there."

"Unless someone stole one."

Natassia activated her data-com. "Call B-Tech."

"What are you doing?"

"I need to find out if the inventory has been tampered with."

While Natassia made her call, Jasi studied a photo of Winkler and Marilyn. They looked happy enough.

"Bad news," Natassia said behind her.

"There's an IHD missing?"

"Two. He must have taken an extra one for backup."

Frustrated, Jasi stepped away from the window. "The entire population of Ottawa, plus every law enforcement agency in Canada and the US knew about the IHDs."

"Yeah, but not many people know who designed them or where to get one."

"Jesus," Jasi said, rubbing her forehead. "What the hell is going on?"

"Your guess is as good as mine."

Jasi gave a nod. "Good work."

"I had a little help." Natassia held out her hand. A second IHD rested in her palm. "Take my backup IHD. You might need it."

Jasi frowned. "I'm terrible with modern technology."

"Plug it into your data-com and practice opening the hotel room door. After you plug it in, enter 911 on the keypad, then push the call button. It'll do the rest. Piece of cake."

Jasi tucked the IHD into her inner jacket pocket.

# 24

Porter Sampson's office was as immaculate as the one in his home. The only noticeable difference was that the books on the built-in bookshelf were filed alphabetically by title this time, rather than by author.

"Sampson has way too much time on his hands," Ben observed, withdrawing a blue binder from the shelf. "I wonder if the binder from home is here."

He checked the label. It was from last year.

Sampson had said he'd misfiled the binder, but everything here seemed organized. Right down to the man's pens. Red, blue and black pens, all high quality, occupied three compartments and silver paperclips filled the fourth.

The other thing Ben discovered was that Porter Sampson was a consummate list maker. He had dozens of lists posted throughout his office. Lists of books to read, research lists, lists of friends and associates and to-do lists.

"He probably has a list for making lists," he muttered as he returned a laundry list to Sampson's desk.

The evidence team had already been through Sampson's home office and the one here on Parliament Hill. The CFBI had processed fingerprints, trace evidence and phone call logs from his cell phone, home and office. Other than the one payphone call to his cell phone, nothing stood out as being suspicious.

"The only thing suspicious in here," he said, "is the guy's taste in music. New age stuff."

He idly fingered a CD that had been in the small stereo on a shelf by the door. He was about to set it down when the logo on the disc made him hesitate. He studied it. Three multicolored butterflies glimmered on the label, one with wings partially folded as it exited a cocoon.

*Why does this seem so familiar?*

Something niggled at the back of his mind.

His data-com beeped and he dropped the disc onto the shelf. "Hey, did you find anything?"

"Someone hacked into Winkler's computer," Jasi said.

When she told him that a file had been accessed, Ben knew they were closing in on something important.

"Wait a minute," he said. "How did you get into his computer? Didn't you need a password?"

There was a brief pause before Jasi answered.

"Natassia has an IHD."

"How the hell did she get hold of an Investigative Hacking Device? They're not even legal."

"Don't ask, Ben. But now we know about that file."

He let out a sigh. He'd have to talk to Natassia later.

"Well, I've got nothing here." He was about to hang up when he glimpsed the CD. "Wait! Jasi, you still there?"

"What's up?"

"I found something here that's been bothering me."

"What's that?"

"It's probably nothing, but I keep thinking it means something." He picked up the CD again.

On the other end, Jasi let out a little huff. "Spit it out, Ben."

"I found a CD with butterflies on the label. Does that ring a bell?"

"*Relaxation for the Soul?*"

"Exactly."

"We found a CD like that in Winkler's home office."

He sucked in a breath, suddenly recalling Natassia's comment about Winkler liking butterfly music.

"I think I saw the case for this one at Sampson's home," he said. "I didn't pay much attention to it at the time."

"What do you think the odds are that two men from different backgrounds and cultures would be listening to the same CD?" Jasi asked.

"Slim to none. This CD directly connects Monty Winkler to Porter Sampson. We need to find out where they got it from."

"It's our first real break, Ben. I'll take a cab to Winkler Manor and pick up the other CD. Then I'll swing by Porter Sampson's and grab the case. You and Natassia should head back to the hotel and have the CD analyzed for prints."

"I'll have Matthew assign a tech to find out everything about," he glanced at the disc label, "Mind Over Matter Productions. Then I'll call Porter Sampson and ask him about that file and the CD."

At 1:30, Ben pulled into the underground parking at the hotel. He parked the SUV in a stall close to the elevator.

Natassia waved the plastic bag containing the CD in the air. "Your room or mine?"

He swallowed hard, avoiding her gaze. Was her question completely innocent, or did she realize how suggestive it sounded?

"Ben?"

"Uh, mine."

She stretched and gave him a smile. "Lead the way."

In the elevator, he tried to ignore the arousing scent of sandalwood that seemed to cling to his partner like a second skin. He stabbed at the floor number and let out a relieved breath when they reached their floor.

Inside his room, Natassia dropped her purse on the floor and kicked off her shoes. As she moved toward the far bed where he'd left his tote bag open, she said, "You haven't unpacked."

"I never do," he said, pushing past her and zipping the bag shut. "I like to be ready to move at all times."

"Sounds like you're running away from something."

He glanced at his watch. "Sampson should be in the middle of his session with Zane right about now."

"Do you think Jasi's friend will be helpful?"

"No, I think he's going to be a pest," he said dryly. "But who knows?"

"You really don't like the guy, do you?"

"Why don't you call Matthew?" he suggested, ignoring her question. "Let him know we'll express the CD to him first thing in the morning."

"Will do."

While Natassia was distracted by whatever was on the computer monitor, he studied her. She'd proven to be smart, tough and damned sexy. It was the latter quality that bothered him.

Natassia's head jerked up. "Is something wrong?"

*Add perceptive to the list.*

"No. Why do you ask?"

"You seem uncomfortable around me. Is it that you didn't want another partner, or that you like having the one you've got?"

"Honestly? A bit of both."

Natassia grinned. "Gee, don't sugarcoat it or anything."

"Sorry. Jasmine tells me I'm too blunt."

Her gaze was intensely direct. "I appreciate bluntness. I like to know where I stand. With everyone."

The woman was hinting at something. *Damn.* The last thing he needed was a partner who was interested in him. Not that Natassia Prushenko wasn't particularly charming at times.

While Natassia called Matthew to apprise them of their new leads, he quickly dialed the Sampson residence. No one picked up, so he left a message.

"Call me as soon as you get this," he said before he hung up.

His fingers caressed the plastic bag containing the CD. The butterflies on the label glinted as he turned the disk toward the light. Metallic paint on a clean white label. No distinguishable markings other than the name of the CD and the company name.

He searched for Mind Over Matter Productions. There were two website links. One was a film company based in California; the other was the site of a self-help author, Maud Abrams. There were no CDs listed on either site or anything else to suggest the CD had come from either source.

He tried just Mind Over Matter. Thousands of entries came up. He perused the first five pages, then gave up when nothing substantial jumped out at him.

*So who made the CD? A company or a person?*

Natassia's data-com beeped.

"It's Jasi," she told Ben.

"Put it on speaker."

Jasi's voice came across crystal clear.

"We have a problem," she said.

Ben's heart sunk. "What?"

"The disk Winkler had is gone. And so is the case from Sampson's."

"What do you mean, gone?" he demanded. "Did you ask the wives?"

"That's the thing, Ben. Neither of them recalls seeing it. Ever."

"Well, we saw it," Natassia said.

A heavy sigh sounded from Jasi's end. "That means only one thing."

"Someone else was in their homes," Natassia said.

Ben nodded. "It also means that whatever's on those CDs could lead us to the killer."

Jasi propped her chin up on one hand and stared cross-eyed at the computer monitor. It was no wonder that people hated politicians. Everything was so damned complicated.

"I never realized how utterly boring politics is until now," she said with a groan. "Winkler's files are full of legal speak and policies I don't understand. Maybe you should have taken this task, Ben."

"When I'm finished working up the perp profile, I'll take over so you can have a break."

"Thanks."

"Forty-six percent," Natassia muttered.

Her assignment was to copy the hard drive from Sampson's work computer to Ben's laptop. And she was using the IHD to do it, much to Ben's dismay.

"It's illegal to copy government hard drives," he said for the third time. "Not without a court order."

"We don't have the luxury of waiting around for court orders," Jasi reminded him. "If this helps us find Winkler's murderer and Sampson's kidnapper, then case solved."

Natassia smiled. "Besides, Matthew has friends in high places."

Jasi continued searching the files on Winkler's laptop.

"Wait a minute," she said finally. "Winkler was working on amendments to at least three bills. He has a draft copy against one bill, and another copy in favor of it. Looks like he couldn't make up his mind which way to go."

"I noticed the same thing in Sampson's." Natassia said. "Maybe they were working on some of the same bills. Let's cross-reference them, see if something jumps out at us."

Before Jasi could answer, her data-com beeped.

"It's Zane," she said. "Probably with a quick report on his session with Porter Sampson." She moved toward the window for privacy.

"Your guy never showed," Zane told her.

"What?"

"I thought you said he was okay with meeting with me."

"He was. At least he said he was. Did you call him?"

"Of course I did. He wasn't home."

"Aw, damn. Sorry, Zane."

"Don't worry about me, love. I'm more worried about this victim of yours. If he's in as rough a shape as you say, he probably shouldn't be out and about. Let's try to reschedule."

Jasi checked her watch. "You waited for him for over two hours,

Zane. That's more than I'd expect."

"I had some spare time, and I thought he was running late. He is an important man, after all."

"Well, thank you and I'm sorry we wasted your time."

"Having an excuse to talk to you is never a waste of time. I'll see you at dinner?"

She took a deep breath. "I'll have to decline."

"Come on, love. You gotta eat. I'll wait for you in the lounge."

"Sorry, Zane. It was supposed to be a business dinner, to discuss Sampson's session. But since he never showed, we have nothing to discuss." She hung up before she could change her mind.

Ben eyed her. "What's wrong, Jazz?"

"We've got a slight problem."

"How slight?"

"Sampson never showed up for his session with Zane."

"Shit," Ben said with a scowl. "I had a feeling he might bail."

"Did Zane talk to him, find out why?" Natassia asked.

Jasi shook her head. "Sampson wasn't home."

"Sounds like he's avoiding us," Ben said.

"Or he doesn't want anyone to go poking around in his nightmares," Natassia suggested.

Jasi switched mental gears. "Have you got a profile constructed, Ben? I know there's not much to go on yet, but we need to have some idea of who we're looking for."

"Our perp is most probably male, between the ages of 35 and 50, in good physical shape, intelligent and well educated. He poses as a friendly guy and is perceived to be non-threatening. Neither Winkler nor Sampson had defensive wounds, so they either knew the perp or felt they could trust him."

"That's how he was able to drug them," Natassia said.

Ben nodded. "Exactly. And since our perp singled out two politicians, he's someone who had a beef with them personally or with what they stood for."

"But why did he let Sampson go?"

"I don't know."

Jasi mulled over this for a few moments.

"He held Winkler for a couple of days then killed him in a brutal fashion. Then he abducts Sampson and holds him for a few days and releases him. Why didn't he kill him too?"

"Maybe he got what he wanted from Sampson," Natassia said.

"What do you think he wanted?" Jasi asked her.

"That's the question of the day."

"His specific goal is undetermined at this time," Ben said, "Based on the method he used to murder Monty Winkler, I believe he knew the victim personally and was compelled to kill Winkler because of revenge or personal gain."

"But what could he possibly gain?"

"Whatever it is, it has to be something huge," Natassia said.

Jasi nodded. "We have to keep looking for connections between Winkler and Sampson."

She knew they were on the right track. They were closing in on a link that connected both men. She had to figure it out before another politician ended up dead.

"Ready to cross-reference?" Natassia asked.

"Sure. What have you got?"

"Bill 7A."

"Nothing here by that name."

"What about Bill 35?"

"Nope."

"Bill 12CF."

"Yes!" Jasi clicked on the file but it wouldn't open. "It's password protected."

"Same here."

"Damn."

"Not to worry, Jasi. We do know something."

"What?"

"Any bill number followed by a 'CF' designates a highly confidential proposal, one that's related to the CFBI."

Jasi gaped at her. "And you know this because...?"

"I've, uh, hacked into the CFBI database in the past."

Jasi covered her ears. "I never heard that."

"Neither did I," Ben said dryly.

Natassia logged onto the Internet and accessed the CFBI's database. Her fingers flew over the keyboard as she gazed intently at the monitor. "I'm in. It'll take a second to find the file." She paused and bit her lip. "That's odd."

"What?" Jasi asked

"There's no record of a file by that name."

"Then it's a proposal," Ben said. "One that never made it to legislature."

"Now what do we do?" Natassia asked. "This is the first solid connection we've had between the victims."

Ben paced the floor. "If Winkler was killed because of his position on this bill, and Sampson was kidnapped for the same reason, then we need to find out what they were working on."

"And we need to find out what it has to do with the CFBI," Jasi added.

She felt a tingle of excitement course through her body and a surge of energy that she only felt when she was getting close. She thought of the perp. He was conniving and ruthless, and if he was interfering with government policy then he had power in his hands. The kind of power that could destroy a country. He needed to be put down, like a rabid dog, before he hurt anyone else.

*We're coming for you.*

She rubber her tired eyes. If she kept staring at the monitor she'd have to make an appointment with the ophthalmologist for a set of glasses. Or pay a visit to a SEE clinic and have her eyes permanently set to *magnify*. Hell, she might as well get them color-enhanced too.

She glanced at Natassia and wondered for the millionth time if her partner had taken advantage of the new technology to enhance the brilliant blue of her eyes. They certainly didn't look natural. Neither did her over-sized breasts, but Jasi sure as hell wasn't going to say anything.

"I'm tired," she complained. "The two of you may be fine with hovering over these computers all day, but I need to move around, do something."

Natassia grinned. "Be careful what you wish for."

"What I wish for," she said stubbornly, "is a freaking break on this case."

Ben glanced up. "I think that's what we all need."

His data-com beeped.

"We have another body," Matthew said.

Jasi immediately jumped to her feet, strapped on her shoulder harness and grabbed one of three backpacks that were ready by the door. Natassia and Ben were right behind her.

"Where's the crime scene?" she asked Matthew.

"Not far from where Winkler's body was found."

This surprised her. It was a bold move by the killer.

"Any ID on the body yet?" she asked.

"No. Emergency crews just got there. It's not pretty."

Death never is, she thought.

# 25

On the way to the crime scene, Matthew filled them in.

"Four teens in a speedboat saw the fire from the river. They figured someone was having a bonfire party on the shore, and like typical teens, they decided to crash the party."

"I bet that's the last time they do that," Jasi mumbled.

"They found an unattended fire, so they tried to douse it. That's when they found the body. Or what's left of it."

The trees began to thin and a glimmer of water danced between the branches.

"We're getting close," she said.

Smoke hung in the air, cloaking the trees as Ben steered the SUV down a dirt road, past a fire truck. Even the flashing lights on the four police cars blocking the road had trouble breaking through the smoky fog. A couple of officers hovered near an ambulance.

Natassia sighed. "It must be bad."

Jasi grabbed a small cylinder from her backpack and inhaled a deep breath of Oxyblast, while Ben slowed the vehicle and rolled down the window.

A female police officer approached, one hand lightly resting on her gun. "ID, please."

Ben held up his badge. The officer nodded, then signaled two of the cars to move.

"What can I do to help?" Natassia asked.

"You can get out the marshmallows," Jasi muttered.

When she caught sight of Natassia's flustered expression, she smiled grimly. "I'm joking. Just follow me and record anything you see, anything I say. Sometimes it's hazy afterward."

Natassia glanced around. "I'll do a victim reading when the body is at the morgue. There are too many people here for me to concentrate."

"I'm sure the body will wait for you."

"I'll get the X-Disc ready," Ben said.

Jasi took a fortifying breath, lowered an Oxy-Mask over her face and stepped out of the SUV. Her gaze quickly surveyed the area. Two girls, maybe sixteen, sat in the back of the ambulance, the shock of what they'd witnessed worn on their pale faces like identical stone masks. Their movements were slow, zombie-like.

Jasi shook her head. *Poor kids.*

On the river bank she followed the billowing smoke. Even at a distance, she could see that the fire had been a big one. The perp had carefully contained the raging flames by placing large river rocks around the base of the pit. A small cairn of stones was stacked a few feet away, in honor of the victim. But whoever had died here hadn't been honored. It was murder, pure and simple.

"It's Shake 'N Bake time," she murmured.

With Natassia trailing a few steps behind, she moved toward the pile of smoking wood, toward the nameless corpse. There wasn't much left of the body. Someone had made sure of that. All that remained besides the smoldering waterlogged wood and ash were the blackened bones and skull that was once a living, breathing human being.

*Someone's son or daughter.*

She inhaled deeply, and with a nod to Natassia, removed the mask. The pungent odor of burnt human remains hit her hard.

*Focus on your breathing.*

"Record on," she heard Natassia say behind her.

The ground shifted.

*Breathe.*

In the blink of an eye, she was in a murderer's mind, hearing every thought, watching every move, and speaking a ruthless killer's words in her own voice.


*"Come on in," said the spider to the fly.*

*A man filled the doorway and shadows danced over his already dark skin. Stepping forward into the dim light, Porter Sampson's face was a mask of calm submissiveness.*

*"I came as soon as I got your call," he said.*

*"Very good," I said, taking in my most recent unsuccessful project.*

*I glanced at the kitchen counter behind me. A bottle of whisky and two glasses waited for the party to begin. Then my gaze turned back to the man before me. "Did you bring it?"*

*He nodded and handed me a thick envelope.*

*"Sit down," I told him, placing the envelope on the table. "Have a drink with me."*

*Porter sat down.*

*That was a good sign. Maybe he could be salvaged after all. I'd need to test his loyalties first.*

*I poured two fingers of whiskey into a glass and offered it to him. When he hesitated, I scowled. "Drink it."*

*His hand reached out, pausing barely a half inch from the glass. With a gasp, he hastily pulled it back and shoved it into his jacket pocket. "I-I don't drink alcohol. You know that."*

*I shrugged. "Justice is blind."*

*Immediately, he removed his hand from his pocket, but kept both hands beneath the table.*

*"Drink it, Porter."*

*"Yes." He took the glass and raised it to his lips.*

*I held my breath. Maybe I wouldn't have to kill him after all.*

*The glass trembled in his hand.*

*"Go ahead," I said, gritting my teeth.*

*"I can't!" He slammed the glass on the table. Amber liquid splashed over the side of the glass.*

*We both stared at the puddle on the table.*

*"Shit," I muttered under my breath.*

*I resisted the urge to slam my fist into his face. His defiance was proving to be a major problem. Like Winkler.*

*He watched me, afraid to move, afraid to speak.*

*Good. He should be afraid.*

*"I'll get you a cola then," I said, rising.*

*With my back to him, I poured soda into a clean glass. With a sigh of resignation, I reached for a small vial tucked behind napkin holder and added the clear, odorless liquid to his drink. With some regret, I turned, smiled and handed him the glass.*

*I poured two fingers of amber fire in the other glass and raised it in salute. "To justice."*

*Porter Sampson took a long drink of cola and I tossed back the whiskey. The warm burn infused my body instantly, as if I'd been washed clean. I felt no guilt in what I was about to do. The man had determined his own fate by refusing to do what I told him.*

*"You're no longer useful to me, Porter."*

*He watched me in confusion. Then he blinked and his head jerked. I could sense he knew what would happen next. I saw it in his eyes as his head hit the table with a thud.*

*"It's time."*


*Porter Sampson lay next to a gas can on the rocky shoreline. He was fully dressed and motionless, except for his dark eyes. They fluttered and fought for control of his voice and body.*

*"If only you had listened." In the dark, I waved the weapon in my hand. "Why couldn't you have done what you were told?"*

*He stared up at me, helpless as a baby.*

*Rage engulfed me. "You're useless!"*

*Recalling my own personal humiliation, I mercilessly hammered at his head. The skull shifted and cracked beneath the pressure. I had no idea how many times I hit him. I never count.*

*Finally, I stood over his motionless body. Blood pooled beneath his head and spattered his face. Panting heavily, I grabbed the gas can and completely doused his barely conscious body. Then I set the can between his legs.*

*"No evidence," I muttered.*

*I gazed at the Ottawa River. In the distance, tiny lights blinked like sleepy stars on the water's surface. I had no fear of the boat lights. They were too far out to see anything.*

*I glanced at the boat tied to the dock. It was too dark to make out anything except a shadowy hulk.*

*"I wish it hadn't come to this," I said, my voice laced with regret.*

*I lit a long match and tossed it on Sampson's chest. Flames immediately slithered over his body. Staring into his glazed eyes, I saw him blink furiously.*

*The bastard was still alive.*

*I grinned.*

*Fire licked at his clothing, turning them to feathery ash within seconds. I saw his skin pucker and blister, and the air was filled with the scent of burning flesh and gasoline.*

*"No hard feelings, mate."*

*As I made my way to the boat, a waft of thick smoke hit me. Suddenly, I couldn't breathe. I breathed in the acrid air and gasped.*

Jasi drew in a choked breath and was instantly jolted back to the present. Between bouts of coughing, she gagged as if she'd fed a cannibalistic desire and partaken of Porter Sampson's flesh. She could still smell his burning corpse.

She inhaled deeply from the Oxyblast canister, then leaned over, grasping both knees to keep her balance.

"I know who the victim is."

"Who?" Natassia asked.

Before Jasi could answer, Ben said, "Porter Sampson."

Her head jerked up. "How did you—?"

He held out a hand. Something small glistened in his palm. "Sampson had a gold cap on one of his molars."

She told them everything she'd seen.

Natassia gasped. "That's awful."

Jasi bagged the gold tooth. Her eyes flicked toward the fire pit. Porter Sampson had been cremated alive. That was something that would haunt Lorraine Sampson for the rest of her life.

"There's more," she said.

"What?"

"Sampson willingly met his killer. On a boat."

Jasi crouched over the cairn. After a crime scene photographer did his thing, she disassembled the cairn stone by stone, hoping the killer had left a clue.

He hadn't.


"I've arranged for a press conference," Matthew told her an hour later via data-com. "Live feed, on the six o'clock news."

She checked her watch. It was almost 4:30.

"I thought we were keeping quiet on this," she said.

"We have to control what the media releases," Matthew said. "I don't want there to be any unexpected leaks, so we'll feed them the information we want them to have."

"I understand. I'll let Ben know."

"Ben's not going to do it. You are."

Jasi was stunned. Matthew's policy had always been that the team leader was responsible for correspondence with media.

She swallowed hard. "Are you sure?"

There was a brief pause.

"Jasmine, you are more than qualified to lead a team. Just remember what you've been taught. Secure—"

"The scene," she finished. "Interview the witnesses and spin the story to the press in a way that doesn't reveal everything we know."

"You got it."

She could tell he was smiling.

"I can do it, sir."

After she hung up, she called the RCMP.

When a receptionist answered, Jasi said, "I need to speak with Constable O'Malley."

The call was transferred.

"O'Malley."

His voice had the rasp of a heavy smoker.

"This is Agent McLellan. We need to arrange a press conference for the six o'clock news."

"What do you need?"

"I was hoping you'd help coordinate the key players. You know your local media contacts better than I do."

"Fine. Leave it up to me."

O'Malley cleared his throat. "Do you have an ID yet?"

"We're pretty sure it's Porter Sampson."

The constable cursed. "So we *do* have a serial killer on the loose."

"It looks that way."

"Well, let's hope he's gotten whatever he's after."

"I have a feeling he's only just begun."

She disconnected the call, then made her way toward Ben and Natassia.

"They're removing the remains now," Natassia told her. "And I've bagged any evidence I could find near the scene."

"Find anything interesting?"

"A receipt for a case of beer, a used condom, a wad of gum—probably from one of the kids—and a piece of fiber that I found in the bushes. This is a popular place. Apparently most of the teen population hangs out around the river. It's kind of a Lover's Lane."

"Maybe the X-Disk found something."

"Ops is processing the data now," Ben said. "But that'll take a while."

Someone called Jasi's name.

Next to the fire pit, a woman in a heavy white jacket stood slowly, using a broken tree branch for support.

Jasi recognized her immediately. Faith Copeland.

"I wanted to show you something," Copeland said, limping around the edge of the pit.

"Are you all right?" Jasi asked.

"It's nothing. I twisted my ankle in the grass." Copeland leaned over and retrieved the skull. It was charred and there were bits of fried flesh and brain matter clinging to it. With a gloved finger, the pathologist traced the circular impressions in the scalp. "See anything familiar, Agent McLellan?"

"Same wounds as Winkler."

"Same wounds, same weapon."

Jasi sucked in a deep breath. *Same killer.*

Copeland wasn't finished. "There are at least eighteen indentations this time, Agent McLellan. They're embedded much deeper than the last victim's wounds. You know what that means."

"The killer's rage is escalating."

Copeland nodded. "This victim didn't stand a chance. If we could only figure out what weapon leaves this kind of mark." Frustrated, she tamped the ground with the stick.

Jasi stared at the small impression in the earth.

Something about Paul Cahill's actions in the yacht club bar had triggered a glimmer, a thought that had never fully surfaced. Until now.

"Dr. Copeland, do you think the end of a pool cue could make these impressions?"

"It's possible, I suppose."

Jasi reached for her data-com. "Excuse me for a moment." She called Matthew.

"What do you have?" he asked.

"When I was at the yacht club talking to the Cahills, the son, Paul Cahill, was pissed at his old man. He stamped his pool cue into the carpet. I didn't think of it at first, but a cue has a round end and could be about an inch and a half in diameter. Can you get his cue and a sample of the carpet?"

"I'll get the warrants and send an evidence team out to the bar right away. Good work, Jasmine."

She thanked him and hung up.

Paul Cahill definitely exhibited signs of rage toward his father. But was this spoiled kid capable of such brutality?

Immediately, she pictured Winkler's crushed skull.

*Was Monty Winkler clubbed with a pool cue?*

As Faith Copeland sealed the skull in a large plastic bag, Jasi said, "We have reason to believe this victim is Porter Sampson."

Copeland was startled. "The man found unconscious in the park?"

"I'm guessing he somehow got away from his captor."

The pathologist's gaze was intense. "Why do you think it's him?"

"My partner found a gold tooth in the ashes."

It was certainly easier to suggest they'd made a possible ID from the tooth than to try to explain how Jasi had stepped into the mind of the killer and witnessed the murder firsthand.

"I see. I take it Mr. Sampson had a gold tooth, then."

"It's already bagged. I'll have Agent Prushenko turn it over to you."

She called Ben and Natassia over and introduced them to the pathologist.

Natassia gave Copeland the tooth.

"I should have a positive ID for you in a few hours," Copeland said, placing the bag in an evidence cooler. "I'll have a COD in about an hour."

"He died of smoke inhalation," Jasi blurted.

Copeland stared at her. "How do you know?"

"Just a wild guess."

The pathologist gave her a strange look, then hurried off.

Jasi turned to her partners. "The skull has the same wound pattern as Winkler's. Made by the same weapon. I'm thinking maybe Paul Cahill's pool cue."

Ben looked surprised. "What led you to that thought?"

Making her way toward the SUV, she told them about her conversation with Matthew. Then she said, "We have to get back to the hotel. O'Malley is scheduling a press conference for six. I need some time to prepare."

"Whose head is on the chopping block?" Ben asked.

"Mine."

"You?" He chuckled. "You're doing the conference?"

"What's that supposed to mean?"

He held up a hand and took a step back. "Hey, don't get defensive. I'm just surprised Matthew gave you the job of spokesperson. He usually saves that for your first official case as team leader."

"I can do this," she insisted.

"Of course you can," Natassia said. "Why are you giving her such a hard time, Ben?"

"Last time she tried to speak in front of a crowd, she froze up. When she finally said something, her voice came out in a mangled squeak." He grinned.

"That must have been awful for her. And here I thought she couldn't possibly be afraid of anything."

"If there's one thing you'll learn about Jasi, she'd rather be buried alive than speak to a mob of hungry reporters."

Jasi moved to the side of the SUV. "I can hear you two, you know."

"I'm not saying you won't do a good job," Ben said.

He let out a shrill sound that made her cringe. Then he broke into a laughing fit.

The bastard was mimicking her.

She climbed into the back seat and slammed the door in frustration. There was a brief delay before her partners climbed in front. When they did, their expressions were calm and composed. On the surface. But inside, she knew they were having a laugh fest.

"So..." Ben drawled, catching her gaze in the rearview mirror. "I take it you *don't* want to sit up here with me."

Jasi's eyes narrowed. "Oh, bite me!"

## 26

Media personnel from every local TV and radio station, plus the major newspapers, gathered outside the Parliament buildings. As soon as Jasi stepped behind the microphone, the crowd began to buzz. And so did her nerves. Her heart hammered so hard in her chest she was sure everyone could hear it.

Rifling the papers in her hands, she took a few deep breaths. "Thank—" She flinched as her voice cracked. She began again. "Thank you, everyone. I'm agent Jasmine McLellan. I'm with the CFBI, and I'd like to assure you that we're doing our best to solve the two recent murders in your city."

She glanced at Ben.

He gave her a nod and mouthed, "You're doing great."

She gave a brief statement on the two victims, without releasing cause of death or any other forensic information.

"How were they killed?" a Global TV reporter shouted as she turned away.

"We can't answer that question at this time."

"Do you have any suspects?"

"The CFBI, in conjunction with OPS and RCMP, is looking into all leads," she said patiently. "We're interviewing all witnesses, and we ask that anyone who has information regarding these murders to please call the RCMP Tip Line."

A young reporter from the Ottawa Citizen stepped forward. "Does this mean there's a serial killer loose in Ottawa?"

"At this time we have two murder victims who both happen to be politicians. It's too early to tell if they were killed by the same person."

The crowd erupted in fury.

"How many bodies do you need for it to *be* a serial killer then?" someone hollered.

"What about the Prime Minister? Is he in danger too?"

"Is this a terrorist act?

Jasi held her hand up to quiet the throng. "All I can say right now is that it's only a matter of time before we catch whoever is responsible." She thanked the media. "I assure you, as soon as we have something concrete, we'll notify you and issue a statement."

After the conference, Ben patted her on the back. "I knew you could do it. Sorry I teased you before."

She couldn't help but chuckle. She felt good. Relieved.

"And I didn't even have to picture them all naked."

Ben grinned. "So, Miss Public Speaker, what's next?"

"I'll give Ottawa Forensics Unit a call," she said.

She barely got the words out when her data-com beeped. She gulped in a breath when she saw who it was.

Faith Copeland.

"I was just about to call you," Jasi said.

"I must be psychic."

Jasi bit back a laugh. "It would be nice if you were. So what have you got?"

"Confirmation on the wound pattern. Exact match to your previous victim. But the force used was even greater than with the previous victim."

"But there's no doubt in your mind that we're looking for the same person who murdered Winkler."

"Correct. We found something else that links the cases."

"What?"

"The victim was given a large dose of Flunitripazam."

*Rohypnol. The killer's drug of choice.*

"Were you able to confirm ID?"

"DNA was a one hundred percent match to the samples we obtained earlier from Porter Sampson." She paused. "You were right, Agent McLellan."

"About what?"

"He died from smoke inhalation. Lucky guess."

Copeland hung up.

Jasi went in search of her partners.

"DNA is definitely Sampson's," she told them. "And the wound patterns are also a match."

"I wish we could figure out the weapon," Ben replied.

"Have you thought more about your vision?" Natassia asked Jasi.

"I haven't had much time to." She realized something. "I was so distracted by the press conference that I haven't even listened to the voice file."

"I'll forward the file to you once I clean up the sound."

"Great," Jasi said. "I keep thinking there's something I missed."


Jasi stood in front of her hotel room door, the IHD in hand. "Well, let's see if you can figure this out."

She plugged the device into her data-com and immediately a numerical keypad appeared on the screen. She entered 911 and a message told her to point her 'com at the door lock, hit the call button and wait for the light on the lock to turn green before turning the knob.

She was inside in less than ten seconds.

"Holy shit, Natassia," she muttered, carefully returning the IHD to her inside jacket pocket.

In the quiet of the hotel room, her mind flitted to her vision. There was a clue in it somewhere. She knew it. All she needed was to remember what it was.

She massaged her temple. *Nothing.*

With a sigh, she checked her 'com for messages. Natassia had been true to her promise and a copy of the voice file from the crime scene was waiting in her inbox.

*"Come on in,"* she heard herself say.

In the recording she described her surroundings, coached gently by Natassia.

*"Did you bring it?"*

Sampson had given his killer an envelope.

*What was in it?*

She'd seen that he'd been drugged.

There was something odd in Sampson's actions prior to taking the Rohypnol. He'd done exactly what he was told, as if the killer was the puppet master.

What hold did his killer have over him?

Was Sampson being blackmailed? Or threatened?

On the data-com, she said, *"If only you had listened. Why couldn't you have done what you were told like the others?"*

Jasi gasped. "What others?"

Winkler...Sampson. Who else was involved?

She recalled seeing the vague shape of a boat.

"That's how Winkler ended up in the river. That's why there was no evidence on the shore. The killer lured him on board a boat and then dumped him."

The next thing she'd said on the 'com made her blood run cold.

*"No hard feelings, mate."*

And there it was. The thing that had bugged her. She knew exactly who had murdered the two politicians. She just wasn't sure she could say it out loud.

*Oh God...*

The air in the room suddenly seemed devoid of oxygen and she couldn't breathe. She rushed to the bathroom, splashed cool water on her face.

"You know who it is," she said, staring at her reflection.

With a deep breath, she returned to the table and plopped down in front of her laptop. For a moment she did nothing but think.

She'd have to tell Ben and Natassia.

"Shit."

Logging into her laptop, she brought up a medical paper on Rohypnol. It confirmed what she'd been told, that the drug was a muscle relaxant, sedative and paralytic. Plus it wiped the memory clean during the time it was in a person's system.

So why couldn't Porter Sampson recall the phone call? Was Rohypnol somehow administered while he was still at home?

The report on her laptop stated that Rohypnol was illegal in North America.

"It might be illegal, but it's all over our streets," she muttered. "You just have to know where to look."

*Or buy it overseas.*

She knew one person who'd been overseas recently. He could get the drug easily, and he knew how to administer it.

*Zane Underhill.*

In her vision the perp had said 'mate,' a common expression in Australia. Zane was the only Australian with even a remote connection to the case.

She jumped to her feet and paced the room.

*Why would Zane do this?*

She called him, but there was no answer.

Frustrated, she called Matthew at Divine Ops.

"I need the file on Zane Underhill," she told him.

"Your psychologist friend? Is this for business reasons or personal?"

"A bit of both. Will you send me his file?"

There was a lengthy pause.

"You're not involved with him again, are you?"

Matthew's concern left her feeling a bit peeved.

"My personal life is my own," she said firmly. "But thanks for thinking of me."

"I'll have the file uploaded to your data-com right away. Just...be careful. Zane Underhill is not receptive to PSIs. He—"

She cut him off. "Any word on the carpet sample from the yacht club? Is Paul Cahill our guy?"

"No. The cue impressions don't match the wounds."

"I had a feeling that would be the case."

*Because Zane's the guy we're after.*

"Sorry, Jasmine."

"Thanks, Matthew," she said, quickly disconnecting.

She called Zane again. He didn't pick up. That made her nervous. She chewed her bottom lip and stared out the window. "He can't possibly know I'm onto him."

*Maybe he's closing in on his next target.*

"Maybe I'm wrong," she murmured.

But logic suggested she wasn't. Zane had to be brought in. Immediately.

She groaned. "Why, Zane?"

As if in answer, her data-com beeped. It was Ben.

"We've got another victim," he said.

Jasi's heart sank to her toes as she moved toward the nearest bed. "Shit! I was hoping we'd get to him first."

"Jasi..."

She took a breath. "I should've told—"

"Jasi, I need to tell you something."

"What?"

"First, you should know he's alive," he said, his voice calm and soothing. "Ottawa General is running some tests, but his prognosis is good."

"What are you talking about?"

"It's a good thing they found him when they did," he said, as if he hadn't heard her.

"Found who?"

"It's Zane."

She sank into a chair. "What?"

"OPS discovered him an hour ago on a bench in Britannia Park. Someone drugged and assaulted him."

"This doesn't make any sense."

"We think he was targeted because of his involvement in the case. Someone must have leaked that Sampson was going to see him."

"Jesus." She massaged her forehead. "I was so wrong about him."

"What do you mean?"

"I thought he…" She sighed. "Never mind."

"Are you all right, Jasi?"

"No. It's my fault. I dragged him into this."

"Zane agreed to help us," Ben said firmly. "You didn't coerce him into it. He knew the risks."

She knew he was right, but it didn't change the fact that she had been ready to accuse Zane of two murders.

She restlessly paced the floor and thought of her vision.

*The killer must have meant 'mate' as in shipmate.*

"You said Zane was drugged," she said.

"Rohypnol. Same as Sampson and Winkler."

Sampson had been dumped in the park too—alive—but the killer went back for him. That meant one thing. Zane was still in danger.

"He needs a guard on his room," she said. "Our perp might come back and try to…finish what he started."

"I already took care of that, Jasi."

She batted away a tear, thankful her partner couldn't see her. "I'm an idiot, Ben."

"Why would you say that?"

"I thought it was Zane," she said in a quiet voice.

From her data-com came a muffled reply. "What?"

"In my vision, the killer said 'mate.' Zane says that all the time. You know, it's an Australian thing."

"He's going to be fine, Jazz. He has a gash on his forehead and doesn't remember anything, but he's stable."

"I'll head to the hospital." She paused. "And Ben?"

"Yeah?"

"Don't tell him I thought it was him."

She hung up, knowing that the last thing she wanted was for Zane to know she thought he was capable of murder. After all, what kind of future could they hope to have then?

She hesitated at the door.

*Future? Is that even possible?*

There was only one way to find out.

By the time she'd navigated her way to the hospital, it was nearly 8:00. She had to take a few deep breaths to calm down, and to keep from speeding. At the hospital, she parked the vehicle in a clearly marked No Parking zone. If she got a ticket, she'd call Constable O'Malley.

She hurried through the hospital, barely stopping to ask for directions. Her heart raced almost as fast as her feet, and she only slowed when she approached Zane's room.

She had to. Someone was blocking the door.

A muscular CFBI agent, armed with a standard issue Glock, 50,000-volt taser and baton, watched her through squinting eyes. In his twenties, he looked appropriately intimidating. His name tag read *Agent Michael Greene*.

"I'm with the CFBI," she told him.

"ID?" His soft voice didn't match his gruff looks.

She held out her badge and he carefully scrutinized it.

"You're cleared," Greene said, handing back her badge.

"CFBI and his doctor only," she reminded him. "You're to keep anyone without clearance out of this room, Agent Greene. That means no family, friends, city police or anyone else. Do I make myself clear?"

"Yes, ma'am."

She turned on her heel and entered Zane's room. When she checked over her shoulder, Greene was watching her through the window.

She gave a nod of appreciation. *No one will get to Zane without going through Greene, even if he does look like he just got out of basic.*

Zane was sleeping when she entered the room. A thick bandage was wrapped around his head, but other than that there was no other sign of injury.

She sat down in the chair and studied him.

*He looks so helpless.*

He stretched suddenly and his eyes opened. He seemed startled to see her. "Jasmine. What are you doing here?"

"Visiting a sick friend."

"Aw, is that all I am to you?"

She blushed. "I don't know what you are to me, Zane."

He patted the bed. "Come here and give me a kiss."

She couldn't say no to an injured man.

His lips were warm and inviting. She'd give anything to curl up beside him.

She pulled away first. "I'm here as a friend, but also on business."

"You want to know what happened," he said. "Honestly, love, I haven't got a clue. Like I told your partners, I don't remember anything except waking up in the park."

"Like Porter Sampson."

"The first thing I thought of was you."

This surprised her. "You get clobbered on the head and drugged and all you thought of when you regained consciousness was me?"

He grinned. "Well, it's not all I thought about."

She smacked his arm, then moved away from the bed.

"Last thing I remember, I was in my hotel room waiting for Porter Sampson to show up," he said.

"He never made it. You called me around four and told me that."

"Oh, right."

"What did you do after you called me?"

"I don't know." A look of bewilderment crossed his face. "The doctor says I have short term memory loss, but it should come back eventually."

"What I don't get is why you?"

"Because I'm charming and good looking?"

Her eyes narrowed. "But you're not a politician."

"Lucky me," he said, grinning.

"This isn't funny, Zane." Her voice wobbled. "You could've been killed."

He reached for her hand. "But I wasn't, love." His thumb drew distracting circles on her skin.

"Next time you might be," she said, reluctantly pulling her hand away. "I don't want that on my conscience."

"You can't control everything, Jasmine." There was a roughness to his voice. "Sampson was coming to see me. Maybe whoever abducted him was worried the man would tell me something incriminating. Who knows? Maybe he will, when he actually shows up for a session."

"Uh, Zane?"

"In my professional opinion," he continued, "I think we need to wait until Sampson seeks out counseling on his own, whether with me or another therapist. Perhaps without you pressuring him, he'll remember something on his own."

"No, he won't."

He gave her a questioning look.

"Porter Sampson is dead, Zane."

"What?" He tried to sit up.

"Stay still," she warned.

"How did he die? What happened?"

"I think the killer wanted to tie up any loose ends. Sampson was burned to death."

Zane flinched. "Good God, that's atrocious. Were there any witnesses?"

"No."

"Did you find anything at the scene?"

"Not one clue."

Zane let out a loud sigh and sank back into the bed. "Poor bloke. First he's kidnapped and drugged and left in the park. Then the maniac comes back and finishes him off on the beach."

"That's the part I don't get. Why let him go only to kill him later?"

Zane shrugged. "Who knows?"

She walked to the window and peered out over the streets below. Evening rush hour was in full swing.

"You were only missing a few hours," she said. "What would someone hope to accomplish in that time?"

"Your guess is as good mine."

She turned and studied him. "I wonder why he left you on the bench, right out in the open. Even with Porter Sampson, he chose a secluded spot to dump him."

"Maybe someone saw him with me. He'd want to get rid of me quickly."

She shivered at his words.

"Or maybe he thought he'd killed me." Zane touched the bandage. "He hit me pretty hard."

"I wonder how he got you out of the hotel. Did he meet you there? Do you somehow know this person?"

Zane shrugged. "There's nothing in my data-com. No appointments after Sampson's. And we know he never showed. I guess now we know why."

"I'll check with hotel security. There should be cameras all over the hotel. Maybe we'll get lucky and see you with someone. It could jog your memory."

"Perhaps."

Zane studied her for a long moment.

"What?" she demanded.

"You are truly lovely, Jasmine McLellan."

"And you should be Irish, for all your blarney." She shook her head. "You look like hell."

"Thanks." He flinched.

"Are you okay, Zane? Should I call someone?"

"I'm fine, love. Other than some memory loss, I have a bit of a headache."

"When are you getting out?"

"Tomorrow afternoon. They want to keep me overnight to make sure I don't have a concussion. Or a reaction to the Rohypnol." He shivered. "At least I wasn't burned alive."

"Jesus."

She stood quickly, batting away the mental image of Zane's burning body. Pacing at the foot of the bed, she thought about everything Zane had told her. Someone had gotten to him.

*They could get to him again.*

"Did the CFBI assign you protective detail?"

"Yeah. Mickey."

"Who?"

"Agent Greene." He jerked his head toward the door. "Young Mickey got stuck with the gig. When I'm let out of here, the poor bloke will be parked in a chair outside my hotel room. Lucky him."

"Good."

"I can look after myself, Jasmine."

She rolled her eyes at him. "Yeah, I can see that."

"So what happens now?"

She wanted to say, 'Now we get into that thick skull of yours and find out who did this.' Instead she said, "We need to find out who took you, and why."

*Which means Natassia would have to read him.*

That bothered her. Zane knew about the PSI Division. He'd testified at cases where PSIs had been part of the investigation. In the past when she'd broached the subject of psychic investigators, he'd always been less than receptive. That was one reason why she'd never told him what she really did. She knew without a doubt that he would flip. He'd see her as a freak.

"What if I arranged for a PSI to visit you?"

He scowled. "No, thank you. I don't want some nutcase poking around in my thoughts. Besides, I don't believe in psychic voodoo."

"You always were close-minded," she grumbled.

"Thanks for the compliment."

His stubbornness frustrated her. Although PSIs were authorized to read anyone related to a case without consent or a warrant, she knew that anyone with a strong negative feeling toward psychics could potentially build up a mental wall that could prove nearly impenetrable, not to mention exhausting for any psychic, even for a Level 1. Plus Zane was a psychologist. He'd know how to put up those walls.

No, Natassia wouldn't have a hope in hell of getting anywhere near Zane. Neither would Ben. *Damn!*

"So what do you want to do when I break outta here?"

She shifted awkwardly. "I'm going to be busy, Zane."

"Well, I think you owe me a dinner."

She took in his bandaged head and pale face. "You're right. I do owe you."

"It's settled then. I'm hungry for something with more flavor than congealed pudding and dry chicken."

The look in his eyes told her exactly what he was hungry for. It wasn't food.

"Tomorrow then," she said, backing out of the room.

"If you have any more questions, feel free to come back," he called after her.

She battled feelings of guilt as she left the hospital.

In the SUV, she slapped both hands against the steering wheel. "I was so far off!"

She slipped the key into the ignition and started the car.

"Of course Zane's not involved. He's not a killer. I'd know if he was."

*I need a drink.*

What she really needed was to immerse herself in the files from the case. There had to be a clue, something to steer her in the right direction. But what?

She gazed up at the handful of stars in the twilight sky.

*If I were a sailor, I'd be charting my course by the stars.*

Too bad it wasn't that easy in real life.


The security office was on the main level of the hotel, tucked in behind the front desk. Before knocking on the door, Jasi took notice of all the cameras in the ceiling. Anyone who came in or out of the hotel through the main doors would be filmed.

The door was opened by a young woman in uniform.

"Are you the CFBI agent?"

Jasi flashed her badge. "I need to look at your security footage."

"This way, ma'am."

Jasi flinched. That was twice today someone had called her that. If there was one thing she loathed, it was being called *ma'am*, especially by someone who looked only a year or two younger than her.

At the far end of the room a vid-wall took up most of the wall. Currently it showed twelve separate camera views of the inside of the hotel. A sign on the wall requested that all visitors completely power down all cell phones and data-coms.

Jasi did so with some reluctance.

"Thank you, Miss."

A man with a bad comb-over unfolded his lengthy frame from a chair parked in front of a half dozen monitors. When he stood, he towered over her. He was close to seven feet tall.

Jasi suddenly felt very small. "Are you Cliff Atkins?"

"Yup, chief of security. You must be Agent McLellan."

He motioned her to sit in the chair he'd vacated.

"So what do you need?" he asked, towering over her.

"I need this afternoon's video surveillance, from four o'clock on, inside the hotel and out."

"Computer, rewind to four o'clock," he said loudly.

"Ah, voice activated," she said, impressed. "My partner's been trying to convince me to get one, but I'm a bit tech-challenged."

Atkins smiled, his eyes crinkling in the corners. "It sure makes my job easier."

The screens depicted the interior of the hotel. In the bottom right hand corner, a time stamp rolled silently as time passed by.

Atkins scratched his nearly bald head and dislodged the long strands of gray hair. "What are we looking for exactly?"

"A man. One of the hotel's guests."

"We could find him faster if you have a photograph."

She thought of the photo she and Zane had taken when they were dating. She'd ripped it to shreds when he'd gone to New York.

"Sorry. I don't—uh, hold on a sec."

She pulled out her data-com and scrolled through the recent file uploads. There it was. An entire file on Zane Underhill. She'd forgotten all about it since Zane had moved from suspect to victim.

"Will this do?" She showed Atkins the photo.

"He doesn't look happy," the security chief remarked.

"Government photos are always serious. You know that."

Atkins moved to a desk in the corner. When he returned, he had a portable scanner in one hand. "Do you mind?"

She shook her head.

Seconds later, Zane's photograph was scanned into the system and his image projected onto the upper right screen.

"You have facial recognition software?" she asked.

"All the hotels around the Hill do. Can't take any chances nowadays."

Atkins was right about that. Terrorism had run rampant after the 2008 Recession, when multinational economies tanked. The crash hit Canada, the US, Germany and many other countries, resulting in outrageous gas hikes, home foreclosures, businesses filing bankruptcy and thousands of people loosing jobs as companies restructured. 2008 made history as the biggest disaster in the financial world since the 1929 Wall Street Crash. Now, four years later, they were finally out of the depressing grip of recession.

Atkins pressed a button. The screen switched to a 3-D image of Zane's face and the computer analyzed his facial contours.

"When did he check in?"

She gave him the date and watched as the guard filled in the parameters, including Zane's floor and room number.

"We're ready," he said finally.

Jasi gave a nod. "Run the search."

He gave a simple command. "Match face."

She held her breath.

"Uh, this could take an hour," he said with a grin. "You might want to relax. And breathe."

"I am breathing," she said tightly.

Atkins paced behind her.

Half an hour later he let out a whoop. "We've got a match, Agent McLellan. Now we'll see only the footage of your guy here."

Zane's handsome face filled the monitor screen and Jasi swallowed hard as she watched him move down a hallway, toward the elevator.

"That's him."

"What's his name?"

"Zane Underhill."

Atkins labeled the search. "I can make you a copy if you want."

"Can you upload it to my data-com?"

"Sure."

Zane disappeared into the elevator. The camera switched off as another camera picked up Zane's trail. He was coming out of the elevator on the lobby floor.

The timestamp read 4:30 p.m.

Another camera picked him up as he exited the elevator. As he moved across the lobby floor, Jasi studied him carefully. Zane was casually dressed and seemed perfectly at ease. No one had coerced him or made him leave by force.

*He'd left of his own free will and the concussion blocked the memory.*

The monitor faded and an outdoor camera picked him up as he left the hotel and ducked into a taxi.

"Which taxi company is that?"

"Capital."

She did a quick search on her data-com, then dialed the number. When the dispatcher answered, she said, "This is Agent Jasmine McLellan with the CFBI. I'm looking for some information on one of your pick-ups from this afternoon." She checked the timestamp. "At four-forty, outside the Embassy Hotel. Single passenger, male. I need to know where he was dropped off."

"There were two pickups around that time, ma'am. Both were single male passengers and both paid with cash."

"Where did they go?"

"One was driven to the airport. The other was dropped off at Patty's Pub on Bank Street."

Jasi thanked the man and hung up.

"Do you know Patty's Pub?" she asked Atkins.

"Yeah, it's a popular place for the younger crowd. It's not far from here."

A quick glance at her watch told her it was too late to check out Patty's Pub.

"I'll go in the morning. It'll be busy now and the day staff will be gone."

She strode toward the door. "Thanks for your help, Mr. Atkins. I appreciate it."

"Agent McLellan, is this Zane character involved in something illegal? If he is, I have to let hotel management know."

"He's a victim of a crime."

The color instantly drained from Atkins' face. "Dear God. He's dead?"

"No, he's not dead." *But he could have been.*

She stepped into the hall, but Atkins' voice trailed after her. "I sure hope you find whoever's responsible."

She already knew who was responsible.

*I put him there.*

# 27

Patty's Pub was southeast of the hotel, and Jasi could have driven it easily, but she decided to call Capital cabs. It was a short drive, maybe five minutes. She was dropped off right in front of the pub door. Outside the building, planters hung from hooks and displayed a variety of colorful spring blooms. To the left was a dentist office and on the right was a salon. Zane wouldn't have gone to either.

Jasi opened the door and stepped inside.

The young woman setting glasses on the shelves behind the bar looked over her shoulder. "Uh, we're not open for another hour. Sorry, I forgot to lock the door."

"I'd like to speak to whoever's in charge."

The woman glanced around the empty room. "I guess that would be me. For now anyway. I'm Abby, the assistant manager. What do ya need?"

"I have a few questions about a man who might have stopped in here."

"CFBI?" Abby said when Jasi showed her badge. "That's kinda like the cops, right?" A small silver lip ring twinkled with each word.

"Kind of."

"Is this about the fight last night? Cause if it is, I…like, never got the dude's name. Manny threw him out."

"This isn't about last night. It's about the day before. Do you usually work the day shift here?"

"Yeah. Nights too, sometimes. The owner is really good with us. If we need more money, we can work more hours. I'm trying to pay off some student loans."

*And an expensive tattoo habit.*

Abby had a Celtic cross tattooed on the right side of her neck, a coiled and fanged cobra on the inside of her left wrist and some kind of floral design under her left sleeve.

"Nice ink," Jasi said.

Abby smiled wryly. "Wish my mom would agree. But you know how mothers are?"

No, actually I don't, Jasi was tempted to say. There was no mother figure in her life. Never had been. The closest person to that role would be her aunt Eileen, who was eight years older than Jasi's father and could never remember Jasi's name.

While Abby watched over her shoulder, Jasi placed her data-com on the bar and scrolled through a few photos. She stopped when she found Zane's photo.

"Did you see this guy here," she tapped the data-com to enlarge, "the day before yesterday, around four-forty?"

"In the afternoon? It was busy here that day."

"So you didn't see Zane."

"Who?"

"Zane Underhill. The guy in this picture. He's from Australia, speaks with an accent."

Abby grinned. "Hey, if I met a dude that hot who spoke with a sexy accent, I think I'd remember. But like I said, it was crazy busy."

"What was going on that made it so 'crazy busy' here?"

Abby pointed to a team photo behind the bar. A group of hockey players in jerseys raised their beers in the air.

"One of our local teams. We sponsor them. This place was packed, wall to wall. My own brother could've walked in and I probably wouldn't have noticed."

"Who else was working that day?"

The woman shrugged. "Pete, Kelsey, Monica and Rica. Had to call two in at the last moment."

"Do you have their contact information?"

"I'll get it for you."

Abby disappeared into the back and Jasi took the opportunity to call Ben.

"I'm striking out here," she told him.

"Maybe Zane never actually went inside. Did you check the buildings next door?"

"I will, but I doubt he went to see a dentist or a hairstylist. Besides, the taxi driver was given the pub's address."

She heard Ben sigh.

"This case is getting stranger by the minute," he said. "Zane got into a cab, gave the driver an address and yet he doesn't remember leaving his hotel room." His voice was tinged with anger, and maybe a trace of disbelief.

"I know it doesn't make any sense, Ben. But the doctor did say he's probably suffering from a mild concussion. That could be affecting his memory."

"I guess."

"You guess?" Jasi was pissed. "Look, Ben…I know you hate Zane—"

"Hate is a bit strong."

"Well, you distrust him then."

"And for good reason, Jazz."

She released a pent up hiss. "Stop it! He's a victim, for crying out loud. He didn't ask to get mixed up in this case. *I* brought him in. Look where that got him! Abducted, assaulted and lying in a hospital bed."

"Jasi—"

"Don't *Jasi* me, Ben. He could've died." She hitched in a ragged breath. "Regardless of your personal feelings about Zane, we have to find out what happened to him, get some justice for him."

"What about justice for you," he said softly. "He left you hanging for months. No phone calls, no text messages, no nothing."

"I'm not holding a grudge against him. Zane left me. I got over it and moved on."

"Did you?"

"Yes." The word scraped the back of her throat.

There was a brief pause before Ben said, "I think you've gotten reeled back in, hook, line and sinker. He'll move on again, Jasi. He's not one to stay in the same pond."

"Skip the fishing analogies," she said dryly. "I'm not taking the bait, nor am I flopping around helplessly. When this case is over, Zane'll be out of my life." Out of the corner of her eye, she spotted Abby approaching. "Look, Ben, I have to go."

"Jasi, I—"

"Whatever else you want to say on this subject, don't," she warned. "I'll see you and Natassia later."

Abby handed her a slip of paper. "Everything okay?"

"It will be."

"Sorry I couldn't be more helpful."

Jasi headed toward the door. "No problem."

"Agent McLellan," Abby called after her. "I didn't see the hot one and

I don't know if this means anything, but I did recognize one of those photos."

Jasi turned on one heel. "What?"

"It's probably not important..."

"Let me be the judge of that."

"Okay, well, that photo of the Ebonic dude? On your cool cell phone? I saw him here."

"The Ebonic guy."

"Yeah, an older dude. Like, maybe he's got grandkids."

Jasi hissed in a breath. *Sampson.*

Hauling out her data-com, she showed Abby the photo.

"This guy?"

Abby nodded. "He was here a week ago, maybe two. It was late, maybe midnight. Dude was with a *white* guy."

Excitement bubbled up from Jasi's stomach.

"Can you describe him?"

Abby gave her an apologetic smile. "He had a dark moustache. Wish I could tell you more, but that one was bundled up like there was a freaking blizzard outside."

"What was he wearing?"

"A dark jacket, I think. Jeans, maybe."

The girl could have been describing half the male population in Ottawa.

"Anything else?"

"He wore a baseball cap."

"Any logo on it?"

Abby shrugged. "Maybe. I'm not into sports."

"Anything else?"

"The ball cap guy wore sunglasses too."

Someone had gone to a lot of trouble to hide his appearance.

"Kind of dark in here for sunglasses," Jasi said.

"That's why we noticed him."

"We?"

"Me and Manny. We thought Ball Cap was weird. He kept leaning forward and whispering. The black dude barely said a word, except for ordering their drinks. Two Southern Comforts on the rocks."

"Do you have Manny's phone number?"

"Yeah, but you won't need it." Abby smiled. "He's in the back room stocking the shelves."

Manny—aka Manuel Rodriguez—was maybe eighteen, with a shaved head, beefy build and an assortment of street tattoos and scars. In a stained white muscle shirt and a pair of faded jeans, he turned in Jasi's direction and immediately flaunted his muscles with the air of an ex-gang banger, someone who could hurt you bad with his eyes closed.

She didn't want to find out.

"Why you wanna talk to me?" he asked, his head cocked to one side. "I ain't done nothin' wrong."

Jasi smiled slightly. "I never said you did." She showed him Sampson's photo. "This is the guy you saw the other night?"

"Yeah." Manny flicked a nervous look at Abby.

"She's *aight*, Manny," the young woman said, slipping into street lingo. "She cool. Just wants to know about that black dude and Ball Cap."

"So, Manny," Jasi said. "Tell me what you remember about these men."

"Not much," Manny said, shaking his head slowly. "They was into some serious shit. You could tell by lookin' at 'em. Maybe talkin' business. Didn't look like either of 'em were out for a good time."

"Did you hear anything?"

"Nope. Nada." He scratched his head. "They talked, then they left. Ball Cap left first."

"Did you notice a logo on his cap?"

"Yeah. It was something gold. Couldn't make it out though. Too dark in here."

"Did you see if either of them got into a cab?"

"Nope." Manny looked at Abby.

"Me neither," the young woman said.

Jasi sighed. "Any chance you have security cameras?"

Abby shook her head. "Sorry."

Jasi thanked them and made for the door.

Outside, she glanced at the buildings on either side of the pub. No cameras. She looked across the street. Nothing there either.

She'd struck out.

*Damn!*


"Jasi's pissed," Ben said, gripping the steering wheel.

It ate at him, this feeling of helplessness when it came to Jasi. He could sense impending doom and she was the last person he wanted to see caught up in it.

Natassia eyed him, one brow raised. "She's pissed because you keep bashing her boyfriend."

"Zane's not her boyfriend."

"What is he then?"

"He's, uh...well…"

"Yeah, right."

He glanced out the side window. He didn't want Natassia to see how much it hurt him that Jasi wouldn't listen to him.

"Let her make her own decisions, Ben. Otherwise she'll resent you."

"I know. I do." He changed the subject. "Did we get the report on the evidence found at Sampson's crime scene?"

Natassia shook her head. "The lab was backed up. They said we'll have it sometime tomorrow. You think the gum or the receipt belonged to our killer?"

"We can only wish. It would certainly give us the break we need."

"And the condom?"

"This wasn't a sex crime. And I don't think the killer boinked someone right before he set Sampson on fire."

"You never know."

Natassia was right. When it came to murderers, some had perverse habits, behaviors that make normal people cringe.

Take the Parliament cases. Whoever they were looking for took great pleasure in inflicting pain. That's why he drugged his victims, bashed their heads in and then set them on fire while they were still breathing. He wanted them to see their own deaths.

Ben thought of his vision. Flags were everywhere, but why he'd seen one falling into water, he hadn't a clue. And they still hadn't determined the meaning of the shining silver sun.

"Mind if I turn on some music?" Natassia asked.

"Go ahead. CDs are in the glove compartment."

He studied the road ahead and navigated a turn.

A glint of light made him look at Natassia. She was holding up a CD and the light reflected off it, creating a silver glow around the edges.

"A silver sun," he whispered.

"What?"

The SUV lurched to a stop in a church parking lot.

"In my vision. The silver sun!"

"*Relaxation for the Soul,*" she said.

"Exactly."

"But we already had the CD analyzed, Ben. They didn't find anything suspicious. No prints, no manufacturer's address."

"Maybe the tech didn't look close enough."

"What do you mean?"

"I don't know," he said. "It's just a feeling."

"You think the music is covering up something?"

He nodded. "That's exactly what I think." His data-com beeped. "Yeah."

"I checked the businesses on either side of the pub," Jasi told him. "No one saw Zane."

"What about the girls who worked that day?"

"I called them and emailed Zane's photo. I'm waiting for their calls."

"Let us know if you get anywhere," he said, glancing at Natassia. "We're on our way back to the hotel."

"Where'd you go?"

"We were headed for the hospital." Before Jasi could interject, he added, "I wanted to speak to Zane myself, see if he remembered anything yet."

"So why'd you change your mind?" Jasi sounded wary.

"You know that CD we found at Sampson's?"

"Yeah."

"I'm sure it's the silver sun I saw in my vision."

"But Matthew already had it tested."

"We need to go deeper, have the music analyzed."

After he hung up, he steered the car in the direction of the hotel.

"The silver sun," he said, glancing at the CD. "Now all I need to figure out is what the flag in the water means?"

"Any ideas?" Natassia asked.

"Not really."

Approaching Parliament Hill, he caught sight of the Canadian flag that waved high atop the center spire that housed the clock tower. He felt an overwhelming sense of patriotism. Men fought for and died for this flag, this country. Yet, somewhere close by, a killer wasn't feeling so patriotic.

*Why?*

If he could figure that out, he'd know who to look for.


He paced in front of the window in Jasi and Natassia's hotel room. The longer he examined the disk, the more certain he was that it held a clue.

"I need the disk," Natassia said, holding out a hand.

When he gave it to her, she slipped it into the drive on the laptop.

"Do you think there's something hidden on it?"

"You mean like terrorist plans?"

He chuckled. "I'm thinking more like subliminal messages."

"Matthew said he could have someone on it right away, if you want."

"I have a feeling you might find the answer quicker."

"Why is that?"

"I don't know. A hunch maybe. You seem to know your way around a computer. Inside one too."

Natassia gazed up at him with her sapphire eyes, eyes he could swim in…or drown in.

"Why, Agent Roberts, I do believe you've given me a compliment."

He could feel the fire under his skin. "Don't get used to it."

"Yes, sir."

He could hear the laughter in her voice. It wasn't such a bad sound. It made him think of the wind chimes his mother had hung in the back yard when he was a kid.

*Whoa! Where did that come from?*

He squelched the childhood memory and spent the next ten minutes wondering why Natassia affected him the way she did. It wasn't something he could ignore. He felt the pull.

*Does she?*

# 28

The following day, it rained continuously. Actually, it was more like the torrential downpours Jasi was used to in Vancouver. Moody weather. That's what she called it.

She hadn't liked missing her morning run, but she wasn't prepared to freeze her butt off in the cold rain, so that morning while Natassia slept, she had slipped quietly out of their room and headed for the gym on the main floor. A half hour of weights followed by an hour on the treadmill made her feel a bit better. After her run, she had showered and dressed for whatever the day would bring.

Jasi watched the rain through the window. It was finally thinning out, the entire city washed clean, sanitized.

"I hate the rain," she muttered

"You live in Vancouver," Natassia said behind her. "You should be used to it."

"Does anyone ever get used to rain?" Jasi turned away, still tired from her nap. "Why couldn't it rain at night, when we're all sleeping?"

"It'll pass."

"It's not just the rain," Jasi admitted. "I feel like we're going around in circles and I'm worried someone else is next on this killer's list. I can't stand waiting. I need to stay busy."

"I have a feeling we'll be very busy soon enough."

"Why do you say that?"

Natassia shrugged. "Just a feeling."

"Is this another psychic gift you have? Premonition?"

"No." Natassia chuckled. "A regular old feeling."

Jasi studied her partner for a long moment, wondering if she was being truthful. Did Natassia know something?

Her data-com beeped. "It's Ben. He'll meet us in The Study Lounge for coffee. Says the place is empty."

Natassia disappeared into the bathroom.

Outside, the rain rattled against the window, adding to Jasi's somber mood and thoughts.

*If we don't solve this case soon, we might have to tell another family that they've lost a loved one.*

She shivered at the thought.


Ben looked up when he felt Jasi's presence in the lounge. She was alone. He watched as she crossed the room in quick strides and sat down across from him.

"Where's our charming partner?" he asked.

"She had to iron a shirt." Jasi grinned. "So you think she's charming, do you?"

"I said that sarcastically."

"Well, our charming partner is getting changed. I wonder what she'll wear. I don't know how she manages to look fashionable and still conduct an investigation."

She was needling him and he didn't want to rise to the bait. "Natassia's okay," he said. "She's a hard worker."

"Hmmm."

He removed his gloves. "What's that supposed to mean, Jazz?"

"You like her."

"I said she was okay."

Thankfully, his data-com beeped. "Yeah?"

"No fingerprints on the CD," Matthew told him.

"What about the music?"

"We haven't found anything definite, but the tech said there were some unusual frequencies he wanted to look into."

"Let us know as soon as you know."

"Of course," Matthew assured him. "You're dealing with someone very cunning, Ben. I have to tell you, I'm getting some real heat here, from the powers that be. We need to get this guy before he kills again."

"We will."

"Matthew?" Jasi asked after he hung up.

Ben nodded. "He's under pressure from the higher-ups. They want us to wrap up this case."

"We've got nothing new to go on."

"Something will turn up. It always does."

Jasi stared past him. "Here's our *charming* partner."

He tried to resist looking over his shoulder. He failed miserably. Natassia gave him an apologetic smile and sat down beside Jasi.

He said the first thing that came to mind. "You look nice."

*Nice?* Was that the best he could come up with?

At least Natassia was dressed more appropriately. She wore a pale yellow blouse buttoned almost to the top and a pair of navy slacks. Was she trying to win him over? If so, it was working.

Or it was until she said, "It's the only clean blouse I had left."

They spent the next two hours trying to reconstruct various crime scenarios, but nothing led to a viable suspect. They combed through the Winkler and Sampson files, looking for anything they might have missed.

Discouraged, Jasi called Constable O'Malley at OPS.

"They've got nothing," she said when she hung up. "They're as stumped as we are."

It wasn't until they reached the topic of Zane Underhill that Ben found his patience wearing thin.

"We still don't know why he was taken," he said.

"He was supposed to see Sampson," Jasi reminded him. "He was a threat, especially if Sampson remembered anything while under hypnosis."

"But who else knew about Zane's involvement?"

"Besides us and Matthew? No one."

"Unless there's a leak," Natassia suggested.

"At Divine Ops?" He shook his head. "I don't think that's it."

"What are suggesting?" Jasi asked, her eyes shooting daggers. "You think Zane told someone he was going to see Porter Sampson?"

"I don't know."

"That's right. You don't."

The anger in Jasi's voice cut through him. He thought back to the time Jasi had been seeing the guy. She'd been happy then. Even he had to admit that. Until Underhill disappeared without a word or phone call.

*She deserves better.*

"I have some calls to make," she said, standing.

"We'll survive without you," Natassia replied.

Jasi eyed Ben. "I'm sure you will."

"Is Zane on your list of phone calls?" he blurted.

"I want to see if he remembers anything."

"I'm sure he'll call you if he does."

For a second he was tempted to leave with her.

He grabbed her arm. "Are you sure everything's okay?"

"I'm fine."

Without thinking, she peeled his hand away. The contact of her hand on his bare skin sent him mentally reeling. After she left, he studied his bare hands and swore softly.

"Ben?" Natassia eyed him. "Is something wrong?"

"No," he lied.

"You touched her and you saw something, didn't you?"

Tugging his gloves over his hands, he said, "It wasn't so much a vision as a sensation."

"What kind of sensation?"

He didn't answer.

"Ben?"

He tried to smile. "It was probably nothing."

Natassia let out a sigh. "You don't fool me a bit."

"Fine then. I'm worried."

"Why?"

He stared into Natassia's eyes. "I think Jasi's in danger."


In the lobby, Jasi sat on a bench and called Zane.

"How are you feeling?" she asked when he picked up.

"I'm fine. The CFBI got me all settled in my room."

"Do you remember anything?"

"Yeah, one thing."

Her heart pounded. "What?"

"We have a date in a couple of hours."

"I meant about your abduction, Zane."

"No. Everything's still a blur."

"But the doctor said you'll be all right?"

"As right as I'll ever be." He chuckled. "Were you worried about me, love?"

"I worry about all my friends."

"Ouch. That's how you think of us then. As friends?"

She gave an irritated sigh. "I don't know what we are. Let's not rush this, Zane."

"Who's rushing? Take as much time as you need."

"That's awfully nice of you," she said dryly.

"Forgive me for being facetious. I'm in a bit of a funk."

"I can tell."

"Hey, you would be too if you'd been stuck in a hospital room. The beds were like concrete and the Jell-O was simply atrocious."

She chewed her bottom lip. "Maybe we should hold off on having dinner."

"Not on your life. A guy's gotta eat, and I'm craving *real* food."

She glanced at her watch. "Listen, I have to go, but I'll see you later. Dinner only, right?"

"Actually, I was thinking that maybe Nurse Jasmine and I could play doctor. I assure you, I'd be a most compliant patient."

"Behave yourself. Remember your promise?"

"Yeah, I remember. I might have forgotten some things, but I do recall agreeing to keep us strictly professional."

"Zane, you've got to stop getting under my skin."

"Under isn't where I plan to be, love."

She shivered. "Goodbye, Zane."


Jasi had tried to quell her excitement. It was date night.

While Natassia and Ben remained in the dining room, she'd had a quick shower, then slipped into stylish dress pants and a simple mauve blouse with a flowing cowl neckline. She rarely ever packed a dress. Corpses usually made lousy dates.

Rummaging through the tote bag, she found the box with her mother's pearl necklace and small pearl studs. They were the finishing touch after she blow-dried her hair as straight as she could get it and applied some makeup.

"Well, Zane," she muttered. "You'd better appreciate the trouble I took."

On her way up to Zane's room, she inspected her makeup one last time in the small compact she kept in her purse. With a fortifying breath, she exited the elevator and headed down the hallway.

A man sat in a chair at the end of the hall.

*Zane's bodyguard.*

"Agent Greene," she said with a nod.

The CFBI agent smiled. "He's excited about your date."

She blushed.

Greene knocked twice on the door. A minute later Zane opened it, his smile widening the second he saw her.

"Come in, love."

She stepped inside, saying, "I'm not sure you should be going anywhere, Zane."

Seeing Greene had reminded her that someone might be looking for Zane. Someone with murder in his or her heart.

"It's already been cleared," Zane said, taking her hand. He raised it to his mouth and his lips lingered warmly on her skin. "We're only going downstairs. Besides, we'll have Mickey."

The fact that a CFBI bodyguard would be with them on their date was both satisfying and disappointing.

Zane grinned. "He promised to sit at another table."

"Great."

Dinner went smoothly. Mickey sat close to the entrance, while Zane and Jasi sat at the end of the room, partially blocked by a decorative screen. Every now and then Mickey would discreetly saunter past them, checking to make sure his protégé was still breathing.

"So much for privacy," Zane said wryly. "Sorry about this, Jazz."

"Hey, don't apologize. It's not your fault."

"I told the CFBI I didn't need a babysitter."

Her mouth thinned. "Of course you do. What I don't understand is why you're not holed up in your room. What are you trying to do? Get yourself killed?"

"Of course not."

She gaped at him. "You're not playing bait, are you?"

"Me? I have too much to live for."

She blew out a relieved breath. "Good."

Zane wiggled his brow. "So...your place or mine?"

She chuckled. "You're incorrigible. I have a roommate. And you have your bodyguard."

"Mickey won't be in my room. Or my bed."

His words sparked an internal heat wave.

"Zane..."

"I want you, Jasmine." His voice dimmed to a whisper. "I need you."

*Be smart, Jasi,* her inner voice warned. *You're still on duty. You can't afford another lapse.*


Ben returned to his room to review the files Matthew had sent to his laptop. The first one was on evidence found at Sampson's murder scene. At first, it seemed like useless information. The receipt had one unidentifiable fingerprint; the condom wasn't a match on the international sex offender database, and the gum had DNA, but without a suspect there was no one to compare it to.

Then something jumped out at him.

*Gum contains nicotine.*

That bothered him for some reason.

Turning to the second report, he read carefully.

"Bingo."

Divine Ops had conducted an investigation into the emergency broadcast channel, and at first glance everything seemed normal. It wasn't until a tech started analyzing the frequency that something strange jumped out. The channel exhibited constant static, but between 6:30 and 7:00 every night, the static was interrupted.

"By an unidentified satellite transmission," he read.

The origin of the transmission was unknown. Ops techs were working on retracing the route back to its source.

"Why would someone transmit through the emergency broadcast channel?" he murmured.

*And why would Winkler and Sampson watch it?*

Monty Winkler went to his home office every night after supper. At around 6:30 he received a call from a payphone, by an unknown caller. Winkler then turned on his television and watched a transmission from an unknown origin. Afterward, he'd fall asleep, later awaking with no memory of watching TV or the phone call. Porter Sampson's story was the same.

*Why?*

There was only one reason he could think of, and it sent a chill through his bones.

"They're being brainwashed."

He grabbed his data-com. "Call Jasi."

Five rings led him to her voice mail. He left a hurried message, asking her to call him back immediately.

Then he called Natassia.

"Where's Jasi?"

"Out." Pause. "Is something wrong, Ben?"

"I think Winkler and Sampson were being brainwashed through the television."

"Can that be done?"

"Definitely."

He told her about the report from Divine Ops.

"Satellite transmissions?" Natassia voice grew excited. "There's one place we know of that deals with that kind of thing."

"Paragon," they said in unison.

"Deirdre Dailey is the one in charge of satellite transmission research," Natassia said.

"And Marilyn Winkler could be involved too."

"Where exactly is Paragon located?"

His mouth tightened. "Shirleys Bay. About twenty minutes from here."

"I'll be right over."

Next, he called Matthew.

"We need a search warrant for Paragon Research Corporation," he told him. "I know it's late, but how long do you think it'll take?"

"You'll have a warrant within the hour."

Ben disconnected the call just as Natassia knocked on the door. He let her in. She had her laptop open and set it on the table.

"There's no Ops file on Paragon," she said, her voice tinged with excitement. "But Paragon's website says that Shirleys Bay started off testing magnetic and radio noise disturbances—high frequency soundwaves—in the early 1950s. The entire area is leased out to the military and an assortment of private research organizations, like Paragon."

He peered over her shoulder. "Sounds like top secret work."

"It does, doesn't it?" She glanced back at the monitor. "Shirleys Bay has been involved in a number of endeavors, including Project Magnet."

"Project Magnet?"

"An investigation into possible UFO transmissions. Over the years, some of Paragon's laboratories have built and tested communication and scientific satellites. And God knows what else."

"Something that someone would kill for?"

"Maybe."

Ben called Jasi again. He got her voicemail.

"Jasi, we found something. We think Porter Sampson and Monty Winkler were being brainwashed through transmissions sent to their televisions. That's why they were watching the emergency broadcast channel. Messages were sent via satellite. And you'll never guess who holds the contract on that particular satellite. Paragon Research Corporation." He glanced at Natassia. "We're heading there now. Call me as soon as you get this message."

"Where do you think she went?" Natassia asked.

He shook his head. "I don't have a clue."

"Zane's maybe?"

"I hope not."

"Why don't you like him, Ben? Are you jealous?"

He laughed. "Of Zane? No, I just don't trust him. Any time I've heard anything about Zane Underhill it's been nothing good."

"And you don't want to see Jasi hurt."

"Exactly." He studied Natassia. "You think she's with Zane?"

"What I think isn't important. Jasi's a big girl, Ben. She can take care of herself."

He nodded. "You're right. I'm being overprotective again."

Natassia walked to the door. "She's lucky you care."

"I care about everyone on the team."

"Really?" Her blue eyes glinted. "I'll remember that."

As they stepped into the hall, Ben mentally kicked himself. *Our relationship is strictly business.*

## 29

Shirleys Bay was dead quiet. The only sign of life came in the form of a beefy armed guard standing by the front gate. The man went into high alert mode when he saw the SUV approaching.

Ben pulled up slowly and stopped the car. When he flashed his badge through the glass, the guard gave a nod.

Ben rolled down the window. "This is official CFBI business. We need access to Paragon Research Corporation."

"Do you have a warrant, sir?"

"It's being faxed to you as we speak."

The guard folded his arms across his chest. "We can wait."

"We can't," Natassia said, leaning across Ben. "Some serious stuff is going down. I'm sure you can help us out."

The guard frowned. "Okay, ma'am. But if the warrant isn't here in half an hour I'm coming to get you. Until then, leave everything in its place."

"We won't be removing anything from the property," Ben assured. "Not until we get the warrant. But we'd like to prevent possible evidence from being destroyed. Is anyone working late at Paragon?"

"Don't think so, sir. Should I call ahead?"

"No," Ben said hurriedly.

"Have you got a key card, sir?"

Ben glanced at Natassia, who nodded. "Yes."

They drove through the security gate and proceeded to the far end where the laboratories were located. There were no signs of activity on the grounds and from the outside the building windows remained dark. When they reached Paragon, he noted the lack of vehicles in the parking lot.

*That's a good sign.*

He parked the SUV next to a smaller building. Then he retrieved his data-com from his jacket pocket.

"Power down, Natassia."

"On vibrate, or completely?"

"Completely."

If someone *was* inside, the soft buzz of a data-com could still warn them, and he didn't want that. Better to get in and out undetected.

"What about Jasi?" Natassia asked.

"We'll probably be out before she returns my calls." He couldn't keep the bitterness from coloring his voice.

"You're pissed at her," Natassia stated unnecessarily.

He shrugged. "She should be here with us."

"We can handle this, Ben."

Natassia was right. It was a re-con trip. Nothing that two agents couldn't handle. If they did find anything incriminating, all of Shirleys Bay would be swarming with CFBI agents, RCMP and OPS within twenty minutes.

"I'll try Jasi later," he said. "If she doesn't call first."

"So we're going to snoop around, see if we can find a link to the transmissions, a file or something?"

"Yeah. It'll be easier without anyone here. If they knew we were coming I'm sure they'd hide whatever they could." He pulled out his data-com.

As they approached the front door, he noted that there were no vehicles parked in the lot.

"I think we're in luck."

Ben led the way, sticking close to the bushes and shadows. Their approach was met with no resistance, and as expected, the door to Paragon was locked.

He glanced at Natassia. "You can get us inside, right?"

"No problem."

He watched as she plugged the IHD into her data-com and pointed it at the door. She punched in some numbers and hit a button. Seconds later, they were inside.

"Wow," he said. "I'm impressed."

"Thanks," Natassia replied.

They moved stealthily through the doors into a small waiting area. It was empty except for a couple of chairs and a magazine rack. A hallway led to three doors.

A sign on one door read *PRC – Main Lab.*

"Let's start here," Ben suggested.

In less than six seconds Natassia unlocked the door.

"IHD rocks," she whispered.

"You rock," he said without thinking.

Inside, they turned on flashlights and started at opposite sides of the room. Individual desks were divided by tall partitions and filing cabinets.

"What are we looking for exactly?" Natassia whispered.

"I'm not sure. But I think we'll know it when we see it."

At least he hoped so.

He was tempted to call Jasi again, but he was sure she wouldn't answer. Besides, she was probably back at the hotel, bored out of her skull.

Boredom was the least of Jasi's worries.

She stood in Zane's bathroom, trying to control her breathing. Why had she agreed on coming back to his room?

"Because you're weak," she whispered to her reflection.

There was a knock on the door.

"Jasi?" Zane called. "Are you all right, love?"

*No.* "I'm fine."

She mentally kicked herself for not bringing her purse with her. At least then she could have used the excuse of needing to reapply her lipstick.

She opened the door.

Zane was leaning against the wall by the door. The sight of him stirred her and she resisted the temptation of stepping into his arms and giving herself to a night of passion.

He smiled. "What shall we do for the rest of the evening?"

She thought about Ben and Natassia. She really should call and let them know where she was.

*And if you'll be back tonight.*

"I have to call Ben."

"Come on, love," Zane said coaxingly. "No more business tonight."

She strode across the room and pulled her data-com from her purse. She blinked at the display.

*Damn! I must have turned it off without thinking.*

"Sorry, Zane. I have to call Ben."

Her partner had left three messages. When she heard what he and Natassia had discovered, she gasped.

"We're almost at Paragon," Ben's recorded message stated. "We're going to do some snooping around first to confirm my suspicions. I'll call you if we find anything."

*Shit!*

Zane moved beside her. "What's wrong, Jasmine?"

"Ben and Natassia have found something."

"What?"

"Call Ben," she said, ignoring his question.

Five rings later and the voice mail kicked in.

"I'm on my way, Ben."

"Jasmine," Zane said, visibly frustrated.

"I have to go." She stuffed her data-com in her purse and strode toward the door. "I'm really sorry, Zane."

"Hey, don't worry about me. But tell me, what did Ben find out?"

She hesitated in the doorway.

Zane grinned. "Come on, love. One hint."

Faced with his irresistible charm, she sighed. "Fine, but don't mention this to anyone. There's a connection to Paragon Research Corporation, the company run by Monty Winkler's widow."

"What kind of connection?"

"That's all I can say. Ben and Natassia are heading there now, and I'm going to meet them." She gave him a hasty kiss. "I'll call you in the morning."

"If I don't see you before then," he said seductively.

As Jasi hurried to meet her partners, she wondered how long Zane would stick around this time. Would he leave her again for the excitement of the Big Apple? Or was he finally ready to settle down?

One thing was certain. She needed an answer.


Ben studied the computer monitor in front of him.

"This is all gibberish to me," he admitted.

Natassia had hacked into a hidden password-protected folder. There were dozens of files listed.

"Where do we begin?" he asked.

"Allow me," Natassia said, opening the files one by one until she came to a locked file labeled *ProC*. "Double security. This could be what we're looking for."

Her fingers flew over the keys and the screen went black. Seconds later, she typed in a series of codes, bypassing firewalls until she reached a file with an intriguing name.

"Project Chrysalis," Natassia hissed.

"You're a damned magician, Agent Prushenko."

She stood up, waving a hand at the computer. "Ta da!"

Ben sat down. Plucking a flash drive from the desk, he plugged it in and copied the file.

"I thought we weren't taking anything until the warrant comes in," Natassia said in a disapproving tone.

"I'm not removing it, I'm copying it. It could be gone by tomorrow." He shrugged. "And who says we didn't retrieve it in the morning?"

"You do realize that techies can find that info in two clicks," she said dryly.

"Then it's a matter of national security."

"Wait!" she said. "Scroll back."

He'd almost missed it. Halfway up the previous page was a familiar design. It matched the logo from the CD they'd discovered in Sampson's home office.

"Butterflies," he said.

"Chrysalis," Natassia murmured.

"This file talks about *ghost transmissions* and *subliminal data inductions*, but they make it sound like it's in relation to experimentation on butterflies. Listen to this…"

*"Larva subjects 1 to 26 show indications of conscious submission and receptiveness. This early stage of development is conducive to audible impressions."*

"Suggestion or hypnosis," Natassia murmured.

*"Pupa subjects 1 to 17 show varying degrees of success, with 7, 15 and 16 being the most resistant to direct suggestion or orders. Side note: Pupa 15 and 16 have been exterminated."* He eyed Natassia. "I think we know what that means."

He clicked on the next page. *"Greater exposure to audible impressions over a longer duration is warranted, with mandatory follow-up and re-evaluation of all subjects. Testing on Pupa subjects 1 and 2 show unwavering loyalty and easy manipulation, making them the best case subjects for this experimental research. Side note: Pupa 1 and 2 - RELEASED."*

Ben struggled to tamp back his horror. "I think they're building their own private army, and at least two of them are already out in society somewhere with another thirty-nine unaccounted for."

"So let me get this straight," Natassia said. "Larva subjects are people being conditioned through hypnotism via the CDs, and Pupa subjects are the ones watching subliminal mind control messages on their televisions." She shook her head slowly. "Sounds like something off a sci-fi channel."

"Yeah, Invasion of the Body Snatchers meets Stepford Wives."

Scrolling to the end of the page, Ben caught sight of a familiar name. The signature was perfectly legible.

Beside him, Natassia let out a small gasp.

"Now we can prove who's responsible," he muttered.

A loud bang made them jump.

"Behind that door," Natassia whispered, indicating a door marked *Lab 3.*

He nodded and they both drew their guns.

"You follow," he whispered.

He reached for the door knob. It turned without making a sound. Slipping into the cavernous lab, he ducked behind a partition and waited for Natassia. She was right behind him. With his gun raised, he crept along the wall, then crouched behind a long counter. He couldn't see a thing. Somewhere up ahead, he heard the sound of something sliding along the floor. He moved along the counter in the direction of the noise.

A half-open door came into view.

He signaled Natassia and she moved to the opposite side of the door. A scraping sound covered any sounds they made and they sipped into the room, the only light coming from a closet in the far corner.

Ben peered from behind a desk. A few yards away, a shadowed form was hunched over a haphazard stack of boxes. The form grabbed something and the sharp scent of gasoline wound its way back to Ben.

"CFBI!" he called out. "Put the gas can down and keep your hands where I can see them."

Before Ben could raise his flashlight to identify the face, the shadow darted toward a back door.

He fired a warning shot. The shadow fired back.

*Damn! I missed.*

However, he hadn't been so lucky. As Natassia moved toward him, a dismayed expression on her face, Ben felt blood trickle down his forehead. His vision clouded and he slumped to the floor.


It took a phone call to Matthew before the guard at the gate would allow Jasi to pass through. Once on the Shirleys Bay grounds, she steered the car west toward Paragon Research Corporation, which was at the end of the street near the Ottawa River. Moonlight glimmered off the water, and to the west the city's lights were reflected in the mirrored surface.

She spotted Ben's SUV and parked behind it.

When she climbed from the car, the first thing that struck her was how quiet and dark it was. There were few outdoor lights, enough to cover the perimeter of the facility, which was surrounded by a fifteen-foot high voltage fence.

Shirleys Bay was nearly deserted at night, but come tomorrow morning it would be filled with scientists, research assistants and government officials working on top secret assignments.

She strode down the sidewalk that led to Paragon. It was an impressive brick building that housed Marilyn's company, plus two other research firms. She eyed the building, noting that the rooms beyond the windows remained dark.

A muffled shot rang out. From inside Paragon.

*Shit! Ben and Natassia are in there, somewhere.*

She quickly sent Matthew a data-com message calling for backup. Then she clipped her data-com to her jacket. She tried calling Ben, but there was no answer. She tried Natassia's 'com and got the same result. She settled for a silent message, hoping they see it even if they were in vibrate mode.

With her Beretta in hand, she reached the main entrance.

The door was locked

*Don't think you're gonna stop me.*

She hastily retrieved the IHD from her back pocket. Natassia's expertise in areas of subterfuge was going to come in handy. Now all she had to do was remember how to use the damned thing.

"Okay, insert the hacker card thingy," she said, trying to remain patient. "Then 911."

Nothing happened.

"Shit! 911, then the call button, dummy."

The light on the IHD turned green and the door opened smoothly. She passed through the waiting area. The door to the main lab was open just a crack. She slipped inside and hid behind a filing cabinet.

*Where the hell are you, Ben?*

Her ears perked at the sound of voices. They were barely audible and she couldn't make out what was being said, but at least she knew they were up ahead somewhere.

On the wall was a security camera, but the indicator light was off. She frowned. Someone had disengaged the security system.

*You're in the right place.*

A few yards down the hall, a shadow sat on the floor. She couldn't make out who it was, but as she approached, the shadow turned and metal glinted.

She raised her gun.

*"Jasi?"*

It was Natassia.

"Are you hurt?"

"Not me."

There was a tremor in Natassia's voice that made Jasi hurry to her side. That's when she saw him.

Ben was stretched out on the floor, his eyes fluttering with pain. On the left side of his temple, an angry red wound sliced through the skin.

"Hi, Jazz," he said weakly.

She dropped to her knees beside him.

"There's no bullet hole," she said after examining the wound. "The bullet grazed you pretty deep."

The pallor of Ben's face didn't look good. They had to stop the bleeding and get him to a hospital.

"Look for something to staunch the blood flow," she told Natassia.

Minutes later, Natassia returned with a package of sterile gauze she'd found in the washroom.

"You might have a concussion," Jasi said, wrapping Ben's head with the gauze. "We need to get you to a hospital."

"Have to get the shooter first," he said, breathless.

"Who shot at you?"

"Don't know. Too dark."

"It happened too fast," Natassia said, pulling her aside. "But whoever it is, they're still inside." She quickly told Jasi about the hypnosis CDs and Project Chrysalis.

"Brainwashing?" Jasi was stunned.

"Imagine the control someone would have."

Jasi nodded. "And the power."

Muffled thumps came from further down the hall.

"I'm going in," she said, taking a deep breath. "Get Ben out of here while he can still walk."

"You can't go in there alone!"

"There's no time for arguing. Get Ben to safety and call the paramedics. I already called for backup. They should be here any minute."

As she moved down the hall, Jasi flicked a look over her shoulder. Natassia looked like she was ready to cry.

"Don't you dare die on me, Benjamin Roberts," the woman said, helping their injured partner to his feet.

Jasi activated the recorder of her data-com and clipped it to her jacket. Then she moved down the hall toward the door that led from the Main Lab to the Satellite Research Room. That's where she'd find the mastermind behind the Parliament Murders.

She stepped through the doorway, focused on the task at hand. She had to end this, once and for all. Crouching close to the concrete wall, she was careful not to make a sound.

But her stealth was all in vain.

*"We meet again, Agent McLellan."*

# 30

At the far end of the room, Deirdre Dailey paced the floor, tossing CDs, folders and binders into a duffle bag. Ignoring Jasi's presence, she moved quickly, her motions deliberate, the actions of someone who had a plan. If she was going to run, Jasi would have no choice but to stop her.

"So you finally figured it out," the woman said without turning. "Good for you."

"The agent you wounded figured it out. Not me."

"Well, I knew one of you would figure things out. Eventually. I was too careless." She flicked a look over her shoulder, hesitating only a second when she spotted Jasi's weapon. "I apologize that I'm too busy to greet you, but I have to get my things in order."

Jasi surveyed the room. Two exits. One a few yards from Deirdre, the other the door she'd just come through.

*Does she have a weapon?*

She inched closer to Deirdre. "I need you to turn around and keep your hands where I can see them."

"Sorry, but that's not going to happen."

"It's over, Deirdre."

The woman spun on one heel, her mouth curved into a bright smile, her eyes filled with tears. "Yes, I know that."

"Put down the bag and step away from the shelves."

Deirdre went still. "I'm going away, Agent McLellan."

"Yes, you are."

"Life behind bars isn't for me."

"You don't have a choice now."

"We always have a choice."

"And you made yours the day you started this," Jasi replied. "It's your legacy. Is this how you want people to think of you? As a murderer?"

"Well, at least one person knew me and loved me for who I am," Deirdre said, sniffling.

"Your sister."

Deirdre sneered. "Marilyn will be more than happy to see me out of her life."

"I'm sure that's not true. She loves you."

"Love?" Her laugh bordered on maniacal. "Marilyn hates me. She always has."

*Keep her talking, Jasi.*

"Why do you say that, Deirdre?"

"Because I tried to ruin Monty's career," the woman whispered. "And because she knew the truth about Daddy's death."

"What truth?" she asked.

The woman closed her mouth.

"What happened with your father, Deirdre?"

The woman grinned. "I killed him."

"Your father died in a boating accident."

Deirdre's eyes gleamed. "Really? An accident?"

"Your sister said there was an explosion onboard. An engine problem."

"Bombs aren't that difficult to construct," the woman said. "You can learn how to do just about anything on the Internet. Daddy never thought I was as bright as Marilyn. Well, I showed him."

Jasi shuddered at the satisfied gleam in the woman's eyes. The situation was critical. She had to get Deirdre to surrender.

"I wish I'd been there to see the look on his face when he realized that someone had cut the gas line," Deirdre said with a laugh. "And when he found the bomb onboard. Too bad I only gave him ten seconds once he lifted the engine hatch."

"You thought you'd get your inheritance," Jasi said. "But what you didn't know was that your father had drawn up a new will making your sister the executor of the estate and the one holding the purse strings."

Deirdre pouted. "Marilyn had everything I ever wanted. Brains, beauty, a respected husband, wealth, power…and Daddy's love. I wanted her and Monty to split up. I thought she'd pay some attention to me, listen to my ideas about Paragon's future, maybe even let me have the money Daddy left me." She looked around the room. "Now she has nothing. Like me. There *is* justice after all."

"What I don't understand," Jasi said, "is why you'd concoct a scheme to brainwash a couple of politicians. What have you got against them?"

"Nothing."

"What do you mean nothing?"

Deirdre shrugged. "I had absolutely nothing against those men."

"There are few motives for this kind of crime. Money—you'll get that from your sister—revenge or love."

"Yes, I'd do almost anything for love. Wouldn't you?"

The question caught Jasi off guard.

"You would murder innocent men for love?"

"They weren't all that innocent, Agent McLellan. Monty messed around on my sister."

"What about Porter Sampson? What was his crime?"

Deirdre gave her a sour look. "Like Monty, he was going to make decisions that would affect everyone, including future generations. Justice needed to be served. Their decisions would have resulted in more deaths, more corruption."

"What *you* did was corrupt. Where's the justice in your actions?"

"Justice is blind. And sometimes plain stupid." She laughed. "You think you're going to cuff me and take me off to prison where I'll wither away and die." Her voice dimmed to a whisper. "I'll die alone."

"Maybe you should've thought of that before you decided to brainwash government officials into obeying your twisted agenda. What you did will be viewed as a terrorist act. That's quite an accomplishment, Deirdre."

"What do you think *you're* accomplishing here?"

"I'm stopping you."

Laughter echoed in the room and Jasi shivered.

"You think you can stop this? You fool! You have no idea how far this goes."

"What do you mean?"

"We've been doing this for nearly a year."

"Let me get this straight," Jasi said, praying that her data-com was getting every word. "You've been messing with Sampson and Winkler for a year?"

"And others. We didn't just manipulate a few homegrown politicians. It started with a few test subjects, but now there are people in every department of government, in the courts, in every official capacity. People in power."

"It shouldn't be too difficult to find a few wayward Canadian government officials."

Deirdre laughed again. "Don't you get it, Agent McLellan? This crosses borders. Canada, the United States, Britain even. The funny thing is you'll never know who is affected."

"And these people have all been brainwashed."

"*Transitioned.* That's what we prefer to call it. With Project Chrysalis, the subjects' brains were exposed to months of high frequency sound waves. This allowed us to implant the next phase."

"Which was?"

"The sound waves activated dormant areas of their brains and made the test subjects susceptible to suggestion."

"You make them sound like nothing more than lab rats."

The woman's mouth curved into a deadly smile. "It was a highly successful experiment in neural conditioning, Agent McLellan."

Jasi fought the sudden urge to pound Deirdre to a pulp.

"So these suggestions altered their normal impulses or desires and made them do what you told them."

"That's correct," Deirdre said with a nod.

"And the CDs?"

Deirdre flinched. "My boyfr—*investor* came up with that idea. He created a disk that helps reinforce the subjects' openness to suggestion, makes them relax. We're talking about using the power of suggestion with high tech frequencies that humans can't hear but that alter their brain waves and activate parts of the brain that are normally dormant. It's quite a fascinating process."

"And the phone calls?"

"Instructions that induced a hypnotic trance, allowing certain suggestions to activate."

"Then why kill Winkler and Sampson?"

"They were our failures."

"So your entire team here at Paragon was in on this?"

"No, they knew nothing about we really did. They ran the tests and studies, then activated the frequencies when I told them. They thought it was all part of our research."

But one person, Deirdre had admitted, knew everything.

"What's your boyfriend's name?"

Deirdre clenched her lips tight. She wasn't telling.

"Come on, Deirdre. Cooperate and things might go easier for you. We need to know who else is in on this."

"And if I don't? What then, Agent McLellan? Are you going to use that gun on me?"

"Not if I don't have to." She raised the gun. "It's over."

"Not quite, Agent McLellan. There's one thing stopping you from taking me in."

"What?"

Deirdre opened her hand. "This."

Jasi swallowed. *Oh shit.*

The detonator in Deirdre's hand made her heart stop.

"What are you doing, Deirdre?"

"What do you think I'm doing, Agent McLellan?"

"Look," Jasi said, holding up her hands and stepping back. "We can all leave here in one piece. It doesn't have to end this way, Deirdre."

"Of course it does," the woman shrieked. "I'm ruined. Everything I've worked for this past year is destroyed."

"But what about your family?"

"I have no family!"

"Marilyn—"

"She'll be happier when I'm gone."

"But you're in love. What about him?"

"I'm in love, yes. But he doesn't love me. He used me and I let him. He raped my mind and twisted my ideas. He called it a partnership of the soul, what we had. He said we were helping mankind."

"Who said?"

But Deirdre wasn't listening. "He said my research would exist for generations to come. That one day we'll not only be communicating with extraterrestrials, we'll be able to modify human behavior right through their television sets." Her eyes flared insanely. "Think of how this would affect war."

"What do you mean?"

"We'd have the power to extinguish a war with a single transmission to terrorist leaders. Saddam, Bin Laden, all of Al-Qaeda. Terrorists watch TV too. We could've stopped 9-11 from ever happening again. He said whoever had this technology would hold all the power."

"Who said this?"

"He thinks he's a God, but he's not even close."

"Who?"

Deirdre stared at the ground and Jasi was tempted to take her down, but something made her hesitate.

*"Jasi!"* a voice hissed to her left.

She turned her head a few inches.

Natassia squatted beside the door, her gun readied. Beside her was the security guard from the gate.

She jerked her head subtly, signaling her partner to circle around behind Deirdre.

"Let's end this, Deirdre," she said, trying to smile.

The woman held out the hand with the detonator. "I wasn't planning on taking anyone else with me, but feel free to join me." Her thumb hovered over the red button. "Or you can leave now."

"Deirdre, think of your sister."

"You have less than 5 minutes." Deirdre pushed the button. "I've activated the bomb."

*Shit!* Jasi had to make a decision.

"Natassia! Get out now!"

Natassia and the guard flew toward the doorway.

With sad eyes, Deirdre watched them. "You'd better run too, Agent McLellan. There's only one place I'm going."

"Please, Deirdre. Let's walk out of here. Both of us."

Deirdre gave her a cold smile. "There's enough C-4 in the basement to turn Paragon into dust." The woman glanced at her watch, then darted for the doorway to the back stairs. "You have four minutes left," she hollered.

Jasi didn't have a choice. She'd never be able to get the woman out of the building or disarm the bomb in time. So she did the only thing she could do. She ran.

Fleeing down the hallway, she prayed that Natassia and the guard had made it out. She was almost to the front door when an explosion rippled through the building, its force so powerful that it blew the door behind her off its hinges and sent it airborne into the waiting area.

"Shit!"

She hit the floor as the door smashed into a wall. Scrambling to her feet, she raced out of the building just as a second explosion rumbled. Shattered glass rained down on her and she ran toward the parking lot where Natassia, Ben and the guard waited inside the idling SUV.

Jasi dove into the back seat of the SUV. "Drive!"

The guard shifted the vehicle into gear and sped off down the road. Behind them, a thunderous explosion shook Paragon Research Corporation. Two smaller blasts caused the building to implode. Walls buckled and folded inward, collapsing on decades of research and destroying the final pieces of evidence in a case that had proven to be far more insidious than anyone had ever guessed. The silence of the night was broken by the crackling of a deadly fire.

Jasi glanced at Ben. It seemed like he was barely breathing. Even worse, blood blossomed through the gauze.

"Ben! Wake up!"

"Is he okay?" Natassia asked from the passenger seat.

"I don't know."

Ben moaned. "Stop making all that noise you two. I'm all right."

"Pull over," Jasi told the guard.

They stared out the windows of the SUV, surveying the research facility. Or what was left of it. Fire licked at the mound that was once walls, floors, offices, computers, hi-tech equipment, and enough paper to wallpaper the House of Commons. Above the smoldering ruins, smoke billowed thick plumes of gray, and caught by the wind it suddenly wafted into the SUV.

Jasi breathed in a mouthful of acrid air. "Oh God," she said, wheezing. "I can't—"

"Shit!" Natassia grabbed Jasi's backpack from the floor and withdrew the Oxy-Mask. "Quick! Put it on!"

Jasi reached for the mask, but before she could get it over her head, her mind connected with Deirdre Dailey's. The woman was trapped beneath the rubble. And she was dying.

Jasi was transported through Deirdre's eyes, the eyes of a killer.

*"They think they're so smart," she snapped. "Stupid, stupid people."*

*"Calm down, love," a man whispered.*

*"I am calm!"*

Someone pulled the Oxy-Mask over Jasi's face and a blast of oxygen whisked away the vision, but not before she saw the face of the man who had manipulated Deirdre Dailey.

*"Then the maniac comes back and finishes him off on the beach,"* he'd said the day before.

She should have figured it out then. She'd never told him where Sampson had been killed. The actual crime scene location hadn't even been released to the media. A rumor had been planted that had explained police presence on the beach—someone had left an unattended bonfire. Other than the teens who found Sampson's remains, only the murderer would have known about the corpse on the beach.

"Aw, shit."

But there was no denying it.

Zane Underhill was a killer.

A beeping sound brought Jasi out of the fog. With a nod of thanks to Natassia, she glanced at the 'com display. It was Matthew.

"What's your status?" he asked her.

"There was an explosion at Paragon."

"Jesus. Is everyone all right?"

She glanced at Ben. His face was pale.

"Jasi?"

"Ben's been shot, Matthew. In the arm. An ambulance is on its way."

"Is he the only casualty?"

"No. Deirdre Dailey was inside the building when it exploded."

"So case closed?"

She glanced at Natassia and Ben, then moved a few feet away. "Not quite. I'm pretty sure Deirdre had a partner."

"Why do you say that?"

"She had the technology to transmit the subliminal messages, but someone else had to program them, plus trigger the victims to turn on their televisions. That's what the phone calls from the payphones were all about."

"Do you have any idea who else is involved?"

Jasi's heart sank at the question. "I do. Someone with training in hypnotherapy. Someone who rigged it to look like they were a victim too."

There was a pause on the other end.

"You're thinking Zane Underhill is involved," he said in a quiet voice.

Jasi blinked back a tear. "Yes. Zane is highly trained in hypnotherapy."

"Did you read his file?"

She sucked in a breath. "No. I pushed it aside when he was found in the park. I didn't think…"

"It's not your fault, Jasmine. Zane played you. He played all of us. Read his file."

"I will."

"And Jasi?"

She swallowed hard. "Yes, sir?"

"Don't go after him alone. Wait for backup."

Flashing lights approached.

"I have to go. The ambulance is here."

"Jasi, wait!"

"I'll call you when we get to the hospital."

She disconnected the call.

"Jasi?" Natassia waved her over. "He needs to get to the hospital right away."

"It's a flesh wound," Ben grumbled. "It doesn't even hurt."

A paramedic rushed to his side. "Is this the only injury?"

"Yes, I—shit!" He groaned. "Okay, that hurts."

"Stop being a big baby," Jasi said, stifling her fear.

The paramedic was joined by another and they carefully loaded Ben onto a gurney and maneuvered it inside the ambulance. Natassia climbed in, then glanced over her shoulder at Jasi.

"You coming?"

"I'll meet you at the hospital in a bit. I have something to do first."

"Wait! Why aren't you coming with us?"

"I have something to take care of first."

Natassia's gaze widened. "What?"

"I know who the mastermind is behind all this. And I have to stop him before he kills again."

"You shouldn't go without backup," Natassia warned. "I'll come with you."

"No. I need you to stay with Ben. Make sure they take good care of him. I can bring this one in myself."

Natassia gave her an anxious look. "How do you know?"

"He has no idea that I know."

"We have to get moving," the paramedic interrupted.

She headed toward the SUV.

"Jasi, get in the ambulance!" Ben hollered.

"Sorry," she yelled over her shoulder. "I have some unfinished business to attend to. I'll see you later."

She watched as the doors closed and the ambulance sped off, sirens wailing and flashing. One thing was certain, if Ben knew who she planned to visit, he'd never let her go without him.

*Please let Ben be okay.*


As she approached Zane's hotel room, she breathed a sigh of relief. Mickey was sitting in the chair, guarding the door. That meant Zane was inside.

"Hey, Mickey," she called.

The CFBI agent didn't answer.

She quickened her pace. "Agent Greene?"

The man remained slumped in the chair.

"Shit!" she said, feeling for a pulse.

Greene was a lucky man. Unconscious, but lucky.

She called for an ambulance, then checked Zane's room. There was no sign of him. Even his clothes were gone.

She called hotel security. On her way down to the parking garage, she called Matthew.

"The agent assigned to watch Zane has been drugged." She caught her breath. "And Zane's gone."

"You have no idea where he is?" Matthew asked.

He's on the run, she was tempted to say.

She sighed. "He knows about the Paragon connection."

"How?"

"I told him." She bit her bottom lip. "I didn't know Deirdre would lead us back to him. He must have taken off the second I left."

"So he's involved." Matthew paused. "He probably knows we're on to him."

"Matthew, this is my fault. I gave him information that he never should have had. I'll find him."

"Jasi, wait until I send you some backup."

"He could be gone by then."

"Jasi, don't!"

"I'll call you as soon as I have him." She hung up.

This was her mess. She'd fix it.


Jasi pulled the SUV into traffic, nearly sideswiping a delivery truck that decided to change lanes at the last second. The driver, who was busy yapping on his cell phone, blasted the horn and raised a hand in anger. She palmed her badge against the window and he lowered his hand and slowed the truck.

She activated her data-com. "Call Zane."

Zane picked up on the fourth ring.

"I'm heading back to Vancouver in the morning," she told him.

"The case is closed?"

"Yeah, Deirdre Dailey was behind it all." She gritted her teeth at the lie.

Pause. "Really? So you've got her in custody?"

"No. She's dead. She blew herself up. At Paragon."

"That's awful," he said.

"I know. I'll tell you all about it when I see you."

Zane chuckled. "One last romp, my love?"

"I'll be at the hotel in half an hour."

Silence.

"Zane?"

"I'm not at the hotel, Jasmine."

"Oh. You and Mickey are sightseeing?"

"You could say that. I needed some fresh air."

She thought of the unconscious Agent Greene. "I'm sure you did. It must have felt like prison being cooped up like that."

*And soon that'll be your life, twenty-four-seven.*

"Where are you, Zane?"

The address he gave her was the Britannia Yacht Club.

"Slip 89, pier 6, number 12," he said. "Look for *Freedom Surfer*. But give me an hour. I have to clean up."

"That's okay. You don't have to clean for me, Zane. I'll be there in about twenty minutes."

"Uh, okay then. See you."

After she hung up, she considered calling Ben and Natassia. Ben would probably insist on joining her, even with a bullet wound. At the very least he'd send Natassia. That would mean another gun in the picture.

Regardless of what Zane had done, she didn't want him dead. No, she'd bring him in quietly. Once she confronted him, he'd realize he didn't have a choice.

*He's not the man you used to know.*

That he wasn't. Zane Underhill had moved up in the world. He'd gone from respected hypnotherapist and brilliant psychologist to a serial killer with a boat.

My own personal Dexter, she thought with a shudder.

*Except Zane isn't going after criminals.*

## 31

On the way to the Britannia Yacht Club, Jasi suspected she was running out of time. Zane would be on the run the minute he heard about Deirdre Dailey's death.

*If only I'd read his file.*

If she'd done that as soon as Matthew had sent it, they might not be in this mess. Now there was no time for reading.

To her left, dozens of lights glinted on the river. It made her think of Pop and his love of boats and the ocean. He'd been a commercial fisherman for a couple of years, after high school. He used to tell her 'tall fish' tales and stories of fierce squalls, especially his survival during three frightening tsunamis. He'd build up the tsunami stories with such intensity that she'd hold her breath. Then he finished with, "And the water rose three inches. We were saved!"

She had loved his stories. They had made her feel safe.

After her mother was murdered, Pop had grown more protective, to the point of smothering her. He wouldn't allow her to ride her bike on the sidewalk. Gone were the days when she could run down to the mailbox at the end of the street and get the mail. She wasn't even allowed in her own backyard by herself until she turned fourteen.

Pop had been relentless in his vigilance. When she was a teenager, he always wanted to know where she was, who she was with and what she was doing. He questioned every choice she made and set stringent house rules. No friends over, no booze, no smoking, no boys, no parties.

What kind of life was that for a teen?

Pop had encouraged Jasi and Brady to stay home after high school and save money for whatever career they each chose to pursue. Her brother, who was only two when their mother was murdered, had dreams of becoming a "hero like Pop," so he enlisted in the Canadian Armed Forces. Six months in, Brady realized that military life wasn't for him and he got out, much to Pop's chagrin.

"Your sister is doing her part for our country," Pop would grumble. "Don't know why you gave up so easily."

Brady and Pop always butted heads, about anything and everything. They'd sip beers out on the deck in the summer and bicker about Canadian and US policies and the war in Iraq. Pop had enough experience with deceitful politicians that even now he had nothing good to say about any of them. They were all 'thieves and man whores,' as he called them. She'd grown up listening to him argue about policy and policing and how they never mixed.

She'd tried to stay on until after Brady left home. She couldn't imagine how Pop would cope once they were both gone, and it hurt to think of him in the house, all alone, with nothing but memories. But he'd made it impossible to stay. She'd had no choice but to pack her bags and leave home. It had never been the same there anyway. Not after her mother's death. And Pop was never the same either.

Jasi's lips curved into a soft smile.

No matter how overprotective he was, she loved her father. Pop was always there for her. He'd even come to accept her 'gift.'

It hadn't always been that way.

She shook her head, shedding the past with the motion.

"You can't live in the past, Jasi. What's done is done."


Since it was after midnight, the Britannia Yacht Club bar was closed and the parking lot was only half full. She pulled into a spot close to the entrance. Leaving the parking lot, she passed the clubhouse and manicured lawn headed for the entrance to the marina.

Descending the steps, she watched for movement along the floating piers below. Antique lamps atop iron posts lit the way, shining soft light on the various craft tied to their respective slips. Some vessels were permanent residents, while others enjoyed a brief holiday in the country's capital.

Her ankle high boots thudded along the damp wooden planks, announcing her presence in the quiet gloom. On high alert, she checked the shadows for sudden movements, but the only movements were restless waves lapping at the sides of vessels.

She found the *Freedom Surfer* berthed, nose in, at the end of Pier 6.

About a hundred feet in length, the sleek white craft was lit on its starboard side by a dock lamp and two rectangular porthole windows along the side emitted golden light.

What was Zane doing on such a magnificent craft?

A flicker of movement in the cockpit caught her eye.

"Zane?"

"Down here, love." His voice rose from below the deck.

With a glance at the cockpit, she shrugged and walked the short gangplank to the gunwale.

"Permission to board, Zane?" she called, thinking of the boating lessons Zane had given her. Along with more intimate lessons.

"Granted."

She stepped onto the deck, then followed soft music down stairs that ended in the aft salon. A passage took her forward, past a closed door and stairs to the staterooms below and cockpit above. The passage opened into a luxurious and spacious salon. Beyond it was the galley with a dining room table and chairs on the port side. An ornate wood partition separated the galley from whatever lay beyond.

When a shirtless Zane stepped from behind the partition, Jasi held her breath. From the muscular calves to the tanned smooth skin on his bare arms, to the resilient angle of his jaw, the man was an Adonis, and Jasi couldn't stop the racing of her heart, or the warnings that flashed through her mind.

*No man should look that good.*

"I thought you'd never get here, my love." Zane smiled and moved toward her, holding two glasses of red wine. "It's Australian."

"I can't. I'm still on duty."

"But I thought the case was closed."

"We still have a few loose ends to tie up."

His blue eyes fastened on hers. "Cola or ice tea then?"

"Ice tea sounds good."

"Make yourself comfortable. I'll be back in a minute."

Jasi sat on the plush sofa. Classical music filtered through the speakers, but the music did nothing to calm her nerves. Her hands were sweating and she wiped them on her slacks. She had to put to rest the niggling suspicions that had bothered her ever since she'd confronted Deirdre.

She took a moment to survey the stateroom. The polished brass accents and African mahogany must have set Zane back a bit.

"Quite the posh setup, Zane."

"It does its job," Zane called from behind the partition.

When he reappeared, he handed her a heavy crystal glass and settled into the seat beside her.

"Cheers, love."

"To what, Zane?"

"To us being back together again."

She gaped at him. "Are we together, Zane?"

"I hope so." His mouth curved into a smile. "We are very good together."

"I'm sure you say that to all your women."

He gave her a hurt look. "You're the only woman for me, Jasmine."

"Really?" The glass hovered near her lips and she could smell the tartness of the tea. "Sometimes I wonder how many women are in your life."

He watched her intently.

"What?" she asked.

"You're so damned beautiful."

Her eyes were drawn to the partition. There was a bedroom back there. She was sure of it. If things had been different, she would have gladly gone back there with him. But everything had changed.

"I hope you aren't thinking I'm going to sleep with you."

He grinned. "While that's a very enticing thought, I have something else planned."

She cocked her head. "Oh? And what might that be?"

"You'll have to wait and see." He clinked his glass against hers. "Drink up."

"You know I don't like surprises, Zane."

"I know." He took her glass. "I'll get you a refill. Back in a minute, love. I have more ice tea in the pantry." He strode down the hall and entered one of the rooms.

Restless, Jasi wandered around the salon, picking up a knickknack here and there. Her fingers trailed across a shelf, over the stereo system and toward a horizontal metal rack filled with CDs. She pulled one out.

*Bach. The same music Sampson said he heard.*

"I thought this was your yacht," she yelled.

"I borrowed it from an old friend," Zane called out.

A CD protruding from behind the music rack caught Jasi's eye. She plucked it out and stifled a gasp when she read the label.

*Mind Over Matter Productions.*

She reached behind the rack and withdrew a dozen more CDs, all with the same label, all undoubtedly carrying the same hypnotic suggestions responsible for manipulating men and women in power. She slipped a CD into her inside jacket pocket and tucked the others back in their hiding place.

She was about to sit down when a curio cabinet in the corner drew her attention. A light inside illuminated a six-inch brass bell. It was inscribed with the name of a sailing race and a date. More importantly, a name was engraved on the bell. A name she recognized.

"Chief Justice Victor Cahill."

Zane's "old friend" and the father of young Paul who worked at the Britannia Yacht Club. The day bartender had said Victor Cahill was a judge who owned three yachts. *Freedom Surfer* was obviously one of them.

Below the bell was an object in a satin-lined box.

A silver gavel.

She opened the glass door and withdrew the gavel. It was pure silver from the weight of it. She held it up to the light and blinked at the brightness.

*What have we here?*

Someone had taken care to clean the gavel and polish it, but they'd missed the groove where the head met the handle. Embedded in the groove was a line of crimson.

*Blood.*

She knew without a doubt she was holding the murder weapon, the one that had killed Winkler and Sampson. But was the murderer really who she suspected?


Jasi returned the gavel to the cabinet and shut the door. After a quick look over her shoulder, she examined the walls of the cabin. Above a window, she found a small spray of crimson.

*Blood spatter.*

She'd bet her next paycheck that Monty Winkler and Porter Sampson were killed right here.

She recalled Victor Cahill telling his son to buy a new dingy. Something had happened to the old one. It had been used as a fiery coffin. Winkler's body would have been cramped, which would explain the burn pattern. And since there wasn't a dingy for Sampson, he'd been set on fire on the beach, not far from a dock.

But Victor Cahill wasn't the murderer.

She didn't like where her mind was going. She wanted desperately to be wrong.

A small table with a single drawer sat beside the cabinet.

"Well, let's see what's in here," she murmured.

The drawer held a variety of items. A deck of cards, a set of keys, some change, a pack of cigarettes with three left and a package of nicotine gum. There was only one person she knew of who was trying to quit and she'd bet her badge that the saliva on the gum found near Sampson's remains would match Deirdre's DNA and this brand.

Underneath the gum was a rectangular piece of plastic.

The missing IHD.

She slipped it into her purse, at the same time catching sight of the Gemini lighter someone had sent her.

Had Zane sent it? If so, what did it mean?

Footsteps approached.

"What are you doing, love?"

She turned, smiling innocently. "I love the décor."

His brow arched as he studied her. "It's okay, I guess."

"Why be so modest?" She laughed stiffly. "You're moving up in the world."

He handed her the glass of iced tea. "Maybe you should move with me."

Ignoring the innuendo, she said, "Did you send me a lighter a few weeks ago?"

"A lighter?" A look of genuine confusion crossed his face. "No. Why would I? You don't smoke. Unless you've changed your habits. "

She shook her head. "Forget it. I'll figure it out eventually."

"You must be disappointed this case is over. I know how you love a good mystery."

"Actually, I'm *glad* it's over," she said, taking a tentative sip of the tea. "I just wish we'd been able to find Sampson's missing blue binder."

Zane glanced at the TV. "I guess it's gone now."

"Too bad. If we'd known what bill Sampson was working on last, we'd have a better idea of what Deirdre was trying to accomplish."

"I still find it hard to believe that she was the mastermind behind the Parliament Murders."

"Don't forget," Jasi said, "someone also put you in the hospital."

He seemed caught off guard. "Yeah, of course. I guess that goes to show that women really *can* do anything if they set their minds to it."

"She's a lot smarter than we gave her credit for, Zane. She's been studying high frequencies and communication satellites far longer than even her sister was aware of. Deirdre got caught up in the power." She stared him right in the eye. "But she wasn't the mastermind behind everything."

"Why do you say that?"

She took a long sip of iced tea. "Deirdre wasn't smart enough to think up something this devious, much less pull this off alone. Someone had to convince her she could use satellite transmissions to infiltrate the human brain."

"Sounds complicated."

"It would be for the average person. And Deirdre was average. Her partner, on the other hand, is far above average."

"If you say so."

"I do. Deirdre needed someone to help precondition each victim. They had to be programmed somehow to turn the television on every night at the same time in order to receive the transmissions."

"Precondition. You mean like brainwashing?"

She smiled. "Or hypnosis."

"Really?"

"That *someone* recorded CDs to keep victims compliant and—" She broke off. "Why does it feel like we're moving?"

Zane smiled like a Cheshire cat. "Because we are, love. We're going on a little cruise."

"I'm not going anywhere with you, Zane."

His eyes narrowed. "Too late."

Jasi rushed toward a small window and pushed aside the curtain. There was no sign of the dock. Instead, a gap of rippling water separated the yacht from the shore. With a curse, she moved to a window on the other side. It gave her the same view.

She had to remain calm and not tip him off.

"I don't have time to go sailing, Zane. Take me back."

"There are no sails on this boat, love. Besides, you need a break."

"Don't tell me what I need."

"I'm afraid you have no choice, Jasmine."

Zane's voice was low and threatening. When she looked in his eyes, she saw desperation. He knew that she knew.

Fear gripped her. She hadn't told a soul where she was going. Not even Natassia.

*Stupid, stupid idiot.*

With all her training she should have known better than to confront a killer without backup. They looked out for one another. That was their strength. Now she was on her own.

With a murderer.

"Where are we going, Zane?"

The smile he gave her made her shiver.

"Have you seen Parliament Hill from the river? It's quite beautiful." Moving toward the stairwell, he paused and blew her a kiss. "Make yourself comfortable, love. I'll be back in a second."

As soon as he was gone, she opened the cabinet underneath the television. And there it was. Sampson's blue binder. She rifled through the pages and found the last bill, one that could potentially eradicate the PSI Division from the CFBI. Sampson's final vote was for it, not against, and he'd already signed it the document.

*Damn.* "Time to call in reinforcements."

She was about to send Ben a message on her data-com when she heard Zane returning. She had barely enough time to slide the 'com beneath the sofa cushion.

"Don't you have to navigate this thing?" she asked him, hoping he'd return to the deck.

"I leave that to the captain."

Her heart hammered. Someone else was aboard the yacht.

"Who—?"

"I'm so happy you're here, love."

The smile on his face and the way he said this made her wonder if he suspected that she knew.

"Why is that?" she asked him.

Zane took her hand and she let him lead her to the sofa. He sat down, patted the seat beside him and said, "Now that your case is solved, we can pick up where we left off. You know that I love you."

Her breath hitched at his sudden declaration. Years ago she would have given anything to hear those words. But now…?

"The case isn't quite over," she mumbled.

He feigned surprise, and he didn't do it well. "Really?"

"Deirdre didn't brainwash two prominent politicians and commit murder without help."

"You're right," he said in an even tone. "She had a research team."

She shook her head. "They just followed her instructions and none of them knew enough about her secret project to comprehend what she was really doing. No, Deirdre had a partner."

"Hmm, that's an interesting theory. Any idea who?"

"At first I thought it was her sister." Wishing she had a stronger drink, she downed some ice tea before continuing. "Marilyn knows a lot about communication satellites and radio frequencies. I thought maybe she was after her husband's insurance benefits."

"But all the clues pointed away from her."

"Yes, and I almost missed the most important one."

"Which was…?"

Here it was. The crux of the case.

"Deirdre had a boyfriend."

Zane's gaze dimmed. "Are you sure about that?"

"Marilyn mentioned it the first day I met her. Something about her sister being in love." She gazed into his eyes. "People will do almost anything for love."

"So you think this boyfriend is somehow involved?"

"Deirdre had help."

Zane shrugged. "So she had a lover—"

"A lover who conspired with her to manipulate government policy. And who helped her commit murder."

As Zane finished his ice tea, she could see in his eyes that he was conflicted. Their little cat-and-mouse game was about to end.

She glanced out the porthole again. When she saw how far out they were, her pulse quickened. They were heading east along the Ottawa River. Toward Shirleys Bay. Toward Paragon.

"You need to take me back, Zane."

"Why? What do you plan to do now?"

"I think you've already guessed."

Blue eyes twinkled. "You think you know something? You know nothing, Jasmine."

"I know you're not the person I thought you were."

Zane placed a hand over his heart. "I'm wounded."

There was a cold edge to his voice.

She subconsciously placed a hand on her stomach and thought of the tracking chip that had been implanted behind her bellybutton. Every CFBI agent had a tracker—standard procedure.

*Come find me, guys.*

The only problem was no one knew she was in danger.

One look in Zane's eyes told her he knew that too.

"So what now, Jasmine?" he asked softly.

She thought about her answer before saying, "Well, I can't allow a killer to go free, now can I?"

"No, not you."

"I'll have to turn him over to the CFBI."

"Or he could disappear, leave Canada."

"I don't think that would be good enough."

"You could forget all about the boyfriend."

She shook her head. "I'd be lying then. I'd have to pretend I never saw the connection."

"And you're too smart. You don't miss a thing."

"No," she said with a sad smile. "I don't."

"Well, before you're ready to turn in this final piece of the puzzle, I'd like to do something."

"What's that?"

"Kiss you." He stood in front of her, took her hand and gently pulled her to her feet. "I'm really sorry things had to work out this way."

"Me too."

"One last kiss then? For old time's sake?"

She knew she shouldn't, but her heart pulled her toward the man she thought she knew, thought she loved. As her lips met his, she wanted to cry out, 'Why, Zane?'

"I'm sorry," he whispered in her ear.

"Me too. But we need to end this."

## 32

"Exactly what I was thinking," Zane said, releasing her and taking a step back. "Although I have to admit, I'd hoped it would never come to this. I never expected to run into you here in Ottawa. Hell, I never expected a lot of things."

"Did you really think you could get away with this?"

He shrugged. "I hoped. At least for a bit longer."

"You're too smart for your own good."

"Sorry, love." He turned away.

"You will be, Zane."

Her threat amused him. "Really?"

"Turn around," she said. "Slowly."

When Zane complied, his gaze dropped immediately to the gun in her hand. "What are you doing, Jasmine? Put that down."

"Don't think I won't shoot you."

Zane shook his head in disappointment. "Why'd you have to go and mess things up, love?"

She refused to answer him.

"You really should put that thing away," he warned.

"Why'd you do it, Zane?"

"Don't go and ruin everything with your questions. It doesn't have to be this way."

"Of course it does. You broke the law. You're responsible for two murders, Zane. And Deirdre wouldn't have killed herself if it weren't for you."

"Poor Deirdre. She must have been overwhelmed with guilt."

"And you? Do you feel guilty?"

He smiled at her and it turned her blood cold.

"I did what was necessary," he said. "Now what?"

"You've left me with no choice. I have to bring you in."

"That's not going to happen, love."

The calmness of his voice made her furious.

"Tell me why, Zane. Why did you kill those men? I deserve to know the truth."

He gave her a sad look. "I suppose you do."

"Tell me."

"I met Deirdre when she came to me for counseling. She was a mess. She'd killed her father and was having problems dealing with the guilt. When she started talking about her research, I was intrigued." He shrugged. "I had a score to settle and she gave me a way to do it."

"What score?"

"Didn't your beloved Benjamin Roberts tell you?" he snapped. "My career was trashed when I was booted off my last CFBI case. And all because of a freak."

"What are you talking about?"

"The CFBI brought in some psychic who claimed she had visions about the case. I had written up a solid psychological profile, but this bitch said it was based on a witness's lie."

"Was she right?"

"It was a good guess," he said, visibly exasperated. "But my profile and my reputation couldn't hold up in court after that. She made a fool of me. Once the case was over, I knew that our judicial system was going to be corrupted by people pretending they could see things the rest of us can't."

"Maybe they do have a gift."

He held out his hands. "You're a CFBI agent. Doesn't it piss you off that your case could be undermined by one of these PSI freaks? They've got to be taken out of the system, and short of killing them all, the best way to do that is to have a new law in place that will disallow any PSI testimony in court."

Jasi was stunned. "You murdered innocent men so you could take down the PSI Division? Because you were embarrassed?"

"It was more than that!" he said. "They made me look like an idiot. I lost all credibility. Your beloved agency cut me off. No more cases. No income."

"Then you work somewhere else," she snapped.

Zane's jaw tightened. "No one would hire me after that. The psychic contradicted my report. She's nothing more than a lying freak. These psychics make up crap and people believe them. It's time our government stopped relying on psychic bullshit. They wanted to spend millions of researching psychics and hire them more publicly. But it's time for some real change in Canada."

"And you're going to make this change happen?"

He smiled secretively. "You have no idea how big this is. My methods have already been tested."

"What do you mean?"

"What I've developed is a way to control government, to influence major decisions. Do you know how much other people—other governments—are willing to pay for that?"

"So you're doing this for money," she said in disgust.

He shrugged. "Money is power. And right now I hold the power to control even our basic laws. Take Monty Winkler's gun vote, for instance."

She laughed. "You're trying to say you had something to do with that?"

The smile he gave her sent a shiver up her spine.

"You brainwashed him to vote yes," she said slowly.

"There were others before him too." Zane gave her a smug look. "And others after him."

"And now you want a vote to oust the PSI Division."

"PSI-0512," he said with a content sigh.

"The file you deleted from Winkler's computer."

"It was everything the government was proposing regarding the PSI Division," Zane said, his mouth twisting bitterly. "You should've seen what they intended to do. We would've been inundated with psychic freaks."

Jasi flinched. "They aren't freaks. They have a gift."

"A *curse*!" he shouted. "What do they really know?"

"They know more than the average person, Zane. PSIs see things that others don't. They don't ask for it. It's just a part of them. And they're all highly trained CFBI agents."

"Trained, my ass," he sneered. "They *see* things that aren't there and—" He froze, gaping at her in disbelief. "Oh my God, Jasmine."

She held her breath.

"You're one of them, aren't you?" Zane's mouth turned down in disgust and his eyes raged with fury. "That's why you're defending them. That's why you could never fully discuss your cases with me, even though I had regular CFBI clearance." He muttered a curse. "I should've known. You're a freak of nature, Jasmine McLellan. Just like the rest of them."

His words cut her. Deeply.

"I thought you loved me, Zane."

"I do. You'll always be in my heart."

Reaching into her jacket pocket with her left hand, she withdrew a set of handcuffs and tossed them on the floor at Zane's feet. "Put them on."

Zane smiled coldly. "I don't think so." He took a step forward.

"Don't move, Zane!"

But he did.

He lunged for her, grabbed her around the waist and dragged her to the floor. Plucking the gun from her hand, he kissed her again, and in the turmoil of bitter emotions of longing, regret and betrayal, Jasi didn't feel the prick of a needle in her arm until it was too late.

With a cry, she jerked away. "What did you do?"

"I gave you a small dose of Rohypnol."

Fear gripped her by the throat. "You drugged me?"

He held up a hypodermic needle. "Lucky for you, I only gave you half of what's in here. I wasn't expecting you to visit me tonight. This dose was intended for someone much bigger than you."

"You said you loved me, Zane."

He shrugged. "You win some, you lose some."

"So I was just part of your game?"

"Not at first. I was hoping we'd continue our relationship afterward. But I know now you'd never let me walk away." His blue eyes narrowed. "How are you feeling, love?"

"Fine."

But she wasn't. The movement of the boat combined with the drug in her system made her dizzy.

"Don't fight it, love. It'll be over before you know it."

Confident that the Rohypnol would make her unable to fight back, Zane released her.

That was his first mistake.

Jasi jumped to her feet and landed a well-placed kick to his left knee, the one she knew had been injured in college. With a grunt, he collapsed on the ground. His hand lashed out, catching her foot, but she whirled on him. Her boot struck the side of his head and down he went, the gun landing a foot from his hand.

She'd never reach the gun before he did.

Jasi grabbed the handcuffs and ran for the stairs, praying that Zane wouldn't shoot her in the back.

"There's nowhere to go," he called after her.

On deck, she held tight to the starboard rail and tried not to look down into the swirling river.

Zane was right. There was nowhere to go.

Glancing up at the cockpit, she froze. She recognized the man at the helm.

*Chief Justice Victor Cahill.*

"Judge Cahill!"

He didn't seem to notice her.

Shit! Think, Jasi!

When Zane's head appeared from the stairwell, Jasi nailed him with the only thing within reach. A metal bucket. The gun skittered from his hand and she grabbed it before it ended up overboard.

With shaking hands and blurred vision, she aimed the gun at Zane's head. "Don't move!"

He laughed.

"Get up!" she shouted. "Now!"

An energizing surge of adrenaline fired her veins, mingling with the Rohypnol. She could feel its effects now, the dizziness, the weakness in her body. She knew she had maybe ten minutes before the drug would immobilize her. She had to get the cuffs on him and call Ben before that happened.

Zane slowly rose to his feet. "Now what?"

She was about to answer when she caught sight of something in the water behind the yacht. A small dingy with an outboard engine. Similar to the one Winkler had been virtually cremated in.

She swallowed hard. "Were you going to put me in that and set it on fire?"

Zane shook his head. "It's for me, for my getaway."

"So you were going to drug me and leave me on the yacht?"

"It's not the drug you should be worried about."

"What do you mean?"

"The yacht is sinking."

A wave of terror washed over her. He planned to drug her and leave her aboard a sinking yacht. She'd fall asleep and drown. No one would find her. She'd become another missing person, a statistic in someone else's report.

"You'd let me drown?" she asked in disbelief.

"Yes. Sorry, Jasmine."

"Cahill too, I suppose."

Zane nodded. "Vic's in his own little *Perfect Storm* world. Anyway, the captain is supposed to go down with the ship." His eyes drifted to the Beretta. "Are you going to shoot me, love?"

"If you make me." She blinked as his body split in two, and then three.

He gave her a twisted grin. "I don't think you can. You love me." He took a step toward her.

"Stay where you are!"

"You won't shoot me." He moved closer.

She waved the gun at him. "Stay back!"

He laughed and reached for her.

"Zane!"

*Crraack!*

The bullet caught Zane high in the chest and a blossom of crimson petals spread across the pale blue shirt. But it was his astonished expression that made her heart ache.

"Jasmine?"

He pitched backward and flipped over the rail.

"Zane!" she screamed.

She dropped the gun and clutched the rail.

*There!*

Zane floundered in the water behind the yacht.

"Hold on!" she yelled, adrenaline flooding her body.

*I have to stop this yacht.*

She glanced up at Cahill. "Stop the boat!"

The man barely blinked.

Scrambling up the stairs to the cockpit, she grabbed the judge's arm. "You have to stop the yacht. Zane's in the water."

"Zane?" Cahill looked confused. "We're going fishing, dear."

"The boat is sinking! And there's a man overboard."

"Man overboard?"

She slapped him hard across the face. "Stop the boat!"

Dazed, he stared at her, then slumped to the floor.

"Shit!"

She ran panicked fingertips over the control panel and tried to remember what Zane had taught her three years ago. *Levers forward to increase engine speed.* She pulled the two main levers downward. The vessel slowed immediately. Relieved, she turned the wheel and maneuvered the boat into a turn.

Finally, she could see Zane's head bobbing on the surface. With the boat at a crawl, she navigated the route until she was a few yards away.

Then she stabbed at two large red buttons, hoping to God they were the ones that would shut down the twin engines.

They were.

Relieved, she hurried down to the deck. She grabbed a life preserver and tossed it into the river, but she threw it too far to his right.

Zane's head was still above the water. Barely.

A wave of dizziness made Jasi drop to her knees.

"Come on, get up! He needs you."

She thought of jumping in after Zane, but that would be stupid. They'd both drown.

"Swim to the boat!" she yelled.

Zane's gaze caught hers. "I did love you, Jasmine."

A sob caught in the back of her throat. "Just swim, damn it!"

She swiped at her eyes and when she opened them, Zane was gone. Her heart raced as she leaned over the rail.

"Zane!"

A hand broke the surface. His fingers reached out for her. Then his hand sank slowly out of sight.

In a heart beat, Zane Underhill was gone.

Jasi struggled to stay conscious. But her mind wanted to float away on the current.

*Fight this, Jasi.*

An overwhelming wave of weakness made her knees cave. She dropped to the deck, first on her knees, then on her back. Staring up into the night sky, she watched the twinkling of the stars as paralysis slithered over her body until all that moved were her eyes.

This was it. Her final moments.

She drifted with the river, up, down, up...

How long would it take the boat to sink? Would she feel the chill of the water, or struggle to breathe? Or would death claim her quickly and painlessly.

She hoped for the latter.

*"Jasi..."*

Had someone called her name? Was it Death?

In her mind she reached out a hand, just as Zane had. But this time someone grabbed her hand and pulled her to safety.

*"Jasi, we're here."*

# 33

"Jasi, open your eyes."

She was too afraid to obey.

*Where am I?*

She tried to lift her arms, but they refused to budge. Were they strapped down? Why couldn't she move her legs? Or lift her head?

She strained to open her eyes. A light gleamed and she groaned at the invasion. She blinked again and when her surroundings began to take shape, she wished she'd never opened her eyes.

Wolf-like shapes crowded around her, their distorted faces elongating and darkening. They spoke in an unrecognizable language and she wondered for a moment if these were the mythical bodachs from Dean Koontz's *Odd Thomas* series, the creatures that warned of terrible death.

*Am I dead?*

She resisted the urge to cry and thought of Brady. He'd miss her terribly. Then Pop's face swam before her. She wanted to hug him.

She smiled. "You're right, Pop. 'The water rose three inches. We were saved!'"

She had no idea what that meant, but it was important.

The creatures terrified her and she wanted to slink away, but her body wouldn't cooperate. She watched them, praying they'd go away. She didn't want to be their feast tonight. When paws poked her, she whimpered, more from fear than any pain.

"Is she waking up?" a voice whispered.

She wanted to say, *No, I'm not waking up. I'm dying.*

What did she have to live for now? A man she thought she loved was lying at the bottom of the ocean. And it was her fault.

*Zane…*

She would have let him into her life—if he hadn't betrayed her first. But even his betrayal didn't warrant a gunshot to the chest.

Yes, it did, her conscience argued. *He was going to kill you.*

Pain pierced her arm. She wondered why. Other than the sedative in her system, Zane hadn't physically hurt her. Even thought he had intended to.

The pain subsided and a gaping void pulled her in. Before she was swallowed by it, she had one final thought.

*Zane...I'm so sorry.*

The void released her, slowly, one cell at a time. In a haze of half-consciousness she felt the pain in her arm intensify. She cried out and was surprised to hear her own voice.

"Can you hear me, Jazz? Wake up."

*Ben.*

"I think she's trying to say something," a soft voice said.

"I'm trying to tell you to get off my hand," Jasi croaked.

"Jasi!"

The loud voices made her cringe.

She swallowed. Her throat hurt.

"I need some water."

Ben held out a plastic cup with a straw.

She took a sip, then glanced behind Natassia and Ben.

Her vision cleared and a sterile white room came into view. She saw the heart monitor and other equipment.

She smiled. Or tried to. "Why am I here?"

"You were shot," Ben said.

Natassia's face appeared. "Don't you remember?"

Jasi swallowed. "Zane shot me."

"Who?" Natassia said, throwing Ben a worried look.

"Not Zane," he said. "That was months ago."

Natassia moved to the door. "I'll get the doctor."

Jasi would have argued with her to stay if she had more energy, but she felt completely drained. And a bit confused.

"What do you remember?" Ben asked.

"Zane...and Deirdre Dailey," she said, closing her eyes.

It all came racing back.

She'd shot Zane and he'd fallen into the Ottawa River.

Meanwhile, Ben had figured out the last symbol in his vision. The flag falling into the water suddenly made him think of the flags on boats, and that led him back to the yacht owned by Justice Victor Cahill.

Shortly after he'd made the connection, Divine Ops picked up the signal from the tracker surgically embedded in her navel and an RCMP helicopter lowered a crew, including Ben and Natassia, onto the yacht.

When the Rohypnol had kicked in full force, she'd passed out on the deck, fracturing three ribs in the process, and leaving a one-inch gash on her chin. Because of a mild concussion, she'd spent eleven days in the hospital that time.

Meanwhile, search teams spent days dragging the river and calculating currents so they could monitor the shores, but Zane's body was never found.

"How long have I been in here?" she asked weakly.

"A while."

She rubbed her head. "I keep thinking of the Parliament Murders. It's like it all happened yesterday."

"The doctor said you might feel a bit disoriented."

Disoriented? She felt like she'd just come off the damned boat. *I swear I'm still rocking.*

After they'd found her on the yacht, the Honorable Ravinder Sharma and Chief Justice Victor Cahill had been brought in for questioning. They were shocked when it was explained that they were victims of brainwashing. Sharma resisted the news and had to be forcibly removed form his position as MLA. Cahill was more reasonable. He stepped down from his position voluntarily when it was explained that he was compromised and putting the country at risk. It would take months to deprogram the two men, and even longer to find anyone else who'd been subjected to Zane's hypnosis and Deirdre's transmissions.

Darlene MacKenzie was brought in, and after further questioning, it was determined that although her VISA placed her at the bed and breakfast, she hadn't actually gone there. Without her knowledge, she'd been an innocent participant in Project Chrysalis.

Zane had planted the false memory of a quiet getaway to explain her absence. MacKenzie chose to step down, rather than risk being influenced by Zane's programming. She later sought out a therapist to help her cope with feelings of violation, something she described to be as traumatizing as rape.

Marilyn Winkler had received a hefty life insurance policy and was somewhere in the Caribbean enjoying a lengthy vacation. James had also left town, possibly for warmer waters.

*But Zane and the Parliament Murders is a closed case.*

"Do you remember the Gemini Murders?" Ben prodded.

Memories of the recent case came back in flashes. Child abuse and abortion had affected the lives of many, including Ronald Scott, Cameron, Washburn, Allan Baker…

*Brandon.*

"I remember," she said. "I was shot this time."

Ben grinned dryly. "Your first bullet wound."

"Lucky me." She frowned. "Do I have a scar?"

"A small one." He sucked in a breath. "Matthew is giving you two full weeks this time. He wants you to take a holiday."

After the Parliament Murders case was closed, she was given a promotion to team leader. Permanently. She wasn't happy about the news until Matthew told her that her new team comprised of Ben and Natassia. Their new Russian partner had requested a permanent transfer to the CFBI.

"Two weeks is what he gave me last time." She grinned. "I think I deserve three this time around."

"I'll see what I can do," Ben said.

"I thought I was out of the woods, going home. What happened?"

Ben straddled the chair by the bed. "An infection happened. It hit you in the middle of the night the day before you were going home."

"How long have I been out?"

"A week and a half."

She gasped. "Jesus! That long?"

He smiled. "You must like all the attention."

"Yeah, it's so much fun to be unconscious, dreaming about murder and wolves."

"Wolves?"

"Forget it. Long story."

She tried to sit up, but Ben reached out. "Stay still. At least until the doctor examines you."

"I want to sit up."

He glowered at her and she sank back into the pillow like a chastised child. "Yes, sir."

Natassia entered the room, followed by a doctor with a familiar face.

"Dr. Habib," Jasi said.

"I see you've finally decided to join us again, Agent McLellan."

The doctor checked her pulse, disconnected the monitors and examined the bullet wound. He wrapped a clean bandage around her arm, then jotted something down in her file.

Jasi eyed him nervously. "So what's the verdict, Doc?"

"Your stats are all good. The wound is healing nicely and I expect you'll make a full recovery."

"Hear that, Ben?" She gave him an overly sweet smile and shifted until she was sitting up. "Dr. Habib, I have one last question."

The man grinned. "Let me guess. You want to know when you can go home."

"Yes."

"I'd like to keep you here two more days. For observation. And I'd advise you take a few weeks off." He looked at Ben. "Can she do that?"

Ben nodded. "I'll make sure she does."

When the doctor left, she crossed her arms and scowled. "I'll only need a couple of days off."

Natassia cut in. "Take the time, Jasi."

"Doctor's orders," Ben added.

"But what am I supposed to do for two weeks?" she whined.

Natassia grinned. "Well, you could get together with that hunk who's been by your side almost every day."

"What hunk?" As soon as the words were out of her mouth, she knew. "Brandon Walsh?"

"Yup," Natassia replied.

"But he went back to Kelowna."

Ben leaned forward. "Don't get mad at us, but we called him."

"You what?"

"We told him you were in a coma," Ben explained. "He was on the next plane to Vancouver."

Jasi wasn't quite sure what to make of that. The last time she'd seen Brandon, she'd told him to leave. And he had. She'd been positive that she'd never see him again.

*And now he's back?*

A faint hope began to brew. She'd been too hasty. She should have realized after Zane that good men like Brandon don't come around often. She'd be a fool to let him go without at least trying to make things work.

*But what if he doesn't want to? What if he's here out of pity?*

Ben stood, stretched, and Natassia scooped up the empty chair.

"Brandon will be here in about a half hour," she said. "We sent him away so he could grab a bite to eat. Poor guy's hardly eaten a thing."


The *poor guy* stood in the doorway, a bouquet of pink roses in hand. The look in his eyes was a mix of yearning and apprehension.

"Well, don't just stand there, Brandon," she snapped.

"How are you feeling?" he asked, moving into the room.

"Like a train wreck, but don't let that stop you from giving me those flowers."

He glanced around the room and grabbed the only thing that could hold water. A bedpan. He took it into the bathroom and she heard the tap running. A minute later, he emerged and set the bedpan on the side table. The roses hung over the edge, their stems in the water.

"Sorry," he said. "It was the best I could do."

"You never asked if I just used that," she said wryly.

He grinned. "I see you have your sense of humor back. You haven't changed a bit."

"Should I have?"

His expression grew serious. "You were in a coma, Jasi. We were all worried that it would affect your memory."

"I remember just fine." She finally smiled. "It's amazing how something like a little coma can put everything in your life in perspective. I see a lot of things more clearly now."

Brandon sat down beside her. When he took her hand, she resisted the impulse to pull it back. This was the time to lay the cards on the table, not wimp out.

"Why are you here?" she asked in a quiet voice.

"Do you really have to ask?" He glanced down at their hands. "I never wanted us to end."

"I know. I pushed you away."

He heaved a sigh. "I've had a lot of time to think while I've been here. I realize that a long distance relationship isn't something you want. I don't think I want it either. But I do know one thing I want."

"What's that?"

His gaze captured hers. "You. In my life. Now."

"Then you have me," she said simply.

His eyes narrowed. "I'm not walking away this time."

"You'd better not," she warned.

He leaned forward, careful not to put pressure on her arm. "We'll figure this out, make it work."

He kissed her then, and it was as if she'd been waiting for his lips all her life. The kiss was soft, loving, and full of promise.

"Yes, we will," she said with a sigh of contentment.

# 34

This was it. The day Jasi got to go home. She was more than a little relieved. And a bit excited. Brandon was coming home with her. At least for the night.

*Maybe a few.*

She muffled a giggle as Dr. Habib entered the room with a clipboard in hand. His smile stretched from ear to ear.

"Well, that's a good sign," she said. "So?"

"We need you to sign this so you're good to go."

She hurriedly scribbled her name. She caught sight of a nurse pushing a wheelchair toward her. "Uh, what's that for?"

"It's hospital policy."

"But I'm fine. I don't need a wheelchair."

Dr. Habib tipped his head. "Hospital *policy*, Agent McLellan. You know how that works."

Before she could argue further, Ben entered the room and steered her by the shoulders toward the wheelchair.

"She'll take the ride," he said firmly. "Or she'll be staying another night."

"But Ben—"

"No buts." He glared at Jasi. And waited.

"Fine," she muttered.

She sat down in the wheelchair and kicked the footrests into position. Propping her bandaged arm on the armrest, she tried to ignore the throbbing pain.

Dr. Habib handed her a glass of water and two pills. "For the pain," he said.

"Any special instructions?" Ben asked him.

"Yeah, but I doubt she'll listen." The doctor chuckled.

"Hey!" Jasi waved a hand in the air. "I'm in the room, people. Right here."

Dr. Habib passed the clipboard to her. She signed the release form, added a happy face, then handed it back. The nurse and doctor left the room, and Jasi gave Ben an impatient look.

He laughed. "Time to escape from Alcatraz?"

"What time is it?"

Ben checked his watch. "Two-fifteen. Isn't Brandon supposed to be here?"

"He's late."

"When's he coming?"

Jasi shrugged. "I don't know. He isn't answering his cell phone. Maybe we could wait for him."

"Sorry, but we have to go now."

"Just a few more minutes," she pleaded.

"We can't, Jasi. I have a meeting with Matthew and Natassia later." He pushed the wheelchair toward the door. "Maybe Brandon's downstairs."

She grabbed onto that thin string of hope. "Maybe."

"Let's get you home," he said, steering the wheelchair toward the elevator.

"Did you come in my new car?"

The Mitsubishi Zen had been an unexpected bonus, a gift from Premier Allan Baker—for saving his life.

"Sorry," Ben said. "You'll have to make do with my old Mercedes."

When they reached lower level, an attendant at the information desk flagged them down.

"I was told to give this to you," the woman said, handing Jasi a folded sheet of paper.

Jasi opened it.

And her dreams went out the window. Again.

*Jasi,*

*Sorry I didn't say goodbye. I didn't want to wake you.*

*I have to head back to Kelowna. I'll explain everything soon. Just give me a few days.*

*For now, trust me.*

*Yours, Brandon*

"Trust him?" She crumpled the note in her hand. "He's got to be kidding." But even as she said this, she felt a pulling sensation in the pit of her stomach. She did trust Brandon. And that was foreign territory for her.

"Maybe you're being too hard on the guy," Ben said, shuffling his feet. "Why not trust him?"

"Maybe because the last guy I trusted drugged me and tried to kill me. Zane told me everything I wanted to hear. He used me. Then he tossed me away. Or tried to."

"Brandon wouldn't do that to you, Jazz."

She whirled around, her fist gripping the note. She stared Ben in the eye and said, "How do you know? Can you guarantee me that? Can you guarantee he won't rip my heart to shreds and leave me floundering?" She was panting now.

"There are no guarantees in life." His voice softened. "You know that. All you can do is trust and live every day to the fullest."

"Well, tell that to Mr. I'm-afraid-of-commitments."

"Did he say that?"

She opened her mouth, then closed it. "No, but—"

"But nothing, Jasi. You were the one who sent him away the first time. He came back though. That says something for the guy." He patted her arm. "And you're the one who's afraid of commitments."

She blinked back the tears. He was right.

"It's time, Jasi. Time to let go of the fear that's holding you back."

"But you know what happens when I get too close to someone. I'm not good for anything then. I can't even do my job."

"You said it was different with him."

"It is."

"Then stop looking for excuses not to be with him. Life's too short for that. You of all people should know that."

He was right. And they both knew it.


The drive home was tiring, but Jasi couldn't sleep, even though the dismal, overcast sky and pounding rain should have been conducive to at least a catnap. While Ben drove, Jasi gazed out the car window at the passing scenery.

Vancouver spread out before her like a lighted blanket of sounds, smells and movement, something alive and ready for action. Everything was so familiar, yet so different somehow. It was like she was seeing her city for the first time.

Her thoughts wandered to Zane Underhill. It wasn't easy to mourn

him, again. Still, she'd put him to rest once. She could do it again.
*Can't I?*

She yearned for someone to ease her conscience.

Brandon's handsome face came to mind.

*What did you really expect? A long term relationship?*

She banished Brandon from her mind. He'd only done what she'd asked him to. Right?

When they arrived at her apartment building, she brushed aside all thoughts of Brandon. Suddenly, she wanted nothing other than to sleep for a week. In her own bed.

"Thanks, Ben," she said at the front door.

"Do you want me to come inside for a few minutes?"

She shook her head. "I'm fine. I just need to sleep."

Entering her loft, she dropped her purse on the floor and headed for the shower. She barked out the temperature and pressure settings, stripped, then stepped into the shower and leaned against the wall.

When she emerged a half hour later, she felt disinfected and sterilized. Sometimes it was hard to feel clean after a case; sometimes it was impossible. This time seemed even more impossible. She was dealing with memories of two cases—one just weeks ago and one from the past.

Naked, she shivered. "Welcome home, Jasi."

She crawled between the cool sheets, hugged her pillow and fell asleep on the first breath.


The dream started off as a warm, happy memory.

Jasi's mother stood at the kitchen sink and the sunlight glinted in her shoulder-length fiery hair. She was humming a tune along with the radio while washing the dishes by hand.

"Mommy?"

Her mother turned. "Yes, baby girl?"

Eight-year-old Jasmine smiled. Her mother was so beautiful.

"When's Poppa and Brady gonna be back?" she asked.

"Soon." Her mother swiped at a strand of hair and tucked it behind her ear. "It's beautiful outside, honey. Why don't you play in the backyard? Take some toys outside in the sun."

"But I want to stay with you. Maybe we could bake cookies together or watch Free Willy again."

"I-I can't, Jasmine. I'm expecting company in a bit. Business stuff."

Little Jasmine scowled. She studied her dirty runners and got angrier and angrier by the second. Mommy was *always* busy lately. Half the time she was busy with Brady, changing his diapers and getting him his special food. And she was always going out and leaving Mrs. Gagnon from across the street in charge. Mrs. Gagnon smelled like old cheese.

Someone banged on the front door.

Her mother jumped. "Run along outside, baby girl."

"I'm not a baby."

"You'll always be my baby, Jasmine."

Her mother scurried down the hall toward the front door. Jasmine saw her leaning against the door. The look in her eyes was one of fear. This wasn't a welcome visitor.

"Go outside and play," her mother yelled at her.

Jasmine walked toward the sliding door that led outside. But then she did something she'd never done before. She disobeyed her mother.

She ducked into the closet near the bathroom. Leaning against Poppa's winter jacket, she took a deep breath and listened. She heard voices. Her mother and a man. He sounded really, really mad.

"Calista, this has gone on long enough. It's time."

"I can't," her mother said.

"For Christ's sake, what's it going to take?" the man yelled. "Where's the kid?"

"She's not here," her mother said.

Jasmine heard the man swear. He yelled something and her mother yelled back. She was crying.

*Mommy?*

She pressed her eyes to the door slats. A flash of mauve raced past. Her mother's slippers. Mommy always said never to run in the house. So why was she running?

"No!" her mother shrieked.

A bulky blur ran past the closet. It happened so fast that Jasmine didn't know it was the man until he stopped a few feet away, his face partially turned away. She couldn't make out his face. He wore a baseball cap pulled low over his brow.

"Cali!" the man growled. "Don't even think of running from me."

They were in the kitchen now. Jasmine heard the shattering of glass. Was her mother throwing dishes like she did sometimes when she was mad at Poppa?

Tears pooled in her eyes. That scared her too.

*Don't cry.*

A sharp bang echoed through the house.

She held her breath. She had to. The air smelled funny.

Finally, she reached out to push the closet door, but footsteps overhead made her pause. Someone was moving around upstairs. Doors opened and slammed.

Jasi listened, her heart pounding in her chest. Something wasn't right. She could feel it. Her mother's business meeting wasn't going so well. But Poppa would be home soon and he'd tell the mean man to go away.

Footsteps stomped down the stairs.

She was about to call out to her mother when she saw the man through the slats. He carried something shiny in his hand and he smelled like a campfire.

No smoking in the house, she wanted to say. That's what Mommy always told Poppa.

The man paused in front of the closet.

Could he hear her breathing?

She hoped not.

Through the slats, she studied the man's feet. He wore shoes like Poppa's.

The shoes turned, suddenly facing her.

Shivering, Jasmine shrank back into the shadows.

*Please don't find me. Please.*

The man jerked his head as if he heard something.

*Mommy! I'm scared!*

"It didn't have to be this way, Cali," the man said, turning away. "But you left me no choice."

Her mother must have answered him because Jasmine saw him nod. Then he said, "I'm sorry, Cali."

There was another loud bang, followed by silence.

Jasmine closed her eyes, trying hard not to cry. She opened them when she heard the front door slam. She waited a few minutes. When there was no sign of the man, she wiped the tears from her face and slipped from the closet.

"Mommy?" she whispered.

No answer.

*She must be in the kitchen.*

"Mommy? He's gone now."

Silence.

Jasmine stepped into the kitchen. As she approached the counter island, she saw something strange. A foot. It poked out from behind the island.

"Mommy?"

She rounded the corner and stood frozen in place.

Her mother was lying on her stomach on the floor, one hand stretched out as if she were reaching for something. Her face rested on one side and her bright green eyes were open. So was her mouth. There was a funny hole on the back of her blouse and another in the middle of her forehead. Dark red liquid pooled on the floor by her head, and a smear of red streaked across the floor.

"What are you doing, Mommy?"

No movement.

"Is this a new game?"

Silence.

Jasmine touched the limp hand. "Mommy, wake up."

Trying hard to be brave, she sat down on the floor and took small breaths until the coughing stopped. She stroked her mother's face. She wasn't moving. Or talking. She just kept staring at Jasmine.

She sniffed the hole in her mother's forehead. It smelled smoky like the fireplace. She started coughing and it was hard to catch her breath. The room pulsated around her and a peculiar sensation washed over her as a dense fog crept into her mind.

Suddenly, she was transported in her mind to the front door. She felt as though she were much taller, an adult. Worst of all, she could clearly see her mother. Mommy opened her mouth in a terrified scream. She lashed out, her fingernails raking the side of Jasmine's face.

Jasmine cried out and touched her cheek. It was not the soft skin of a child. Confused, she rubbed harder. It felt like Pop's face did first thing in the morning. That's when realization hit her. It wasn't *her* face. It was a man's unshaven face that she touched.

With the man's long legs, Jasmine ran after her mother. When she caught up, she reached out, but it wasn't her own small hand she saw. This hand was big and gloved. In it was something she'd seen her father holding.

A gun.

The hand pointed the weapon at her mother's back. Jasi felt her body jerk as a sharp sound echoed through the house. A burnt smell made her nose burn.

Her mother fell to the floor.

Jasmine screamed, and in a flash, the vision was gone.

Confused, she blinked. What happened? Who was the man? And why had she seen through his eyes?

The sight of her mother's cold corpse numbed her.

She wanted desperately to forget everything. The horrible man, the gun…her mother's body.

*Blood. So much blood.*

She didn't want to see it, so she closed her eyes against the carnage and pushed the terror of the past half hour far from her mind. Then Jasmine did the only other thing she could think of.

She let out a heart-wrenching scream.

*"Mommy!"*

# 35

Jasi awoke with her pulse racing. "Shit."

Panting, she thought of the nightmare. She'd seen everything so clearly. Except the killer's face.

"My God. I remembered more this time."

She recalled the man's angry voice.

*Cali.*

All these years everyone thought it had been a random home invasion, that a stranger had murdered her mother because they weren't expecting her to be home.

"But he called her by name. They knew each other."

There was no doubt in Jasi's mind that her nightmare was a symptom of her unconsciousness finally releasing the terrible memories she'd stuffed down deep inside.

"I'm starting to remember."

Something creaked downstairs.

She sat up and turned on the lamp.

The clock beside her read 2:54 a.m.

She listened for a minute, then laughed softly. "You're imagining things."

Another creak made her heart skip a beat.

Someone was in her apartment.

Throwing back the blankets, she reached into the side table drawer. Her fingers paused of their own accord. The last time she'd fired a gun, someone had died.

A horrifying thought gripped her. What if Zane was still alive? She'd been thinking about him a lot lately. Ever since she'd woken up in the hospital. She'd been confused at first, still lost in the past with Zane, until

Ben told her that had been months ago.

She'd loved Zane. Once. There was no denying that.

*What if he somehow survived?*

Her hand began to shake as an image of Zane floundering in the water came to mind. He'd called out to her. *Help me!* But she was too drugged. The last thing she'd seen was the terror in his eyes as his head disappeared beneath the water's surface, a trail of blood from the bullet wound in his chest the only thing to show his passage.

She swallowed hard. But what if he'd faked his inability to swim? Whoever heard of a guy from an island not being able to swim?

Gathering her courage, she grabbed the Beretta. The gun felt alien, and that bothered her. She'd always thought of her weapon as an extension of herself, at least when she was facing danger.

Her senses tingled, suddenly alive, receptive.

She could hear the clock ticking in the hall. She could smell the cleaner from the gun cloth she'd used the night before.

With the Beretta in hand, she tiptoed down the stairs, hesitating at the landing, listening. A shuffling sound came from the living room. Then all was silent.

She waited.

Who the hell was in her apartment? And what did they want?

Determined to find out, she inched down the stairs. Her heart pounded and she fought to contain shallow breaths. When she reached the archway that led to the living room, she pushed her back against the wall and peeked around the corner.

The room appeared empty, but she could feel another presence. Slowly, the intruder emerged from the shadows and moved toward the fireplace mantle. Moonlight from the window over the sofa illuminated a tall, daunting form.

Jasi could tell by the build that it was a man. A big man.

*Zane?*

Startled by her thoughts, she bit back a gasp.

*What the hell, Jasi! Zane is dead.*

Besides, the intruder was taller, broader in the shoulders.

The man had his back to her, his attention fixed on the display of photographs on the mantle.

She frowned. *He broke in to steal my photos?*

He was staring at a photograph that her brother had taken of her, the one where her hair was loose in a spring breeze and where for one brief moment she had forgotten that she entered the minds of deranged killers for a living. On that one perfect day, Jasi and Brady had gone to Stanley

Park and picnicked in the grass. They were goofing around when Brady snapped the picture.

But what did this man want with the photo?

Silently she approached him, her trembling hands gripping the cool metal of the gun. She took two steadying breaths, then moved closer, aiming the gun at the middle of the man's back.

"I have a gun aimed at your head," she said between her teeth. "I advise you to put down the picture and raise your hands where I can see them."

The man silently obeyed.

"Now turn around," she said. "Slowly."

The hands held up in surrender were strong hands, familiar hands. Hands that had held her, touched her, caressed her.

"I thought you said you were aiming for my head," Brandon Walsh said with a smirk.

She raised the gun. "What the hell are you doing here?"

"I came to see you, silly."

With the gun still trained on him, she glanced at the H-SECS display panel. There was no sign that he'd tripped the alarm.

"How'd you get in?"

"Ben gave me the code."

"He wouldn't do that," she scoffed.

He shrugged. "Okay, I guessed the code."

"That's impossible," she said dryly.

"Eight digits. I knew there was only one date that would be permanently etched in your mind."

She flinched. "The night my mother was murdered."

"And here I am."

She lowered the gun a few inches. "But...but you left."

"I had to tie up some loose ends." He frowned and moved closer. "You should put that thing away."

*You should put that thing away, Jasmine.*

Her mind shifted to the last time she'd held a gun on a man she loved. *Zane.* He'd said the same thing to her. And she'd shot him.

"You're not going to make me shoot you, are you?" she said, her voice stretched thin like a worn elastic band.

"That wasn't in my plans, Jasi."

She lowered her hands. "What exactly are your plans?"

Brandon tipped his head. "Well, for starters, *this.*"

He strode toward her, grabbed her and kissed her hard. The kiss softened and his lips caressed hers with driving passion. And something else. Longing?

"Brandon…" Her words were carried on a sigh.

"And this." His mouth followed the arch of her neck down to her shoulder where, with nibbling kisses, he nudged aside the thin strap of the teddy.

Heat spread throughout her body, flowing downward, a cascading waterfall of emotions. Somewhere in the heat of the moment the gun fell to the floor and she kicked it aside, thankful that the safety was still on.

She pulled away and took a breath. "And?"

He backed her against the wall. She stopped breathing and watched his hooded eyes swoop down. His mouth claimed her again, this time soft and sweet. A moan started in the back of her throat and found its way to the surface.

His hands explored her, and she didn't want them to stop. When he slid the straps of the teddy down her arms, she made no protest. His hot hands swept under the teddy, capturing her breasts and lifting them. His prize.

"God," she said with a moan.

He raised his head, grinned, then his tongue trailed down her neck, over her chest where her heart was beating rapidly, toward her breasts. She closed her eyes as his mouth clamped down on one hardened nipple, eliciting a wave of pleasure that rose and ebbed like a tide.

Then suddenly the contact ended.

"No," she said with a whimper. "I want more."

The look he gave her melted away any reservations she might have had, and then his head swooped down between her breasts. She moaned at the contact and he raised his eyes to hers.

In a husky voice he said, "Then more you'll get."


Much later she watched Brandon sleep. Through the sheers at the far end of the bedroom, faint rays from the rising sun painted his skin with streaks of pale yellow and peach. In the tangle of sheets, he'd thrown one leg over hers and his hands clasped one of hers under his chin.

She took a moment to study the angular line of his jaw, the finely arched brows, his sensuous mouth. She snuggled closer, allowing a smile to cross her face. Slowly, she reached out and lightly traced his lips. She wanted to kiss them.

*Every day for the rest of my life.*

The thought surprised her.

She wasn't one to plan too far ahead, but suddenly she couldn't think of her life without Brandon in it. When he'd left after the Gemini Murders, she was lonely—although she refused to show it. For the days before the infection had set in she'd told herself it was better that way. Better for both of them.

Watching him, she knew now that she needed Brandon. It was time to let someone back into her life. Time to live in the present, to rid herself of the past.

She closed her eyes and recalled her coma nightmare. She'd relived an awful time in her past, one she longed to forget. She'd thought of Zane often over the months following his death. Every time, she was left with an overwhelming sense of guilt.

Now Zane's face swam before her, his pleading eyes, his outstretched hand. She couldn't help him back then. She realized that now.

*You made your choice, Zane. Now I'm making mine. I'm letting you go once and for all.*

In her mind, she saw her hand reach out toward him, but instead of trying to save him, she pulled her hand back and watched his head dip below the surface.

*Goodbye, Zane.*

"Penny for your thoughts."

Her eyes flared open.

Brandon was watching her from half-hooded eyes. "I hope you're thinking of me."

"How'd you know I wasn't sleeping?" she asked.

"You breathe differently when you're sleeping." He grinned and kissed her on the nose. "So…have you got anything to eat? I'm starved."

"There's one thing you should know about me. I don't do domestic."

"I should've known. Martha Stewart's granddaughter you're not." He chuckled and threw back the blankets. Scooting to the edge of the bed, he pulled on his boxers. "I could make breakfast. Providing you have something edible in that fridge of yours."

"How about breakfast out?"

"We need to talk first." His voice was ominous. "And I'd prefer to do it here."

"What, as opposed to in public?" She bit her lower lip.

*Here it comes. The brush off.*

He studied her intently. "I'm leaving my job in Kelowna."

Her heart fluttered, then sank.

"Don't go," she said in a quiet voice. "I was wrong before. I thought

I'd be better off alone. But I'm not."

"Jasi, I—"

"I *need* you in my life, Brandon Walsh. I *want* you in my life. You...you..."

"Complete you?" Brandon grinned.

"Stop making jokes," she demanded. "This isn't funny."

He grabbed her hands and lifted them to his lips. "I'm not leaving you. I'm moving here. To Vancouver."

He took a visible breath and she wondered what he could possibly say that would make him this nervous.

"Jasi, I had a meeting with Matthew Divine."

Confusion scored her forehead. "Why?"

"I told him that every talented Pyro-psychic needs a trained arson investigator on her team."

She gaped at him.

"You can close your mouth, Jasi."

"But you're not..."

"Psychic?" He grinned. "I knew you'd say that."

She couldn't help the smile that crossed her face.

"No, you're right. I'm not psychic. But I have a lot to offer. I'm trained in arson profiling. You and I together will make an unbeatable team."

Jasi was stunned. This turn of events was the last thing she expected. With Brandon joining her team, she'd see him every day. They'd work on the same cases. He'd be taking orders from her.

For a second, she experienced a surge of doubt.

He kissed her. "Don't worry. We can make this work."

"Does Matthew have a rental for you?"

Brandon shook his head. "There's nothing vacant yet."

Jasi hitched in a breath. "So where will you stay?"

The smile he turned on her made her melt.

"Well, my little pyro-psychic, I was kind of hoping I could stay here. At least until something comes available." He cupped a hand against her cheek. "Besides, I think you'll need someone here to help you extinguish the fire."

"What fire?"

Brandon's head lowered. "This one."

Hot lips seared hers, and she welcomed the flames of desire that consumed her. This was one fire that could take some time to put out.

*But we'll have fun trying.*

# Epilogue

*Emily emerged from the shadows of Jasi's closet. She drifted forward, her feet barely touching the floor. Her head lolled at an awkward—strangled—angle.*

*In this dream, an adult Jasi gasped in surprise.*

*The pink skipping rope noose was gone.*

*"You're ready, Jasmine."*

*"Ready for what?"*

*"To start looking for me."*

*Jasi stood still, mesmerized by the bruises around the girl's neck. They were fading before her eyes.*

*"The skipping rope is gone," she said finally. "And your bruises are disappearing."*

*"Yours will too," Emily said.*

*"I don't have any bruises."*

*Emily led Jasi to the mirror. When she peered into it, her image shifted from a young Jasmine back to her adult reflection. One arm was bent in front of her, throbbing as though someone was squeezing it hard then letting it go. Old yellow bruises dotted her arm.*

*Emily tried to smile. "In time all your bruises will fade. But first, ya have to set things right."*

*"And how do I do that? Oh, right, I have to find you."*

*"Yes. Find me." The dead girl floated backward.*

*"Wait!" Jasi cried out. "Why did your bruises fade?"*

*"Because you're one step closer to finding me."*

*"How? I don't know anything more than I did before."*

*Emily blended into the shadows. Before they swallowed her, she said, "You may think you aren't any closer to finding me, but trust me, you*

*are." Darkness closed in around her.*
   *Jasi took an anxious step forward. "Emily?"*
   *Silence greeted her.*
   *And a mystery.*
   *She took a deep breath. "I'll find you, Emily."*

~ * ~

*If you enjoyed this book, please consider writing a short review and posting it on Amazon, Goodreads and/or Barnes and Noble. Reviews are very helpful to other readers and are greatly appreciated by authors, especially me. When you post a review, drop me an email and let me know and I may feature part of it on my blog/site. Thank you. ~ Cheryl*

cherylktardif@shaw.ca

*Family life itself, that safest, most traditional, most approved of female choices, is not a sanctuary: It is, perpetually, a dangerous place.*
—Margaret Drabble

# *Prologue*

Emily emerged from the shadows of Jasi's closet. She drifted forward, her feet barely touching the floor. Her head, with its long blonde hair, lolled at an awkward—strangled—angle.

In this dream, an adult Jasi gasped in surprise.

The pink skipping rope noose was gone.

"You're ready, Jasmine."

"Ready for what?"

"To start looking for me."

Jasi stood still, mesmerized by the bruises around the girl's neck. They were fading before her eyes.

"The skipping rope is gone," she said finally. "And your bruises are disappearing."

"Yours will too," Emily said.

"I don't have any bruises."

*Emily led Jasi to the mirror. When she peered into it, her image shifted from a young Jasmine back to her adult reflection. One arm was bent in front of her, throbbing as though someone was squeezing it hard then letting it go. Yellowed bruises dotted her arm.*

*Emily tried to smile. "In time all your bruises will fade. But first, ya have to set things right."*

*"And how do I do that? Oh, right, I have to find you."*

*"Yes. Find me." The dead girl floated backward.*

*"Wait!" Jasi cried out. "Why did your bruises fade?"*

*"Because you're one step closer to finding me."*

*"How? I don't know anything more than I did before."*

*Emily blended into the shadows. Before they swallowed her, she said, "You may think you aren't any closer to finding me, but trust me, you are." Darkness closed in around her.*

*Jasi took an anxious step forward. "Emily?"*

*Silence greeted her.*

*And a mystery.*

*She took a deep breath. "I'll find you, Emily."*

*Sanctuary: a (1) : a place of refuge and protection (2) : a refuge for wildlife where predators are controlled and hunting is illegal*
*—Merriam-Webster Dictionary*

# 1

<u>Tuesday, July 16, 2013</u>
*Vancouver, BC*

In the smoky ruins of what had once been a flophouse for methamphetamine tweakers just off Hastings Street in downtown Vancouver, CFBI agent Jasmine McLellan stared at what was left of Tara Kincaid's smoldering corpse. The young woman's body had been reduced to a twisted, blackened mass of tendons and bone. From the gaping hole that was once the victim's mouth, Jasi deduced that twenty-one-year-old Tara had been alive when her killer poured some kind of accelerant on her and set her on fire.

"Ready?"

The question came from Benjamin Roberts, a Psychometric Empath and the only Psychic Skills Investigator—*PSI*—who could pull off wearing a well-fitted Armani suit to a crime scene.

Her lips tightened. "As ready as I'll ever be, Ben."

Beside Ben stood Natassia Prushenko, a former Russian SVR agent and gifted Victim Empath, and Brandon Walsh, an arson expert they'd met during a previous case. Brandon was the only member of their team who did not have a psychic gift. He had other *gifts* though, ones she preferred to think of in the privacy of her bedroom.

*Focus!*

The corpse beckoned her closer. Though the Oxy-Mask protected her, she knew the smell of death permeated her own hair, skin and the very air around her. It was a pungent scent, like no other, and she knew it all too well. Some smells were impossible to wash away, no matter how much bleach one used.

"When you take off the mask, inhale slowly," Brandon said. "Don't rush it."

"This ain't my first rodeo, you know."

"No, but I know how badly you want this guy. I don't want you passing out."

For Jasi, the scent of a fire set by a killer triggered something mysterious—a psychic gift, the ability to view a scene from a killer's mind and memories. A Pyro-Psychic and covert government agent for the Canadian Federal Bureau of Investigation, she knew these killers more intimately than anyone else.

Sometimes the visions were so strong they knocked her unconscious for a few minutes.

"Not this time," she murmured.

She inhaled the smoke-free air from the mask, gave her team the thumbs-up signal and tucked her auburn hair behind her ears. *Okay, give me something—anything—so we can confine this bastard to a windowless cell in Matsqui Institution.*

She removed the Oxy-Mask, inhaled two shots of OxyBlast from a mini-can she'd strapped to her chest and tentatively sniffed the smoky air. "I'm fine. It's Shake 'n Bake time."

*Breathe...in...out...in—*

The vision hit her hard, knocking the air from her lungs.

*"No!" the young woman screamed. "Please don't! I'll go back. I'm sorry. Let me go back!"*

*Didn't she know how pathetic she looked? I'd bound her legs and hands, trussed her up like a calf waiting to be slaughtered. Poor little cow.*

*"It's too late, Tara," I said. "You know the rules."*

*"But I can do better. I'll do what I'm told. I can be useful. You'll see. Someone will want me."*

*I smiled at the stupid child. "No one wants you. Not your parents, not any of us, no one. You are weak. You are a traitor." I spat the last word at her.*

*"Please!" she begged, her face dirty except for the path her tears took down her cheeks. "Forgive me."*

*"I told you when you joined us that it was a life choice. You chose."*

*I reached for the gasoline can, unscrewed the cap and began to pour it over her body as she lay writhing on the ground. She was shivering from the cold night air and her lips had a bluish tinge to them. It's not difficult to get hypothermia when you're practically naked and lying in the middle of a clearing at two in the morning.*

*"Mercy!" she cried.*

*I had shown her mercy. I hadn't let the others have her first.*

*"I'll do anything!"*

*I scowled at her. It was too late. "Soon you won't feel a thing."*

*Tara coughed and sputtered as I poured gasoline over her head. When I lit a match, she screamed and the sound echoed in the night.*

*With barely a backward glance, I headed to the nondescript gray sedan I had borrowed, lifted the trunk, pushed aside a small white bag and removed the blanket I'd used to wrap around Tara's unconscious body. I returned to the hellish mass that was once Tara and tossed the blood-soaked blanket into the fire. I watched it smolder and ignite.*

*After a minute or so, I returned to the car and climbed inside. Against my will, I peered into the rearview mirror. Behind me, several yards away, flames scratched at the air like hungry claws grasping for food.*

*Lighting a joint, I took a long drag. The deed was done.*

*I drove away, knowing I had made my point, one the others would clearly get. There was only one way out.*

Jasi gasped as hands secured the Oxy-Mask over her head once more and her vision cleared. Blinking back tears, she said, "We've got him."

"Are you sure," Natassia asked, her sapphire eyes widening.

Jasi clenched her teeth and stared down at her hands. "I saw his hands. And I saw his vehicle and his eyes in the rearview mirror." She described everything she'd seen.

Ben handed her a folder containing an assortment of suspect photos. It took her seconds to find the killer, a beefy guy with thick arms and an oversized bald head.

"Him."

"Boris Lipinski?"

She nodded. "I saw his tattoo, a cobra, inside left wrist."

Lipinski was one of the head guys of the Black Cobras, a ruthless gang originally from Denmark that had set up camp in the Vancouver area. He'd been investigated multiple times for theft, illegal weapons and drugs. A few cold murder cases were thought to be his work, but no one had been able to gather enough evidence to prosecute him. Until now.

"He drove a gray Ford Fairmont, late '70s or early '80s," she said. "BC plates, but I didn't get the number. There will be trace evidence in the trunk. He was sloppy."

Natassia glanced up from the palm-sized, government-issued data-communicator and brushed aside jet-black bangs. "According to my data-com search, Lipinski doesn't own a car. I checked vehicle registrations Canada-wide."

"Look for one of his older relatives. Someone on heart medication. I saw a pharmacy bag in the trunk. I only caught the last name. Same as his. You'll find blood on the bag too, so tell forensics to check the relative's garbage if they don't find the bag in the relative's house."

"Got it!" Natassia said. "A 1979 Ford Fairmont is registered to a Regina Lipinski, age 83. Boris's mother. She underwent heart surgery a week ago."

"I'm positive this is the vehicle he used for all four body dumps. He would've had access to it while his mother was in the hospital. We've got him." Jasi threw Brandon a sad smile. "The four women that were lured into this gang will be avenged."

"You always said Boris was the enforcer," Brandon said.

She shrugged. "He had that look. Kind of like Schwarzenegger meets

Stallone—on elephant steroids."

With the task at hand completed, she headed toward the SUV parked on a side road near the secured crime scene. She removed the Oxy-Mask and stowed it in a backpack along with two cans of OxyBlast. After gathering her smoke-infused hair into a ponytail, she withdrew a small photo of Tara Kincaid. The woman's mother had given it to her a week ago when Tara hadn't shown up for a planned family get-together. In the photo, Tara was smiling.

"This is how you'll be remembered," Jasi whispered.

She dreaded the visit she'd have to make later—the one where she got to tell a mother that her child was dead. There was no easy way to break that kind of news.

Brandon loomed over her. "Are you okay?"

"Yeah."

"You seem rather quiet."

"I was thinking about Tara's mom. Her life is going to change completely."

"It's going to be tough, but at least she'll have closure. She won't be wondering if her daughter is out there somewhere, in pain or alone."

She thought of Emily, the dead girl in her closet, and blinked back a tear. "I guess there's that. We found Tara." *But will I ever find Emily?*

Though she had shared many things with Brandon, she hadn't gathered the courage to tell him about her dreams. They were too horrific. And she couldn't admit to him that she'd seen a ghost while she'd been wide awake either. He was still getting accustomed to her psychic abilities.

"How often does it happen this fast?" he asked.

"Clear visions? Not often. I'm not sure why this case was an easy one, but I'm glad it was. You and I still have that date you promised. And don't think you're going to get out of that."

Brandon gave her a half grimace, half smile. "I can hardly wait."

"I'm not water-boarding you, so stop acting like you're being tortured."

"I was expecting a different kind of date. One with less—"

"What, culture? This is going to be the best date ever."

"If you say so," he mumbled.

She almost laughed out loud at his downtrodden face. They had been dating for just over a year now, ever since they'd been thrown together in an arson investigation. He'd annoyed the hell out of her when they'd first met, but he'd proven his loyalty to a fault. And although he didn't have a psychic talent, his expertise in arson investigation was advantageous, and her feelings for him had blossomed into something she'd never before experienced—something more than pheromones and physical attraction.

They didn't always see eye-to-eye on what constituted a "date." He'd dragged her to many a hockey game and monster truck event, and she suspected they may have permanently affected her hearing. Now it was her turn to plan a date. She'd eventually convinced him to see *Phantom of the Opera*. He'd even bought the tickets. For tonight. But when Matthew Divine had called them in to consult on a string of four brutal killings, she was pretty sure Brandon had been relieved.

She looked at her watch. "We have lots of time to get ready for Phantom."

"I don't know, Jasi. What about our reports?"

"Ben and I'll write them up," Natassia called out as she and Ben joined them. "What? Not my fault you two were talking so loudly that I could hear."

Jasi laughed. "I swear you'd hear a leaf fall in the woods from five miles away, Natassia."

"Seriously, I don't mind. You two go out and have fun. Ben and I will take care of the reports. After all, you did crack this case wide open with a single vision. Didn't even need me to read the victim. Not that I mind."

"Didn't need me either," Ben said, adjusting his black gloves to ensure his skin was fully covered.

Jasi knew what he was doing—preventing the chance of an unexpected vision. As a Psychometric Empath, he had visions when he touched an object or person. But the visions were symbolic and enigmatic, and translating them wasn't always easy.

"No," she said, "but you did get us closer to finding Lipinski. You were the one that picked up the gang connection on the second victim when you touched the necklace she'd been wearing."

Ben patted her shoulder. "I think we all agree that this win is really yours."

"We're PSIs. Credit goes to everyone on this team, not just me. Now, go write your reports."

She watched as he and Natassia drove off with a city detective.

She climbed into the passenger seat of the SUV. "Come on, Brandon. We have one stop to make. After that, we've got a date with the Phantom and some champagne."

He gave her a mocking salute. "Yes, ma'am."

Sitting on the sofa in Jasi's living room, Brandon raised his champagne glass. "To an evening of mystery…without serial killers or corpses."

"Amen to that." She clinked her glass against his. "Cheers to two days of downtime and a night out like a real couple."

His pale blue eyes twinkled with mischief. "We've still got about two hours until the show starts."

She arched a brow. "Any ideas on how we can fill the time?"

"A few. One involves a long, hot…" he grinned, "shower."

"That works for me. And we can discuss that…uh, *thing* I mentioned a few days ago."

He frowned. "What—oh, right. The living in sin idea."

She set her glass down and leaned in for a kiss. "If this is sin, I'll go to confession later." Her lips met his.

On the coffee table, her data-com rang.

"Ignore it," Brandon murmured against her mouth. His tongue traced her lips then swept inside, searching.

The ringing persisted.

"You changed the ring tone," he said.

"I thought the buzz was more irritating."

*Ring-ring! Ring-ring!*

She scowled. "I guess I was wrong."

The 'com went silent, the call directed to voicemail.

"There," she said. "Now where were we?"

"Getting ready for our shower. You have too many clothes on."

His tanned fingers moved to the button on her blouse. Bit by bit, he exposed more skin, leaving a trail of kisses from her neck down to the top of her breasts.

She moaned. Lifting his face, she traced the zigzag of the scar that crossed his right brow. She kissed it.

Her data-com rang again, but they both ignored it.

Brandon peeled the blouse away, unhooked her bra and flung it behind him. With her breasts free, he caressed them, teasing her nipples until they were hard.

Jasi grabbed the sides of his shirt. "Take this off." Her fingers couldn't move fast enough. When his chest was bared, she reached for the snap of his jeans.

They rose as one—mouths and limbs entwined.

Somehow they made it to the bathroom, where they quickly shed the last of their clothing. Naked, their bodies collided, their passion primal and urgent. It had been too long.

She reached for him.

"Jasi," Brandon said with a grimace.

"Am I hurting you?"

"No. I wish that were all it was. Your 'com is ringing again."

"I'm off duty. It's probably Natassia wanting to know if you've managed to worm your way out of going tonight. She'll figure we're otherwise occupied."

The 'com began another round of ringing.

He playfully nipped at her bottom lip. "Whoever it is, sounds like they're going to keep calling until you pick up."

She groaned now. "Fine. I'll make it quick, especially if it's a telemarketer. Then we can get back to discussing your living arrangements."

She wrapped her robe around her and headed for the living room, thinking about her offer to Brandon. A few days ago, before they'd been called in on the gang case, she'd asked him to move in. It made sense. To her, at least. Her apartment was more secure and much larger, one of the perks of being in the

CFBI. And it was closer to Divine Ops, making it an easier commute to work for both of them now that Brandon was a permanent addition to her PSI team.

But he seemed hesitant about the idea. She wasn't sure why. He practically lived there already anyway. What was the big deal? They always used her place for overnights—which had turned into most nights.

*Maybe he doesn't want to commit.*

She fumbled for her data-com and listened to her messages. There were three frantic messages, all from the same person. Cameron Prescott. Cameron was a television reporter for *CTBC News*, and she had a nasty habit of getting involved in some tight situations.

Jasi called her right away.

"I really need your help!" Cameron's voice was shaky, frightened. "My friend Sheral Downham is missing. She's a reporter for *The Vancouver Sun*, covers the Lifestyle section. She's involved in something...dangerous." She lowered her voice. "I can't talk about it on the phone."

"Where are you?"

"Parked across the street from your apartment building."

Brandon entered the room, dressed in the ratty white robe he'd brought over after their first overnight. As soon as he saw her serious expression, the sexy grin was wiped from his face. "Ah, damn..."

She gave him an apologetic look. "Come on up, Cameron. Brandon is here too."

# 2

When Cameron entered Jasi's loft apartment, she gave Brandon a brief nod and then sank into the sofa as though she hoped it would swallow her whole. Her face was pale, her blonde hair a tangled mess and the shadows under her eyes suggested she hadn't slept in days.

"Start from the beginning," Jasi said, handing her a glass of water. "And tell us everything."

Twisting the straps of her handbag, Cameron let out a slow breath. "Okay, I need you both to understand that I tried talking Sheral out of this. I knew it would be too dangerous, and she had no backup except me. But she told me she *had* to do it." She stared down at her purse and bit her lip.

Jasi sat down beside her. "Do what?"

"Go undercover."

"Where?"

*"Sanctuary."*

That one word, though spoken as a whisper, made Jasi shiver. Sanctuary was rumored to be a safe harbor for rapists and pedophiles. A cult for the damned, created by the damned.

"Sheral went in without any backup," Cameron said, her voice breaking.

"Shit."

Cameron sighed. "Yeah."

Brandon sat in the chair across from them. "Since I'm not originally from here, what's Sanctuary?"

"A cult," Jasi said. "It's located on an acreage just outside Mission, about an hour's drive from here."

"Religion based?"

"If you count Father Jeremiah's beliefs as religion."

"I think I've heard his name before."

"Father Jeremiah has been in the news before," Cameron said. "Most recently he was advocating rehabilitation for addicts, no matter their predilections."

"His real name is Giles Christiansen," Jasi added.

"Interesting last name for a religious zealot," Brandon said.

"I know. It's ironic. Christiansen has been suspected of having his hand in a number of criminal activities, but no one's found any concrete evidence against him."

"That's why Sheral went in," Cameron said. "Said she wanted to sink her teeth into a story that would give her a top priority byline, maybe even front page. Journalism is a tough industry, and if you don't get ahead of everyone else, you end up on page sixty—or worse."

"When did your friend infiltrate the cult?" Brandon asked.

Cameron let out a soft sob. "Twelve days ago."

"I know this is difficult," Jasi said, reaching for her hand, "but the more we know, the more we can help."

"Thank you."

Jasi took out her 'com. "Voice record on. I hope you don't mind, but we need to be thorough and do this right."

"We can't go public with this." Cameron stood up and paced the room. "None of what I'm telling you can be made public. Not yet. If Christiansen gets wind that she's there undercover, who knows what he'll do to her. Maybe her data-com died and that's why she hasn't contacted me."

"I don't think you really believe that. Otherwise, you wouldn't be here."

"I just don't want to do anything to make it worse for her."

"You won't. I'll get Matthew Divine to agree to a discreet investigation."

"How will you do that?"

"He owes me a favor. Don't worry. We'll find out where your friend is." *If she's still alive.*

She didn't reveal her thoughts, but one look at Brandon told her he was thinking the same thing. Chances were, so was Cameron.

"Why don't you sit back down and tell us what the plan was. Start from the beginning."

Cameron sat, her shoulders sagging as though she had the weight of the world on them. "Sheral's plan was to get inside Sanctuary, get to know some of the people there, gain their trust and come back with dirt on Christiansen."

"I take it she didn't use her real name?"

"No. Too many people read her column, Jasi. That would've been suicide."

"What name did she use?"

"Nancy Davison. It's her mother's first name and her sister's last name."

"What exactly was she expecting to find?"

"People." Cameron swallowed hard. "Sheral had been investigating a number of missing persons cases. Family members had called her at the paper, begging her to look into it. Over time, she noticed that many of the cases had a common connection."

"Let me guess. Sanctuary."

"At least a dozen people have gone missing after visiting Sanctuary. Sheral thought they might be imprisoned somewhere on the property. Or worse."

"When she reported in to you," Brandon said, "did she give you any idea if she'd found anything to substantiate this idea?"

"No, but she'd done her homework before going there. Whispers on the street suggested there was something more to these disappearances and that Christiansen was involved. It's like everyone *knows* it's true, but no one can prove it."

"Who did she report to and how did she communicate?" Jasi asked.

"Only me. She had a mini spy-com, one of those new models with the camera. She called me every other day at 1:00 PM like clockwork."

"Was this her regular 'com?"

"A burner. She didn't want it traced back to her if they found it." Cameron recited the phone number. "She managed to sneak the 'com in even though they're forbidden at Sanctuary. No phones, no computers, no TVs or radios."

"Christiansen doesn't want his *sheep* to have contact with the outside world."

"Exactly. Sheral strapped the spy-com to her thigh before they picked her up. I have no idea how she kept it concealed in the complex though. I never thought to ask her." Fear flickered across her face. "I've tried calling her a half dozen times, but there's no answer."

"When was the last time you heard from your friend?" Brandon asked.

"Five days ago."

"Perhaps something happened to her 'com," Jasi said. "Maybe she lost it."

"Or someone found it," Brandon added.

Cameron flinched. "That's what I'm afraid of. She told me they have strict rules at Sanctuary, and anyone who disobeys is punished."

"How?"

"Sheral didn't know exactly, and she was afraid to ask or draw attention to herself. But she did say there was a commotion a few days after she arrived. A woman named Jennifer Phillips—Jenny—bunked in Sheral's cabin. Apparently she broke one of Sanctuary's commandments, and that was the last anyone had seen of her. Father Jeremiah said she'd be in isolation for a few days, and if she didn't learn her lesson, she'd be exiled."

"Did you see Sheral the day they picked her up?" Brandon asked.

"No. I only know she was posing as a hooker. She'd been hanging around downtown, waiting for them to notice her. You know, in the red light district. Sanctuary has a white-panel van they use to pick up recruits. People call it 'the pedo-van.' I'm not sure who drives it."

"Christiansen, maybe?"

"No. A younger guy. I saw him once when Sheral was doing her research and I camped out in her car with her. When the van stopped to pick up a young girl, we saw a guy in a navy-blue suit get out."

"Describe him," Jasi said.

"Good-looking guy, maybe in his thirties. Shoulder-length, dirty-blond hair and a moustache and goatee. He kind of reminded me of Brad Pitt. When Sheral called me the first day, she said, 'You'll never guess. Pitt picked me up.' As if it were a great thing."

"But she didn't mention the guy's real name?"

"No. Anyway, Christiansen renames all of his flock when they're reborn."

Brandon lifted a brow. "Reborn?"

"Not the typical Christian rebirth as in accepting Jesus, blah, blah. Sanctuary has their own process. Members have to pass a trial period of fourteen days. 'To cleanse them of their sins and shed them of their former lives,' according to *Father Jeremiah*. Sheral was supposed to have her 'rebirth day' in three days. At that time, she'd be introduced to everyone at Sanctuary, and she'd be given a new name for her new life." Cameron's words dripped bitterness.

Jasi touched her arm. "We'll find her. I promise."

"Thank you. I didn't know what else to do. I couldn't go to the police because I don't want this to get back to Sanctuary."

"What exactly did Sheral tell you when she called you?" Brandon asked. "Did she uncover anything that would put her in danger?"

"She said she was housed in a cabin with two other girls who had been picked up the week before. One was Jenny, the woman I already told you about. She's an addict. The other was a fourteen-year-old runaway named Katie. Every day they're given chores to do, and at meal times they have to sit together, ostracized from the other members. They're told not to talk to anyone except Father Jeremiah."

"Part of their trial," Jasi said. "To see if they can follow orders."

"The more docile they were, the more he'd ease up on the chores and invite them to their group rituals."

"Sounds like brainwashing to me," Brandon said. "A bunch of Kool-Aid drinkers."

"You can't really blame them," Cameron said. "Most of the people who end up at Sanctuary are outcasts in one way or another, separated from their family, living on the streets, addicted to drugs, alcohol or other things. Sanctuary poses as a safe haven for anyone who wants to change their life."

"What about Sheral?"

"What do you mean?"

Brandon's expression was doubtful. "Maybe she drank the Kool-Aid too."

"Sheral is happy with her life. She'd never willingly give up everything she has, and all that she's worked for, to live in a reclusive cult."

"Cults can be pretty persuasive," Jasi said. "Especially with a charismatic leader like Christiansen."

"She went in for a story, one that could *make* her career. She's a bulldog that way. She'd never allow anyone to brainwash her." Cameron stood. "Find her, Jasi. *Please*."

"We'll do what we can."

"Thank you."

"One more thing," Jasi said.

"Yeah?"

"Do you have a photograph of Sheral?"

Cameron rummaged around in her purse. "Here. This was taken last month at Vortex." She looked over at Brandon. "It's a popular nightclub in North Van."

Jasi studied the photo. Sheral Downham was a beautiful young woman. Tall and slender, she had the presence of a consummate and confident professional, especially when dressed in a tailored gray skirt and jacket that accentuated her curves. Rich brunette hair draped down her neck to below her shoulder blades. In one hand she held a martini glass that contained a blue liquid that glowed, and around her wrist was an amethyst-studded bracelet in either silver or white gold.

"Sheral couldn't let this go," Cameron said, her chin quivering. "She said she had to know for sure what was going on at Sanctuary."

Jasi stared at the photo. *Let's hope you didn't find yourself a victim of curiosity.* "We'll check out Sanctuary tomorrow morning, Cameron. We'll do it discreetly, in case Sheral is still there."

Cameron looked her in the eye. "I didn't tell you quite everything."

"Go on."

"About an hour ago, the RCMP was called out to Sanctuary to investigate a suspicious death. They found human bones inside an incinerator. One of my contacts in Mission called me right away because she owes me a few favors. She said the bones are from a female, about twenty-five to twenty-eight years old." Cameron took a deep breath. "I think it's Sheral."

As soon as Cameron left the loft, Jasi and Brandon headed to Divine Ops, a top-secret warehouse that accommodated the PSI division. Situated in Vancouver's West End, Divine Ops didn't look like much from the outside. Worn signage touted it as a condemned fish-packing plant, but inside was a different story.

After handing their weapons to the tech on duty, they keyed in their security access codes, passed through Voice Recognition and the Retinal Scanner, and a full body scanner that examined the tracking devices implanted in their navels. They followed a narrow corridor to Ops One, the primary operations station, and Jasi submitted to the routine paranormal electroencephalograph scan, while Brandon's body stats were scanned and recorded. Then they took the elevator down to the PSI floor.

"Every time I come here I feel like I've been stripped naked and made to walk a runway," Brandon whispered in her ear.

With a chuckle, she pushed him away. "You'll get used to this eventually. As Matthew keeps telling us, these precautions are designed to keep us safe."

When they reached the Command Office, Matthew Divine greeted them with a grim smile, his gray hair slicked back in his customary ponytail. "I wasn't expecting to send you out again so soon, Jasmine. You both deserve some downtime."

"The Cobras' case is now closed," she said, sitting down at the conference table. "We barely got our hands dirty with that one. Besides, I promised Cameron we'd help her. After all, she's helped us in the past."

Matthew's face shuffled through a range of emotions. "The CFBI has been after Giles Christiansen for years, but the man always manages to slip through our hands."

"Did you get our warrants?"

He handed her a manila folder. "A search warrant for the property and structures within the property of Sanctuary, warrants for individual evidence collection and a faux arrest warrant for prostitute Nancy Davison. I had to do a bit of convincing to get the paperwork in Sheral Downham's fake name." He slipped off his ancient tortoise-shell glasses and wiped them on his shirt.

"I appreciate it, sir. Thank you."

"If this woman is at Sanctuary, and if she hasn't been found out, she's putting herself in a lot of danger. I want you to convince her to leave with you."

"Unless she's the victim in the incinerator," Brandon said, taking a chair across from Jasi.

Matthew slid his glasses over his ears and sat down at the head of the table. "Christiansen told RCMP officers it was an accident, that whoever died in there must have wandered inside and couldn't get out. He says the incinerator is only turned on once a week and everyone knows the schedule."

"What does the medical examiner say?" Jasi asked.

"That's the strangest thing. When the bones were collected, no one noticed at first."

"Noticed what?"

Matthew flicked a switch on a control box in front of him and two panels in the wall slid open, exposing a mammoth video-wall. He pulled up a photograph taken inside the incinerator. It showed an assortment of bones that had been set on top of a white cloth and pieced together like a jigsaw puzzle.

"See anything missing?" he asked.

"The skull," Jasi and Brandon said in unison.

Matthew diminished the photo. "There were no other remains found inside the incinerator."

Jasi winced. "Someone cut off her head?"

"With a very sharp weapon."

"Someone didn't want us to be able to identify the victim."

"Any defensive wounds found on her?" Brandon asked.

Matthew shook his head. "Not that the ME could tell. Of course this is only the preliminary report. We'll know more once the body has been transported to the morgue."

Jasi stood and paced in small circles. "So we're looking at a murder here."

"Most definitely."

"Has anyone left Sanctuary in the past week?"

"That's what you'll have to determine. Christiansen swears he doesn't keep track of who comes or goes."

"So this victim *could* be Sheral Downham."

"Yes, it could, Jasmine. Or it could be someone entirely different."

"Perhaps Sheral left Sanctuary and is laying low somewhere," Brandon offered.

Jasi stared at the photo on the screen. "As with Boris Lipinski and his Black Cobras gang, there's usually only one way out of a cult like Sanctuary. In a body bag."

~ * ~

## Message from the Author

As with my other novels, I have used authentic Canadian settings. Shirleys Bay *is* actually a research facility, one with a rich history of research projects, including the real *Project Magnet*.

According to Wikipedia, "Project Magnet was an unidentified flying object (UFO) study programme established by the Canadian Department of Transport (DOT) on December 2, 1950, under the direction of Wilbert B. Smith, senior radio engineer for the DOT's Broadcast and Measurements Section. It was formally active until mid-1954, and informally until Smith's death in 1962."

I found it interesting that Canada has been involved for decades in UFO investigation and communication satellite technologies. I never know what I might unearth when researching a novel.

Paragon Research Corporation and their specific research projects are entirely fictional. *Project Chrysalis* does not exist.

Or at least, I hope it doesn't...

*~Cheryl Kaye Tardif*

**Novels by Cheryl Kaye Tardif**

Whale Song
Whale Song: School Edition
The River
Children of the Fog
Submerged

**Series by Cheryl Kaye Tardif**

*The Divine Trilogy (in order):*
Divine Intervention (Book 1)
Divine Justice (Book 2)
Divine Sanctuary (Book 3)

**Short Stories by Cheryl Kaye Tardif**

Remote Control
Skeletons in the Closet & Other Creepy Stories
Dream House

**Novels by Cherish D'Angelo (AKA Cheryl Kaye Tardif)**

Lancelot's Lady

## About the Author

Cheryl Kaye Tardif is an award-winning, international bestselling Canadian suspense author. Her novels include *Divine Sanctuary, Submerged, Divine Justice, Children of the Fog, The River, Divine Intervention*, and *Whale Song*, which *New York Times* bestselling author Luanne Rice calls "a compelling story of love and family and the mysteries of the human heart...a beautiful, haunting novel."

She is now working on her next thriller.

Cheryl also enjoys writing short stories inspired mainly by her author idol Stephen King, and this has resulted in *Dream House* (short story), *Skeletons in the Closet & Other Creepy Stories* (collection of shorts) and *Remote Control* (novelette eBook). In 2010 Cheryl detoured into the romance genre with her contemporary romantic suspense debut, *Lancelot's Lady*, written under the pen name of Cherish D'Angelo. And she even has a children's picture book published, *The Elfling Princess*.

Booklist raves, "Tardif, already a big hit in Canada...a name to reckon with south of the border."

Cheryl's website: www.cherylktardif.com
Official blog: www.cherylktardif.blogspot.com
Twitter: www.twitter.com/cherylktardif

You can also find Cheryl Kaye Tardif on Facebook, Goodreads, Shelfari and LibraryThing, plus other social networks.

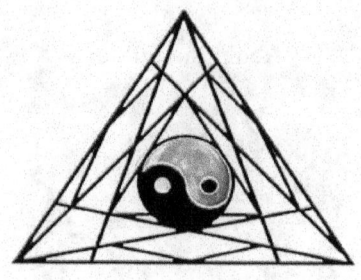

**IMAJIN BOOKS**
*Quality fiction beyond your wildest dreams*

For your next eBook or paperback purchase, please visit:

www.imajinbooks.com

www.twitter.com/imajinbooks

www.facebook.com/imajinbooks

www.ingramcontent.com/pod-product-compliance
Lightning Source LLC
Chambersburg PA
CBHW051522260626
47170CB00003B/735